heaven

Blood. There was blood everywhere. It trickled in rivulets, it ran in torrents. It was intermingled with a hundred other fluids of what had once been living organisms. Now there was just a contorted heap of their dissected organs, bones, exoskeletons, skin, antennae. Thick slabs of tissue lay in open trays, mucus and slime dripped from towering racks of offal. The smell of excreta was everywhere.

It looked like a charnel house. It looked like a vision of Hell.

But this was Heaven...

ACCLAIM FOR *HEAVEN*

"HEAVEN is terrifyingly good, profound, and brave. A cracking pageturner packed with great characters—only some of them human!—spectacular incident, marvelous ideas, and some of the best-conceived aliens I've ever come across. This is a very important book, which deserves huge success."
—Stephen Baxter, author of *Coalescent*

"Fascinating and original aliens, compelling religions, and far-out technologies—Stewart and Cohen probe horizons and push limits. That's what readers of futuristic science fiction want."
—David Brin, author of *Kiln People*

more . . .

heaven

IAN STEWART
AND
JACK COHEN

ASPECT®

NEW YORK   BOSTON

Cover design by Don Puckey
Cover illustration by Steve Stone

The Aspect name and logo are registered trademarks of Warner Books.

Warner Books

Time Warner Book Group
1271 Avenue of the Americas, New York, NY 10020
Visit our Web site at www.twbookmark.com

Printed in the United States of America

Originally published in hardcover by Aspect
First Paperback Printing by Warner Books: May 2005

10 9 8 7 6 5 4 3 2 1

Everything that man seeks in the world: someone to bow down before, someone to entrust one's conscience to, and a way of at last uniting everyone into an undisputed, general and consensual antheap, for the need of universal union is the third and final torment of human beings.

Fyodor Dostoyevsky, *The Brothers Karamazov*

The order that emerges in enormous, randomly assembled, interlinked networks of binary variables is almost certainly the harbinger of similar emergent order in whole varieties of complex systems. We may be finding new foundations for the order that graces the living world. If so, what a change in our view of life and our place must await us.

Stuart Kauffman, *At Home in the Universe*

Memeplexes are groups of memes that come together for mutual advantage. Once they have got together, they form a self-organizing, self-protecting structure that welcomes and protects other memes that are compatible with the group, and repels memes that are not.

Susan Blackmore, *The Meme Machine*

heaven

1

NO-MOON

Identifying with other creatures' feelings is only one part of the problem. The more important question is, how can you make effective use of your knowledge of what they are feeling? Emotions are straightforward. Motives—those are quite another matter. And without an understanding of motives, there is no true empathy, no predictability, and no power.

Archives of Moish

The lion-headed Neanderthal woman sat at the end of the pier, dangling her feet in the sea to cool them . . . but her mind was elsewhere. Usually, she was composed and carefree, but today she was troubled by an apprehension to which she could not put a name.

She shook her thick mane, trying to clear her head. It was a beautiful day on a beautiful planet, and everything was right with the world.

For a few moments, she almost believed it.

Small wormlike animals circled around her toes, occasionally probing her skin with thin tubes, only to withdraw as soon as they sensed alien biochemistry. There was no nourishment here, and the ancient evolutionary bargains were null and void. Newcomers arrived, made the same mistake, and retreated in their turn, baffled. The woman laughed, a gravel-throated chuckle: The worms tickled, and she liked that.

Her trading name was Smiling Teeth May Bite. Her friends called her May. Her enemies could call her what they wished. To both, throughout the Galaxy, she and her kind were "lion-headed"—not literally, but because their ocher skins, their flamboyant sunbursts of marmalade hair, and their wide noses gave them a decidedly leonine appearance. In May's case, the effect was enhanced by tawny eyes and a tendency to snarl.

She wore a short olive green tunic, cut diagonally to leave her left shoulder bare. Several small packages were arrayed around her waist, as if hung on a belt, but with no visible means of attachment. Precursor technology, like most inexplicable things in the Galaxy.

A pair of hand-woven sandals, which she had picked up the previous year on Nothing Ventured, lay next to her at the pier's edge.

She was waiting for a sail. Not any sail, but a particular one: lateen-rigged in a motley patchwork of colors, torn and repaired many times. She redirected her gaze from the swarming worms to the haze where sea met sky. The motion was graceful and haughty. There was an economy to her movements that made her powerful frame seem always perfectly balanced. She sniffed the air laden with the characteristic smells of rotting algae and salt dust; her eyes flicked to left and right, instinctively noting every movement.

She could see a few sails on the horizon, and more of them closer to the port, but none were the sail she was waiting for. Despite her uneasiness, she laughed again, this time in amusement. Second-Best Sailor was late. As he had been last year, and the year before, and would be next year. The reason was always the same. His route would take him along at least three foreign coasts and through several of the innumerable archipelagos that infested No-Moon's world-girdling ocean. At some point of his voyage he would be distracted by the dubious attractions of one of the more exotic ports, find himself behind schedule, and try to invent a shortcut to catch up. Then, entirely predictably, he would be thrown off course by the Change Winds.

May knew this, and she also knew why he was called Second-Best Sailor, and that meant that there was no point in trying to make him see sense. So, as she did every season, she had left extra time in her schedule for him to find his way into port from wherever his latest episode of irresponsibility had led him. He would turn up soon . . . unless his boat had sunk. But he was Second-Best Sailor, not Thousandth-Best. He would never allow his boat to sink.

She didn't mind waiting. She liked the port and the natural sea breezes, just as she liked being immune to the depredations of the carnivorous worms. It made sense to hang around for a few more days until Second-Best Sailor turned up. The trading would surely be up to expectations.

Would it not?

A foot scuffed the timbers of the pier, and without turning her head May knew that her companion had returned from her foray into the maze of narrow floating walkways that constituted the above-water part of Isthmus Port.

"I have reregistered our credentials with the Trade Authority like you told me," the newcomer said. Her voice was in a slightly higher register than May's, but her orange mane was just as luxuriant and her nose was, if anything, even more like a lion's. Her eyes were an improbable royal blue, exactly the same color as a species of electric eel on one of the hubworlds where Neanderthals often traded. The coincidence had given rise to her trading name of Eyes That Stun the Unwary—usually abbreviated to "Stun."

Her tunic was a deep, dusty purple. She was accompanied by a fat, goatlike creature on a braided lead. A yullé—clever but not sentient. The animals were bred in a variety of shapes and colors, and this one had a dramatic pattern of large and small spots, black on gray.

There were many Neanderthals in the ports of No-Moon, and following habits laid down thousands of generations ago, most of them kept pets. Over the centuries, their unique empathic sense had allowed them to tame several dozen species, from as many worlds. May, a rare exception, didn't keep any pets on No-Moon—land animals occasionally upset the customers. But back on board Ship, she had quite a menagerie.

"It went as I expected," said May. It wasn't a question: The Neanderthals had an innate ability to sense one another's emotional flow-patterns, and those of most other creatures. It was why they had been prized as

Beastmasters, back before the Rescue, 116 generations ago.

"The permission fee was adequate, as you foresaw," said Stun. May snorted. Even a flatface would have been able to appreciate that a small increase on last year's fee would be acceptable. And Stun had been given latitude to offer quite a bit more than that if previous custom no longer applied.

Stun bobbed her head in affirmation, and her mane rippled. She joined May on the edge of the pier. The worms quickly discovered this new target for their affections, and were equally disappointed by it.

"The Change Winds must've started early," Second-Best Sailor protested. "Not my fault. Nothin' anyone could've done to see *that* comin', ain't I right, boys?"

He had been publicly congratulating himself on weathering the storm without inflicting too much damage on the boat, when Short Apprentice had noticed that the stern thole-boards had come loose and were trailing behind, with a danger that their staylines might get tangled in the steering gear. Then, when Short Apprentice had been dispatched through a sallyport to secure the thole-boards temporarily to the planking-rail, Fat Apprentice had cast doubt upon the wisdom of their three-day stopover in Coldcoast Docks, and Second-Best Sailor had felt obliged to defend his judgment. Even the reefwives, he pointed out, found the vagaries of the weather difficult to fathom, so he could scarcely be blamed for the freak storm that had come from nowhere and driven them many miles from their intended course.

Fat Apprentice didn't argue. He didn't point out that although the precise timing of the Change Winds was unpredictable, their occurrence around that time of year was entirely to be expected. He did not point out the obvious, because he had no wish to be sent out to join his fellow crew member in the heaving turbulence of the ocean roof. It could make you airsick. Fat Apprentice had cultivated a deceptive air of somnolence and absent-mindedness, but behind that facade he was surprisingly intelligent. He just hadn't had much of an education. He was smart enough to hide just how smart he really was. Sailors didn't go much for smarts.

As he looked around the underwater cabins where he and his crew lived and worked, Second-Best Sailor consoled himself that below the ocean roofline his vessel was pretty much intact—save for those annoying stern thole-boards, which must have been inadequately tensioned when their staylines were being storm-lashed.

'Bovedecks, well, that was another matter entirely. No marine creature was ever completely at home out of the water, and Second-Best Sailor was no exception. But he had to find out how much damage the boat had sustained above the roofline, and that meant putting on his sailor suit and going 'bovedecks to inspect the garden, which had been at the mercy of surges for the better part of a week. Right now he was in no hurry to do that. He *knew* that there would be squids in the lemon trees again, and most likely crabs in the sagegrass as well. Those things always happened when the boat was exposed to a gale-strength airstorm.

It had been the worst storm he could remember. For several days he had been at the helm, relieved only for a few short rest breaks, trying to control the heavy boat as it pitched and yawed its way through outrageous waves. The constant rush of aerated water past the hull hurt his siphons and made him feel sick. The boat had tossed in the crushing surges, creaking and shuddering as if it was about to fall apart entirely.

It had been bedlam. His apprentices had no sooner tied down an errant hunting net than half a ton of cargo had torn loose from its mountings. And as soon as they had improvised secure fastenings for the cargo, the steering gear had seized up and had to be freed with pry bars and massive applications of boiled blubber lubricant. And all the while, the waves and the wind jerked the boat in so many directions that he was sure some of them didn't exist. Second-Best Sailor had very nearly been sucked out of the helm cabin into the surrounding ocean at least a dozen times by surging pressure-waves, and his tentacles were bruised and sore from trying to hold on to safety handles, furniture—anything that was solidly bolted down. Short Apprentice had very nearly been washed out through a broken sallyport. If he had not grabbed hold of Fat Apprentice at the last moment, they would have been down to one crew member, and Short Apprentice would have been faced with a long swim to rendezvous at their next destination.

What made it all the worse was that the jib halyard had jammed when the first gales hit, making it impossible to bring down the jib sail, and the air currents hitting the coarse cloth triangle had made steering next to impossible until the sail had ripped away altogether. By then they were already well off course, and the winds and currents were becoming less favorable by the minute. It had been a race against disaster, and disaster had romped home.

Right now Second-Best Sailor had little idea where they were, except that it had to be a long way to the west of where they ought to be. As soon as the waves reduced to a rough swell, he would have to make an excursion 'bovedecks and carry out some navigational observations. Until then . . . He instructed Fat Apprentice to keep the boat on its present heading, except to avoid rocks. He took another look through the maze of periscopes that No-Moon's sea captains used to check the set of their sails and the state of their ropes, and it didn't look good. The sheets were tangled, and the mainsail, hastily lowered, was a crumpled heap. The jib, he already knew, had ripped into shreds and blown away. Short Apprentice had watched it go, and a few tattered strips of sailcloth straggled across the deck in mute confirmation.

This kind of thing always seemed to happen to him—something that Second-Best Sailor found unfair and irksome.

The mast, at least, was still attached to the airside face of the boat's deck.

The gale had subsided to a strong breeze, just right for sailing if he could get the mainsail up and replace the missing jib. He opened one of the sallyports that flanked the sides of the hull below the roofline, and swam out into the tumbling ocean to find out how Short Apprentice was getting on.

Second-Best Sailor's squat body pulsed as water

squirted through his siphons, propelling him away from the shell-encrusted planking of the hull. The keel, a large triangular lignoid slab, hung down from the hull to catch the ocean currents. Through the air-bubbled water of the ocean roof he could see enough to be satisfied that the keel's integrity was unbreached.

He swam closer to the keel and brushed away some tangled weed with an expert tug of one tentacle. Then he headed for the stern, to assess the results of Short Apprentice's efforts.

Second-Best Sailor was a polypoid, a free-floating male belonging to a coral-like species. The females formed vast reefs, and only their husbands were mobile. He was shaped rather like a shortened squid, and slightly smaller than a 'Thal trader. His body was a cylinder of highly viscous jelly, tapered at one end and dividing into nine strong, flexible tentacles at the other. Every third tentacle trifurcated at its tip, for more delicate manipulations. Three large hemispherical eyes were arranged at equal angles around the cylinder, just forward of the base-ring, where tentacles met body. Between them, at the front center of his body, was a sphincter that could open to ingest food or expel digested waste. Three longitudinal fins, each aligned with an eye, ran from just aft of the tentacles all the way to the tip of the tapering tail, where they narrowed and merged into a complicated fan-like structure. Clusters of siphons were arrayed between the fins, where they ran into the tentacles. Most of them were devoted to the extraction of oxygen from the sea and the ejection of seawater to control movement. A few were more specialized. At the moment Second-Best Sailor's skin was mottled in patches of brown and gray, and it was as smooth as silk . . . but those features could change in an instant to reflect his mood.

He arranged his approach to keep him in Short Apprentice's blind spot, which would be quite big in one of such youth. To his surprise and relief, he quickly saw that the youngster was making an excellent job of tying down the thole-boards. Five of them were already secure, and the young polypoid was swarming all over the sixth and last, using three tentacles to braid a strong net of ropeweed while the other six held the board in place against the planking-rail. A few of the nodes were tighter than they ought to be, but Second-Best Sailor was content to let the apprentice find that out later, when he had to replace the temporary repair with permanent bindings. After he'd struggled with the tight nodes for a few hours, his captain would impress him with one of the lesser-known uses of an awlfish spike and fix the problem in seconds.

Second-Best Sailor was a great believer in the positive approach to training apprentices, and he turned until his speech-siphon pointed straight at the youngster, bellowing encouragement. Short Apprentice displayed the stripes of gratitude for a few seconds and carried on braiding his net.

Second-Best Sailor returned to his boat, entering through the nearest sallyport and closing it behind him. The seas were calming, and it was time to don a suit and penetrate the alien world 'bovedecks.

May and Stun tired of dabbling their toes in the ocean swell, and put their sandals back on.

"You are troubled," said Stun. "But you do not know what you should be troubled by. And that troubles you further."

May stared blankly toward the horizon. "I feel that something terrible is going to happen."

"Here?"

"I am not certain. I know that it involves this world, though I have no idea how I know. We have been taught to be rational, Stun, as our kind has spread between the stars. But you know, as do I—as do all Neanderthals— that there is more to the mind than the rational."

Stun agreed and offered an explanation. "Our minds evolved to recognize patterns, for survival. And many are the patterns that cannot be captured by rational thought. It is not so strange that we can sense patterns that have no rational basis. It does not mean they have no basis at all. Is a friendly touch rational? A mother's love? An enemy's hatred? Yet these things have been obvious to our minds since the time our monkey ancestors swung from the branches of trees. Rationality is a tool, not the sole reliable style of thinking."

"I would like to argue against you, but what you say makes too much sense," said May. "Our ancestors were Beastmasters before the Rescue opened the universe to them. They knew the minds of animals; they could sense a leopard's bite before the cat itself began to flex its jaw muscles. We have inherited that talent." Her tawny eyes went wide. "I fear, Stun, that a great beast is coming to this world, and its bite will be terrible and sudden." She paused. "And yet I doubt my fear, for I cannot find anything to support it."

She got to her feet. "We are wasting our time waiting here; it is as we expected—the mariner is late as usual. He will not make port today, the tides are running against him. And I am getting old and my mind is wandering, and I am seeing shadows where there is nothing to cast them."

Stun laughed, but her laugh was quickly silenced.

She was seeing shadows, too.

Polypoids are sea creatures, and their boats are mostly underwater. But being boats, they float, and their upper parts protrude into a more alien environment—air. And air holds its own new possibilities, though it took many generations before the polypoids began to understand them, and even longer before they learned to bend them to their will. The No-Moon boats had evolved from simple wooden structures, the equivalent of underwater carts, barely protruding from the water into the air above, propelled by the polypoid "sailors" who towed the unwieldy vessels behind them as they swam through the ocean. Later, the carts became more elongated, like a galley, and trained teams of sailors coordinated their siphons to direct the boat wherever it was intended to go. The reason for having a boat at all was to carry cargo; even a small crew could convey many times their own weight of goods to ports hundreds of miles away. They topped up basic food supplies by hunting whenever they got the opportunity.

Soon the rudimentary carts became transformed into more elaborate structures, underwater homes where the sailors could live and work unhampered by the vagaries of the ocean just outside the solid hull. Sallyports, underwater doors, offered instant access to the ocean whenever the fancy took them. They had the best of both worlds.

The first really big breakthrough in technology was the invention of keels—flat boards of dense, strong lignoid, which caught the current and improved the vessel's stability, at the expense of drag. Keels were raised when moving against the current, and angled when moving cross-current. It was a difficult skill.

The second and more significant innovation was to take advantage of air currents as well as water currents. The triangular sail, initially an expanse of heavy shugskin and later of thick, specially woven cloth, was attached to an assembly of wooden poles so that it could catch the wind. The boat was rolled on one side to rig the sail from the safety of the water, and then tipped upright again so that the sail could catch the wind. It was adjusted by ropes that ran over the bulwarks, down the side of the hull, and underneath to the main deck. If anything jammed or broke, the boat could be temporarily capsized to make repairs, or sailed into port if that was easier.

At first, sails were used for added speed in the same general direction as the water currents. But as the centuries passed, No-Moon's sailors learned to combine the forces of wind and waves to perform astonishing feats. They could sail against the water currents, provided the wind was coming from the right quarter, and they could even tack up-current in favorable winds. An important (and difficult) step was to redesign the keel as a rigid fixture, which went against the grain of centuries of sea lore but increased the vessel's speed dramatically.

Now major voyages thousands of miles long became practical. And direct two-way trade supplanted the previous cumbersome circumnavigation of the globe, simplifying commerce and creating a new business in passenger boats.

This was only the start. The sail opened up regions of the planet that had previously been accessible only to superfit, specially trained teams of polypoids. New ports festooned the continental coastlines and the countless archipelagos. And where the sailors went, so did their sessile, coralline wives, though these could take up residence only in shallow, warm waters.

Like all of No-Moon's mariners, Second-best Sailor always carried a piece of his wife with him, locked away in a mesh closet in his cabin so that the waters could flow over her and keep her healthy. A wifepiece was the best way to maintain mental equilibrium and physical condition on the long voyages away from the home lagoon. Many a new colony had been established from just such a "seed" in the past, but those pioneering days were long gone.

On this particular voyage, however, his usual chunk of female company had been supplemented by a second piece of living coral, also part of his wife. And this second wifepiece wasn't just there for sexual companionship.

Second-Best Sailor had been spawned in a rocky crevice beneath the warm, shallow waters of Crooked Atoll, one of the hundreds of tiny islands belonging to the Mosaic Isles, some four hundred miles southeast of the jutting sickle of rain forest known as The Claw. To its north, the rainforest gave way to the rock-strewn tundra of the Cloudless Continent. Few mariners had ventured inland of The Claw's jagged coastline, and fewer still had penetrated to the spine of the rain forest, but Second-Best Sailor's father, Talkative Forager, had won a sailor suit in a game of float-the-cube.

Talkative Forager was the kind of person who always got value out of anything he owned, so one day he had set off in a small skiff alone; and half a year later he had returned with several scars and wondrous tales of brightly colored creatures that swam through the air like the familiar coastal buzhawks and ocean-faring blannies but made their nests in tall woodweed trees. And weird things covered in fur that lived in holes in the ground and collected fruit husks. And much else, little of which was believed by anyone who listened to him. But they were wonderful tales nonetheless, and Talkative Forager became extremely popular.

Second-Best Sailor knew none of this, for he was fertilized in a mass spawning by the light of the Quadricorn meteor shower, along with a billion other microscopic prepolyps. He had no idea who his father had been. But his mother knew. His mother knew everything.

Second-Best Sailor's mother was Crooked Atoll. All of it.

Individual polypoid wives were only corals,

reefwives, completely immobile. But when these corals became a reef . . .

Like most of the reefs on No-Moon, Crooked Atoll was an episodic network coral. Sometimes it was much like any normal coralline reef on any of a million planets: a seething slow battleground of chemical warfare, in which dozens of different species of coral-like organisms competed for space, nutrient, and light. No two corals on different worlds were ever the same. But the universals of life were similar on all worlds—the environmental constraints gave rise to the same interlocking systems of self-defining niches, and on any world with an ocean there automatically arose a niche for organisms that could grow their own reefs.

Yes, sometimes Crooked Atoll was a coral reef like any other. But the rest of the time it was like nothing anywhere else in the Galaxy. Acting on a common impulse, the separate corals could link their rudimentary nervous systems into a gigantic web that spanned the entire atoll. And when they did, their combined brain outperformed the most intelligent individuals anywhere else by a factor of billions.

The network was linked now. And the separate reefwives became one, and the one was like nothing ever seen on any other world in the vast universe.

Across the planet, each atoll's collective consciousness functioned like the brain of a single organism, the reefmind. And the separate atolls were also linked, by thick cables of nerve fibers that wandered across the sea beds. These cables conveyed information from each atoll to her neighbors. It was a small world network, and no two atolls were ever separated by more than eight links.

The exceedingly mobile males were also part of that network, communicating with their wives using a language of molecules. Every wash of the waves brought news from the boats, the bars, and the trading posts of the seaports. Crooked Atoll sensed the pulse of the planet; by communicating with her fellow atolls she could make herself aware of almost everything that was happening in the oceans and ports of No-Moon. And, by picking up gossip from the spaceport bars and swimways, she could also keep tabs on what was happening off the planet.

Only the mariners knew that their wives possessed such an ability. It was a racial secret, and the polypoids never talked about it around other sentient species. Not that they would have been believed if any of them had accidentally dropped hints. An intelligent reef? Nonsense. Just another typical sailor story.

The reefwives had an unbroken history of collective perception that went back half a billion years, and they remembered all of it.

And now the reefwives were becoming concerned. Some of the Neanderthal traders were telling the males about a large space fleet that might be heading their way—purpose uncertain. In a corner of their perception the reefwives watched potential events unfolding that would have dire consequences for their mates and their world. And the group mind could segregate itself into separate entities so that different parts of the reef could "discuss" their perceptions and compare them.

The reefwives had an unusual sense of time. They perceived an "extended present" which caused them to "see" in a single "timechunk" about two weeks either side of what other beings, including their husbands, were aware of as "now." However, they did not know the future; they foresaw it, constantly and unconsciously extrapolating from the first two weeks of the timechunk, which they updated from sensory input and relayed news and gossip. To them the future was as real as the past, and distinguished only by its position within the static expanse of frozen time.

Now, in one corner of the "future" section of their perception, they saw events unfold that disturbed them on an atavistic level.

Not because they were unfamiliar events. On the contrary, the reefwives had witnessed this menace many times before, in many forms. Now it was happening again. The inbound fleet was host to a religion. Not just any religion—a special kind. A benevolent memeplex, a mental hook baited with tolerance and love, which, as it gained adherents, would sometimes rigidify into pure evil. How far along that path had this particular memeplex progressed? It might still be benign, but it might be malignant, well into its runaway phase. The reefwives could not yet decide which; they needed more detailed information. But there was no sense in being complacent—not when they remembered what had happened when a benevolent memeplex had tried to infiltrate their previous homeworld of Three-Moons.

Age-old contingency plans flashed across their collective consciousness. For a fraction of a second, the collective mind that was Crooked Atoll debated a million alternatives, and came to a decision.

Implacable resistance.

The rigging was a tangled mess, and the garden was a wreck.

No one knew which mariner had first decided that it would be a good idea to grow plants in the otherwise useless 'bovedecks area. The fashion probably started out as decoration—a few salt-tolerant flowers and trailing vines. The polypoids had long grown fruit trees on the more accessible shores of their islands, especially the Isles of the Heliponaise. They had bred them for more succulent fruit, tended them with loving care. Fruit trees were symbols of an untroubled life. Later, various types of root and grain had augmented their horticultural repertoire. Add to that the obvious point that the flat upper surface of a boat was otherwise mostly wasted space, and matters arranged themselves. Gardening quickly gained popularity: It was a relaxing hobby on a long voyage. Of course, it had to be done in a suit, but every boat had at least one of those. And the garden had to be carefully laid out so as not to obstruct the rigging. But those were minor details and easily taken care of.

Second-Best Sailor had specialized in fruit: every spare yard of the above-sea deck of his vessel was crammed with stumpy trees that grew lumpish blobs of concentrated *taste* that were rather like lemons. These "lemon trees" were planted in tubs, and apart from twice-yearly pruning they needed little attention. Mariners adored lemons, and any surplus could easily be traded for cash or kind in the ubiquitous sea bars and markets of the ports.

Second-Best Sailor felt his propulsive organs tighten involuntarily. His garden had been comprehensively ruined. Most of his lemon trees had been washed overboard, and those that remained had lost most of their fruit. They were covered in sticky squidlike creatures, which were common in surface waters around the time of the Change Winds. Second-Best Sailor uttered a robust mariner curse and set to work.

Before the wind could get up again, or other calamity befall, he made a series of observations of the sun's position, the directions of wind and waves, and any visible landmarks. When these were combined with underwater observations of the ocean floor, it should not take him long to work out the boat's position. He was pretty sure he recognized two of the distant islands anyway, particularly the one with the three jagged cliffs, a small one between two larger ones.

Then he began to pluck the dead but still-sticky squid from the branches of the lemon trees, tossing them over the taffrail. Soon a herd of spiny tallfins gathered in the boat's wake, attracted by the prospect of an easy meal. They were harmless unless they in turn attracted one of the large predators, but shugs and gulpmouths were unlikely in these latitudes at this time of year.

He hoped.

Once the squid were cleared away, it became possible to disentangle the rigging from the trees. Second-Best Sailor could see at once that there was no point in trying to save any of the lines except for the main halyards, which had been coiled and secured when they lowered the mainsail. Those apart, the whole boat would have to be rerigged, and that required a wet-dock and a week's hard work. But the mainmast was still standing, and he could jury-rig the mainsail by running staylines out along the cross-pole. This temporary fix would last until they reached their scheduled destination, and proper repairs would have to wait until then.

He busied himself with the crumpled mainsail, pulling it flat and inspecting it for rips. When he was satisfied, he looped runners from the staylines through metal-rimmed sockets in the edge of the sail, thumped the deck twice to alert Short Apprentice to the need to turn the boat into the wind, and hauled the makeshift sail into place. The sailor suit, sensing the heavy forces acting on his muscles, reconfigured itself to take most of the strain.

Second-Best Sailor tied off the halyards to a convenient cleat and ran his eye over the jury-rigged sail as a final check. He made a few more navigational observations—the way the sun's angular height changed with time, for instance. Then he stepped off the side and swam back through a sallyport to the main cabin.

He regretted having no lemons to trade, but those were of small importance. He usually traded them to other mariners or used them as gambling tokens when the mood took him, though he'd intended on this occasion to give a few to the Neanderthal women to lubricate the trading. Tough.

For a moment he wondered if it would be worth trying to sell his small but exquisite collection of fanworm tubes. It was a kind of coming-of-age ritual for the most daring mariners. The beautiful secretions were to be found in the ocean depths near No-Moon's rare volcanic vents, where superheated mineral-laced water spouted from the sea bed. Here, in the eternal darkness, lived dense clusters of delicate fanworms, which peeped from protective tubes and flashed colored lights at one another. The tubes were convoluted and roughly square in cross-section. Each tube bore intricate patterns of colored deposits, no two the same, and they were prized as natural works of art.

A sufficiently bold polypoid, equipped with a suit, could dive to the bottom of the ocean, brave the dangerously hot waters near a vent, and liberate a few fanworm tubes. Second-Best Sailor had done just that, on a dare, and he kept his treasures locked away on his boat.

They were valuable. Could he bear to part with one?

No. Trade was important but not *that* important. Even though the damage to his boat would set his income back considerably, this was going to be a very profitable voyage, as long as he could reach port before the Neanderthals moved on. Based on past performance, he was sure that Smiling Teeth May Bite would wait for him, provided he didn't take *too* much time. And, safely stowed away in a locker of solid metal, he had the stack of datablets that the reefwives had extruded, containing valuable simulations for offworld customers. The reefmind traded in information, and the Neanderthal women would pay enough for it to outfit his boat for a dozen voyages.

The Neanderthals thought that the mariners prepared the simulations themselves, no doubt using some high-powered Precursor computer, and the mariners made no attempt to disabuse them. The secret of the reefmind must be *kept* a secret.

Later, when night had fallen, Second-Best Sailor made another excursion 'bovedecks to observe the stars. Their positions would confirm his navigational calculations, but mostly he just got a kick out of stargazing. So many worlds, so much life. And tonight there was a bonus, a sight so rare that he knew of it only through legend.

Stretched across a huge arc of sky were hundreds of lavender lights, arranged like beads on strings, forming a fan that pointed straight toward the horizon, where the sun had just set. He knew what they must be, and excitement surged through his whole body. He had been waiting all his life to witness the passage of the fabled magnetotorus herd. It was even more beautiful than he had imagined from the stories—bejeweled patterns of living light, emitted by streams of wild magnetic creatures migrating under the guidance of their inscrutable herders. He gave thanks to the Maker and counted it a privilege to be alive to witness the herd's arrival.

To an observer on the outer fringes of the system, the herd announced itself as a faint patch of monochromatic lavender light. As it approached the outermost world of the No-Moon system, an outpost of loose rubble held together by nitrogen ice, the patch resolved into a sprinkling of random spots, all glowing with the same spectral hue.

Seen from the side, as they passed, the spots became chains of glowing pearls, neatly stacked in line astern, all pointing straight at the nearby star, Lambda Coelacanthi. Although they varied in size, every pearl was ring-shaped, aligned at right angles to the axis of the chain, with their matter—if it was matter—spiraling smoothly into the central hole and out again.

There were hundreds of these chains, irregularly distributed in a teardrop-shaped cluster, and each chain contained anywhere between eight and sixty pearls.

The pearls were magnetotori, primitive organisms made from magnetic plasma, living Bussard ramscoops that devoured the thinly spread hydrogen of the interstellar medium, sucking it up atom by atom, fusing the atoms into helium to create energy. Every two hundred thousand years this herd of wild magnetotori repeated the same nomadic cycle, migrating from star to star in a pattern whose origins were lost in the abyss of deep time.

Elsewhere, other herds followed their own cycles, longer or shorter. And for the past few million years, all of the migrating herds had been accompanied and regulated by itinerant herders, whose physical form was a pattern of standing electromagnetic waves confined in cocoonlike metallic nets. The herders drew sustenance by absorbing radiation from their toroidal "cattle." Without this life support, the herders could never have survived in the dark voids between the stars.

They accompanied their herds in ramshackle ceramic vessels, floating junk piles assembled according to rules that only a herder could comprehend, and controlled their beasts with pulses of magnetic force. The herders could not change the migratory routes, but they could make sure that the journey was timed to their own advantage.

The magnetotori were coming to graze in the photosphere of the system's sun, where the local plasmoids were roosted.

The herders had a longstanding arrangement with the

plasmoids. They could direct their beasts to feed on selected regions of magnetic vortex-fields, where their presence would be most beneficial to the dynamics of the star. There, too, the magnetotori would mate. Before the fields became overgrazed and turned into sterile magnetocrystals, a process that took a few centuries, the herds would move on to the next star in their itinerary.

At this distance from the star, their passage was slow and leisurely. As they neared their destination, their speed would pick up. Now they sailed gracefully past two moderately sized gas giants: the enigmatic green mist of Ghost and the blotchy blues and purples of Marsupial. Next they traversed a dangerous belt of rocks and snowballs to cross the orbit of Bandicoot, timing their passage to stay well clear of its fuzz of radio noise. Bandicoot, too, was a gas giant, a protostar that had failed to ignite. It was made of hydrogen, helium, and a hundred other gases. It spun so slowly that the normal equatorial bulge was distinctly subdued, and its clouded atmosphere crackled with electrical discharges as a matched pair of never-ending storms circled its north and south equatorial zones, pursuing each other as if in some bizarre ritual hunt.

The next three planets were tiny, all much the same size but differing wildly in physical constitution. Baugenphyme was a sulfur desert, pockmarked by the calderas of long-dead volcanoes. Hilary was a cracked ball of ice, coated in a thick layer of dust, dominated by a spectacular impact crater whose radiating arms wrapped themselves right round the little world, overlapping one another in a fishnet pattern. Jones was a mottled ball of pink and lemon, with pale gray lakes of frozen phosphorus hydride.

Fourth from the sun was No-Moon, a typical aqueous planet with extensive oceans of liquid water surrounding five large island continents, liberally sprinkled with archipelagoes. Unusually for a planet of its size and position, it had no naturally occurring satellite, hence its name. It had a flourishing biota, including a variety of sentients, mostly nonnative. For most of them, the spectacular appearance of the herds against the night sky was a deeply spiritual experience.

The herd sensed the gradual steepening of the sun's gravitational gradient and plunged onward, seeking pasture. The herders' only remaining task was to make sure that they chose the pasture that the plasmoids preferred.

It was Stun who spotted the sail first. May was busy arguing with a couple of suited mariners who thought that she was interested in scrimshawed bottlewhale teeth, and who wouldn't accept that she wasn't. She finally got rid of them by criticizing the carvings, pointing out that they were primitive and poorly formed. They were, but there were plenty of worlds on which these features would have been a virtue—indeed, the sole reason for owning such artifacts.

When Stun shouted the news of Second-Best Sailor's arrival, May unslung her ansible and selected the correct encryption disk. There was an exactly matching disk among those in Will's ansible. All ansible communication required such disks—not for security per se, but because that was how the Precursors in their wisdom had built them. Security was a side effect. Another side effect was that although an ansible link conveyed messages instantaneously, the link could not be set up any faster than a ship could carry an encryption disk—unless you used a transible, but those were prohibitively expensive. Anyone with an ansible could receive messages from anywhere in the Galaxy, but the only messages they could understand were those that came from a disk that matched their own.

Now set up for instant communication, May signaled to the orbiting starship that was their home: "I have just spotted a sail. It is ripped to shreds, but the colors look very familiar."

Her mate, Sharp Wit Will Cut, responded after a few seconds' delay: "He must not have been diverted *too* far from his course by the Change Winds, then." Over the ansible, May could hear mewling sounds from the furry crevit that habitually draped itself across Will's broad shoulders. It was a handsome beast, like its master. By Neanderthal standards, anyway.

"No, he is several days earlier than I expected," said May.

"At least we know he did not sink."

"Apparently not. He really is a very good sailor, you know. Just irresponsible."

Sharp Wit Will Cut reviewed what May had just said. "I am not sure that those two sentences go together."

She decided not to rise to the bait. "I hope he carries the datablets; otherwise this will have been a wasted trip."

"Not entirely," said Will.

"What do you mean?"

"We have been picking up transmissions from some distant craft that seem to be approaching this world."

"The wild magnetotori and their herders?"

"No, the herd passed by last night, on their way to the sun. This is something else. The rumors have been circulating for a while. Now they have been confirmed."

May's sense of foreboding heightened. This would interest the mariners, assuming they didn't already know it. "Craft? Do you know how many, or what size?"

"A fleet. We think there are between sixty and eighty of them, all powered by tame magnetotori. There seem to be a dozen command vessels, among them a mother ship, about the same number of heavy transports, and a lot of smaller support craft. The command vessels are *big*—conveyor-class, top of the range. They are making no attempt to conceal their approach. Some of our fellow nomads picked up bits of their interfleet communication traffic when they passed nearby. Radio messages, some unencrypted. They have sent me copies by ansible."

"Can we put names to any of them?"

Will snorted. "No, the messages mention no individual names. But they repeatedly use a collective name. It is almost a chant, a mantra."

"What is it?"

"They call themselves 'Cosmic Unity.' Ever heard of them, May?"

"Possibly. Does Ship have any records under that heading?"

"Yes, it has. Lots. We are reviewing them now."

"Copy them to me immediately, Will. I think my

sailor friend will place high trading value on a datablet containing information about this fleet."

As his boat drifted slowly into port, Second-Best Sailor left most of the handling to his apprentices. They knew the routine, they knew the port, and if anything went wrong, then he could blame *them* for it. They in turn were well aware of this tactic, which had been used against them many times, and were careful not to make any errors.

"Luff the mainsail," Second-Best Sailor commanded at the precise moment that Short Apprentice was moving to do just that. It was always a good idea to remind subordinates who was in charge. "Neatly done." It was also a good idea to praise them when they performed unusually well. Second-Best Sailor had learned such tactics from his mother, who had passed them on from Talkative Forager as part of a routine method for maintaining cultural continuity among the males.

The waters around the shore of the port were a jumble of docks, boat's chandlers, warehouses, and bars—all b'low-water, naturally, but most had 'bove-water extensions for commerce with landlubbers. These extensions could be used by polypoids wearing simple water-masks, provided they slipped back into the water at frequent intervals. Longer periods out of the water required suits, but the duplicators had made those widely available—though still quite pricey. Duplication was not cost-free. It took time, raw materials, and most of all, expertise.

The boat slid neatly alongside two others moored to

the posts of a dock. Short Apprentice went through the side to tie it up securely. Fat Apprentice began to stow any gear that wasn't needed in port. Second-Best Sailor went to his private cabin, convinced himself that the two fragments of his wife were in good health, and checked the fan that would ensure a continuing flow of fresh water to their polyps. Then he rummaged in the cupboards until he found the datablets that his Neanderthal contacts were expecting.

He locked the cupboard and left the datablets where they were. He would come and get them once trade negotiations were completed. Then he grabbed a watermask and headed for a bar he particularly liked, known as Wild Weed Wasted. Smiling Teeth May Bite and Eyes That Stun the Unwary would meet him there shortly. He'd looked through the periscope and seen them on the pier as he approached.

The underwater parts of the bar were crowded with sailors celebrating landfall in the traditional manner. Several were obviously getting very high on sticks of concentrated algae, and at least three had lost consciousness altogether and fallen into a stupor. He slipped underneath a group of mariners from the Sharptop Peninsula who were playing a raucous game of float-the-cube, and located the up door at the far corner of the bar. Pulling on his water-mask, he headed toward the surface.

He emerged in what appeared from above to be a small swimming pool—impossibly blue water contained by tiled walls and floor. But the tiles were ceramic shells, imported from the Cool Isles, where they were extruded by trained mollusks. And the blue was mostly the effect of squads of cleaner-algae.

May and Stun were already there, sitting on dockchairs beside the pool.

"Late again, I see" was May's greeting.

"Not my fault," protested Second-Best Sailor. "Change Winds come early this season."

"Again."

"Yeah. Funny, that. Don' understand it at all. It ain't normal." He gestured with splayed subtentacles, as if struck by a thought. "Do ya think the arrival of the torus herders might 'ave something to do with it? Some say their animals can disrupt normal weather patterns."

"Not the timing of the Change Winds, Second-Best Sailor."

"Oh. But did you *see* them? Amazin'! Makes ya realize what an astonishin' universe we live in!"

The Neanderthals, too, had seen the strings of magnetotori, but they were unmoved by events that stirred most other species' spirits. "An unusual sight," said May, as if it were an intellectual proposition. "Pale violet lights in a fan. Pretty." She didn't sound very enthusiastic.

"You guys just don't appreciate the finer things of life," the mariner stated with mock disapproval. "You need educatin'."

With a quick glance at Stun to confirm tactics, May decided to cut short the banter and get down to the trading. It might just throw Second-Best Sailor off his guard. "We trade information for the edification of the mariners of No-Moon. What do you trade?"

"Information? What kind of information?"

May sighed. She'd known it was pointless. Nothing could throw Second-Best Sailor off his guard when he was sober. And there was no point in offering him anything to eat: He'd save his eating until he had clinched the deal.

"First tell us what *you* have to trade. Then we will describe the nature of our information. Do you have the datablets?"

"Might have. I was gonna throw in a few lemons, for free, but the airstorm destroyed most of 'em."

Stun giggled. "Just like last year."

Second-Best Sailor failed to see the joke and looked hurt. "Well, 'smatterofact, yeah. I suppose I might have a datablet or two somewhere, if that's what grabs ya. . . ."

The bargaining began.

Not only were the reefwives highly intelligent, they had long ago evolved the ability to extrude ceramics, metals, and minerals to any desired pattern, right down to the molecular level. They had developed this ability by modifying the chemical systems and genetic controls that enabled their distant ancestors to make carbonate solids to construct their own hard parts, just as mollusks can secrete shells that are virtually monocrystalline. But the reefmind was intelligent, so the reefwives' extrusions could be deposited according to a plan. They could make ceramic insulation, impervious to water, one molecule thick. The datablets, capable of cramming huge quantities of information into a very small space, were constructed in the same way. And the datablets could be read by land-entity computers, suitably programmed and equipped.

The reefmind made many other kinds of ceramic, waterproof electronic circuitry, too. Some of the best electronics in the Galaxy were reefwife extrusions, though they were universally assumed to be of mariner manufacture. The most widely accepted theory was that the mariners had stumbled across some hitherto unknown Precursor gadget. All attempts to steal it had failed, but this was attributed to the high security of an underwater lifestyle, not to the gadget's nonexistence.

In this manner the reefwives, using their husbands as a front, could market their most important product: simulations. The same ferocious computational abilities that powered their remarkable timechunk extrapolations could be turned to other tasks, and routinely were. The reefmind placed great value on information, and to its delight, so did the rest of the Galaxy. The datablets still on board Second-Best Sailor's vessel were accurate simulations of the forest ecosystem of the aqueous planet Beta-2 Tigris, which was suffering from an epidemic of tuber rot and in serious danger of ecological collapse. The simulations offered guidance on management strategies to eradicate the infection and return the forests to their former state, including all the important subecosystems, from microorganisms to ponderous fellingtooths.

In return, the reefwives wanted information about Galactic politics and society. Inside information, the kind of thing they could not get from public sources. With this, their extended-present perceptions of wider events would be more accurate.

They were especially interested in anything the Neanderthal computers held relating to new arrivals in the vicinity.

And so it was that a rambling, confused dossier on Cosmic Unity was handed over to Second-Best Sailor, and the forests of the aqueous world Beta-2 Tigris were thrown a lifeline.

But before the deal could be concluded, Second-Best Sailor had a private request. "May, what I really need right now is new lemon trees 'bovedecks. Mine were *wasted.*"

"You can buy those from many sources."

"Yeah, but you Neanderthals can work in air, so ya could plant 'em for me a lot more easy, and a lot better, than most jobbin' gardeners."

Stun feigned reluctance. "We *could*, if offered sufficient inducements."

"Oh, I can pay."

"With what? You have already agreed a trade for your datablets. The lemon trees were your spare trade goods."

Second-Best Sailor laughed. "Lemons—they're nothin'. I got somethin' better. Somethin' no one has ever offered ya before. Somethin' I wants ya to hold in sacred trust for me, until—if ever—I ask for 'er back."

Her? The lion-headed Neanderthal women were intrigued. This was no bargain; if anything, it was an obligation. But their sense of empathy was screaming at them: *accept, accept.* "What?"

"I want to lend ya a piece of my wife."

2

COSMIC UNITY MISSION FLEET

Wickedness, selfishness, vanity, greed, arrogance . . . Yes,
I have known all these, have been guilty of all these . . .
But they are obvious faults, easy to recognize and to
combat. They are nothing compared to the evils that
have been inflicted by sincere bigots obsessed with their
own version of Good Works.

The Wisdom of Chalz

The galaxy was a mere stripling.

*But despite its comparative youth, it had already ac-
cumulated dangerous residues of its past, and it could
not be rid of them. There were idiosyncrasies and anomalies, complications that would not normally have been
expected in such a young specimen. Not just the gross effects of gravitational disruption, which could afflict even
a young galaxy. These peculiarities were subtler, and
they normally took a long time to develop.*

This galaxy had suffered from what can best be de-

scribed as a series of childhood infections. It was chronically infected with a plague of life. Reproducing entities, leaping from planet to planet and from star to star, had diffused along its spiral arms, taking the path of least resistance. Occasionally, the more virulent strains had crossed the relatively starless voids between. Now life forms had become endemic and moved through the galaxy's substance at will.

And as they spread, they changed the nature of the habitats that they infected, until those accumulated changes affected the nature of the galaxy itself.

It was not clear whether these spreading patches of change were a disease or a natural progression toward maturity. Or both. There was no obvious place in the laws of quantum gravity for this fifth state of matter, sticking out at right angles to the conventional four of solid, liquid, gas, plasma: the spontaneous appearance of organized complexity. The physics of a galaxy seemed, at first sight, to imply a lifeless future. But the inner workings of those laws, propagated through the Middle Kingdom of the material mesoscale, led inexorably to persistent outbreaks of self-complication. When allied to the potent ability to replicate, this tendency gave rise to emergent structures that could only be described as living. And when replication made mistakes, becoming reproduction, those entities acquired the ability to evolve. Natural selection preserved some mistakes, destroyed the rest; this accelerated the process of change and offered a natural route to ever-greater complexity.

During the galaxy's infancy this potential for complication had run riot. It had been realized in a billion different ways—as carbon chemistry, plasma topology, dislocations in high-gravity neutron crystals, diffraction peaks of electromagnetic radiation, herds of entangled electrons, communities of graviton orbitals. Each instance formed the nucleus of a separate infection with its own characteristic etiology, but the overall course of the galactic disease was much the same, whatever physical form the entities took. This was no disorder, however. On the contrary, it was an insidious, metastasizing outbreak of order. Order where none should exist, order that danced to its own tune. Impossible, wonderful, unavoidable life, clinging to existence with a robustness that defied all expectations.

Especially interesting complexities came into being at the boundaries where distinct infections collided and competed. Those boundaries could be temporal as well as spatial. The past could influence the future. Expectations of the future could influence the present.

In this galaxy, the dominant influences had been of just these kinds. While still in its early childhood, the galaxy had experienced a virulent infection by an unusually potent form of intelligence. The Precursors, as they were named by those with whom their legacy collided, had spread through almost all parts of the galaxy, avoiding only the Black Hole jungle at the galactic core. The agent and the consequence of this cosmic diaspora went far beyond mere intelligence, to become extelligence: the interactive, collective knowledge that is shared by a culture of intelligent, communicative beings. With breathtaking speed, Precursor extelligence became self-sustaining, self-propelled. It gave rise to a brand of technology so advanced that it bordered on magic.

All things end. When the Precursor contagion had run

its course, and immunity had set in, the infectious intel-
ligences vanished from the universe. But they left behind
relics of their extelligence, scattered enigmatically
across huge swaths of intragalactic space like the scars
of long-healed wounds.

Later infections picked at those scars and metabolized
them in their own ways. The relics of this childhood dis-
ease affected the symptoms, and the spread, of a thou-
sand later, milder ones.

One of those relics was currently being employed to
create several thousand copies of a mechanism so primitive that the Precursors would have been profoundly
embarrassed by the use to which their technology was
being put. The construction was being conducted by
Servant-of-Unity XIV Samuel Godwin'sson Travers on
board *Disseminator 714*, one small ship in a huge Cosmic Unity mission fleet that was soon to bring the
memeplexes of universal joy and tolerance to yet another
grateful world, a planet known locally as No-Moon. He
hummed a tune of indeterminate provenance as he
packed the resulting devices into plastic containers,
sixty-four to a box.

For a normal human, Sam was tall—not with the exaggerated elongation often found in people who lived in
microgravity, but a head higher than most. His bones
were slender and lightly muscled; his face was a little too
wide for its jaw, with the eyes set close together on either
side of a narrow, straight nose. He wasn't ugly; he wasn't
good-looking; he was just ordinary.

The depth of his devotion was not. He carried out his allotted tasks with the keenness of a true zealot. Performing the duties of Cosmic Unity gave him a deep spiritual satisfaction. His lifesoul felt cleansed and sparkling, vibrant with transcendent love. Ever since early childhood his life had been dedicated to Service, for his parents knew that their son had been born to serve. They knew that through Service all species would eventually become One, and the sacred prophecies would be fulfilled, as had been ordained by the Founders. And soon, under their kind but firm tutelage, XIV Samuel came to know it, too.

The prospect sent a shiver along his spine. *If only Unity would be attained soon! So that I am alive to witness it!*

Absently he buffed the Precursor duplicator with the sleeve of his robe, removing a faint trace of sweat left by a previous, less careful servant. The machine functioned without noise, vibration, or indeed any external signs save for the appearance, in a steady stream, of the copies that it made. It had no evident energy source, but some kind of conservation law seemed to govern its functions, for it had to be fed an occasional meal of matter. It did not seem important what kind of matter—save for a few essential elements like praseodymium, which presumably could not be synthesized—but there had to be *enough* matter.

An original of the object being duplicated lay in a shallow depression on the machine's surface, where Sam had placed it. The duplicator created such a depression automatically, to fit whatever was deposited there. Sam's job, in which he had undergone extensive training, was to operate the duplicator and persuade it to disgorge endless replicas of that one original.

He did not have to know how the duplicator worked, which was good. *No one* knew how any Precursor technology worked—not the giant orbital fortifications encircling Rigel, not even the handheld devices that had been dug from the frozen nitrogen plains of the fifth moon of Zeta Camelopardi 14, the ones that could both crack nuts and graft new limbs on silicon-based creatures in low gravity. But that technology had been designed by master engineers, who did not expect the user to understand what was being used. Every Precursor machine was controlled through a user interface based on metaphor. It must have been entirely intuitive to any Precursor. But even with extensive and arduous training, it took their successors many years to become accustomed to the rudiments of the system—and half a lifetime to become proficient. Even experienced operators often made mistakes.

Mistakes were unimportant. The material could be recycled, the task repeated until it achieved the desired result. When it did, the duplicator could churn out perfect replicas, apparently identical down to the molecular level, indefinitely.

In a replicative economy, anything that works is free.

Duplicators were a gift to younger species from the long-dead Precursors. The Precursors built to last. Perhaps they had intended to leave a legacy for those that followed them. Perhaps it was the merest accident that anything useful survived. No one knew how Precursor minds worked; they had left their artifacts but no record of themselves.

This particular gift was not easily acquired, even so. A quarter-million years before Sam's lifetime, a Thunchchan expedition along a section of the Galaxy's Trailing Spiral Arm had investigated a world whose atmosphere was rich in the sulfur oxides so necessary for metabolism. Hoping to found a new colony, they had stumbled instead on something of far greater value: the separate components of an unused duplicator, still in their original wrappings.

It took more than 230,000 years for the combined intellect of the Thunchchan Empire to figure out how to provoke those components into self-assembly. It took only a few months more to get the device running, producing poor but recognizable copies of small items like skin clips and crest jewelry.

It took more than a century to refine their control of the device to make perfect copies of any inert object no larger than their own heads.

Life forms? Those were different. The duplicator could *copy* them, but the copies came out dead. Many religions took this as proof that life was infused with something special, some nonmaterial essence. But Cosmic Unity held to a simpler, more prosaic explanation: The Precursor machine could duplicate form but not dynamics.

One duplicator, however, is little more than a curio. The Thunchchans searched their entire region of the cosmos for a second—or, better still, for another set of components, waiting to be assembled. The components would be small enough to be copied faithfully with their current skills.

The search proved fruitless. The Thunchchans were the sole owners of one solitary item of Precursor magic, and all they could use it for were party tricks.

It was frustrating.

Thunchchan technocrats studied the duplicator until there were no ideas left to test, learned nothing useful, and consigned the artifact to an archaeological museum. There it was prominently displayed but seldom operated. It remained there for three thousand years . . . until one morning an inquisitive youngling, climbing over the exhibit, triggered a second mode of operation, in which the duplicator accessed a presumably preinstalled database of constructs. It began turning out copies of a limited range of devices without the presence of an original.

It then took Thunchchan science less than a year to discover how to access the default templates that generated all the components of a duplicator. Complete with wrappings.

Duplicates of these components could also self-assemble. The result was a fully functional duplicator. There seemed to be no loss of fidelity: The product of a chain of copies thousands of generations long seemed to do everything that the original could.

Within ten years, the machines were in use on a hundred worlds. All attempts to control their spread failed, even—especially—when they fell into the hands of Thunchch's enemies. Within a century, there was not a solid-matter civilization in the Galaxy that could manage without them.

Like life, the duplicators were a disease, and they

spread like wildfire. They needed only three things to function: nutrients in the form of matter; a small but essential supply of rare elements, notably praseodymium; and a host mind to configure them. The duplicators were not self-reproducing life forms, but they reproduced nonetheless. They were viruslike parasites, or more probably symbionts—the verdict was not yet in.

Sam turned to the duplicator and knelt before it, his head bowed. He made a series of graceful gestures with his hands.

It was not some religious rite, although there were plenty of those on board *Disseminator 714* as it spread the Good News of Cosmic Unity, namely, the Oneness of All Life. It was how the machine's user interface—its *metaphace*—worked. Presumably, the Precursors had used a language of gesture, or possibly that was merely how they communicated with their machines. All Sam knew was that this particular series of movements would (he hoped) increase the size of the output by approximately 12 percent. It did seem to help if the duplicator was approached in a reverential frame of mind, but he suspected that was because such a mood slowed his gestures down and made them clearer. Or smoother. Or more confident.

Sam didn't really care; all he cared about was serving Unity, as he had been trained to do by his revered parents, XIII Samuel and his partners XVI Eloise and II Josephina.

Sam drew a short breath of pleasure. The new devices

were larger, just as he had intended, but otherwise they were identical to the original. He had no idea of the purpose for which Cosmic Unity needed them, and it never occurred to him to ask. They were just the next item on a very long list: 65,536 copies of original AZ-F-4933, the second half of them to be made one standard increment larger. He uttered a short but heartfelt prayer to the Lifesoul-Cherisher, and experienced a flood of satisfaction as he fulfilled his assigned role of servant.

While its operator prayed, the duplicator continued to disgorge identical devices, one every few seconds.

Sam rose to his feet and picked up an empty container. The boxes themselves were made by a colleague in an adjoining chamber. Methodically he packed the box with the devices he had made. By the time he had finished, another boxful was ready. Occasionally, he conversed with the box-maker, another human male. *Disseminator 714* had the fifteen types of species that the Church had determined were ideal to maintain social harmony, but repeated attempts to mix species on technical tasks never seemed to work very well and had been abandoned.

In this manner Sam's morning passed. It was fulfilling work.

In the belly of *Disseminator 714* was a large open space, once a cargo tank. The vessel had originally been built to carry freight, mostly liquids that were common in some parts of the Galaxy and rare, but essential, elsewhere. When the market in liquid neon collapsed, Cosmic Unity had purchased the ship at a bargain price and converted it for creatures warmer-blooded than its previous Gra'aan owners. The cargo tank became a sanctum for the rites of the Community of the United Cosmos, and the vessel became yet another agent for the dissemination of the Memeplex of Universal Tolerance to a receptive Galaxy.

His duties temporarily suspended by command of the high acolyte, Sam hurried through the bowels of the ship as he always did on such occasions, trotting securely in the ubiquitous artificial gravity. He was hastening to take his place in the Assembly of Joy so that he could renew his faith in the essential oneness of Life—be it a magnetic plasmoid in the surface of a star or a fragile bag of molecules like himself.

It was the high point of his existence, a daily reaffirmation of his reason for being.

To Sam, the atmosphere in the sanctum was pure poison. So, as he entered, protective Precursor machinery sprang into action. A puff of mist condensed and enveloped him in a molecule-thick membrane that would filter out toxic compounds from the air. If his skin had been unprotected, these would have had the same effect on him as nerve gas: He would have died within seconds of entering the room, his skin becoming a mass of giant pus-filled blisters. He knew this, but he seldom even thought about it anymore. It did not disturb him. Precursor gadgetry never failed.

The environment in the Assembly was deliberately selected so that it suited none of those present. That was fair and just, reflecting the essential nature of the Community of the Cosmos. Each sentient entity present, in its own way, was protected by technology, be it endogenous or Precursor. Unity came at a price, the price of constant discomfort and reliance on machines, coatings, membranes, and magnetogravitic fields. All this served as a valuable reminder that Unity was not the natural state of the universe, but one that could be attained only through sacrifice, humility, faith, and tolerance.

Tolerance was more than just a state of mind. It was an ever-present act of reaffirmation. You had to work at being tolerant.

Sam looked around, trying to find a place to pray. Worship rings painted on the bare metal floor tacitly told ground-seeking species where to station themselves. Smaller rings, on the walls, were occupied by metallomorphs, which clung like lichen to flat surfaces and moved by hitching a ride on other, more mobile creatures. In appearance no more than shiny quasicrystalline patches, metallomorphs actually housed a quick electronic intelligence.

Other areas of the walls were hung with strips of fabric from many worlds, forming an abstract representation of the striped clouds of a gas giant, in memory of the Founders. There were no other artworks, nothing ostentatious in any way. The only smells were those of a working starship, mostly the characteristic odors of its varied inhabitants.

Sam slipped along the rows of worship rings until he found an unoccupied one. He folded his legs beneath him in a yogic pose and emptied his mind of all save a proper humility and respect for the unfathomable diversity of the Lifesoul-Giver's creation. As he waited for the high acolyte to commence the rites, he mouthed a silent prayer to Moish the Firstborn, a simple prayer that every Child of Unity learned almost before it could transduce energy.

The high acolyte's entrance was low-key, almost demure, and all the more effective for the absence of pomp and panoply. The priestess was a blimp from a gas giant's cloud layer, possibly even a Jovian descendant, though no one seemed to know for sure. She was enveloped in a Precursor wrap to protect her lumpy skin from the radiant warmth of the inner-world life forms whose veins flowed with liquid ice, and a breathing bulb hovered beside her as she floated to her place at the rostrum, buoyed up by the mixture of hydrogen and helium that was almost universal in gas-giant balloonists. Her many tentacles—also a universal on such worlds—hung down her sides, and she spun lazily as she advanced, spying out her surroundings in an unconscious reversion to evolutionary habit.

She was followed by a dozen lesser acolytes, each from a different species. Every day they were chosen by lot. Today the first was a tall, spindly creature, all black twiglike legs, supported in what for it was high gravity, by a Precursor exoskeleton. Sam recognized it as a linecrawler from one of the rare rock webs—clusters of small asteroids linked by thick cables, extruded over the eons by a variety of arachnoid organisms that obtained their energy directly from infrared light. It was followed by a Wymokh, a representative of a species that he had never seen before, which resembled a tangled ball of wool. Surprisingly, it moved not by rolling but by squashing itself flat and suddenly expanding, so that it hopped along in a series of rapid bounds. He found it difficult to imagine what habitat might cause such a form of locomotion to evolve. Third in line was a steel blue Hytth insectoid. Next was something rather like a stubby centipede, then a metallic construct with what looked like wheels, then a procession of three apparently identical creatures like giant butterflies with teardrop bodies—but in fact these had originated in totally different spiral arms of the Galaxy and used totally different genetic material. It was a strange case of convergent evolution and vivid affirmation of the Unity of Life. Sam was pleased to see an Earth-norm humanoid, possibly even a true human—until he realized that the creature just looked like a human. It was a metamorph, and it could mimic anything from a neutronium tetrahedron to a beautiful human female—which was today's choice. The informal procession was completed by a chlorine-breathing Illensan, which dragged a spherical powerball behind it on a trolley to run its life-support systems.

So many species. Sam remembered his childhood priest explaining how much the Church valued a diversity of cultures and species. Universal tolerance involved having something definite to be tolerant toward. It was not enough to love one's fellow species in the abstract. They had to be present in the flesh—or whatever else they were made of. The Church made sure that they were present, by creating a suitable mixture of species on every converted world and in every space-going vessel that it operated.

There were, of course, no exotics—no plasmoids, no neutron-star crystallines. As yet, no way had been found to include them in such company without destroying it, the ship, and anything else within lethal range. That was beyond even the Precursors, or at least beyond the known capabilities of any of their gadgetry that had yet been discovered.

It was a serious theological embarrassment to Cosmic Unity that some of its adherents were so incompatible with planet-dwellers that there was no conceivable form of protection that could permit them to coexist, and the paradox had inspired several heresies. The orthodox view was that somewhere in the Galaxy there must exist powerful, compact Precursor force fields, antigravity hypergenerators, or whatever, that would permit even these entities to join the planet-dwellers in Full Convocation.

Without a doubt, the Lifesoul-Giver would have arranged this, and it was only a matter of time before suitable devices were discovered. Until then the planet-dwellers, even though they were a minority, necessarily represented all other fellow participants in the One.

As a compromise, several exotics were always present as holograms, and the entire ceremony would be broadcast by ansible to selected audiences—three stars that hosted converted plasmoid colonies, a band of nomadic believers herding their magnetotori across the cold and dark of the interstellar vacuum to solar-wind pastures, and four orphan planets, worlds without any accompanying stars. Such planets, long ago expelled from nascent stellar systems, were common in the celestial voids. Typically, they possessed high-pressure atmospheres, in which a kind of greenhouse effect could sustain life for tens of billions of years. On one of these orphan worlds, flat creatures like pancakes had evolved an advanced culture beneath a high-pressure atmosphere of molecular hydrogen that retained nearly all the heat from decaying thorium and other radioactives. Cosmic Unity planned to help them spread to the other three orphan worlds, as soon as appropriate inducements could be found.

They were working on it.

No challenge was too great to prevent dissemination of the Memeplex and the way of life that went with it. Cosmic Unity would not be denied to any sentient creature, however great the challenge.

The blimp spread her tentacles, and the Assembly fell silent save for the gentle hiss of air pumps here and there and a gurgle of body fluids from those unable to suppress this evidence of their material nature. Those who spoke in light toned down their emissions. Pheromone production was contained within barrier fields produced by specially duplicated generators.

The representative selection of acolytes positioned themselves in various rest poses at the high acolyte's feet. The last to settle was the Illensan, which hesitated before deciding to sit down on its powerball.

All attention now focused on the high acolyte.

The light from No-Moon's sun filtered down onto the reef, refracted into ever-changing caustic patterns by the ripples and waves that coursed across the lagoon of Crooked Atoll. Corals were wedged in huge convoluted mounds or scattered haphazardly across underwater clearings of open sand. Giant purple fans sprouted from thick lumps of pale jelly, undulating in the gentle currents. Shoals of brightly colored fish gathered in clefts between the rocks or patrolled the open waters alongside the reef, alert for any hint of a predator. The predators took them anyway, but enough survived their attentions to keep their species in business.

Here, faint traces in the sand told of a lurking trapdaw buried under the lagoon floor, waiting for its open jaws to be sprung by any unwary crustacean that walked into the trap. There, just visible behind fronds of algaweed, was the double snout of a rigid eel. Tiny free-swimming polyps created huge semiopaque clouds, often forming spontaneously into grotesque shapes.

The reef formed a huge dented ellipse, broken in four or five places as the result of bleaching by too-warm seas during unusually hot summers. It was about three miles from end to end, half that from side to side. It contained roughly fifty million corals.

One, not distinguished in any notable way from any of the others, was Second-Best Sailor's wife.

Unconnected, as she was right now, her mental abilities were rather weaker than those of a desert cactus. She could feed, transduce energy, and—when the night was luminous and the mood was right—breed with her husband. She could compete for territory with her neighbors, exuding toxins to keep them away, or—if that failed—to kill them. Some of her neighbors had another weapon: They could turn themselves inside out and eject their stomachs, still attached to their main bodies, toward any suitable victim . . . and eat it. When satisfied, they would draw their stomachs back into their more usual position.

This was how Second-Best Sailor's wife got on with the other reefwives—who also had the brains of a cactus, so it worked out fine. Every coralline reef is a battleground, but the unending guerrilla warfare has a positive consequence. The reef thrives. In a web of mutual enemies there must be many accidental cooperations. As the old saying goes, "My enemy's enemy is my friend." In literal terms, the saying is nonsense, for my enemy's enemy can perfectly well have a go at me, too, but whenever it has a go at my enemy, it does help me. When the webs become more complex, ecological support groups cannot avoid coming into existence. Wars cannot be fought on too many fronts at the same time.

Dormant neural connections activated. With no warning, Second-Best Sailor's wife, and millions like her, suddenly became united to create the reefmind.

The reefmind determined that she was in need of multiple viewpoints, and she segregated herself into four separate conscious modules: North, South, East, West.

North: You will remember from our recent-immediate unison that I/we expressed concern about a potential threat on the fringes of our joint perception?

East: Agreed.

South: Confirmed.

West: I would kind of go along with that, yes.

East: And now we are all distinctly apprehensive, for the threat is no longer potential. Our males send news from the ports. The disturbing activity is migrating toward the center of our perceptions.

North: Am I justified in sensing invasion of our territory?

West: Too true. And I am sure that I speak for us all.

East: I believe we would do well to unite for a moment and pool our resources and recollections. I want to make certain . . .

. . . Yes, it is as I suspected. I/we have encountered such a threat before.

South: Many times. A benevolent memeplex, perhaps already turned malignant. And now we have a name for it: Cosmic Unity.

North: The name alone is worrying. How can a diverse cosmos ever become united?

South: Unified.

West: Uni*form*. Regimented.

South: That is what I fear. It is a pattern as old as the Galaxy. Apologies, I exaggerate. *Almost* as old as the Galaxy.

West: I think it's older. There are other galaxies.

East: But no means of transport between them.

West: That we know of. Yet.

North: Whatever—it is an ancient pattern. More ancient even than the Precursors. And a precondition for its appearance is infestation by extelligent life forms.

South: The *only* precondition.

West: You realize, it was just this threat that forced us to leave our beloved Three-Moons and flee across the void to this unpleasantly moonless world, where only the light of sporadic meteor showers exists to stimulate our mating urges?

East: Agreed.

South: Affirmed.

West: Right on.

For a moment the reefmind remembered the great evacuation as if it had happened yesterday—the bargaining to secure allies, the transfer of males and females, the restructuring of their new home's ecology. And the war that had destroyed their original world.

West: So, uh, we ourselves may be at risk—again.

North: Permit a minor correction, West. The dynamic of history is emergent. No algorithm can predict its long-term course. It can only be left to unfold. However, some courses are more probable than others, and there are heuristic procedures to compute those probabilities.

West: And your point is?

North: The risk to me/us cannot yet be quantified.

South: Ah, yes . . . I/we am/are not at risk as long as my/our existence remains unsuspected by Galactic civilization, and as long as the incursion follows its less malign course. My/our own destruction would occur only if there were widespread disruption of our planet, such as the release of a pan-oceanic biotoxin.

North: Correct. But I perceive no such activity.

West: Yet.

South: Pessimist! Let us assume the less malign course. It is still a disaster. But not, directly, for us.

North: No. It is for our husbands that we must fear.

East: For they are individuals, and recognizable as such.

North: And evidently sentient.

West: There are times when I would beg to differ. Consider the example of Second-Best Sailor! But technically speaking, you are right. So our polypoid husbands are obvious targets for the approaching memeplex.

East: We must protect them from the coming menace. Look, even now it becomes more central in our perceptions!

West: Yes. We will speed up our implementation of the usual contingency plans, then, fellow reefwives? Vaccinations against viral attacks, the formation of covert guerilla groups? Large-scale plans to mobilize the husbands? An improved capacity to wage ecological warfare on a planetary scale?

East: Affirmed.

South: Emphasized.

North: Obligatory.

By the time the wild magnetotorus herd passed close by No-Moon, it was definitely speeding up. Ahead was the orbit of Chromatistes, a smaller, predominantly purple world. This was home to a complex ecology of archoid pseudobacteria and Belousov perennials—mobile meadows that formed patterns of concentric rings.

As the herd sensed good grazing up ahead, the herders made final careful adjustments to its trajectory, let slip the magnetic reins, and concentrated on positioning their improbable ceramic craft in a stable, high-radiation orbit. The magnetotori ignored the innermost planet of the system, technically classed as a slag asteroid. They stampeded toward the designated areas in the photosphere of Lambda Coelacanthi, guided by solar flares lit by the indigenous plasmoids. Down, down, down the gravity gradient the herds plunged, sensing the granular magnetic patterns of ripe vortex-fields. They plunged into the star in a spectacular light show. As the last of the chains disappeared, strange ripples coursed through the hot plasma of the photosphere, sending short-lived flares looping out into the corona and temporarily disrupting electromagnetic communications throughout the system. Soon, only the plasmoids and the herders would know that the herds were there.

The herders adjusted the orbits of their ceramic homes, the better to keep watch over their beasts. Soon the magnetotori would start broadcasting radio-pheromones, which would trigger the strange topological dances of mating. Until then, the herders could leave their beasts to browse on magnetic field-lines while their owners floated in the health-giving radiance of the solar wind.

After a long journey between the stars, it was good to relax, sunbathe, and recharge one's frequencies.

Sam relished the familiar words as the high acolyte recited the central tenets of the Church of Cosmic Unity. Its high-pitched squeals were translated into comprehensible signals by a variety of electronic aids so that all could understand.

The origins of his religion were uncertain; according to the best scholars it had appeared about twenty-five thousand years ago on a small number of solar systems closely associated with the System of the Original Sun. Three or four sentient species had stumbled upon the first intimations of a new, species-transcendent philosophy—that no sentient being was superior to any other. It

followed that cooperation, rather than mutual antago-
nism, was the righteous way to live. The model for this
form of coexistence was symbiosis, a universal evolutionary trick familiar to all sentient species on their own
worlds. The resulting belief system encouraged a multicultural, multispecies vision of the future. And it was so
evident that this system was *right* that its main objective
naturally became its own propagation and expansion.

"The many shall become the One," the blimp intoned
solemnly. "The ways of the many shall become the way
of the One."

The assembled creatures all performed one of the few
motions that most of them had in common, a brief duck-
ing movement. The Wymokh acolyte flattened slightly
and then returned to its normal, slightly oblate spher-
oidal shape. The metallomorphs on the wall twitched.
Sam bowed his head momentarily. He understood the
meaning of the words: that every species should recognize the existence of every other and respect its ways.
That was the entire basis of Cosmic Unity: mutual respect and tolerance.

"This is the inevitable course of the Lifesoul-Giver,
and none shall be excluded from the Fellowship of the
All," said the high acolyte. "The Memeplex of the One is
all, and the Memeplex of the One shall be conveyed to
all. And all shall receive the Memeplex, and believe,
and obey."

Sam translated this as "Every sentient species must be
persuaded to adopt the beliefs and ways of Cosmic
Unity. It is the duty of every servant to ensure that no
species fails to be converted to the sole true religion,
with its morally uplifting focus on mutual tolerance. It is

the duty of every servant to promote the pan-specific symbiosis."

And the servants had not flinched in their duty. From Cosmic Unity's early beginnings, with the conversion of a few solar systems in one remote corner of the Galaxy, it had spread like wildfire. The Memeplex of the One had succeeded beyond the Founders' wildest dreams. The evangelists had expected resistance, possibly violent resistance. It had not materialized, not then, back when it all started. There had been dissenters, of course—there are always dissenters. But they were few and easily overcome. The Memeplex was so strong, so sensible, so self-evidently *right*. Who could argue against tolerance and respect? Who could support intolerance or non-cooperation?

The Memeplex had been partly designed, had partly evolved. At first by accident, later by intent, Cosmic Unity's Founders had laid down a collection of memes—concepts that could propagate themselves in the medium of intelligent minds—so attractive that it traveled between stellar systems like a celestial gale. The more sophisticated designer memes of the Church's main expansion phase were proof against the commonest antimemetics, and only very unusual cultures could resist them. Paramount among these were the wandering Neanderthals, whose lack of any spiritual dimension rendered them immune to all religions.

Instead of wasteful, terrible interstellar wars, the priesthood of Cosmic Unity preached the word of peace. And that made sense, because any intelligent organism can understand that there is no way to protect a planet. A single large asteroid, set on a rough collision course, could destroy a world. And it could come from any direction, anywhere in the celestial sphere. Once diverted into a planet-bound orbit, an asteroid would be virtually unstoppable, especially one protected by an armed escort. Attempts to change its trajectory could be wrecked by a hundred easy tactics—biological weapons, booby traps, or merely surrounding the weapon with a cloud of smaller rocks and gravel so that nothing could approach it. Even if the planet possessed gravitic repulsors, these clumsy, slow-moving devices could be overwhelmed, taken out, or sabotaged. And defending against such an attack by preventing the enemy from gaining control of an asteroid was almost impossible. Most solar systems had their own version of an asteroid belt, and if necessary the invaders could bring their own rocks with them.

And that was just one tactic, the most primitive. There were others. Suicide squads of plasmoids could turn a star into a giant laser and sterilize its system. Organisms causing virulent diseases could rain down from the darkness of space, as virtually undetectable spores tailored to the sentient inhabitants. Seas could be poisoned, icefields melted, acid oceans neutralized, mountains flattened, forests set ablaze. Atmospheres could be infiltrated with corrosive oxygen or stripped away with blasts of energetic particles. Protective magnetic fields could be stolen. Stabilizing moons could be abducted.

A planet was a fragile place to live if someone wanted you and all your kind dead.

The only defense—if that was the word—was a preemptive strike. Kill your fellow being before it kills you. And *that* philosophy would get everybody killed.

It would rid the Galaxy of its infections. But the infections didn't want that.

Mutual coexistence, pan-specific symbiosis—it was such an obvious idea. There was no rational alternative. For perhaps the first time in history, anywhere in the Galaxy, a religion had arisen with an entirely rational basis. Its dissemination was a precious trust, and no effort, however extreme, would be spared in bringing it to every corner of the Galaxy.

The high acolyte's voice, explaining these well-known facts, ended in a squeal of triumph. The blimp pivoted and settled into its relaxation pose. After a short, democratic vote of the entire congregation, the Illensan was chosen to speak next. The translation devices automatically reset to pick up the ultrahigh frequencies employed by its kind.

"Fellow servants, as we approach the next recipients of our message of cosmic harmony, those poor benighted lifesouls on the ocean world without a moon, we must not allow the excitement of our mission to deflect us from the foundations of our faith. Let us all remember this," the Illensan declaimed, "when we talk of the Memeplex of the One." To his horror, Sam found himself fighting a sudden attack of boredom. Hadn't they just been over that ground? Oh, how weak he was, despite his devotion to the Church. He tried to banish the unwanted thoughts. "But, by definition, a memeplex is multiple," the Illensan continued. "How, then, can a multiplicity represent a unity?"

Good point, Sam realized. Hadn't thought of that. Maybe this was going to be worth hearing. Anyway, he wasn't supposed to be here to enjoy himself; he was here because it was right to be here, and to prepare for the task ahead.

The Illensan waited for the paradox to register with the assembled lifesouls. "What is a memeplex? It is a network of mutually supportive ideas, which collectively cause each other to be propagated. Old-style religions did not understand the means of their own success, but the Church of Cosmic Unity suffers no such delusions. It is entirely aware of the reasons for its universal appeal, and it celebrates them! A memeplex is not simply an accident, my fellows. It makes a statement that intelligent minds are eager to hear—a statement so compelling that it must be passed on to others.

"And not just one statement: an entire system of them. Not any memeplex, but *the* Memeplex. So powerful is the Memeplex that through it, and it alone, entire worlds can attain the ultimate bliss of Heaven! Many have done so. More will follow them. And to advance that process, we will now contemplate the two Great Memes, the twin pillars of the Memeplex." The Illensan paused to adjust its powerball. "Huff Elder herself enunciated these twin memes in the earliest days of the Prime Mission. They are mutually complementary, and between them they form the basis of everything we do. And *that* is how many can be one."

Unbidden, the Great Memes rose to the forefront of Sam's mind. He had been trained to recite them since before he could walk.

The First Great Meme, the Illensan reminded them, asserted the supremacy of the collective over the individual. What mattered was the Church, not any single member. Not even a Founder, not even an ecclesiarch.

"And what is the Second Great Meme? It concerns the role of the individual within the collective. What is important for the lifesoul of any one of us here is not bodily comfort. We can be cold, or hot, or wet, or dry . . . happy or sad, consensual or consumed. None of those matters! All that matters is spiritual completeness. We must be fulfilled; we must follow the precepts of the Originals. We must follow the path of tolerance and love for all sentient beings, everywhere in the universe. For that is the path that leads, if all play their part, to the ecstasy of Heaven! Remember, Heaven is no abstraction. Already, for a ninesquare and seven worlds, Heaven is a reality. And the Church's ultimate task, toward which every one of you strives with every fiber of your being, is to make *every* world a Heaven!"

The Illensan's oratory had risen to a strident climax. Suddenly drained of energy, no longer able to sustain such heights of emotion, it switched mood, never missing a beat. Previously, the words had tumbled out in a rush; now, they came one at a time, like the steady drip of liquid. "But Heaven is not quickly attained. The path to bliss is strewn with obstacles. Before you can aspire to Heaven, you must come to grips with"—pause for effect—"*perversion*. What is fittest will thrive; what is least fit will decay: That is a basic evolutionary principle. . . ."

It was gripping stuff, solid doctrine. Wise words, indeed. It needed to be said again and again, and listened to as if it were ever fresh. Yet, as the Illensan droned on, Sam felt his mind slipping away . . . and awoke with a jolt as the Fyx on his left alerted him to the unwanted attentions of a sharp-eyed acolyte. Sam surfaced from his daydream to find that the same speaker still held the stage. The Illensan, who had been rehearsing the eight varieties of perversion, resettled itself on its powerball, winding up to a conclusion: "Cosmic Unity tells us to tolerate all differences *except* perversion. Perversion is a great evil and must be rooted out at any cost. So we need feel no shame in performing the lesser evil of eradicating perversion at the root, before it becomes established."

Of course, Sam thought. *The lesser evil is always preferable, for in that manner do we minimize the total evil.*

Which is itself an evolutionary principle, he suddenly realized. He fought to quell the flush of false pride that the discovery engendered. The Lifesoul-Giver must have provided him with the insight.

Its truth was too compelling for it to be otherwise.

3

NO-MOON

Plans? Rubbish. The trouble with plans is that something unexpected always happens. So then you have to be able to throw away the plan and improvise. Ready, fire, aim—that's my motto. Look where it got me.

The Little Book of Prudence

Second-Best Sailor awoke and wished he hadn't. He felt as though he had been chased by a gulpmouth, ingested, digested, and excreted. He tasted as if he had been, too. And his body, currently mottled in irregular patches, ached all over.

It was a familiar feeling. He had overcelebrated as usual, swapping sailors' tales in the bar at Wild Weed Wasted and eating too many algae sticks. But he was entitled to a bit of fun, wasn't he? The trading had been profitable beyond his wildest dreams.

As the world came into focus, he began to notice more than just his aching cartilage. The boat was rocking slightly in its moorings—there must be a squall outside. Or maybe a big cruiseliner was about to leave port. Whatever it was, right now he didn't give a squirt. He rummaged through the cupboards for some medication but found none. He must have used it all up in Coldcoast Docks. Make a mental note to get some more before setting sail . . .

Mental note! He struggled to remember whether he had performed some essential duties, and failed. He set off through the boat, looking for Fat Apprentice, and found him in the cargo hold, scraping barnacles off the walls.

"Did ya send an eel like I told ya?"

Physically Fat Apprentice was scraping the walls, but mentally he was somewhere else entirely. He was trying to work out how to distinguish knowledge from opinion, and it took him a moment to realize that his captain was talking to him.

"An eel, I said! Did ya send one?"

Fat Apprentice believed in delivering more than he was asked to, a habit he had developed as a child. It had gotten him into trouble with his fellows on many occasions. "Better, Cap'n. The post office had some silver marlon, freshly fed and ready to go. They cost a bit more, but at least one copy ought to be there in three days. I hope that was right; it seemed real urgent. I would've asked ya, but I couldn't find y'anywhere."

Second-Best Sailor had been touring the bars, and was probably unconscious by the time his apprentice went looking for him. And he doubted that his crew member had made much of an effort to find him. The sooner Fat Apprentice discharged his duties, the sooner he could hit the brightlife himself.

"Ya got copies made like I told ya? Silver marlon c'n get eaten by predators, y'know, Fatboy, even if the zygoblasts *are* quick as wormshit. Eels're more cautious, hug the crevices. They ain't so overconfident as marlon."

"You told me to get the 'Thal datablet about the approaching fleet to the reefwives as quickly as possible, Cap'n. So I sent five marlon, each with one copy."

Second-Best Sailor did a quick mental calculation. Eels were safer, but best for nonurgent mail. The chances were about eight out of nine that at least two marlon would get through, and only one out of eighty-one that none would. Fat Apprentice had made a good choice.

He wondered if he had made an equally good choice when he'd entrusted a piece of his wife to the Neanderthals as instructed. He guessed it had been a clever way to place an obligation on them. Now they were more likely to empathize with the intentions of the reefwives of Crooked Atoll, as expressed through their husbands, and that gave the mariners—especially *him*—a trading advantage. He was sure they'd keep her safe, and after all, it was only a *piece*. And he still had a second wifepiece, so he wouldn't lack female company and consolation on the return voyage.

He kept telling himself this, but it saddened him to lose even a piece of his wife. It was a kind of betrayal. He felt like a monarch who had married off his favorite daughter to a rival for political gain. Still, it was the reefwives themselves that had told him to lend her to the Neanderthal traders, and he certainly wasn't going to disobey *them*. He wondered whether he had correctly guessed their intentions.

He doubted it.

She was a deep one, the reefmind.

In the end, four copies of the Neanderthal datablet got through to Crooked Atoll, and the first took only two days. One marlon had been netted by fish hunters while taking a shortcut across Season's-End Bay, and the message that it carried had gone into the cooking pool unnoticed. The rest straggled in a day later.

The Neanderthal starship's data reinforced and complemented what the reefwives already suspected from other sources. It also required them to dismantle the "future" half of their existing timechunk, which had been seriously wrong in several respects—in particular, its guesses about the content of the Neanderthal datablet and the effect of its reception upon the reefmind. A new extrapolation inserted itself smoothly and automatically as more accurate information was fed into the network of shared neurons, and it was as if the false perceptions had never existed. The reefmind was completely unaware that this subconscious revisionism was going on at all times. In effect, the currently active timechunk was a constantly updated contingency plan, seamlessly joined to a genuine historical record. It gave the reefwives a two-week head start before the invasion was due to begin, though they did not think of things quite that way. By now their timechunk contained an extrapolation of their actions over the succeeding two weeks, so as far as they were concerned, what they were about to initiate had already happened. To them, past, present, and future were meaningless distinctions: Time was a fixed block of events. But the contents of that block were ever-changing.

They knew this because they remembered previous timechunks, as they remembered *everything*. But it was in the nature of the reefwives' perceptions that the only timechunks that could pass into long-term memory were those that had been fully realized by actual events—the left-hand sides, so to speak, of earlier timechunks, re-grouped in consecutive pairs and arranged in temporal order. A "live" timechunk still subject to revision was held in a different region of the collective brain.

The replanting of the lemon trees was about half fin-ished, and Second-Best Sailor had slipped on his sailor suit to go 'bovedecks and supervise the placement of the new roots, where mistakes were most likely. Stun was heaping compost into deep tubs set in the foredeck and ready to receive the grafted rootstock, currently lying on the dockside, swathed in rolls of dampened cloth. May had taken an ansible from the invisible belt at her waist and was talking animatedly to Ship about the latest news.

"Ya needs to tamp the compost firmer 'round the edges," the mariner observed. "Otherwise the lemons'll suffer from foot rot if we hit too many fog banks 'round the tip of Cape Destruction."

The Neanderthal woman smiled. She could sense that he was nervous, and not just about his precious fruit trees, so she did her best to reassure him instead of pointing out that she knew a lot more garden-lore than he. Anyway, on this particular item he was right: The compost did need tamping. She had been about to do just that when he had clambered out from the 'tweendecks well.

She watched, intrigued, as the water slid off his suit. It didn't trickle in random rivulets, as she would have expected—it was more like a sock being pulled off a foot. When the mariner had first emerged, head vertical, tentacles trailing beneath him, he had been encased in a thin shell of water, which seemed stuck to the suit. Then the water peeled back from top to bottom, as if the suit itself had decided to remove it.

It made a perfectly normal puddle on the dock.

She picked up a soil hammer and began to firm up the compost while Second-Best Sailor watched over her shoulder.

"Soon's ya finish the gardenin', Stun, I'll be slippin' port," he said. "Like to stay longer—nice places here—but it's important that we get back before late-season air currents set in; otherwise we'll be weeks late and miss the meteor shower that'll trigger the next fertilization window." He leaned closer and said in a hushed voice, "I been practicin' for that with the other bit o' my wife, ya understand. The one I didn't lend to you 'Thals. Reckon as how I might acquire some sons, if any survive their time in the plankton. Not that I'd *know*, y'appreciate, but it'd be nice all the same, if you catch my drift."

Stun straightened her back and tossed the soil hammer aside. She glanced at May, who had finished talking with Will on board Ship and seemed agitated. "The intruders are definitely coming this way. Their infleet transmissions say that they bring a memeplex of peace and goodwill, which is distinctly disturbing." Her eyes narrowed.

A psychic shiver ran up Stun's spinal cord. "You can never be sure with memeplexes," she said. "They are reproductive. For good or evil, they multiply. Assuming they take hold at all. Most do not . . . but the few that do make up for all the failures."

"According to Cosmic Unity's records, its memeplex has proved itself a fount of goodness on more than ten thousand worlds."

"According to *their* records, yes . . ." Stun could *feel* May's skepticism. It matched her own. "And what does Ship say, Will?"

"Ship reckons that the total number of affected worlds is 14,236, provided you count plasmoid stars and magnetotorus trails as worlds. Plus seventeen more, currently in the process of conversion to true believers. Information on converted worlds is remarkably scarce, almost as if it has been subjected to self-censorship. They are all closed worlds—no trading, few reasons for anyone outside Cosmic Unity to visit them. What information there is about them is benign, possibly unbelievably so. 'Banal' is a better word.

"Hardly any ansible transmissions have been detected from worlds that were undergoing the conversion process. No one except Cosmic Unity would have been able to decrypt them anyway, but there were none to decrypt. The communication blackouts appear to have been voluntary, triggered by the need to concentrate on conversion." Did he really believe that? May doubted it. "But one thing is definite. Every one of those fourteen thousand worlds has been totally peaceful ever since adopting the creed of Cosmic Unity. There have been no interplanetary wars and no international or civil wars. Not so much as a riot. The Community of the United Cosmos is a haven of peace and tranquillity."

Second-Best Sailor gaped at her. "What are you talking about?"

"Our new visitors."

"Are they willing to *trade*? What goods've they got?"

Stun wrinkled her nose at him. "Do not ask me to help a potential competitor, Second-Best Sailor."

"Surely ya c'n give me a few *hints*—" He broke off. His apprentices were splashing in the sea next to the boat, jabbing excitedly at something in the water. To the amusement of the Neanderthals, he shot off down the well instead of just jumping into the sea. A few moments later, he appeared between the two apprentices, just visible in the polluted dockside swell.

He had taken this sudden action because he'd noticed that Fat Apprentice had found a jellyfish. Short Apprentice was trying to spear it with a bilgehook. They obviously thought it was a jelloid, whose stings could be fatal, but Second-Best Sailor recognized it for what it was. And he had an idea why it was there.

"No!" he bellowed. The sound waves generated by his speech-siphon were strong enough to be audible from the air, despite the ripples that broke along the boat's hull. "Leave it out, boys! That could be a letter from *Mother*!"

If it was a message from the reefwives, it had either been dispatched long ago or it had traveled unusually quickly—probably piggybacking on a messenger hawk flying at high altitude to catch the fastest air currents, and dropped into the ocean near its destination. By its size, the jellyfish must have endured an arduous journey, much of it out of water, for its substance was almost entirely dehydrated. If it *was* a message, had it survived? Would it rehydrate without serious molecular damage?

Leaving the apprentices to quiet the creature and make sure it did not get washed away by the current, Second-Best Sailor returned to his cabin. There, he slipped out of the sailor suit and swam back outside. Even though the jellyfish was starting to rehydrate, it seemed on the point of expiring.

He reached out one of his more sensitive tentacles, to stroke the animal's gelatinous surface. . . .

"Ooosh!" The expulsion of water through his siphons was involuntary. That *hurt*. The little beast had stung him.

According to plan, then.

Now he must wait while the toxins coursed through his circulatory system, up into the midbrain, and then . . .

Second-Best Sailor, said a faint voice. *Remember this message with care, for it can be told only once.* Second-Best Sailor had no idea how this magic worked—it actually involved tailored neurotoxin chains that caused sequential inflammatory reactions in parts of his sensorium. A molecular message system, a kind of long-distance chemical telepathy.

There followed a complicated series of instructions, but their general gist was simple. "We suspect Cosmic Unity to be a malignant benevolent memeplex. We are making contingency plans in case we are right. Select a few nines of fellow mariners, and persuade the 'Thals to convey them offplanet immediately and evacuate them to a suitable *safe* home for an indefinite period. Reveal our existence to them. Repeat: *Tell them that the reefmind exists*. The ingrained social prohibition is lifted, but only as far as this group of Neanderthals is concerned. The danger is great, and concealment would now be counter-productive. Send an encryption disk to our males at Atollside Port that will link them—and, at one remove, us—to the 'Thal ship's ansible. We will then handle the task of convincing the 'Thals that a coral reef can house a conscious mind. That will be easy, for our intelligence cannot possibly be attributed to you males. Tell the 'Thals to confirm their choice for the evacuation world with us. As payment, offer them free simulations for life; do *not* delay action by attempting to bargain."

The prohibition on bargaining went even more against the grain than the instruction to reveal the secret of the reefmind to offworlders, but Second-Best Sailor had long ago learned the hard way that the wishes of the reefwives were not to be denied. He wondered what could possibly have caused such a panic. The sun about to go nova? A comet strike? With a heartfelt flush of his siphons, he headed for his cabin, to put the suit back on.

It was a lot to ask. He hoped the Neanderthals would agree. But he never doubted for an instant that the reef-mind would persuade the 'Thals of its own existence. Second-Best Sailor knew from personal experience ex-actly what his mother was capable of.

The Neanderthal ship didn't really have a commanding officer—it pretty much took the decisions itself. As far as the crew were concerned, Sharp Wit Will Cut behaved as a leader, but the ship took its own counsel and seemed generally to respond to the overall consensus. In fact, experience with Precursor starships showed that the more diverse a population the crew members were, the better the ship seemed to function, and the easier it was to control.

This particular vessel had been part of a fleet found drifting in the vicinity of Iota Ursae Majoris by a band of magnetotorus herders, and it had taken part in the original Neanderthal evacuation from Earth, forty thousand years ago. Its official name was *Talitha*, the name that ancient Arabic astronomers had given to the star where it was found, but the Neanderthals called it "Ship." *Talitha* was a generation ship: Its crew lived the main part of their lives on board, and their families traveled with them. And most of the time it traveled at just below the speed of light. However, unlike a true generation ship, it also possessed a Precursor faster-than-light hydrive. But the hydrive consumed large amounts of energy and so could be used only when it was really necessary.

Despite its gigantic size, the ship was a village, not a city, housing some six hundred crew, along with their families—maybe fifteen hundred altogether. Of the half dozen or so species on board, the majority were Neanderthals, Tweel engineers, and Cyldarian ecologists. A lot of the space on the ship was taken up by life-support systems for their varied environments—oxygen, nitrous oxide, chlorine, and so on. Cargo holds occupied much of the rest. Even so, the ship could have housed a city, had that been necessary.

Like all Precursor ships that had ever been found, *Talitha* had no weapons. But its size alone was intimidating.

Ancestral Neanderthals had inherited the ship forty thousand years back, along with several others, from their rescuers, and had been using it ever since to travel the length and breadth of the Galaxy. Because of relativistic time-dilation, the crew had lived through a mere three thousand years of subjective time since the evacuation.

They generally traveled for subjectively short periods—a few shipboard years, long enough to reach the nearest worthwhile star, maybe fifty light-years away—and then based themselves in that region of the Galaxy for a generation or so, trading goods and facilitating the exchange of valuable information. They were in no great hurry to go anywhere in particular or achieve anything special, but they were wanderers at heart and seldom stayed anywhere for more than twenty years, fifty at the outside.

Like most of the Galaxy's nomads, they mainly followed the spiral arms that wound outward from the Galactic Hub. In the arms, stars were more densely distributed, so travel times to the next habitable system were less. A few adventurers had struck out across the interarm voids, with mixed success. Most had never returned.

Along the way, the Neanderthals had made contact with many civilizations, and occasionally representatives of some of these had been added to the crew. Now Will was faced with a problem. The reefmind had convinced him that she existed, and his ansible had a new encryption disk to prove it, a direct link to Atollside Port. This was a big secret, and he would probably be able to exploit it to advantage at some future date. In the meantime, May and Stun had negotiated a potential deal with that strange little polypoid Second-Best Sailor. It was a very favorable deal from the Neanderthals' point of view. But the rest of the crew weren't convinced that they wanted to move again yet, and Ship was sensing that majority opinion and refusing to budge.

There was no point in arguing with Ship. Instead, over the years, Will had developed several effective techniques for persuading the crew to go along with his wishes. If he could develop a consensus, Ship would go along with the decision, he was sure. So he bustled about the mile-long vessel, arguing and persuading, cutting side deals if necessary, wheedling and disputing, reminding his crew again and again of the astonishing revelations about the reefwives' collective mentality. And the innate empathic sense that all Neanderthals possessed gave him such an edge that soon Ship was positively enthusiastic about the whole idea and was offering unsolicited advice and assistance.

May and Stun, waiting patiently, got word that the deal was on.

"*How* many transpods?" May asked Will, almost shouting into her ansible.

"Ship says it is sending three. Plus a small one to communicate directly with the reefmind."

"We were only expecting one."

"I know. But you know what Ship is like when it senses a really strong consensus. I guess I must have oversold the evacuation analogy. Everyone seems to think that it would be a great idea to make a symbolic gesture and repay the universe for arranging our rescue. The Tweel in particular like the sense of closure in that, and they seem to have inspired the others with a sudden sense of cosmic brotherhood and historical fitness."

"That sounds dangerously like Cosmic Unity."

"No, just a harmless, spontaneous upwelling of good-will. It will not last. Anyway, you had better tell Second-Best Sailor to round up another forty of his friends. And get busy duplicating sailor suits."

"We will not be using a transible, then."

"No, the power drain would not be justified, and the recycle time is too long for us to transport enough mariners by that means," said Will, confirming May's own unexpressed judgment.

"Transpods will be more effective," she replied, speaking her thoughts out loud.

"Correct. Ship is creating a suitable environment on board, where space is all but limitless, but the transpods cannot carry enough seawater." Which reminded him. "Tell Stun to get the analysis of dissolved minerals in No-Moon's oceans sent up to Ship as quickly as possible. And pay careful attention to the isotope proportions. The reefwives say that their husbands are very sensitive to deuterium imbalances."

May hung the ansible back on her invisible belt and set off in search of the polypoid captain. The strange sense of apprehension that had dogged her these past few days was much sharper now that she could put a name to it. But were the approaching strangers truly a menace, as the reefwives feared? Even they were unsure.

The uncertainty worried her. Cosmic Unity's declarations of universal love worried her more. It all added up to impending trouble. But what *kind* of trouble? She hadn't a clue.

Her mind returned to the task at hand. She had left Second-Best Sailor on his boat, kitting out his two apprentices and fifteen other mariners. He had had enough difficulty persuading those to accompany him offplanet, even with dire warnings of impending—but unspecified—doom. Now she was going to have to tell him to find twenty or thirty more.

It wasn't only Will who needed to be very persuasive.

While she was doing that, Will was delving through Ship's records, trying to find the best choice of a destination. It shouldn't be too close—there was no point in evacuating the mariners to a world that would shortly suffer the same fate as their own. But it shouldn't be too far, either.

He had called up a three-dimensional star map of the local zone, a cube of space some five thousand light-years wide. The worlds currently embracing Cosmic Unity glowed lime green, and the frontiers of that religion's expansion were highlighted in yellow. A long streak of yellow, running along the spine of the Trailing Spiral Arm, was pointing straight at No-Moon. They were coming, and they were coming fast. This memeplex was a powerful one, and no mistake. He began to appreciate *why* the reefwives wanted a random selection of their husbands evacuated from their homeworld before Cosmic Unity's peace mission arrived in planetary orbit.

The star map would help him to decide on a good

choice of world to receive the evacuated mariners. The Tweel engineers had well-defined priorities, but these contradicted the advice of the Cyldarian ecologists. It was hard to gain consensus. The Cyldarians didn't help. One of them was adamant that what mattered most was climate and atmosphere; another flatly contradicted this, insisting that what really mattered was the existence of at least one large sea, preferably an ocean. With an acceptable chemical composition, of course—that was one thing they both agreed on.

The only thing, it seemed.

Will valued diversity of opinion, because constructive dissent generally led to more effective decisions and kept everything functioning effectively. Nothing made Ship more sluggish than mere conformity. But dissent cannot continue indefinitely, and eventually he was forced to offer one of the Cyldarians a small inducement to shut up. The bribe worked like a charm, and within ten minutes, Ship had marked out six likely candidates in blue. Another ten minutes' work by the Cyldarians and Tweel reduced that number to just one.

Hoping that further study would not reduce it to zero, Will called up the data for this sole remaining candidate. It was a fairly ordinary world. Its main planetological features were two large polar icecaps. At their fringes they produced copious quantities of meltwater that fed a network of underground aquifers. Much of the land above was tundra, scrub, and desert. The aquifers fed into a single ocean, covering about a quarter of the surface, which was bordered by thick, impenetrable swamps. Water evaporating from the ocean fell as snow at the poles, and this kept the circulation going and topped up the aquifers.

There were no sentients. Nothing even came close. Plants, yes . . . insectoids in abundance, various flying things. Lots of strange beasties in the ocean. Almost anything in the swamps. And funny walking things that lived in ponds and made long treks across the desert.

The climate ranged from freezing cold at the poles to uncomfortably hot at the equator. But it wasn't hot as in *molten rock*—there were places on No-Moon that were just as warm. On neither world would such places be a problem, because the mariners normally stayed in the sea, and if they had to go onto the land, they wore suits.

The atmosphere had a bit more nitrogen and argon than No-Moon's, along with some irritating sulfides. There was a slight methane deficiency. The oxygen level was a bit too low for Neanderthals to avoid wearing breathing apparatus, but there was enough oxygen dissolved in the ocean for the polypoids to feel perfectly at home. The deuterium levels were comfortably within tolerance.

They would need to seed the ocean with the polypoids' food organisms, because the native ones were unlikely to be compatible with mariner metabolism. There could well be dangerous predators in the ocean, so the mariners would have to restrain their natural urge to travel until the Neanderthals had time to carry out a survey of the marine ecosystem. Their records were inadequate on this point, as on many others. Nobody had ever done a full planetological study of the planet. That was a nuisance, but it added to the planet's attraction— unwanted visitors would be unlikely.

All this meant that initially they would have to find a suitable body of water, like a landlocked bay, and seal off its connection to the main ocean. It would have to be swept for dangerous life forms and, if necessary, sterilized. The polypoids would have to remain confined within its boundaries until the wider situation could be assessed. However, all this was relatively simple with Precursor gadgetry.

If it all worked out, then eventually they would be able to transplant reefs to the planet, too. Apparently, that was how the reefwives and their males had originally come to No-Moon. At first they had created protected environments to live in, much as they were doing now, but within a million years of their arrival they had transformed the planet to suit themselves. Now it was as if they had always been there—had evolved there. When it was safe, and necessary, to move the reefs, they would. Until then, the reefwives were confident that whatever effect Cosmic Unity might have on their husbands, it would do their wives little harm. Cosmic Unity didn't even know the reef was sentient. So the wives could wait.

In the longer term, their new home's ocean might be permanently nomoonformed, but there was no need even to think about that step right now.

May was on the ansible again. "Have you come to a decision?" The Neanderthals' empathic sense did not function at a distance. If she'd been with Will on board Ship, she would have known that he had.

Will could hear that she sounded agitated—probably because of the sudden change in plans. Trading one day, in charge of an evacuation the next. "Yes, I have narrowed the options down to just one," he reassured her. His crevit, now curled in his lap, buzzed in blissful contentment. Will tugged its ears affectionately. The contact helped to relax them both. "And it is suitable. Far enough away to be well out of range of the probable future expansion of Cosmic Unity, but close enough for hydrive access without us going bankrupt. It will need some work, and the polypoids will have to exercise restraint for a time."

May chuckled. "There is little prospect of that, Will. Even now, the natives are getting restless."

"It is for their own safety."

"That might possibly get them to behave themselves. At any rate, some specific news will help to calm them down."

Will transmitted the details to her.

"Restless" was an understatement. Second-Best Sailor's trawl of the bars had netted another thirty-one mariners who were willing to abandon their wives and atolls, not to mention their boats, to travel to another star. Most were in late stages of algal inebriation, which was very likely why they had agreed to this crazy plan. Fitting them out with suits was proving to be a complicated business. The suits were ancient and inexplicable technology that carried them in an upright position, doused with recycled water through a kind of showerhead, which kept their siphons oxygenated and their skins damp. The suit's recycling microfilters osmotically removed excreted chemicals from the water, keeping it fresh-tasting and removing any risk of toxic shock. Although the suits were "one size fits all," that is, they adjusted themselves to the form of their wearer, there were some initialization procedures that had to be carried out before the golden sailor suits were fully operational.

This shakedown was not going according to plan, because the mariners kept interfering with it or forgetting what stage they'd reached. Second-Best Sailor had his work cut out calming them down and preventing fights from breaking out, while May and Stun checked off the suits' functions and ran a few precautionary tests. It would not do to get the evacuees to their new home and then find that they dried out because of a suit fault.

Eventually, the forty-nine mariners were ready to be loaded on board the transpods, and with a certain amount of grumbling and horseplay and many good-natured obscenities, they trooped through the wall-irises into the stark loading bays.

The last on board was Second-Best Sailor, preceded by his two apprentices. As they passed Stun and May, Fat Apprentice finally got around to asking a question that he felt he really should have asked sooner.

"Where are we goin', miz?"

May gave him a smile. The fat little polypoid was terrified out of his wits but doing his best to conceal it.

"It is a very suitable world. You will like it."

"What's its name?"

"Uh . . ." May wasn't sure it had an official one, but it would be simplest to invent one rather than explain-ing about official nomenclature. Recalling the planet's specifications, she was about to tell him it was Sand when something told her that would not be sufficiently reassuring.

"Aquifer," she told him. "The planet you are going to is called Aquifer."

4

SPITTLE NEST CLIFF

Praise not the Lifesoul-Giver,
Grim Sower of transient Life,
With its joys, miseries, uncertainty.
Give thanks to the Lifesoul-Cherisher,
Kindly Reaper of the dysfunctional vortex,
Enforcer of the peaceful certainty
Of entropy everlasting.

The Book of Plasms

The cliff was six miles, from its abrupt top edge to the enormous scree slope of dislodged rubble at its base, and the canyon descended a further two miles before it reached the ammonia torrents that had carved it from thick deposits of frozen sulfide, remnants of a long-forgotten period of planetwide volcanism.

All along the canyon walls, on the side facing the setting star, the ledges were piled several stories high with the round-mouthed spittle nests of the Huphun. Adults lined up on the nest forecourts to spread their wings, displaying the varicolored homing symbols that identified each parent to its parthenogenetic young. And as the Huphun watched the star set, they sang to their neighbors about the beauty of their world and the consonance of the city, attributing both to the Wings of the World, which were invisible but must exist in order to carry their planet around its star in what every child knew was a slightly eccentric ellipse. Its resemblance to a breeding-dance flight path was presumably coincidental—the topic had been the subject of continuing speculation for a myriad myriads of starsets.

Flocks of fledglings sported in the cooling skies, soaring in the blissfully dense atmosphere of the high-gravity world, chasing each other's spiny tails, diving on their friends and pulling out horizontally at the last minute in a parody of a direfalcon strike. The shadow of the far rim of the canyon moved up the cliff as the huge orange globe of the star sank toward the horizon.

When the shadow reached a thin but prominent stratum of pale yellow crystals, the play stopped abruptly. The flocks streamed back toward the starlit side, each fledgling heading for its nest. Their homecoming song filled the skies with harmony, and the mothers soon joined the choir.

As each fledgling neared its nest, it picked out its mother's homing symbol and flew straight toward it, slowing to a hover and instinctively clinging to her torso using its tiny, mobile mouth-tusks. The tusks were hollow, and the mother's body fluids, liquid nitrogen laced with strange organics, flowed through some of them and returned through others, delivering nourishment to the fledglings.

When the entire brood had completed the homeward flight, the mother Huphun folded her wings closed around them and stepped backward into the open mouth of the nest. Finally, she used her abdominal claw to push a ball of damp spittle against the hole from the inside, to seal it. The nights on Epsilon Cuniculi 7 were deathly cold, but the warmth of a sealed nest would keep the entire family comfortable and safe.

Unfolding her wings, the mother began to sing a poem to the fledglings, to settle them in the comfortable darkness.

Disseminator 714 traveled with the mission fleet as it sped toward its objective, the aqueous planet of No-Moon. All of the vessels were propelled by tame magnetotori, to which they were hitched by means of magnetic reins. It was a cheap and efficient way to travel between the stars, and the herders usually had surplus stock that they were keen to sell. Small groups of magnetotori were easier to control than whole herds, and a huge industry had grown up to tame them and turn them into docile beasts of burden. Most of the Galaxy's travelers owed their mobility to the torus tamers; the Neanderthal trading ships were an exception. Ships with magnetotori as "engines" also used them as their main source of power, bleeding off energy from their living plasma-fusion reactors. They had limited auxiliary power sources for emergencies.

Activity in the fleet's duplicator cubbies was becoming frenetic. As the azure sphere of the ocean planet loomed ever larger, Sam found himself doing double duty. The list of goods to be duplicated grew ever longer and more complex, as it always did before the fleet's arrival in a new system. The evangelical phase of the Unification of the Cosmos placed heavy demands on the duplicators' capabilities as the high acolyte tried to anticipate obstacles to successful conversion and to devise apparatus to overcome them.

Sam loved these times. He even loved the sacrifice of sleep.

Even though Sam hardly ever left the cubby that housed his beloved duplicator, he always enjoyed the change in shipboard atmosphere when the fleet approached a new world. He reveled in the prospect of helping, in his small but satisfying way, to bring yet another sentient species into the loving embrace of the Lifesoul-Cherisher. The joy of it all filled his entire being. *To work is to serve: to serve is to love.* He knew that his happiness would overflow, probably for weeks. The childhood meme coursed through his mind: *To serve is to bring others to Service.* The elegant simplicity of this positive feedback loop filled his mind with wonder. And he believed in his very bones that serving Cosmic Unity would open the way to universal love, and the harmony of peaceful coexistence, throughout the Galaxy.

There could be no more worthwhile way to live.

Sam had grown up on a typical Cosmic Unity world, living in a huge, graceless housing complex with neighbors of many other species. Life was simple—and dull. Very little ever happened to disturb the daily routine. But then, it never occurred to him that any other lifestyle was possible, so he was content.

Following family tradition, he had trained as a duplicator operator. Then—it was still amazing to think about it—the priesthood had selected him to leave his homeworld and carry out his spiritual duties on board a starship!

As a child, he had seen the stars. Only a few times, but their brilliance was burned into his memory. Never had he dreamed that he might *go* to the stars. None of his ancestors had ever been so privileged. And it was not just any starship, but a disseminator of the Memeplex. From which he had helped to convert unbelievers to the Way of the One. Not just a few lifesouls—entire planets.

He had already served the Lifesoul-Cherisher on three missions. No-Moon was to be his fourth. He fervently hoped there would be many, many more before the Lifesoul-Stealer put an end to his life. And he *knew*—he had no idea how, but he never doubted it—that he was destined for even more than this. He would rise in the Church, in the fullness of time. Then he could serve the One to even greater effect.

It was not something that could be rushed. He must await his moment and seize the chance when it came.

For now, he was content to operate a duplicator and stay in his familiar cubby.

One production run ended, and he consulted his list and performed the necessary ritual gestures to start the next. Equipment boxes piled up faster than the menials could remove them.

Sam had been told, along with the other servants of Unity, that the indigenes of No-Moon were aquatic crea-

tures, male polypoids bred in coralline reefs. Their intelligence was about average, unlike that of their females,
which was zero. And—*praise the Lifesoul-Giver!*—the
target was a trading world. A dozen other species were
regular visitors. According to advance information, tens
of thousands of Neanderthals were transient inhabitants
of the sea ports, all across the seven continents, throughout the myriad atolls and archipelagoes.

Neanderthals. Sam was gloriously aware that, like his
ancestors, they had evolved on one of the Founder
worlds. They had lived in the System of the Original
Sun, along with humans, blimps, and plasmoids. They
were among the most privileged of all races. But, if he
recalled his childhood lessons in Church history correctly—and he always did, for he had remembered them
with arduous perfection—the Neanderthals had been removed from their home planet, leaving only *Homo sapi-
ens*, the stock of Moish, long before the first voyage of
Cosmic Unity had set out to evangelize the Galaxy. They
had departed the System of the Original Sun *before* it
had joined the Cosmic All. They had become vagrants,
nomads . . . and more than once they had fled from the
approach of a mission fleet. They remained infidels—a
continuing challenge to the servants of the Lifesoul-
Cherisher.

He did not believe that the Neanderthals were actually
wicked. They were obstinate and misguided, to be sure.
Instead of believing in their own puny false gods, like
most races, they believed in no god at all. Their empathic
sense was legendary, but their sense of the supernatural
was nonexistent. Infidels indeed: Literally, *they had
no faith.*

How could any sentient being deny the evidence of the Lifesoul-Giver? It was all around them. Every sunrise, every rainstorm, every perfect crystal of frozen methane *shouted* the presence of a benevolent being, creating the cosmic order. The proofs were everywhere, mundane or profound. In fact, that was why he'd seen the stars.

One night, his principal duomother, XVI Eloise, had taken him up to the roof of the housing complex. There, away from the light pollution of the poorly lit streets, it was possible to see the stars. There was still too much light to see the dusty sweep of the Galaxy, but the brighter stars stood out clearly.

Sam had never seen stars before. He had never been outside the complex after darkness had fallen.

Eloise had named some of the nearer stars and the patterns they made: the rabbit, the lizard, the coelacanth. Many of his neighbors, she told him, were from species that had evolved on planets surrounding one or another of those stars. She had explained the words patiently, as a good mother should, until he dimly began to understand.

And then she'd said something that at the time made no sense at all. She had pointed out a bright, slightly reddish star, saying, "We were all born in such stars, Sam. That is where the atoms of our bodies were made. If you need proof that the Lifesoul-Giver is real, that is where you will find it."

The moment had stayed with him, but it was years before he properly understood what his duomother had meant. The star was Omicron Oblatratrictis, colloquially known as Orc Eye. It was thirty-eight light years away, and it was a red giant. Red giants were where the universe made its carbon, an essential element for Fyx and Hytth and humans. Who, except the creator of the universe and its sentient life, could turn stars into living beings? And since there must be a creator, there must also be a maintainer, the Lifesoul-Cherisher. And to keep the cosmos tidy by eliminating surplus lifesouls, there must be a Lifesoul-Stealer. . . .

Which brought him back to the Neanderthals. It was as if they were blind to the presence of the Lifesoul-Giver. As if they felt no need for anything that extended beyond the mundane bounds of the material universe. But, he remained sure, this was ignorance, not evil. With enough effort, even the infidel Neanderthals could be brought into the One Sole Union. And it looked as if No-Moon would afford the perfect opportunity to achieve that holy goal.

There were a few other species, too, in smaller numbers. No-Moon, in its own secular manner, was already started on the golden pathway to multiculture! That boded well for the success of their mission. The indigenes would be converted. The transient population would be recruited to open up new routes for spreading the gospel of the unity of the cosmos, and they would also help the high acolyte to fulfill her assigned quota of love.

The ecclesiarchs back on the Cloister Worlds of Intermundia, the religious leaders at the core of Cosmic Unity's domain, would be well pleased.

"I just can't get over how flouncin' *big* this thing is," said Fat Apprentice, who had spent much of the trip so far exploring *Talitha* in his golden sailor suit.

"Yeah," Short Apprentice responded. It was difficult to find better ways to express the feeling of sheer incomprehension that he felt whenever he tried to come to terms with the Neanderthal vessel—and, even more so, with its builders. The biggest sailing boats on No-Moon were cruiseliners about eighty yards long, thirty broad at the beam; their masts were seldom more than fifty yards tall, and the sail, on the occasion he was fortunate enough to be able to go on board and inspect one of those impressive boats, had been absolutely massive.

Now it seemed puny in retrospect. And *Talitha* didn't even *have* a sail. Not that it needed one.

Stun had been kind enough to show them a graphic of Ship once the routine of quitting orbit for deep space had been completed. It was vast. There were interminable corridors, some straight, some twisty. Huge engines occupied much of the stern. A veritable flotilla of transpods had been stowed in just one of the capacious holds. Apparently, the Precursor vessel housed not just active crew but their families, from the very young to the elderly. But the family areas were off limits to Fat Apprentice and all the other polypoids, to minimize disruption.

Ship was twenty times as long as No-Moon's giant boat—a little over a mile. It was shaped like nothing that Fat Apprentice had ever come across, except maybe a very warty sea slug. Nothing about the starship was geometrically regular or simple; every surface that started to resemble something he could put a name to, like a sphere or a cone, merged into something else or just suddenly stopped.

The reefwives, if they had put their mind to it, would have known why . . . but they had never seen Ship, nor had they ever needed to. However, if they had seen it, they would immediately have realized that the vessel had not been designed but had been evolved. It was closer to an organism than to a machine. Yes, everything about it was mechanical, made from metal and ceramic, but it had been grown more than built. In fact, Ship's automata occasionally decided to modify some part of the vessel, often while it was in transit between stars. The Neanderthals and the rest of its crew seemed used to this. Fat Apprentice had been horrified, the first time he tried to go to a part of the ship that he had visited a few days earlier, only to find that the previous entrance had been remodeled and the layout beyond it changed out of all recognition.

He couldn't imagine deliberately tearing a boat to bits while it was sailing. The wind and waves of No-Moon did enough of that without assistance. *Rebuilding* a boat while it was sailing—ah, that they had to do all the time. But no mariner would voluntarily seek it out. And polypoids could *swim* across an ocean.

Neanderthals couldn't swim through space.

All of this was lost on the crew. They seemed to trust Ship implicitly and never turned a hair when part of it was being melted, crushed, or unglued by robots outside their control.

If the outside of Ship was weird, the inside was even weirder. The "cabins," if that was the word—and Fat Apprentice knew no other way to describe the internal com-

partments of a boat—were of every conceivable shape
and size. Some had gravity and some had not, and this
was very disconcerting because you could easily wander
from one to another without warning. The gravity was
generally no more than a tenth of that experienced at the
surface of No-Moon, though, so even if you accidentally
wandered into a hundred-yard shaft, it was easy to grab
something and arrest your descent. And on the one occasion when his desperate grab for a stanchion (or whatever the eel-shaped protrusion was) had failed, and it had
dawned on him that even in one-tenth gravity he'd hit the
bottom very hard, Ship itself had turned off the gravity-
field before he had fallen more than twenty yards.

For the first few seconds, though, it had been the worst
experience of his young life. So now, when he explored
Ship, even in areas he thought he knew well, he carried a
small lump of rock, which he used to test new cabins for
the presence or otherwise of a gravitational field before he
let his suit roll him through the opened wall-iris.

Many areas of the ship were closed to him altogether.
The wall-irises were there, but they refused to recognize
his presence, staying stubbornly shut. He wondered if
that was because the conditions inside were unsuitable
for him. Occasionally, as he wandered the passages and
cabins, he encountered a crew member. He'd come
across plenty of aliens at the seaports, but a lot of these
guys were of species that were totally unknown to him.
He was smart enough to understand that aliens often
needed different atmospheres, temperatures, humidity,
whatever. The tanks where the polypoids spent most of
their time had been fitted out so that they could live comfortably without suits. Presumably, other parts of the

vessel were designed for the home requirements of chlorine-breathers or radiation-consumers. His suit would have protected him even in such conditions . . . but perhaps Ship didn't know he was wearing a suit.

It was hard to work out what it did or did not know. It seemed aware of where he was and whether he was getting himself into trouble.

It never dawned on him that the latter was the main reason why Ship was keeping him away from the home regions of the alien crew. It didn't want to risk his causing unnecessary damage, so he had been confined to the common quarters, where all the crew were expected, and where it could be assumed that they would be equipped with suitable life support.

And it was on one of his early excursions that he had blundered into a gallery and found the window into space.

Fat Apprentice had never seen space before. He'd seen the stars, of course, but space seemed to have a lot more stars—and these were a lot brighter—than anything he'd witnessed during No-Moon's nights. And he'd found that if he concentrated on some region of the starscape, the window would seem to *bulge*, and the view would be magnified. When he had put a tentacle against the window, he'd felt no movement. The bulge wasn't a change in shape, just a change in optical properties.

Some things that looked like stars, he found, were actually big collections of stars, presumably seen from a great distance. Often these star clusters formed pretty shapes, with spirals being especially commonplace. But they weren't one-armed spirals like the shells that could be found near the shores of No-Moon's landmasses. They were usually two-armed, more loosely coiled, and *flat*.

Maybe a bit bulgy in the middle, but, *Maker! Flat shells made of stars!*

One day May found him staring out the window into space. It didn't take a Neanderthal's sensitivity to other creatures' moods to understand what transfixed him. "Many of the experienced crew find it awe-inspiring, you know," she told him. "And they have made hundreds of journeys in this ship, and seen hundreds of worlds. I can sense their awe. Sometimes it is so strong that I even regret my own inability to share it."

Fat Apprentice hardly knew how to answer. May's leonine features and her graceful movements were overpowering. And her confidence in herself was so much greater than his own. He was still learning his trade, whereas she was mistress of hers, and had been for a long, long time. And here she was, confiding in him.

Not only that: The shipboard pets that habitually followed her around put him off. He wasn't used to land animals.

"You can relax, Fat Apprentice," she said, sensing his awkwardness. "You have nothing to fear from me or my beasts."

He knew that. It wasn't fear, it was . . . No, she was right; it was a kind of fear. Not the kind you would swim away from, though. It was more a respect so enormous that it was frightening to contemplate it.

"Eeesh," he said, evacuating his speech-siphons, and he felt foolish at his hesitation. "It's just that wherever I looks, I sees more and more *stuff*. It's a flouncin' big uni-

verse, beggin' ya pardon, miz. I can't see any end to it."
He paused, trying to express himself better. "And I can't
see what it's all *for*."

May turned thoughtful. "That is either a very clever
question, Fat Apprentice, or a very stupid one. I cannot
tell which. Perhaps the universe is not *for* anything. Perhaps it exists merely for its own sake. Because it is what
it is, because there is no alternative. Can you contemplate the possibility of *nothing* existing?"

"Uh . . . no. But I can't see how things become *real*,
either. When I was tiny, the reefwives told me that everything that exists is there 'cause of the Maker, who made
the world and whose siphons cause time to flow."

"Yes, that is a common solution to the enigma of existence. Do you find it acceptable?"

Fat Apprentice quailed under her level gaze. "Well, to
be honest, miz—no. I don't. Ya see: *Who made the
flouncin' Maker?* I can't wrap my tentacles 'round that
one."

May laughed. "Neither can the finest philosophers,
Fat Apprentice." *Perhaps even less so than you.* "But if
nothing can make a Maker, what can make a universe?"
To spare him further embarrassment, she changed the
topic. "What were you looking at?"

Fat Apprentice gestured clumsily. He still found the
suit uncomfortable if he wore it for long. "There's a star
here that turns into a muckin' great snail-thing when you
look at it close."

She followed his gaze. "Ah, yes. That is a galaxy.
Which is an old word for 'milk,' because when you mag-
nify the cluster even more, it looks as if someone has
spilt milk across the sky." His bafflement was obvious

and should have been predicted, and she laughed again at her own stupidity. Polypoids had little experience of mammalian nutrition. "What is milk? It is like . . . like the sea when the reef spawns. White and liquid and thick. A galaxy is a gigantic cluster of stars, bound together by mutual gravitation."

Fat Apprentice wondered at that. "So . . . is a galaxy what 'appens when a *universe* spawns, miz?"

May stared at him. This was a clever one and no mistake, for all his innocence. "Again, Fat Apprentice, you ask something that would baffle the finest philosophers. But this time you also ask something that to my knowledge has never been asked by the finest philosophers. I cannot answer you now." Her own knowledge of philosophy was limited, but she recalled that on board there was a genuine philosopher; indeed, he was Ship's philosopher. He was a portly little Thumosyne whose name was a purely mental pattern, and he had consequently acquired the nickname Epimenides because they had to call him *something*.

Perhaps Epimenides could answer Fat Apprentice's innocent-sounding question. May turned to leave, then turned again to give the polypoid a strange look. Somehow, his question was linked to her ever-present, unnamed fears.

The words were sucked from her against her will, and they came out as a hoarse whisper. "But, Fat Apprentice . . . you may very well be right."

The pond lay in a shallow depression, which the prevailing winds had scoured from the lee face of one of the great barchan dunes. Seasonal evaporation had left a line of crusted salts against the rocky outcrop that sliced across one end; the rest of its margin lapped against Aquifer's sparkling desert sand.

Ripples on its surface projected shifting blue patterns of reflected sunlight onto the dull grain of the rock. In its depths, swarms of tiny crustaceans darted this way and that, hunting down shoals of medusas no bigger than a pinhead. Blue-brown algal mats carpeted a quarter of the surface in polygonal jumbles like cracked ice. Where the rock shaded the pool from the brilliance of the sun, small humpbacked amphibians peered out of the water with a single slitted eye.

The pond looked normal; its surroundings did not. For ten yards around, the ground was bare sand. Not an insect moved; not a twig or dried leaf disfigured the uniform silver-gray surface.

Farther away, tiny yellow spikes sprouted from the desert in isolated tufts. Beyond them were stunted cacti, scalloped by nibbling mandibles and surrounded by a carpet of fallen needles. A few were in bloom, festooned with patches of soft pink wool. Segmented insects, each with a dozen long, spindly legs, skittered across the hot sand in search of a cactus that was marginally more succulent than the rest. Twin-rotored copterflies hovered around the woolly blossoms, coating their legs and dangling abdomens with thready pink spores.

In most deserts, an oasis would attract vegetation. Not on this world. On Aquifer the vegetation secured its moisture by sending out roots to tap the deep subterranean water table. It stayed away from the ponds. Vegetation that tried to grow too near a pond seldom survived for long, so evolution weeded out such tendencies.

A broad, scuffed track ran through the scrub, making a zigzag ascent up the long windward slope of a nearby dune. At the crest, a walker cast its expert single eye over the terrain ahead of it. Mental processes tens of millions of years in the making unscrambled the shimmering distortions created by currents of heated air, seeing through the labyrinthine refractions to the true landscape behind them. A walker would never mistake a mirage for a pond.

The walker was rather like a hybrid of a millipede, a turtle, and a translucent bag, and about the size of a crocodile. It moved on thousands of tiny tube feet that sprouted from its underside like the bristles of a brush, tipped with soft, pudgy spheres that stopped the feet from sinking into the sand. As the bristles rippled, the body undulated from side to side like a slow serpent.

The walker had no head, no mouthparts, no obvious way to ingest food. At what was presumably the front, its solitary eye was mounted on the end of a segmented trunk. The trunk was translucent like the rest of its body, and small dark shapes moved within it. The eye was hooded by a flap of opaque skin that flicked open and shut every few seconds.

The trunk was held upright, like a periscope. The eye could not move in its socket, but there was no need; instead, the trunk writhed and squirmed so that the eye scanned the way ahead, with an occasional nervous glance to the rear.

The body was divided into segments—this walker had

six, but anything between five and seventeen was common—and it resembled a row of overstuffed pillows, each separated from its neighbors by a thick gelid partition. All the segments were filled with a watery fluid. One contained brown and blue algae. In another, sporulated crustaceans were packed like grains of rice. A third was stuffed with what looked like semolina—the tiny globes were actually dormant medusas.

A shoal of brilliant yellow fish peered through the translucent walls, watching the world go by.

The walker's periscopic eye surveyed the terrain ahead, where a thousand ponds glistened like mirrors in the sharp blue light of the sun. Toward the haze of the northern horizon, the walker could see that the ponds began to peter out as the land reverted to a more uniform silver-gray, speckled with blue-green scrub and patches of the yellow spikes.

Its tube feet picked up the beat, and it plunged over the crest of the dune and down the steep slope beyond. The desert stretched ahead like an ocean frozen at the height of a violent storm; there were many more dunes to climb before the walker attained its goal.

The blinding sapphire pinpoint of the sun began to sink toward the horizon, and shadows invaded the troughs between the dunes. The blue of the sky deepened, turned purple, then black; the stars came out. The walker's eye adjusted itself to the low light, and its tube feet continued their steady, if erratic, progress.

Eventually, the walker emerged from the pond field, heading north. Now the vegetation became a little more lush—nothing obvious, but the cacti looked healthier and more succulent, and the yellow spikes were broader and less glossy. The walker's periscopic eye began to cast about for a suitable place to stop, and shortly it found one—a bowl-shaped depression where the sand had subsided, ringed by slabs of weathered sandstone. At the center was a withered tangle of woody tissue, the desiccated remains of what had once been a clump of marram-grass.

Perfect.

The walker slithered backward until the rear of its body overhung the patch of dried marram-grass, and retracted its tube feet. It lay in the sand like a discarded sack, but its eye continued to scan the surrounding terrain obsessively.

A sphincter beneath the walker's rear opened and extruded a thick proboscis, which inserted itself into the patch of marram-grass. The proboscis poked tentatively at the sand, then settled into a satisfactory position and buried its tip deep into the ground. The walker had found the shriveled remains of the marram-grass's long, tubular taproot, which decades before had drilled its way through layers of sand and soft stone to the aquifer that flowed beneath this part of the planet, filled with meltwater from its ice-clad poles.

The proboscis now extruded a fluid filled with pea-sized blobs—algal cooperatives. The algae began to multiply with astonishing rapidity, forming a branching network of filaments that invaded the hollow space inside the taproot, all the way down to the cool aquifer beneath. Billions of tiny vessels began to suck up water by capillary action, passing it from one tiny valved chamber to the next, channeling it ever higher toward the desert floor. The walker extended its tube feet, crawled away from the marram-grass, and turned around to witness the effects of its labors. Already the sand was damp. . . . Then a squat fountain of water was bubbling up in the center of a small puddle.

The puddle spread, lapping around the walker's body. The walker did not move.

As more and more water welled up from the aquifer, the puddle began to turn into a pond. Soon the walker was completely submerged except for its eye. But the eye no longer twirled on its fleshy stalk. The trunk began to droop until the eye was floating on the pond's surface.

The walker began to dissolve.

Its translucent integument softened and fell away, tearing gaping holes in its body. Spores reverted to crustacean form, and a stream of shrimplike creatures bled from the walker's wounds. Algae seeped from its punctured pillows. Dormant medusas unfolded their multiple rings of tiny tentacles and expelled themselves from the dissolving corpse. Humpbacked amphibians flopped from pockets molded into the partitions between the walker's segments. The shoal of yellow fish scattered as the amphibians splashed into the water, then reassembled.

Now only a few flaps of skin and a half-dissolved eye, bobbing obscenely on the surface of the new pond, indicated that the walker had ever existed. The tough skin melted to thin jelly and became one with the pond. The eye shriveled and burst like an overripe grape; a swarm of crustaceans pounced on the fragments and devoured them. The amphibians took up their customary station at the shady end of the pond.

Windblown sand had already started to fill the walker's tracks.

Sam knew that he ought to feel nothing but joy. He had been chosen to serve the All in a new role.

He had earned a promotion.

The high acolyte herself had summoned him to the office of the local hierocrat so that Sam could be told in person and instructed in his new duties.

Ever since childhood he had dreamed of this day—his first tangible step away from his forebears' traditional duties and toward his own advancement in the Church!

So why did he feel so vexed?

Was it worry about the use of a transible? No, he was looking forward to that. Never in his life had he expected to be assigned a task that would require such an expensive mode of transportation. And everyone said it was painless and instantaneous. . . . *Was* he worried, nonetheless? For irrational reasons? If so, he must search his lifesoul and seek out a preceptor, to eradicate the needless fear. But no, he really was looking forward to passage by transible.

Was it his destination? No, what little they had told him made it sound fascinating, even though it was a fixed world, not a starship. A world was vast, a ship small by comparison. But . . . yes, his concern had something to do with leaving the ship. Not changing his job, for his new post would again involve running a duplicator and manufacturing apparatus according to lists of instructions. But now those instructions would come from a hierocrat!

What, then, was it? Suddenly, he knew. He would miss the conversion of No-Moon. On his three previous occasions, when he had finally been permitted to leave his duplicator to experience the success of the mission, the sheer feeling of joy had been overwhelming. He could still recall the waves of happiness from the inhabitants—the appeal of the Memeplex was truly universal. But this time he would not be present when yet another grateful world became united with the Cosmic All. Just as the time was ripening, he was being torn from the mission fleet and sent elsewhere.

It was an unworthy thought, and he was shamed by it. Yet it would not go away. He consoled himself with another thought: He was being sent to a monastery world, so new that virtually all the monks were novices. Many were still uncertain in their faith. There would be many confused lifesouls to help heal.

He put his duplicator into slumber, where it would wait patiently until a successor was appointed to run it. Then he returned to his quarters, to assemble his few belongings and—most important of all—to tidy his lodging-place ready for that same successor. It would not do to earn a reprimand at this crucial juncture in his career.

Everything he owned packed easily inside his most prized and most expensive possession—a container that followed behind him, immune to gravity, attuned to his own person. Mobile, faithful, personal luggage. It would accompany him to the transible and be with him at journey's end. It was like an old friend, only more dependable.

His heart still heavy at missing the coming conversion of No-Moon, Servant-of-Unity XIV Samuel Godwin'sson Travers made his way through the corridors of *Disseminator 714*, wondering exactly what would await him when he stepped onto the surface of his newly assigned planet. He would wear suitable protective gear, of course; that was understood. He had been told that it was a cold world.

He didn't much like cold. He hoped that the protection would be effective. The ecclesiarchs advocated a spartan approach to the comforts of living, and Sam would not be in the least surprised if his protection left him feeling decidedly chilly. Still, a true servant of the All was expected to ignore discomforts. He was used to them, that was certain.

He arrived at the portal of the transible at the appointed time. The surrectors were in place, performing the ritual gestures that warmed up the machine and programmed it for the correct destination. Sam hoped they were competent—he had no wish to end up on the wrong side of the Galaxy by mistake, just because one of them sneezed at a crucial juncture.

But that was impossible, of course. The surrectors had ways to verify that the settings were correct before the transible was triggered.

So it was said.

To the untutored eye, the transible was little more than a slightly raised platform of irregular shape, but as the machinery approached readiness, it began to glow with a soft inner light. During his period as a novice, Sam had been told that one operation of a transible consumed as much energy as an entire starship did in a month. Later he asked a surrector he knew socially, and was told that if anything, the quantity was an underestimate.

It was indeed an honor to be permitted the use of a transible. It meant that speed must be of the essence, though no one had told him why. But his task was to serve, not to ask questions. He knew that the hierocrats always had good reasons for their decisions, even though they seldom revealed them.

Sam took a deep breath, and stepped onto the platform. His luggage snuggled up beside him, taking care not to protrude beyond the platform edge. To do so would not cause damage, but it would prevent the transible's functioning and waste energy—and merit a reprimand, of course.

After checking that all was in its proper place, the surrector-responsible stepped back and spoke a few soft words to his assistants. In unison, they bowed low, all facing the transible platform.

The transible's metaphace interpreted their movements as instructions. The air above the platform seemed to solidify, freezing Sam and his luggage inside a prism of sheer transparency. His internal organs became visible, but not as if his skin and muscles had turned to glass—more as if he were being observed from a different dimension altogether.

Simultaneously, every particle of his body was undergoing quantum phase recoherence. The particles' wave functions were being rotated in the complex plane until they were all perfectly aligned, perfectly in phase. In this state, his velocity could be observed with absolute precision—which implied, thanks to the uncertainty principle, that his position was completely indeterminate. This was the secret of the transible.

The wave functions phase-locked. The observation was made, and unmade.

Sam's body, and his luggage, surrected—and resurrected.

Their particles' velocities became indeterminate; their Bohm positions reverted to things that had meaning. Only now those meanings had changed. Body and luggage rested on another transible platform, in another part of the Galaxy.

Like all transible platforms everywhere, this one was entangled with all the others, including the one on board *Disseminator 714*. Recohering the phases united Sam and his luggage with that platform, and with all others. By observing their velocities from the frame of any selected platform, those wave functions could be persuaded to decohere in such a way that his classical *self* materialized only on the intended platform. Because interactions between entangled particles were simultaneous, there was no relativistic constraint on the speed with which everything happened. Sam arrived at his destination at the same moment he disappeared from the ship.

A moment later, his luggage arrived too. Nobody knew why Precursor luggage always arrived late. It just did. Precursor technology was like that. It was hard enough discovering how to use it. Understanding how it worked was impossible. And every so often, it did something unexpected.

You got used to it.

Sailing the starlanes of the Trailing Spiral Arm, Second-Best Sailor had decided, was nowhere near as exciting as sailing a boat. Unlike Fat Apprentice, he wasn't greatly interested in exploring the Neanderthals' ship or in talking philosophy. And the myriad pinpoints of light that could be seen outside—well, he supposed it was outside, but with all that intervening gadgetry, how could you be sure?—left him cold. You couldn't open a sallyport and swim in space, and you couldn't hunt a galaxy. He felt superfluous on board the great vessel. There was nothing for him to do, no need for his skills. . . . He was about as much use as a fish 'bovedecks.

Not to put too fine a point on it, he was bored, and he was miserable. Not even his wifepiece cheered him up, however cutely she made her polyps dance. The hastily filled tanks of No-Moon seawater, once cargo spaces, were cramped and lifeless, bounded by stark metal walls.

You couldn't even get a decent stick of high-powered algae.

The trip seemed interminable. Nothing happened; every day was the same as every other. In fact, if it hadn't been for the periodic dimming of the underwater lighting rigs, you wouldn't know where one day left off and the next began.

He wished he hadn't agreed to come. He hadn't wanted to come. The only reason he had signed up for this mad trip was because the reefwives had told him to. Mind you, that was a pretty good reason. Like all mariners, he had learned from childhood to obey the reefwives. Doing what they told you might make you miserable, sure. *Not* doing what they told you would definitely make you miserable.

The really annoying thing was, he had no idea why they wanted him offplanet. He'd been given hints that it was for his safety, but he'd spent his entire life so far on No-Moon without being in the slightest danger. Except for a few close calls with hurricanes, several nasty ramming incidents, one involving a 'viathan, and that trident fight beneath the dockside at Cindercone Grate, which he preferred not to think about. Oh, and that mad descent to the ocean floor to snaffle some fanworm tubes. So why was there such a hurry to leave *now*?

He sucked bubbles through his speech-siphon—a sign of exasperation. A few went the wrong way, and he spluttered, expelling them in an explosive exhalation of foam. His skin turned spotty with embarrassment when he noticed the amused stares of several other mariners. That really worried him—he could usually maintain an impassive, unbetraying float-the-cube-skin. He was losing his grip.

This depressing reverie was interrupted by the arrival of Fat Apprentice, who bore some welcome news.

"Cap'n, Cap'n! The ship's philosopher says we've arrived!"

It was typical that Fat Apprentice should get this news from a pedantic Thumosyne intellectual rather than Ship's captain. And even then, the apprentice did not know *where* the ship had arrived. Moreover, it was unclear what "arrived" meant. The concept of low-planet orbit made very little sense to a creature that expected journeys to end by tying up beside a dock.

Half a mile away from the mariner pool, Sharp Wit

Will Cut was gaining a much clearer idea of the nature of their destination. With the aid of a squad of Cyldarians safely bubblewrapped in chlorine-recycler cloaks, he had talked Ship into an almost circular orbit that approached within 150 miles of the planet's surface at its closest. The orbit was steeply inclined relative to the equator, so that as *Talitha* went around and around, and the planet spun beneath, the ship's footprint traced a sinusoidal curve that ranged over much of the planet.

Their initial surveys showed that Aquifer was a very ordinary world. Its diameter exceeded No-Moon's by about 10 percent, but its mass was correspondingly greater, so that the surface gravity was close to No-Moon norms. Its atmosphere had a lot more nitrogen and argon than No-Moon's did, and slightly more sulfides, but it was the mix of dissolved gases in the ocean that mattered, and the mariners' metabolism would easily cope with that. Patchy belts of cloud girdled the planet in temperate latitudes, with a third belt at the equator, mainly forming at night when the temperature dropped.

Aquifer had two satellites. One was about a sixth the planet's size, and spherical: a glittering ball of spangled metal-rich rock. There would be luminance to spare for mating excitement once the females arrived. The other satellite was tiny, shaped like a dumbbell, and so dark a shade of gray that only smears of paler regolith revealed its presence against the blackness of space.

Three-quarters of Aquifer's surface was a single landmass that spanned both poles, decorated with huge ice caps at each end. At the moment it was unclear whether they were free-floating or rested on yet more land. The continent completely surrounded a lake so vast that it could only be termed an ocean. To north, south, and west, thick swamps stretched a hundred miles inland from the coasts, gradually petering out into a maze of sandbars, then thin strips of grassland, then desert. Some regions of swamp were forested with tall succulents. Others were a tangled mass of floating vines, some of which had grown to a diameter of eight or ten feet.

A spine of mountains ran down the land at the ocean's eastern edge, snowcapped even at the equator. The snow line descended as the peaks got nearer the poles, and there were countless glaciers. Those on the western side fed into the ocean. Those on the eastern side melted to create rivers, which meandered out into the desert only to disappear beneath the surface and join the aquifers. Endless plains stretched away to the east. Most of the plains were desert, but only near the equatorial zone did the sparse vegetation give way to barren rocks and shifting sand. Elsewhere, scrubby bushes and swaths of waxy-leaved plants battled for supremacy in the dune valleys, and in some latitudes the valleys were thickly carpeted with cactals, strangely convoluted assemblies of tough plants like spiny mushrooms. It was obvious that there must be a lot of water under the sand. In some places it could be seen on the surface, as fields of tiny ponds spaced almost geometrically in a random close pack. But there were no large lakes.

Between desert and ice caps were twin bands of tundra, a broad band in the north and a narrower one in the south. Three ring-shaped lines of eroded peaks peeping up from the northern band attested to ancient impacts. The ocean sported five large isolated landmasses and innumerable islands. A few of these were active volcanoes, and there were many dormant ones. The volcanically active region of Aquifer seemed to be confined to the ocean floor.

The ocean was what interested Will, and he had set the Cyldarian ecologists the task of choosing a suitable location for the mariners. Of course, it would be possible to shove the mariners out of the transpods while they hovered over the middle of the ocean, but there would probably be no food for them. The Cyldarians possessed no specific data, but they knew that nearly always, local life forms were incompatible with the biochemistry of invading aliens. Not only that, there might be predators. The polypoids would almost certainly prove incompatible with *their* biochemistry, too, but it would be small consolation to the polypoids that anything that ate them would get rather sick.

Even if there was food and no predators, maintaining contact after dumping the mariners in midocean would be tricky. And part of the Neanderthals' bargain with the reefwives was that contact *would* be maintained. So they had to find a bay—not too big, not too small, not too shallow, and not too deep—with a narrow entrance that could be blocked using a Precursor forcewall.

So *Talitha* floated smoothly through the near-vacuum of low-planet orbit while its inhabitants surveyed the world below, seeking the best place to found a mariner colony. And Second-Best Sailor fretted and cursed, because until the 'Thals came to a decision, he was stuck in a big metal tank, along with forty-eight other, equally bored mariners. Only Fat Apprentice seemed to be enjoying this kind of life, but only Fat Apprentice enjoyed theological disputations and serious stargazing.

Second-Best Sailor was rapidly coming to the conclusion that Fat Apprentice was weird.

According to *Talitha*'s team of Tweel engineers, the big problem was the swamps. They had recognized the difficulty instantly. Managing the flow of water into and out of the mariner settlement would be much harder if the coast was bordered by swamp. A forcewall would keep out any swamp flora and fauna, but it would also affect the flow of water in the swamp and stem the replenishment of evaporated seawater with fresh. Oh, yes, it could be *done*, but the whole setup would be far more elegant if they could find a bay surrounded by solid rock. Those, on the whole, were rare. They were mostly to be found on the eastern side of the ocean, where foothills ran down to the sea. But glaciers tended to run down with them, calving into the bays—millions of tons of ice crashing down into the water as the glacier's base was eroded and melted. Such a bay, the Tweel repeatedly explained to anyone within earshot, would be an exciting habitat for the mariners, but not an appropriate one.

Two days passed before the Cyldarian ecologists, having conferred with the Tweel engineers about practicalities, reluctantly decided that a pear-shaped expanse of water about ten degrees north of the equator, on the western coast of Aquifer's ocean, was the best compromise available. Ship moved to a low circular equatorial orbit to obtain a better view of the bay. Its entrance was walled on both sides by steep cliffs, rather like a fjord, but the cliffs were chalky and crumbling, and they quickly fell away beyond the entrance. The bay itself was broader and shallower than a typical fjord would have been, which was good, but it was a bit smaller than they had hoped. Still, the mariners had no option, and it would be a lot less cramped than Ship. In time, the entire ocean would be open to them, and until then they would just have to put up with what they had.

In partial compensation, the top of the bay was surrounded by a broad chalk beach, firm and—by comparison with a swamp—dry. The transpods would be able to land there, and there ought to be somewhere suitable to set up a forcewall generator.

The invasion of Aquifer's ocean would begin on land, with the establishment of what was, literally, a beachhead.

5

AQUIFER NORTH ICE CAP

One must be aware that to inflict pain is to suffer it.
One must be aware that ignorance is no refuge.
One must be aware that one must be aware.
One must beware of the seductiveness of infinite
regress.

Koans of the Cuckoo

Servant-of-Unity XIV Samuel Godwin'sson Travers reflected on an ancient principle, much repeated by his mothers: that everyone is promoted to his level of incompetence. Had he, perhaps, been promoted to *his*?

He hoped not. He nursed a burning ambition to rise higher than his forefathers had. But—was he up to the challenge?

He had spent his whole working life learning the language of gesture that persuaded Precursor duplicators to disgorge accurate copies of whatever his superiors required. He had never questioned his role or his instructions. He had served Unity to the best of his ability, studying the manuals late into the night, rehearsing difficult gestures in front of a full-length mirror. Naturally, he had expected these skills to be the reason for his relocation from *Disseminator 714* to whichever distant planet the ecclesiarchs had chosen for him. He had expected to be promoted, but not to change his career completely. And for a short time, that's how it had been.

But now his hierocratic mentor, a female Flinger-Erdant with the identifier Hhoortl555mup, wanted him to become a *healer*. He would be responsible for the spiritual health of other sentients. It was without doubt a promotion, just as he had been promised. Having found out what it was, though, he was beginning to wonder if it was a promotion too far. He would go to Hhoortl555mup and tell her. . . .

No. He could not and would not. It was not his place to question the decisions of his superiors. If one or more hierocrats had chosen him for this role, and the local hierocrat had ratified their decision, then there was no possible doubt that he was fit for it. If he were to express doubt, the only result would be a reprimand. And in the strict environment of the ice caverns, it could well be a severe one.

✧ ✧ ✧

"No, Fourteen Samuel," his instructor said, with a patronizing swivel of its olfactory organ. The instructor was a querist, a very senior level of healer assigned to the iconological faction of the Church. He was a serpentine Veenseffer-co-Fropt from the tropical jungles of

Candirossa Twixt. His primary sense was smell—at least, that was the nearest human equivalent. The olfactory organ was a flexible, tapering tube covered in featherlike tufts. A smell that was fading away produced a very different sensation from one that was becoming stronger. For hundreds of millions of years, the predators of Candirossa Twixt had employed such mental impressions to deduce the likely movements of their prey. When the Veenseffer-co-Fropts evolved sentience, their sense of "smell" acquired a social dimension, too. Now the instructor was sensing confusion.

Sam was struggling. The clean certainties of his childhood were being exposed as simplistic and naive. In answer to his instructor's probing questions, he had innocently trotted out what he had always been taught was the essence of tolerance: always to respect the other's point of view, however repulsive or wrongheaded it might be. Respect would lead to spiritual enlightenment; disrespect would lead to conflict.

"No," the instructor repeated. "Conflict can be desirable. Tolerance cannot be taken to such an extreme that it becomes self-defeating." So tolerance was not what Sam had thought it was.

The same went for peace. Peace was a valid spiritual objective—indeed, an overriding one—but not one that could always be accomplished peacefully. Means and ends might be incompatible, and when they were, it was the ends that mattered. So when as a child he had been asked "When is it permissible to kill another sentient being?" the answer had been easy: "Never." Now he began to see that so absolute a stricture was necessarily flawed.

The querist had posed a standard ethical dilemma: "What is the correct action if a crazed criminal holds a hundred younglings hostage, Fourteen Samuel?"

He had thought very hard, trying to spot the trap, but saw none. "The wise person will attempt to negotiate, master."

"And if negotiation fails?"

"No action should be taken that would harm a sentient."

"And what if the hostage-taker is about to detonate explosives?"

"The criminal is insane; the situation is not its fault. Tragedy must be avoided if at all possible."

"But suppose it is *not* possible?" the instructor pressed.

"Then . . ." Sam had no real answer. He had never had to think about such a dire circumstance. In school, where they had acted out such scenarios, the hostage-taker could always be talked into peaceful surrender or, if necessary, bribed into releasing the hostages. It had merely been necessary to explain the ethics of the situation to the hostage-taker, for no sentient would risk its own lifesoul!

Now he was faced with the realization that "crazed" meant what it said. Such a being *would* risk its own lifesoul. It would not value its lifesoul as a rational being would.

"Then tragedy is unavoidable," said Sam. "Prayers will be chanted afterwards for the dead younglings."

"Is that the only action you can devise?"

"Uh, well . . . of course the unfortunate criminal would have to be confined—"

"No! It would have to be *killed*."

Sam was genuinely shocked. "But the *Koans of the Cuckoo* tell us that it is a mortal error to kill another sentient, master."

"That is one interpretation, Fourteen Samuel," the querist demurred. "But the scholars have discovered another. The Cuckoo, as a Founder, cannot be challenged. But the context for his wise words does not always apply as it did then. The leading theologians now teach that it is ethical in such circumstances to kill the mad thing and save the innocent younglings. And to say the prayers for the lifesoul of the *criminal*."

Sam thought about that. "But what of the lifesoul of the being that kills the criminal?"

The querist was impressed. His student had depth, and had seen the moral difficulty. Now he must be told its resolution.

"Sam . . ."

Never before had the instructor stooped to such informality. Sam was touched.

". . . is it not recorded that the greatest service that one sentient can render to another is self-sacrifice?"

"Most certainly, master."

"And is it not a major sacrifice to risk the health of one's lifesoul?"

"Yes . . ."

The Veenseffer-co-Fropt's tufts were quivering, which meant either that he was feeling extraordinarily pleased with his own cleverness or that he was late in readying himself mentally for the simulated onset of his homeworld's lengthy night, which would shortly begin in his private quarters. Sam saw where his instructor was heading. He didn't like it, but he saw no way around it.

"So you see that the killer, by risking the possibility that he has misinterpreted the Koans and has damaged the health of his own lifesoul as a consequence, is making an enormous sacrifice for the benefit of the lifesouls of all those children and their families?"

Sam nodded. It was difficult to disagree with the logic.

"So it is ethical to kill the criminal. *If all else fails*."

There. The instructor had said it. No hedging, no hiding behind euphemisms. So now Sam could give a more subtle answer: "When killing would ultimately result in fewer deaths than not killing."

The one may be sacrificed for the benefit of the many. And sometimes *must* be. It was logical. It made sense. It was, no doubt, the kind of wisdom that a healer must acquire. But it wasn't what he had been taught to see as tolerance or love. It damaged lifesouls.

But not *killing the criminal would damage even more!*

The judgment was relative, not absolute. Simple arithmetic. Count the number of lifesouls that are damaged. Minimize it.

Sam guessed that he was starting to grow up. It had all seemed so simple when he was a child. Now he was learning to weigh options, compute ethical balances. Even so, he mostly felt confused. *"That is when you are beginning to understand,"* he heard his childhood teacher's voice say in his mind. He hoped it was true.

Aquifer's ice caverns housed a monastery of equals. Certain special, selected devotees of Cosmic Unity— "monks," to use an archaic term—spent their days there in total seclusion, dedicating their lives to coexistence with other species. As well as the monks, there were a few technicians and medics, some menials and orderlies to assist them, and a few security guards. Quite a lot of security guards, actually. Sam vaguely wondered why.

It was a harsh lifestyle, as he now knew from personal experience. Above all, the caverns were *cold*. Not because they were beneath the polar ice cap—the caverns could easily have been warmed without melting the ice, merely by applying the appropriate insulating materials. No, they were cold because most of the monks were gas-giant blimps, who could not survive in temperatures that humans would find comfortable without life-support equipment. Higher authority was represented by a wide variety of species, in agreement with the Quota of Love, as was only proper. Like most creatures that lived on gas giants, the blimps adhered to universal phenotypes, and so resembled the sacred Jovians who had taken part in the Prime Mission, the first diaspora of Cosmic Unity. In particular, they were balloonists. But also, again like most creatures that lived on gas giants, they differed from these fabled progenitors in countless ways. The universality of the balloonist phenotype was a consequence of convergent evolution, not identical biochemistry. Just as most sea beings of a certain weight and size had fins and a tail, their body plan was the inevitable outcome of fluid dynamics. There were only so many ways to swim.

Sam had no idea what planet he was on, or where it

was, but he did manage to work out why the Monastery of the Nether Ice Dome was so cold. The religious authorities had been led to a compromise, one that was equally uncomfortable for the main species represented in the monastery. The caverns were distinctly too warm for blimps, and way too cold for several other species present, with the notable exception of the cold-blooded Gra'aan, who were at home whatever the temperature as long as their blood remained liquid. There were very few Gra'aan in Cosmic Unity. Their homeworlds had not yet converted, but like many species they had some members in the Church, often immigrants or passing visitors to worlds undergoing conversion.

In the monastery, each species was permitted to wear minimal life support—not effective enough to reproduce their own comfortable conditions, but effective enough to keep them alive. And uncomfortable. And *equal*, which was the point. Sam quickly understood that personal comfort was irrelevant. Indeed, it was good for one's lifesoul to suffer for the advancement of cosmic equality. That point had featured in his very first lesson as a trainee healer.

Equality itself, of course, was a compromise. Sam wore a lightweight breathing mask to compensate for the planet's low oxygen levels; the blimps, on the other hand, were completely enveloped in translucent sacks and carried heavy tanks of compressed gases. The planet's atmospheric composition was much closer to Sam's requirements than it was to a blimp's, so here the blimp was less equal than Sam. On the other hand, the blimp's envelope was more effective at cooling its wearer than Sam's thin cloak was at keeping him warm, so here the blimp gained an advantage.

It all evened out, and again, that was the point.

Although most of the monks were blimps, quite a few other races were represented. So far Sam had run across some miserable-looking Thunchch, a bunch of distinctly unhealthy Hytth insectoids, a few metallomorphs hitching rides on the other monks, and one solitary Gra'aan. The Gra'aan were social creatures, and became afraid when removed from the safety of the herd; this one was clearly teetering on the edge of terror the whole time, and would eventually suffer a mental collapse. There were no other humans, and only one humanoid, a female Neanderthal child.

Most unusual. Neanderthals were without faith; they hardly ever joined the Church. But this very rarity made them valuable. He would cherish her lifesoul like any other, but he couldn't help feeling she was special. He guessed her age to be about seven. Her face was downcast, and she seemed to take little notice of her surroundings. He had never seen her smile.

The monks all had one thing in common: Their lifesouls were very, very sick. You didn't need to be a healer to see that. It was why they had been brought here, why they had been made monks. Their lifesouls required attention . . . correction. Healing.

He wanted to speak with them and comfort them, but of course he was not yet ready for such sensitive contact. Conversation was permitted only when duties demanded it. In his case, that meant he could talk to other duplicator staff when—and only when—he was duplicating, and to his clients when he was playing the role of healer.

During his training he would be permitted to talk to his clients, but only when a fully qualified healer was observing. Only after he had successfully completed his training would he be free to choose when, and to whom, he spoke. And then not in excess.

The physical and mental state of the monks disturbed him. The cavern complex of the Nether Ice Dome may have been a monastery of equals, but spiritually uplifting it was not. Suffering for one's faith was one thing, Sam thought, but this kind of suffering was unnecessary and upsetting. There was no nobility in it. It was . . . squalid.

Even to think such thoughts made Sam feel ashamed. The ecclesiarchs were the spiritual leaders of a religious movement founded on respect and tolerance, love and universal brotherhood. They were by definition wise and kind. They would never permit such apparent squalor without having a very good reason. The hierocrats would never accept leaders who acted otherwise.

So, Sam reasoned, the discomfort and unhealthy conditions must serve some significant spiritual purpose. The only problem was, he was finding it very difficult to work out what that purpose might be.

Sam spent part of every day running a duplicator, and at those times he was happy. He was happy when he copied sections of metal rod, with screw threads at one end and matching sockets at the other; he was happy when he made smaller batches of pointy things with screw threads, and blunt, rounded things with sockets. He was happy making funny little equilateral triangles in batches of a few thousand. He was happy making coils of wire, nuts and bolts, edged blades, springy semicircles of metallic strip, spikes, metal rings, gas cylinders, brackets, buckets, pots, hammerheads, handles, boxes, irregular lumps of solid steel, plastic badges, ropes, chains, tubes, spouts, switches, funnels, trays, shelves, life-support machinery, floater components, and delicate assemblies of glass and gossamer.

It passed through his mind that many of these items were intended to be assembled in some manner and that they had been designed to be small enough for routine duplication, but he did not attempt to work out how the assembly procedure worked or what its end result would be.

Healer training, by contrast, was a struggle. He found it hard to wrap his head round the convoluted thinking. He had no trouble understanding that the Unity of the Cosmos must transcend the fate or wishes of any individual—that was in accordance with the Great Memes. But the fine points of interpretation were so much more difficult. His mind was in turmoil. He had been trained since birth never to question the motives of his religious superiors. They were wiser and cleverer than he, and there were many things that one as lowly as he was not entitled to know. There were heresies, forbidden questions, and secret doctrines reserved for the eyes and ears of the initiated. On his homeworld, as on *Disseminator 714*, anything not mandatory had been forbidden. Now, though, he had to learn to think for himself.

That was *hard*.

He was racked by doubts. He was only the latest in a lineage of humble duplicator operators, not a healer!

Healers could penetrate people's innermost secrets and passions. They could see through the layers of pretense as if they were the clearest glass. They could lay bare a being's very lifesoul, with all its flaws. And by theological arguments and subtle persuasions, they could correct those flaws and restore the afflicted lifesoul to full spiritual health. How could he, XIV Samuel, hope to attain such intellectual powers, when thirteen previous generations had not improved their standing in the Church? He'd overreached himself. He didn't want the responsibility. He didn't want the spiritual fate of thousands to rest on his unaided shoulders.

He tried to tell himself that his crisis of confidence was just a silly panic attack. He would start to feel better when his instructors moved on to the practical aspects of guardianship. Then he would begin to make more meaningful contact with his fellow monks. It would be good to talk to the Neanderthal girl, for instance. Maybe he would be able to cheer her up.

She looked so sad.

Sam was getting used to the cold now. It was astonishing how adaptable the human body could be. He still felt distinctly uncomfortable, but it was becoming easier to concentrate on his assignments. He was beginning to see how a monastery of equals worked, and why it was set up as such a stark environment. Already it had taught him three important things: obedience, patience, and humility.

Today his instructor had welcome news. "You have

been diligent, Fourteen Samuel, and the time has come for your diligence to be put to the service of the One." No mention of diligence being rewarded, for in the Church of Cosmic Unity diligence was its own reward. Sam remembered a wry remark from his childhood teacher, in a different context: *"The carrot is, we won't use the stick."* Yes, that was Cosmic Unity, all right.

But it was a reward nonetheless, even if nobody called it that. His heart had leaped when the querist went on: "It is time for you to begin practical work. You will be assigned a client, a lifesoul in need of healing."

Praise be to the Lifesoul-Cherisher!

"You will be briefed before each session, to set the boundaries of what you may say and do. For the foreseeable future, Fourteen Samuel, you will not be left alone with your client. Always there will be a querist, or several, observing—perhaps from concealment, perhaps physically present. And after every session with your client, a querist will review your performance and correct your mistakes.

"If you progress sufficiently, you may in time be permitted a degree of independence. Of course, all healing sessions will be recorded and the records placed in the archives. You understand?"

"I do, master."

"And you understand why?"

His instructor was always asking tricky questions like that. Veenseffer-co-Fropts had a penchant for logical traps. Sam tried to decide what answer the querist wanted. It was so easy to say something stupid, or to reveal an unacceptably tentative grasp of doctrine. "Uh . . . because I am but a novice in such matters, master.

And"—he glanced at the querist's face to get a hint of how well he was answering, but the face was impassive—"And I will benefit from correction by my betters." No, his instructor wanted more; those were too obvious. "And . . . I must accept responsibility for the consequences of my actions, however far in the future they arise."

The querist gave him a penetrating stare. "Almost. You *will* be *made* to accept responsibility for the consequences of your actions. So those actions must be available for consideration at any time."

That was really what Sam had meant when he said he *must* accept responsibility. But it was not his place to argue with his instructor. He nodded. "I stand corrected, master."

The instructor rose from his stool and began to slide across the chamber. He looked distracted. Then he slithered in a sharp U-turn and raised his foreparts so that his olfactory organ dangled inches from Sam's face. He had come to some kind of decision.

"There are two lifesouls, among the many that concern me, that are suitable for your limited knowledge of the art of the healer, Fourteen Samuel."

Sam waited.

"One is a Hytth, who has suffered an amputation and has not yet succeeded in coming to terms with her consequent inability to secure a mate. How would you approach such a client, Fourteen Samuel?"

There was a consensual answer to such soulsickness, and Sam had been reviewing the doctrine only a few days before. "There are comforting words in the Reevaluation of Saint Joan the Profane," he said. "An extensive passage on the virtues of enforced celibacy, linked to the inspiring tale of Saint Joan and the seventy virgins."

"That is one way. Obvious, easy, but none the worse for that. The other potential client is more difficult. It is a Neanderthal child. What is the difficulty with Neanderthals?"

"They—well, master, characteristically they lack a sense of the spiritual."

"Go on."

"Before the Neanderthal Exodus, when they were Beastmasters, their empathy with animals rendered them insensitive to the signs of the Lifesoul-Cherisher. Even though those signs are everywhere. To a Neanderthal, a sunset is just a star being occulted by the horizon of a spinning planet. They see no beauty in it, and experience no sense of awe. Their empathic sense seems to have subverted their sense of the spiritual, perhaps by taking over the part of their brain that would otherwise attune them to the marvels of the Lifesoul-Cherisher."

The querist seemed pleased by this comprehensive answer. "Which has what consequence, Fourteen Samuel?"

"Most Neanderthals are deaf to the gospel of the United Cosmos, master. It is notoriously difficult to overcome their skepticism. They seem immune to the usual arguments and evidences. And they can be extraordinarily stubborn."

"Even at the age of seven years?"

"Especially then."

"So you would prefer to teach a suffering Hytth the story of Saint Joan and the seventy virgins rather than at-

tempt the taxing task of bringing Dry Leaves Fall Slowly
to the truth?"

So that was her name. Sam didn't hesitate.

"Master, I prefer to accept the challenge, if you deem
me worthy. I will attempt to heal the lifesoul of the Neanderthal child."

". . . and so the third ornithopt was able to succeed
where the others had failed," said Sam. The Neanderthal
girl's large golden eyes gazed past his face, over his
shoulder, at a patch of wall. She seemed unimpressed by
the story he was telling her, one of his own childhood favorites. A cultural difference? Or was it a peculiarity of
the child herself?

He struggled manfully on. "So, Fall, what does the
story tell us?"

The girl stared at her feet. "I miss my mother. You
have an ugly, flat face. Your nose is too thin. And you
must call me 'Leaves,' not 'Fall.'"

Well, that's me put in my place, Sam thought. *Her second name. Not formal enough to mean that I have any
importance to her; not informal enough to accept me as
a friend.*

"The story tells us that we can learn from the failures of
others and avoid repeating their mistakes. Uh . . . I'm sure
you will be able to return to your mother once we've finished talking about what the story really means," said Sam.

The child's eyes lifted and met his. "My mother is
dead."

Sam's heart sank into his boots. Worse, a querist

would be watching this, and it would be recorded and go into the permanent archives. . . . He should have guessed. He should have dug out the information from the archives. Dry Leaves Fall Slowly was the only Neanderthal he had seen in the Nether Ice Dome. He had assumed that her parents were somewhere around, too—just not happening to cross his path. It was a reasonable assumption; he had little freedom of movement in the monastery, and he was sure that he had encountered only a tiny fraction of its denizens.

He felt a complete fool.

"Leaves, I'm terribly sorry," Sam said. "I didn't know."

The child seemed more puzzled than upset. "But you are a priest. Priests know everything. Why did you not know?"

"No, I'm—" Sam stopped. He *was* one of the priesthood now. He was a novice lifesoul-healer. It was taking some getting used to, and the girl's calm poise floored him. His face reddened with embarrassment; he felt like bringing an end to the session. But the querist was watching, and he had to continue. Anyway, it was his role as a servant to get through this poor child's mental barriers and heal the trapped, damaged lifesoul. A lifesoul deprived all too early of a mother's love, and thus in mortal danger.

"What about your father?" he asked gently, dreading the answer.

"He is dead, too."

Somehow, this information was not a surprise. If her father had been alive, the girl would have said so when she first mentioned her mother's death. This time, though, Sam did not apologize. *"Sometimes,"* his instructor had told him, *"it is necessary to wait in silence. Do not feel a need to fill in gaps in the conversation. Any hiatus should be met with equanimity. It will put pressure on the client to continue talking, and there is a chance that they will reveal something that would otherwise have stayed hidden."*

He waited. So did the child.

If Fall—Leaves—was feeling the pressure, she showed no sign. Feeling increasingly foolish, he stuck to what he had been taught, and remained silent.

An awkward pause, which went on too long. Then: "They killed my grenvil, too."

He wanted to ask who had killed the small, scaly creature that had clearly been the child's favorite pet. Instead, obeying his training, he waited, hoping the silence would draw her out. It worked.

"I miss my grenvil. They hurt it. I felt its pain. And I saw what they did. It was horrible. I hate them." A tear rolled down one cheek—*eureka!* Finally, a response! "I hate you, too; you are one of them, one of the priests!"

She was shouting now. Spittle ran from her full-lipped mouth. Sam tried to take her hand—touching a client was permitted, provided it was nonthreatening. She jerked it away as if his own were red hot.

What has this child witnessed? He could not believe that a servant of Unity would harm a pet. He wondered whether the animal had perhaps been sick and she had misunderstood an attempt to heal it. Not knowing exactly what had happened, he had to avoid putting his foot in it again.

"It is a bad act to harm an innocent animal," he finally ventured. "When I was your age, I had a skirrel. I loved it dearly and would never have allowed anyone to hurt it."

"Could you have stopped anybody hurting it if they were stronger than you?" the child asked, appearing interested in the conversation for the first time since it had started. "I could not help my grenvil. They burned it with a blowtorch." The tears increased their flow; her whole body was shaking. "They . . . they tied me to a chair. I could do nothing. And if I *could* have tried to help my pet, they would have burned *me*."

"No!" cried Sam, discovering that his self-control was more brittle than he had thought. "That's impossible! You must be mistaken!" *Oh, Cherisher help her.* Now he saw the extent of the child's lifesoul damage in all its spiritual deformity. It was far, far worse than it had first seemed. Far, far worse than he had feared.

The Neanderthal girl, a child of seven, was lying. And it was a wicked lie. He made a mental note to find out from the querist just what had really happened to trigger such a malicious accusation. But now he had to put the session back on course. How could he explain? Ah . . .

"What you tell me was done is contrary to the Memeplex, Leaves. The most important things in the world are tolerance, love, peace, unity, and harmony among all sentient races."

The child was unimpressed by the logic. "But a grenvil is only an animal. The Memeplex does not apply to animals."

"That's true . . . but although a grenvil is not sentient, Leaves, any harm done to your pet would also be harm done to *you*. There is no way that a true servant of

Unity could torture a harmless animal, but even if they could, they would never do so in front of someone who loved it."

"Then ... those priests were not true servants of Unity," said the child, wiping her streaming eyes on her arm.

"You must have misunderstood what they were doing," said Sam. "I'm sure of it. I promise you that I will find out the truth, and reveal it to you when next we meet."

The girl sniffed and hung her head. "I am a child. I was there when my pet was killed, but I am merely a child, so I count for nothing. *You* did not even know it had happened. But you are a priest. So ... *I* must be wrong."

Sam observed wryly that for a seven-year-old she had a cutting sense of sarcasm. "Leaves, believe me, I will ask my superiors, and find out the truth, and explain it to you."

"And will you ... will you also find out the truth about my ... my mother? And my father?" she asked, now sobbing openly. "I do not know how they died, or where, but I know that they did. A priest told me." The tawny eyes opened wide; the mouth curled in a snarl. "I saw the priests take my parents away. . . . I think the priests killed them, just like they ... they killed my grenvil."

It was a reasonable enough conclusion, given the girl's twisted logic. If the priests could torture her pet before her eyes—not to mention the effect on her empathic sense—they were capable of anything. So, if her parents had disappeared, then of course a priest had killed them. Probably by a similar method. It was a child's logic, based on circumstance, not facts. But it was terribly seductive.

At least he now knew where to start. The session had not, after all, been a dead loss. He would ask permission to consult the archives and find out what had really happened to the girl's parents. Perhaps they were still alive but had been sent elsewhere and she had not been told. Or, if they truly were dead, he could find out how and where and when. And *finally*, he could also see a point of leverage, a way to get inside that ugly-beautiful leonine head of hers.

He would have to find out the truth about the grenvil and convince her that it *was* the truth. Then, by extension, she would be more likely to believe what he told her about her parents. And then the healing could begin.

Dry Leaves Fall Slowly was going to be a very difficult client. Every time she had opened her mouth, the lies *(call them 'confusions'; euphemisms sometimes help)* had gotten worse. But she was young, and something terrible had surely happened. He wondered what it had been. His outrage at her lies disappeared beneath a wave of affection. Fall had lost her parents, so he, Sam, would become a substitute. A poor substitute, he knew, but better than none.

He had found his true calling.

He reached for her hand again, and this time she did not pull back. He felt terrible, but above all he felt sympathy. And the child was a Neanderthal, with that spooky sense of empathy that they all seemed to have, and she knew *exactly* how he felt—and responded.

He held her, and her tears renewed. But she clung to him as if he were all that existed in the whole world.

And, after a time, she drifted off into an undisturbed sleep.

Let the querists make of that what they wished.

As they had done for a hundred thousand generations, the Huphun broodmothers lined up at starset to welcome home their young, spreading their wings to display their homing symbols in a riot of color. But after the arrival of the aliens, the happy event inspired only mindnumbing fear.

When will it stop? When?

Each evening, the strangers randomly chose one section of spittle nests, the Huphun equivalent of a city block, and walled it off from its neighbors using opaque, impenetrable fields of force. Within the protection of the field, they went about their evil work.

The forcewalls stretched a hundred feet outward from the cliff and stopped. They did not prevent the young from seeing their mothers, displaying beside the home nest. The walled-off section was open to anything that flew.

As long as it was a returning fledgling. When the first force fields went up, several adult Huphun had flown out into the canyon to find out what was happening inside the walls. But as they crossed the line of the wall, *something* plucked them from the sky and dashed them against the rocks. By the strange way that the light nearby was bent, forming a momentary streak like faint, curdled smoke, the Huphun deduced that the aliens were in possession of tractor beams as well as forcewalls.

The Huphun quickly found out what was happening in the walled-off section, and it terrified them. They had to listen for hours to the cries of the trapped mothers. They could not cover their hearing buds; they could not remove themselves from the vicinity, because their own brood were making their evening return to the warmth of the nest. They had to stay and listen, however distressing the sounds might be.

And at starrise, the mothers removed the spittle plugs from their nest openings and looked out to greet the new day, knowing the scene that would await them. The forcewalls had vanished. All that remained were mothers, flattened against the cliff, solidified by the cold of the deep night. And pathetic corpses of fledglings, scattered obscenely at the base of the cliff.

The Huphun knew what was happening inside the forcewalls. Oh, yes. What they still did not know was why this was being done to them.

And now it was happening again. The carnage had resumed every evening since the aliens arrived. Eleven consecutive starsets of unparalleled horror.

Why are they torturing us?

When broodmother PinkStripedLozenge saw the forcewall forming around her, she knew she was going to die a terrible death—but that was not her greatest fear. Over and over again, until her vocal organs were torn and inflamed and her voice was hoarse, she screeched warnings to her approaching young.

"Not here! Not me! To the nest! To the nest!"

The noise of panic-stricken mothers was the worst thing she had ever heard. And through it all, the same questions beat in her head: *Why, why, why? What have we done to suffer such pain? Whom have we ever harmed? Why have the Wings of the World exposed us to this atrocity?*

She knew that even if her fledglings had obeyed her commands, it would have been useless. The young did not know how to close the nest opening, and in any case their spit glands were not yet functional. There was no chance that they would obey. The fledglings were operating on instinct, and they ignored the desperate cries of the mothers. They lacked the mental powers to understand the danger they were in, or to escape it.

Like all the mothers inside the forcewall, PinkStripedLozenge had been glued to the cliff. The alien invaders had tried to force her wings open, and she had fought against them like a maddened bant-eagle until the struggle broke several of her wing bones and dislocated one of her trailing struts, so that the pain became unbearable. Then, ignoring her screams of anguish, they pulled her wings wide apart, tearing skin and snapping skeletal struts. They sprayed the backs of the wings with a sticky chemical, whose very smell nauseated her, and then they held her against the cliff next to her nest.

A puff of gas from a stubby cylinder set the glue like rock. At that moment she finally accepted that she was going to die, as thousands of others had on each of the previous starsets. She hung from the cliff in a haze of pain, knowing that the true horror was yet to come.

The fledglings were too young to reason. Their instinct knew no better than to seek out the symbols of their own nest, flagrantly displayed upon her inner wings. PinkStripedLozenge knew that when her young reached her and clung with their mouth-tusks, she would be unable to fold her wings around them. And even when the whole brood had attached itself to her calluses, she would not be able to step into the nest to escape the bitter cold of the night.

The fledglings' approach was hesitant. They knew something was terribly wrong, but they did not know what. Their panic-stricken mewling drove the mothers frantic, and they renewed their struggles to get free. One, whose bone structure had been severely damaged, ripped away from the cliff and fell to her death, leaving her wings still attached to the rock, dripping body fluids.

"Stay away! Stay away!" PinkStripedLozenge could not tilt her head far enough to see her brood as they attached themselves to her torso, but she could feel their mouth-tusks gripping the toughened calluses that ran across the front of her upper body, and the weight of the youngsters against her breathing cavity. And she knew that they could not hold on for long. Time and again one of the fledglings would fall off, clatter down the cliff until it bounced into open air, spread its ever-more-tired wings, and reattach itself to her.

After a time, they no longer returned.

Barely conscious, awash with pain, and half-insane from the loss of her brood and her own helplessness to prevent it, PinkStripedLozenge watched the last arc of the Evenstar disappear below the canyon rim. At once she began to freeze.

And still she did not know why.

Although he had sounded confident when he'd made his promise to the Neanderthal child, Sam wouldn't have been surprised if his request to consult the archives had been turned down. The regimen at the monastery was very restrictive, and he didn't *need* to find out about Fall's parents to heal her lifesoul. In fact, it was conceivable that she would be more likely to develop spiritually if she just accepted that whatever had happened to them had been a necessary contribution to the pursuit of a united cosmos. But when he made a diffident approach to his instructor, he was immediately granted an hour's access to all unrestricted personnel records and given the necessary qubit crystal to activate it.

It took him a few minutes to find the right section of the archive; after that it was relatively easy to select the glyphics for a primary search procedure to locate the girl's father and mother, and a secondary one to inquire into the fate of her pet. The archive quickly gave him access to Fall's parents' files. What he read there shocked him.

The early part of the record was pretty ordinary stuff. Fall's father, Alert Ears Hear Silence, had been born on board a Neanderthal spacecraft. So had her mother, but on a different vessel. They had met when both ships overlapped on a trade venture, paired up, and jumped ship. This left them trying to make a living in a very ordinary town on an insignificant planet that had not at that time enjoyed the benefit of Cosmic Unity's ministrations.

Seven years ago they had produced their one and only child, Fall.

Four years and five months later, a mission of Unity

had arrived on that world and converted its inhabitants to the cause of universal tolerance and love. Alert Ears Hear Silence had been among the last to convert, but it was well known that Neanderthals lacked the common spiritual graces and were difficult in this respect. His wife, Golden Mane Floats Softly, had proved less awkward and had volunteered to take on the task of bringing spiritual luminance to those members of her species that were finding its concepts confusing. She had enjoyed modest success, but none whatsoever with her husband, Hear—a failure that grew to haunt her. And so she tried harder and argued with him constantly about his indifference to the realm of the lifesoul, the omnipotence of its Giver, and the immanence of its Cherisher.

All of which, Hear told his wife, was superstitious claptrap.

As time passed, the relationship became ever more strained by this spiritual incompatibility, and they separated. Fall remained with her mother, Floats, and the authorities moved her father to a distant city, where suitable counseling was available.

Just over a year later, Hear returned, to be reunited with his wife, but he was a shadow of his former self. He had finally embraced the tenets of Cosmic Unity, but he had also contracted a rare disease, which had left him with a physical deformity to his hands and feet—and, it turned out, a serious but undiagnosed mental instability. One day, when Fall was at school, Hear and Floats had begun arguing. Neighbors heard the shouting, then silence. When one of them became concerned, she found the door open and went in. She found Floats lying dead on the floor, and Hear in another room in a pool of blood, with a knife in his chest.

The neighbor alerted the authorities, who took over Fall's upbringing. She did not return to the house; instead, an order of female monks took her under their wing. She was told that a terrible accident had happened to her parents. The truth—that Alert Ears Hear Silence had killed his wife in a violent argument and then committed suicide—was deemed unsuitable for such a young child. So was the autopsy report, which had found anomalies in Hear's brain, attributed by the coroner to his previous disease.

Sam was greatly distressed by this discovery. He now knew the truth, but he had no idea how much of it he would be able to tell Fall. He would have to ask the advice of his instructor. A mistake could prove very damaging to the child.

In his state of shock, he nearly forgot his secondary objective, but the machine had been hunting through its memory banks, and it had come to a disturbing conclusion.

Of the incident with the grenvil, there was no record. In fact, there was no record that Fall or her parents had possessed any pets. The girl must have imagined the whole thing—maybe dreamed it, then confused dream with reality. He tried to find out whether she was known to suffer from sleep paralysis, which could cause dreams to be confused with reality, but found no record of it.

Several hours after quitting the archives, a nagging thought finally surfaced. Sam reviewed the session in his mind. Hadn't Fall said that she had *seen* the priests take her parents away? He could review the records, but it would be simpler to ask her again at the next session, which was scheduled for tomorrow. Anyway, he was sure that was what she'd told him.

The archives flatly contradicted her statement. They said that she had left her parents in the normal manner and never returned home from school. Had she dreamed about the priests taking them away, *too*?

This was a very disturbed child, but he was sure he could heal her. His love was great enough. He simply needed to keep trying. But in their next sessions, she was immovable. Sam began to realize that it would take a huge effort to correct her misconceptions and bring her to the truth. His slowly building confidence began to drain away again.

Still he stuck to his task. There *had* to be a way to get inside her shell of obstinacy. But Fall simply could not be convinced that her memories were false. No matter how Sam tried, in session after long, frustrating session, she would not be shaken from her story. It infuriated him that she could *sense* his sincerity but took no notice of it. Then he would realize that she could sense his fury, too, and that made him ashamed of his inadequacies as a lifesoul-healer . . . and, of course, she could sense those feelings, too. . . .

It is extraordinarily difficult, Sam discovered, to engage with an empath. They cannot read your mind, but they can read your emotions perfectly, however well you conceal them. Yet, paradoxically, this was what bound the two of them, client and healer, together—for the main emotion that Fall could sense was love. Sam really did want to help her, to heal her, to make her whole again. It wasn't his fault that he didn't believe her. He believed what the priests' records told him.

She didn't. She was convinced that the records were wrong.

He knew they were right. His upbringing and his training left him no choice. All his life he had obeyed the priests, accepted their advice, studied their teachings, and striven to make himself like them.

The contradictions were driving him crazy. And it wasn't only Fall who could sense *that*.

6

NO BAR BAY

The soul is the life, and life shall cherish life. Thus, life shall cherish the soul of life, and strive always to enhance its becoming. There can be no limits to the love of the lifesoul, no restraint on the ways of its preservation.

The Book of Biogenesis

Second-Best Sailor emitted a wild whoop of joy from his speech-siphons and spouted a fountain of seawater into the air in a looping parabola. Gusts of wind ripped it to pieces as it reached the apex. He whooped again. It was so good to be out of the belly of the 'Thal ship and back in a real ocean.

Well, a small bay, really. But that was just temporary. The ocean might be off limits for the moment, but it was *out there*. He could taste it. One day, he and his kind would make it their own. He contracted his ring muscles to squeeze water out through his rearward siphons, and shot across the bay in a cloud of bubbles, stirring up sand from the shallow seabed. His chromophore skin turned yellow and turquoise in slowly drifting chevrons, a sign of overexcited happiness. He sensed the color change, which normally would have been embarrassingly juvenile.

He didn't give a squirt.

The sea was clear today, and visibility was good. No more than half a mile away, out in the deeper water away from the beach, he could make out several of his companions, racing two boats against each other. He would have placed a bet on the outcome if there had been anything to act as currency . . . though perhaps that was all to the good, since he now saw that the boat he had favored was wallowing in a sudden calm. The one that obviously hadn't stood the chance of a jelloid in a riptide was cutting through the water like a marlon in pursuit of its mate, which only went to show that even a completely incompetent captain sometimes got lucky.

He opened his siphons wide and gulped the alien seawater. The taste was strange, but to the mariners the freedom of the bay was infinitely preferable to the restricted confines of the 'Thal spaceship. One reason why Aquifer had been chosen was that the mix of salts in its ocean was similar to that on No-Moon; the differences were evident enough to the mariners' sensitive taste-buds, but not unpleasant. *A taste of the exotic*, Second-Best Sailor had remarked, and not all the resulting amusement had been forced.

The mariners had named their new home No Bar Bay because it was evidently a bay, and equally evidently there were no bars. There were no docks, either, and no access to reefwives, which was a source of some complaint—though, of course, each polypoid had brought along the traditional piece of his wife, which would help maintain his sanity but would not sustain the mariner population until the Cyldarians deemed the ecology sufficiently nomoonformed for mating to be permissible. No Bar Bay was safe from big predators, but dull. Already, though, the mariners were finding ways to liven it up. The ship's crew who were lugging the final pieces of equipment out of the transpods, ready to return to *Talitha,* watched them, by turns amused and bemused. It must be pleasant not to have to think about the longer term. Also dangerous.

The leisurely pace of the voyage had suddenly given way to ceaseless, draining activity. In a short space of time, the bay had been transformed. The differences would not have been evident to the casual eye, but the bay was no longer a native part of Aquifer.

At the southern end of the beach, tucked away among a mass of eroded rocks that had once been part of the cliff, was an ansible. It had two encryption disks: one linking it to *Talitha,* the other to Atollside Port on No-Moon, from which its messages could be quickly relayed to the reefmind. It was housed in an unremarkable gray tentlike structure made from a Precursor fabric that could withstand anything that Aquifer's climate threw at it. The mariners would have to put on sailor suits to use it, but when *Talitha* finally left the neighborhood, they would be able to keep in touch with their Neanderthal protectors. Later, the 'Thals might install a transible as well, but for now all ship-to-surface transportation would have to be by transpod.

The Neanderthals and their mixed alien crew wanted

to make sure the mariners were managing well in their new home, and they expected to be stuck in orbit around Aquifer's equator for quite a while.

Under instructions from the Cyldarian ecologists, a squad of Tweel engineers had installed a small but powerful energy source in a tunnel burrowed in the chalk cliffs, most of whose output was used to maintain a semipermeable forcewall across the mouth of No Bar Bay. It could be set to be impassable to anything larger than some chosen size, and in this first sweep the rotund, tangled Tweel had been conservative, to avoid inflicting too much damage on the ecology of the bay. Their main concern had been the larger organisms; anything less than in inch in length had been allowed through.

Initially, the forcewall had been set up near the beach, and then they had swept it gradually toward the outermost end of the bay so that any of the larger marine creatures that normally inhabited the bay would be swept out with it. Smaller creatures would not be excluded by this procedure, but that was all to the good, because the ecology the Cyldarians were trying to create, with Tweel assistance, would have to take a lot of its ingredients from the local flora and fauna. Once the forcewall reached its intended location, the engineers tightened it up to exclude anything larger than an inorganic molecule. By changing the properties of the forcewall, they could manage the exchange of substances between the ocean and the bay.

Smaller forcewalls similarly barred the few streams that flowed into the bay. The Cyldarians were happy to ignore any rain that fell directly into the bay—the intake was mostly matched by evaporation, and any discrepancy would be taken care of as part of their general monitoring and control of the overall capacity of the walled-off volume.

While this was going on, the Cyldarian ecologists also made a quick but thorough study of the water and organisms trapped within the now walled-off bay, mostly looking for toxins that might be incompatible with the mariners' physiology and metabolism. Bacteria and other microorganisms were less likely to pose a problem, but they tested for those, too, just in case.

Satisfied, the ecologists seeded the bay with a careful selection of essential No-Moon organisms, especially food animals and plants. A small group of mariner volunteers, including Short Apprentice, was introduced to the bay's artificial ecology. After they had survived unscathed for a week and had been subjected to a battery of medical tests, the Cyldarians pronounced the experiment a qualified success. Much more work would need to be done, for many years, but the bay was now fit for the rest of the mariners to occupy it.

The Neanderthals got at least one thing spectacularly right, thanks to some very specific advice from the reefwives. They had brought along some boats in *Talitha*'s capacious cargo spaces. There was nowhere to sail except the bay, and the mariners would have to take turns until they could build more boats, but no No-Moon sailor would ever be happy for long away from a boat.

Talitha's crew watched from orbit as, day by day, the beachhead on Aquifer became more and more established. As far as Ship was aware, the planet had no sentient natives, and in this it was correct. Sentient nonnatives—that was the problem. Concealed as it was beneath the Nether Ice Dome, Cosmic Unity's monastery of equals was invisible to *Talitha*'s surveillance, and the ship's equatorial orbit made the polar regions difficult to observe in any case. If the Neanderthals had suspected that Cosmic Unity had gotten there before them, they would have looked more carefully. But they were reliably informed that the benevolent memeplex had not yet come anywhere near Aquifer. It was not their fault that their information was wrong.

The monastery on Aquifer had been built in secrecy, hidden under the northern polar ice cap. In the outside world, only a few of Cosmic Unity's most senior figures were aware of its existence, and even fewer knew its location. A casual observer could have walked over the top of it and never noticed anything other than natural ice. It was there to play some covert role in the Church, known only to the ecclesiarchs. To the monks and menials that worked there, it functioned like any other monastery of equals. The few who knew how secluded it was were not surprised—*all* monasteries were secluded.

There was a price to pay for such secrecy, and it was ignorance, as the monastery's governing hierocrat was well aware. The problem with covert installations was that they had to *stay* covert. Equipment capable of sensing approaching spacecraft could also be *detected* by approaching spacecraft. If someone bounced radiation off you, you noticed it. So the monastery had no long-range sensors. The hierocrat was effectively blind to approaching spacecraft.

For the same reason, the monastery could not keep spacegoing vessels or even probes in orbit. It had some ships under the ice, for emergencies. And there was always the transible, to evacuate key figures if that ever became necessary. Plans had been drawn up long ago, and rules established to recognize when to put them into action.

The ecclesiarchs' desire for this facility must have been very strong, because they had been forced to take some calculated risks to get it. To be sure, the risks were small. The surrounding regions of space were far from any normal trade routes, with no inhabited planets. There was no reason why this obscure and isolated world without sentient indigenes should attract outside attention. It was mostly barren desert and open ocean. It had no valuable resources. That was why it had been chosen.

Some security measures could be taken without giving anything away. Surface patrols made regular searches for signs of intruders. And the monastery had telescopes, but they had to be small enough to be well hidden, and they had to be readily accessible. Remote telescopes would need servicing and maintenance, and that would leave unnecessary traces of activity. So the few telescopes on Aquifer were all housed within the monastery.

The hierocrat had no more knowledge of the Neanderthals' presence than they did of hers. *Talitha* had come in fast and taken up a low equatorial orbit, well below the horizon of the polar telescopes.

There was no way that this state of mutual ignorance could continue once the mariners arrived. And the

Nether Ice Dome had everything it needed to deal with unwanted trespassers.

XIV Samuel put his hands on the table in front of him and counted his fingernails *again*. He had carried out the ritual many times a day for as long as he'd known how to count. Its object, though he had never been told this, was to instill automatic obedience. But this time, his devotions were interrupted by a commotion in the corridors outside his cell. For most of the morning he had been trying, for the thousandth time, to think of a way to heal the troubled lifesoul of Dry Leaves Fall Slowly, but the noise of tramping feet made it impossible to think at all, let alone about such a difficult problem. So, breaking all the rules about devotional procedure, he tiptoed to the door of his cell and opened it a crack. But by then, whatever was causing the disturbance had gone.

Feeling vaguely guilty—presumably of inquisitiveness—he felt the need to confess his lapse and made an appointment to see his instructor for the purpose of obtaining spiritual guidance. To his surprise, the Veenseffer-co-Fropt brushed Sam's tale of interrupted devotions aside with a brusque "Anyone's devotions would be upset by such a racket, Servant Samuel. If you feel uncomfortable about it, you can practice your deathsong for the edification of the Lifesoul-Cherisher." Sam had not expected to be told what had caused all the noise, and he was right. But the querist had no intention of terminating the interview.

"I am very concerned," he said, "about your client."

Sam, taken aback by the sudden change of topic, took a few moments to collect his thoughts.

"She is proving . . . difficult," he eventually replied. But that wasn't really the right word, and he knew it.

"She is proving obstinate, Samuel," the querist said, dangling his olfactory organ an inch from Sam's nose. "And I am asking myself how a novice lifesoul-healer should respond to that."

Sam tried to defend the child without getting himself into too much trouble. "She needs more love than I can yet summon, I believe, master."

The querist brought his manipulators together so that the tips touched, and sat in silent thought for several heartbeats. Sam tried to conceal his nervousness. He had *tried*, surely. The child, whom he loved dearly, was simply impossible. All Neanderthals were difficult, but this one was the proverbial immovable object. He had made no progress whatsoever on eradicating her errors.

The querist drew a deep breath through his brushlike tufts. "I agree with your diagnosis, Samuel." He paused, as if finding it hard to summon up the necessary words. "There are many kinds of love, Samuel. This you have been taught. Some kinds of love are simple and uncomplicated. Some take a more complex course. And some do not flinch from hard decisions, because their aim is ultimate good, whatever the route to that good may have to be."

Sam understood then that he had failed and that his client would be removed from his care.

The querist seemed to read his thoughts. "No, the failure is not yours. As you say, the child is impossible. I have been waiting to hear such a verdict from your own lips for this past month, because the ability to cut one's losses is an essential aspect of the training of a lifesoul-healer. You are to be commended for your patience in trying every conceivable alternative avenue before making such a judgment.

"Nonetheless, you will be returned to the task of duplication for a time, so that you can reflect on the lessons you have learned from this experience. And the Neanderthal child will be referred to fully qualified healers with the experience necessary to make inroads into her condition. Be assured that they will love her like devoted parents, even as they take steps to correct the deficiencies in her attitude."

Sam bowed his head in silence.

"You may go."

He turned, then stopped. "Er, master—what . . ."

"What techniques will be employed? That is not an appropriate question for a novice to ask."

Sam cast his eyes to the floor and left before he could talk himself into serious trouble. Fall would be in safe hands; of that he was certain.

Patrol Captain VIII Ykzykk-Knazd had been on uninterrupted duty for a month, and this was his fifteenth successive night operation. Like all the others, he knew that absolutely nothing was going to happen. Yes, the floater was heavily armed according to standing orders from the hierocrat, but he would never get to *use* those weapons. He ran an insectile limb over one of the heavy-duty laser cannons, taking satisfaction from its cleverly engineered form and reassuring solidity. It was the only satisfaction the patrol captain was likely to get, this night or during a hundred more. He stared morosely up through the floater's transparent roof, but clouds hid the night sky, as they often did in these latitudes. He would have liked to see some stars.

A device near the floater's nose activated. Ykzykk-Knazd turned lazily to see what it had picked up this time. Another wayward walker? An unusually shaped rock? Then he saw the readings, and all traces of bored cynicism vanished in a rush of fight hormones.

An *ansible*? In the wilderness of Aquifer?

Precursor encryption was unbreakable, so there was no point in trying to decode the message. But Ykzykk-Knazd was well aware that the very *presence* of an ansible meant sentients. Intruders. He extended an angular midlimb and touched his second in command's clawed foot to attract her attention. "I believe we have an EMC, Myzzk-Harradd. Do you concur?"

The subordinate considered the question. An extreme measures circumstance arose if a patrol encountered a small, isolated group of sentient intruders, with no evident backup and in possession of long-range communication equipment. She ran through her mental checklist. "I concur, Patrol Captain. There is no error."

Ykzykk-Knazd clicked his claws, as if already preparing for combat. Extreme measures must be used only when authorized; the penalties for misuse were themselves extreme. But so were the penalties for failing to take such measures when circumstances required them. The tactic was a draconian response to a limited but potentially disastrous threat. He knew the reasoning behind it—the highest echelons of the Church had analyzed the risk cascades and determined the optimal strategy. Typically, in a context like the present one, an isolated group of intruders was most likely to be a scouting party, sent to make a preliminary assessment of an unexplored world. Such parties occasionally disappeared, and if anyone noticed their absence—scouts often acted on their own—then further exploration was usually curtailed. The planet would be flagged in Galactic records as being potentially dangerous, and people would tend to avoid it.

He was aware, as were those who had drawn up the standing orders, that extreme measures could go wrong—by attracting precisely the attention that they were intended to prevent. But several unlikely factors had to combine for that to happen.

"Very well," said Ykzykk-Knazd, reassured that he had assessed the nature of the threat correctly and could justify ordering a preemptive strike. They all knew the form that it would take. First, take out the intruders' means of communication. Then, take out the intruders. If possible, capture one for questioning, but that was a secondary goal. The hierocrat had made the priorities very clear: Destroy the immediate threat at all costs. No spiritual or moral aspects were to be considered—this was to be a military action, not a Church mission. Later, more informed judgments could be made by those who were qualified to assess the nature of the threat and to determine any further response.

There were six floaters in the patrol, flying close to the ground in a tight formation. Under the coordination of Ykzykk-Knazd in the lead craft, they swung in a wide arc and headed for a stretch of coast about 140 miles away, where the brief ansible transmission had originated.

At supersonic speeds, they were there in under ten minutes. The final approach was made in total silence. Through sensitive nightsights they could see obvious signs of the intruders. The bay had been blocked off using a forcewall, and several strange boats bobbed in its shallow waters. No evidence of any backup—just an isolated group. Definitely a case for extreme measures.

Ansible first, then. Sensors had already revealed its location inside a tent at the base of a cliff. The first bolt of laser fire took it out, and much of the cliff as well. The second turned one of the boats into a floating bonfire, which quickly fizzled out as the wreckage sank. Two more boats suffered the same fate. The patrol captain decided to leave the intruders' forcewall intact—for now. It would hinder their escape. After the battle was over, its generator would be destroyed.

Ykzykk-Knazd noticed that some of the intruders were in the water. They were swimming around in total confusion—no doubt still trying to work out what had hit them. Had they escaped from the burning boats, or had they been in the water all along? From their shape, they were marine creatures; he could not put a name to their species, but they had numerous tentacles and thickset bodies.

One of the creatures was making a run up the beach, trying to head inland for cover. He wondered how it could function on land, and realized that it was wearing some kind of life support. That probably meant that this particular creature had some special function among the group of intruders, which automatically made it a prime target for interrogation. Like all the intruders, it was unarmed; Ykzykk-Knazd gave orders for a squad to capture the fleeing creature, if that could be done without killing it.

None of the other interlopers had left the sea. He didn't think they could—as far as he could tell, none of them was wearing life-support equipment. That made things a little trickier, because the water offered a certain amount of protection. But orders were orders, and his had been made crystal clear on many occasions. What the hierocrat wanted, the hierocrat got, and what the hierocrat wanted in these circumstances was total annihilation.

There were standard tactics for dealing with an underwater threat. He quickly assessed his firepower: six floaters, each carrying a dozen heavy laser cannons. The swimmers were confined to the bay by their own forcewall; the bay was shallow . . . He would have power to spare.

He ordered the floaters to deploy around the margin of the bay, three on each side at the top of the cliffs.

This would not take long.

The morning sun had dispersed the nighttime clouds, and the beachhead at No Bar Bay was clearly visible from *Talitha*'s gallery. It seemed tranquil and undisturbed, so Sharp Wit Will Cut was not particularly worried when no one answered his ansible call. No doubt the mariners were racing their boats again. But a closer look at the bay showed no boats out in the deeper waters. In fact—and now he did begin to worry—it showed no boats at all.

Then he looked really closely, saw what had happened to the boats, and *really* began to worry.

He was the first to drop down from the transpod into the trampled chalk sand, and when he did so, he was looking over his shoulder as often as forward, watching out for any threat that might emerge from the landward swamp or the rocks beneath the cliffs. The ansible shelter had been annihilated, and it wasn't alone. He saw at once that the tunnel to the power source had collapsed; rubble of a kind he had never before encountered lay strewn at the foot of the cliff where the tunnel had once been. It was as if the chalk had melted and flowed like syrup before freezing solid and cracking into dangerous needle-sharp spikes and razor edges.

The boats were little more than scattered fragments, charred debris floating among the waves, strewn along the tide line.

A dozen steps, and he saw the first body. At first he failed to recognize it, so blistered and mutilated was the viscous, rubbery flesh. But then he saw the stumps of tentacles and realized that he was looking at what had once been a mariner.

A search turned up more bodies. Most were scattered about the shore; a few were floating in the sea. All bore appalling injuries.

One of *Talitha*'s Tweel engineers bent over one of the corpses and shuddered. "What calamity caused this?" he asked, not to anyone in particular but to the universe in general. He straightened and looked nervously around.

Whatever had done this might still be nearby, hidden in dense vegetation, concealed by rocks.

Will had a sudden suspicion. He put his hand in the water. The sea was warm. Too warm. *Definitely* too warm, given that the forcewall had been turned off and colder water had been diffusing into the bay from the ocean, and running into it from the streams.

"What calamity?" he said, turning to the engineer. "A military calamity, my friend. An energy weapon. The mariners and their wifepieces have been boiled alive." Now that he had some idea what had happened, the evidence around him slotted neatly into place. His theory was supported by the state of the bodies—more accurately, from the fragments of cooked meat that were all that remained of their polypoid friends. Some pieces were streaked with the telltale burns of laser fire. Others were just sickening parboiled chunks.

In his mind he could not avoid reconstructing the scene in all its horror. The attackers must have trained powerful lasers into the bay, either from levitating cars or from the cliff tops. As the water heated up, the mariners would have been caught in a terrible dilemma: Stay in the sea and boil, or emerge onto the sand and suffocate for lack of oxygenated water. Even with a sailor suit, the land was no real option, for anyone exposed on the shore could be roasted with lasers or blown apart by explosives.

It would only have taken a few hours. At night the Neanderthals suspended direct surveillance of the bay because in normal circumstances there was nothing to be seen, even if clouds failed to form. As it happened, last night had been cloudy, but *Talitha*'s records might still show some signs of the attack. It would be easy to check.

There was no point in hanging around on the beach, and the attacking force might come back at any time. He and his companions ran back toward the transpod. Later they would return, if their instruments showed that it was safe, and count the bodies. Right now it looked as if all the mariners had perished.

Once off the ground, Will summarized the disaster for those still on board the huge, ancient vessel. Even now he could not assume the transpod was safe from attack, so *Talitha* had to be told what it was up against, straight-away. Right now there was very little to go on.

A patchwork of bright curves, surging and reforming moment by moment, rippled across the pale sand of Crooked Atoll, playing on the grotesque outlines of coral and weed and scattering shoals of light-sensitive crustaceans, who fled beneath the shadows of the rocks until the brightest concentrations of wave-focused light had swept past their refuge.

Beneath the sand, neural connections switched on, and the reefmind awoke. The husbands in Atollside Port had passed on an ansibled report from *Talitha*. On this occasion the reefwives elected to divide their collective intelligence into three autonomous, intercommunicating parts. The tactic increased the mental power of each participant, but the small number of components reduced the quality of the debate and the diversity of opinion.

The mood was somber.

Sinker: It is as we feared, my sisters.

Line: No, it is worse. Look at the edge of our perception, where it trails off into mist and chaos. You see the pattern?

Hook: Compared to the bright, central clarity of the disaster on Aquifer, this 'pattern' of which you speak is flimsy and impossible to discern. I say there is no pattern.

Line: Then your perceptions are inadequate, sister. The pattern exists. I/we recognize it from long, long ago. Cosmic Unity is a new instance of an ancient evil, awoken again. It is a benevolent memeplex at the apex of its trajectory, rigidified by its own memetic feedback, locked in the straitjacket of its single-valued logic. It is powerful and malignant, a cosmic cancer.

Hook: We have no proof that the slaughter of our husbands on Aquifer was carried out by Cosmic Unity.

Sinker: The threat to No-Moon is the same, whoever is responsible. Share my/our vision, and you will understand.

Hook: (Reluctantly) You are perhaps right. I do see something, indistinct but full of menace. Now I feel uneasy.

Line: Affirmed.

Sinker: Emphasized.

Line: How should we respond?

Hook: Whoever killed our husbands, Cosmic Unity's benevolent memeplex threatens our very existence. That must be our main concern. We must seek an alternative refuge, offworld. Refuges. Many. A nine, a ninesquare. Send nine ninesquares of males to each planet, not nines!

Line: Having changed your opinion, you now overreact. The more ships we dispatch, the more attention we will attract to ourselves.

Sinker: In any case, our stock of trade information is limited. We cannot afford to pay for mass evacuations of our world.

Hook: And we ourselves cannot yet leave this world, sisters, if ever. For the moment we can only send husbands and wives to rebuild our species, slowly, on another world. While we grow to maturity in a new home, our males will lack guidance and advice. And you know what they are like when we are not taking care of their best interests.

Line: Useless layabouts.

Sinker: Utterly worthless.

Hook: Alga-craving sex maniacs.

Together: Males!

Sinker: Much as we love our mates for all their adorable faults, we are becoming distracted from the main threat. The awakened evil approaches even as we debate. Its arrival cannot long be delayed. In some of my perceptions it is already here.

Line: You are too fearful, sister. I/we have survived worse.

Sinker: Yes, but at what price?

Line: Whatever price it is necessary to pay. There are strategies, tactics, devices we can employ. They have succeeded before, and they will succeed again. Look, even now our vision includes their first use.

Sinker: Yes. And it seems to me that they are failing.

Line: That must be a temporary problem, I am sure. Always they have succeeded. Always.

Sinker: Except when our foremother had us conveyed to this world.

Line: That strategy succeeded. We are here.

Sinker: And our foremother died, along with Three-Moons.

Line: It was still a success. Our species survived.

Hook: Past successes do not guarantee present ones. Circumstances can change.

Line: We have no option, for only those strategies are known to us.

Sinker: Nonsense! We must invent a new strategy.

Line: Against an ancient evil? There is no philosophical match there. How can the new defeat the old?

Hook: What else can defeat the old, when the old fails?

The reefmind grew quiet as it struggled without an answer.

Servant-of-Unity XIV Samuel Godwin'sson Travers immersed himself in his work, depressed by his failure with his first client. He missed his daily sessions with Fall, even though they had driven him close to despair, and at the back of his mind he was worried about her. She was so relentlessly logical in her delusions that he could see no possible way to break down her mental barriers. But since there was nothing he could do, he busied himself with the familiar and comforting rituals of duplication and gave thanks that, for a time, his mind need not be occupied by anything more challenging.

Lists of items for duplication arrived, and he performed the necessary gestures at the machine's metaphace. Empty boxes arrived, and full ones were taken away. His days passed without distinction; his nights were troubled only by evanescent dreams. He no longer felt stressed by the need to adapt to new tasks and to learn new skills.

And yet . . .

Now *duplication* was becoming boring. Was it his destiny to be bored by *everything*? He missed the intellectual stimulus of learning to deal with *new* things. He was disappointed not to meet with Fall. His ambition had grown along with his confidence; now he hoped his separation from lifesoul-healing would not last too long. He was certain that given enough time, he could have found a way to heal Fall. Already strategies were forming in his mind. It was frustrating.

Time dragged by.

One evening his instructor left word for Sam to attend him immediately in his quarters. Sam hurried through the frigid corridors of the monastery, hewn from the solid ice and mostly left unclad, so that the walls sucked the warmth out of anything that came near them. Here and there the corridors were damp, where the air temperature was high enough for the ice to melt, but such places were rare, and the dampness just made him feel even colder. He shivered, and not just with the cold. What did the querist want with him?

He would soon find out. He knocked and was bidden to enter.

"Ah, Servant Fourteen Samuel. I trust your sojourn in the duplicating chamber has improved your mental health? Yes, as I expected. You had become too emotionally involved with your young client to serve the Life-soul-Cherisher well, Samuel." The Veenseffer-co-Fropt waved his olfactory organ airily, as if brushing away an errant parasite, to show that the matter was of little importance. "That is only to be expected in a novice. Your persistence was admirable, even if it did border on stubbornness and obstinacy. You may yet attain the glory of Heaven, if any of us live long enough to experience that joyous transformation.

"And you are wondering why I have summoned you here. Come with me, and you will see the reason. And be pleased."

A section of furnishings slid aside, and wall became doorway. Beyond was a well-lit corridor, and Sam followed the querist along the passageway. He had never passed this way before and didn't know that such concealed tunnels existed—though he was unsurprised to find that they did, for there was much about the monastery of equals that he did not know. And there had to be ways for his superiors to come and go, on the business of the Community of the United Cosmos, without their inferiors observing them.

The passage widened into a ramp, which led downward in a tight spiral, coiling into the bowels of the ice dome. Pass lights glowed pinkly to illuminate the way, so that the light seemed to move with them as they descended. They passed side branches and closed doors. There were strange smells and odd little sounds as metal scraped against metal and the ice itself creaked and groaned.

They came at last to a door that differed in no obvious way from a hundred others. The instructor produced a qubit-coded crystal key; the door recognized the sequence of encoded quantum spin states, unlocked, and swung open into a darkened room, which curved in a semicircle. One wall was a transparent membrane. Cupped in the arc of the semicircle was a lighted chamber carpeted with a soft, deep pile, its walls hung with devotional weavings and decorated with scenes of the Prime Mission—a star with emergent magnetotorus herds, a dirigible satellite, a gas giant wrapped in bright stripes of cloud.

Seated cross-legged in a worship ring in the center of the chamber was Dry Leaves Fall Slowly.

Sam caught his breath. She was praying.

"How . . . ? It is a miracle . . ."

"You can speak naturally," the instructor said. "She cannot hear us even if we shout. The membrane has been tuned to be impermeable to any sound made on this side, but to allow sound from the other side to reach us.

"Are you not proud of your client, Fourteen Samuel?"

Sam nodded, close to tears. He suddenly felt foolish that he had worried about her safety, about what might happen to her. And he realized that he still had an awful lot to learn about the healing of lifesouls.

He could not see her face, for her back was toward him. She seemed utterly calm, utterly relaxed. She was chanting a children's prayer to the Lifesoul-Cherisher—one of his favorites—in a slightly lilting voice. There was no hesitation; she sounded word-perfect.

The prayer ended, and she began another.

"You may observe your client from any angle," said the querist. "From the end of this room you will be able to see her face. Observe how serene she is."

Sam followed the curve of the membrane so that the familiar features seemed to turn until they faced him. *Serenity*, yes, that was the word. Not a flicker of emotion passed over the Neanderthal child's face. *Beatific*? Yes, there was such a word. *Saintlike*.

Her hair was thick and freshly washed, her skin glowed with health and vitality. She kept her head bowed and began once more to recite a prayer, the same one he had heard her saying when he first entered the room. It seemed that her repertoire was limited, but there was no questioning her devotion and her concentration.

"It's . . . amazing," he said, his voice trailing off as the immensity of it all hit him. "You—you succeeded."

The querist nodded. "It was the work of many dedicated healers. With enough love, anything can be accomplished. Even the most stubborn and misguided of lifesouls can be started on the road to healing." The instructor's innate sense of emotions guided his words as Sam absorbed the awesome nature of the triumph. "Dry Leaves Fall Slowly was a challenge. She was far too difficult a case for a novice; we should have recognized that right at the start. We tried many techniques, some arcane, before we gained entry to the source of her delusions."

Suddenly, without any change in her expression, Fall stopped praying and rose to her feet. Her hair swung away from her neck, and for an instant Sam saw—or thought he saw—a triangular mark on her skin. Then the hair swung back, and the mark, if there had been one, was hidden once more.

A door opened to reveal a menial; it beckoned silently, and Fall walked meekly out of the room and disappeared from view.

"Her progress is encouraging," the querist said. "Her new, acceptable attitudes still need regular reinforcement, but she has come to embrace the Unity of the Cosmos and the fundamental Oneness of all beings. No longer does she set herself apart from the world. And her delusions about her family no longer trouble her young mind."

"Her pet? The grenvil? She thought it had been killed. Horribly."

"There was no grenvil. It was a dream, an invention. It has been banished from her thoughts. Now she knows that her place is in the Community of the United Cosmos, where she will be loved as a person and cherished as a lifesoul." The querist spread his tufts in the equivalent of a human smile—something Sam had never previously witnessed. It looked as if the serpentine alien was out of practice. Probably he was. But he seemed happy, and his translated voice held a tinge of pride.

Rightly so. Sam was overawed by the display of expertise. He would never be able to match it, he was sure. Never in a thousand years.

"You have seen her; she is well. And soon her mind will complete its healing, and her lifesoul will be whole again. But we waste precious time now she has gone. You have much duplication to perform before your training recommences."

"Can I not restart my training now?" Sam inquired in disappointment. "With respect, master, I feel ready to return to healing. More ready than I have ever felt before."

The instructor "smiled" again. "A worthy feeling, Samuel. But your immediate task must be the duplicator.

An unexpected emergency demands that we all employ all of our skills where they can count for most."

May had been reunited with her shipboard menagerie, and several of her pets were refusing to leave her side. *We missed you. We want company.* They followed her about the ship and got underfoot.

She played with a hornsnake that was curled round her wrist. It liked the warmth. There had been two, but one had disappeared into Ship's superstructure. If it could find enough food to survive, it would give some unsuspecting sentient a surprise one day. Half a dozen furry ant-moles gamboled at her feet, chasing one another's long, trailing hind antennae. The snake ignored them—it ate only worms.

It's good to be home.

Will's thoughts were less happy. "I think the murdering bastards got them all," he said, studying a data summary displayed on his command screen.

The remark brought May back to ground with a bump. "All forty-nine corpses have been identified?"

"We have twenty-two, plus twenty-seven probables. A lot of them were so badly damaged that it's difficult to distinguish them from offal in an abattoir. Until we know it's safe to recover the bodies and genotype them, we won't know for sure. But I'd bet my lifetime trade profits that every last mariner on Aquifer is dead."

"I was getting quite close to the little fat one," said May, sad beyond measure at her loss. "The one apprenticed to that bane of my existence, Second-Best Sailor."

She shook her mane, as if that might undo what had happened and bring the annoying but engaging polypoid back to life. "Fat Apprentice asked such foolish questions . . . yet such difficult ones. He made me rethink some of my most strongly held assumptions. I shall miss him."

"As shall I," said Will, absently stroking the crevit slung across his muscular shoulders, hoping to make it buzz. He had reviewed *Talitha*'s recordings. Nocturnal cloud cover had hidden events in the bay itself, but six floaters had been spotted to the north, where the cloud thinned. They had continued due north until the horizon blocked the view.

"I shall miss the others, too," May added. "Even Second-Best Sailor."

Will took the statement at face value. "There is more to this than personal tragedy," he pointed out. "The reefwives fear that this disaster could spell the end for their race. Cosmic Unity is closing in on No-Moon, and all the patterns point to it being in thrall to a benevolent memeplex."

"Which may not be as benevolent as its adherents imagine."

"Exactly. The memeplex holds itself to be benevolent, but the reality may be different. The worlds that this memeplex has touched all seem to be peaceful, but the reefmind wonders at what price such unnatural peace has been bought. And there are hints in certain Galactic records. . . . Aquifer was a backup strategy, a safe refuge for a small group of husbands who would later be provided with wives, ready to rebuild the polypoid population should that become necessary. But now, if No-Moon is overrun, there is no backup."

May understood that all too well. Like Will, she was terrified out of her wits. Anyone would be.

And to make their immediate problems worse, there was a high-tech race on the loose on Aquifer, completely contrary to Galactic records. Armed and vicious. Willing to attack for no reason, or for reasons of its own . . . reasons so alien that they would make no sense outside that one species. If it was one species. It might be an alliance.

What was it? Who were these murderers?

Could they be Cosmic Unity? The Church might be on the planet already. Could a religion whose central tenet was tolerance boil forty-nine harmless mariners alive merely for being where they were not expected?

Maybe not. But the reefwives were certain that the Cosmic Unity fleet heading for No-Moon represented the biggest threat their world had ever faced. They thought that a religion whose central tenet was tolerance could become twisted enough to enforce that belief through holy war. It was often the religions that boasted most loudly of their love for their fellow beings that most readily perverted their beliefs into cruelty and destruction. Because *they knew what was good for you*, and sometimes they would stop at nothing to make sure that it happened. This, May realized, was the self-laid trap that awaited every benevolent memeplex.

7

THE NETHER ICE DOME

Be cherished, O my lifesoul
free from suffering
free from grief
    free from the perversion of Unbelief
Attended
    mended
    protected until ended
Each cell, each entity, each clan, each race
each species builds a Heaven
    in its rightful place
With rock and cloud and mud and fire and ice—
Until the healer can no longer heal
    Until the Lifesoul-Stealer comes to steal
    the mortal being
    from its self-made paradise

Deathsong of the eighty-first ecclesiarch

Sam's patience was rewarded more quickly than he had expected. Halfway through his third day back on duplicator duty, he was interrupted in the middle of preparing the machine to duplicate a batch of spiky things whose end use was, as always, unknown to him. Previously, such ignorance had never bothered him. Yet now, as he was whisked away before he could complete his assigned task, he found himself questioning the decision. Only within the confines of his own mind, to be sure—he was not so foolhardy as to voice his concerns, in case that should be interpreted as dissent. It was just that—well, the replacement servant would have to start the sequence of ritual gestures all over again, and if he made any mistakes, it might take several hours to get back to the stage that Sam would have reached if they'd allowed him ten more minutes at the metaphace.

The realization that he was questioning received authority bothered him a lot more than what the authorities had actually done. No doubt, they knew best. They must have reasons beyond his limited comprehension. But now, thinking back, he got the distinct impression that, more and more, he was privately questioning the actions of his superiors in the Community. He was thinking about how his instructions fitted into the broader context of the Monastery's work, and the Community's own Great Mission.

He fervently hoped he didn't accidentally voice any of his doubts. He was starting to clamber his perilous way up the ecclesiastical greasy pole, and it would set him back years if he appeared to be acting above his station. Blatant insubordination might well prove terminal to his career, and then he would complete his days carrying out tasks far less agreeable than running a duplicator.

Sam was amazed to find himself thinking any of these thoughts. He never used to think like that. But then, he hadn't been exposed to the training regime of a novice lifesoul-healer. In fact, he now understood in a flash of insight, it was the *training* that had led him to start asking himself such questions. His instructor, he realized with a rush of excitement, *wanted* him to think for himself. Not too much, but enough to have some control over his own direction.

If he was to heal damaged lifesouls, he must first take charge of his own.

But with humility.

That was the key; that was the lesson that the Veenseffer-co-Fropt had been hoping he would learn, but could never overtly teach. It could not *tell* him how to take responsibility for his own life, for then he would merely be carrying out his instructor's bidding. He had to be given the opportunity to think it out for himself. And that would be the next step in his advancement. He had to make it clear that he had made this vital step in his thinking, while continuing to appear humble.

He corrected himself hurriedly. To *be* humble. But even the humble could have plans and dreams.

He was getting used to the cold corridors and the bare, unfinished walls of the tunnels. He was even getting used to the pallid, downcast, hollow-souled beings whose paths constantly crossed his as he threaded his way through the under-ice maze. He passed a squad of Illensan monks, dragging a large chlorine tank along on crude runners, and scarcely noticed how distressed they were at the physical effort involved, or how labored their breathing had become. Had he given the matter any thought, he would have wondered just how effective their breathing masks were; their splutterings and inflamed nasal passages would have suggested they were suffering from a small, nonfatal but irritating excess of carbon dioxide. But such things were commonplace, and his task was to heal the lifesouls of his clients, not to interfere with beings who had been consigned to the care of others.

There were three querists in the room when he arrived and made entry. Never before had he been in the presence of more than one. He was unsure what this meant, but presumably it had to be important.

One he recognized: It was his own instructor. The other two looked older; one was a Rhemnolid, who ran to fat and had pronounced storage pouches, and the other had to be a !t!, for no other sentient being possessed such a slender exoskeleton. Sam had never encountered a !t! before, for they were the rarest species in the Community, but he had seen many images of them, for the same reason.

The Rhemnolid glanced at the knotted silvery braids, identification marks on Sam's maroon robe. A Precursor translation field enveloped the room, and Sam had no difficulty in understanding the sibilant spurts of fetid air, laden with chemical content, that Rhemnolids used for speech. "Thisss is the novice, then. He is a Traversss? That is a name well known and respected in the Church. The Travers women are mostly virtuous, so I am informed; their men are ssseldom of poor faith. The son of Godwin . . . Mmm, I have held awarenesss of several Godwins, all trustworthy humen."

"I read that this young servant," said the !t!, speaking as if Sam were not present at all, "is the fourteenth member of his lineage since his forefathers first embraced the righteousness of the United Cosmos. I have encountered smaller generation numbers, but seldom in a healer-novitiate." Its speech, a rapid-fire sequence of chirruping clicks produced by flexing a special joint in its ventral forelimb, could be heard in the background as a patchwork of frequency textures.

"His family's progress has indeed been of unprecedented rapidity," said Sam's instructor. It was true. Only fourteen generations in the same task. Sam was indeed fortunate for his lineage to have advanced so quickly.

"Yes, and so has his own. You tell me that he handled that setback with that Neanderthal child . . . ?"

"Dry Leaves Fall Slowly."

"Yes, that was its name. He handled it with delicacy and well-directed love. It was not his fault that the child needed . . . *extra* love. Special treatment. No, it was not his fault; he outperformed any novice I have encountered." The !t! flexed its joints, uncomfortable in the relatively high gravity despite the support of its exoskeleton. "He is most unusual, as we had already noticed. He conforms, but that is not his true nature. He is actively engaged in everything he does—he is not merely playing out a role."

The Rhemnolid instructor settled into his slingcouch—a ponderous procedure. "The novice is not yet aware that the child was a tessst?"

"That she was deliberately selected because of her incurable obstinacy? Her wicked lies and delusions? Assigned to him *so that he must fail*? Not until this moment." For the first time the !t! instructor addressed Sam directly. "Do you understand what I have just revealed about our training methods, Samuel the son of Godwin, fourteenth in the male lineage of the Travers clan?"

Sam swallowed hard and tried to regain his poise. "Masters, I understand—now that you have told me—that the child was deliberately assigned to me to . . . to test my patience, my faith, and my . . . uh . . . capacity for love. And I understand that I was expected to fail, that I was bound to fail. That . . . that what counted would be the manner of my failure."

Sam's instructor fluffed his olfactory tufts with pride. "You see?" he said to his companions. "It is just as I predicted."

"That is ssso," said the Rhemnolid. "Do you also understand, Fourteen Sssamuel, that in failing so magnificently, you triumphed? For when you learned that other techniques had saved the lifesssoul of the child, you showed not the slightest sign of envy or jealousy. You were pleased for her, and for those who had begun the long, slow processs of healing her."

Sam remained as he was, head bowed, but his eyes shone. Praise was almost unheard of in the monastery of equals. But he did not wish to be seen to have sought it. Or to take pride in hearing it. He could not trust himself to keep pride from his voice, so he said nothing.

"He is ready, is he not?" said the Veenseffer-co-Fropt.

"For the next ssstep in his training? Undoubtedly.

Now he must face the ethical dilemma that has exercised the Church since its Founders first encountered the wickednesss that infesssts so many souls . . . the sin of intolerance. Can the Church tolerate sin? No. So can it tolerate the intolerant? That is a paradox. For can the sole route to the One be self-defeating? Fourteen Sssamuel, what do *you* think?"

Sam's breath caught. He would need to be careful, but he had to answer, and quickly. It would have helped if he had any real idea of what the querists were talking about. But the general gist seemed clear.

"The . . . Wisdom of Unity cannot be denied," Sam said, reciting a text from *Conversations with Huff Elder* that he had been taught almost before he could walk. "Action that defeats itself is not true action at all, for it contains the seeds of its own annihilation. But—masters, forgive me if I err, but it has long seemed to me . . ." (Here Sam took a golden opportunity to demonstrate that he had absorbed the meta-lesson of his training and that now he was developing a mind of his own.) ". . . it seems to me that it may be possible to meet intolerance with tolerance, and yet overcome it."

The Rhemnolid's thick-lipped eyes stared at him impassively. "How?"

"Uh . . . one may, perhaps . . . be tolerant in one's mind, master, while still enforcing correction in the external world. Wickedness cannot be permitted to continue as a *fact,* but there is no inconsistency in pitying the wicked for the *cause* and accepting that their error may result from cultural inadequacies, not from their own true lifesoul."

The Rhemnolid nodded, and gave the !t! a quick, approving glance. Its spatulate tongue licked quickly over its face and was reabsorbed. Sam, encouraged by the informality of this display, developed his theme. "Of course, an individual's true lifesoul will often be obscured by the habits and . . . uh, the values of their culture. A key duty of the lifesoul-healer is to save the lifesoul from such cultural tarnish. And so . . . I *think,* masters . . . that one may tolerate the *occurrence* of tarnished lifesouls, but not their continued existence in that state." He stopped abruptly. "But I do not wish to overstep my place. This was only an idle thought. If I am in error—"

"No, your thinking is orthodox, though more subtle than anything you could have been taught explicitly," said the !t!. "However, your thinking goes only so far. You are not yet aware of its practical implications, Fourteen Samuel. Thought must be translated into action, if it is ever to accomplish anything, and actions are harder to accept than words. You understand why?"

Sam shook his head. "Master, I do not."

"Words are . . . idealizations. They have no reality. Their consequences are hypothetical. Actions are different. Their consequences are real, and immediate, whether imagined in advance or not. If you speak, the implications of the words may remain concealed. If you act, the implications will be undeniable—even to those who wish to deny them.

"And, Samuel, *those implications may not be anything that you desire.* Does not the Church rest on two Great Memes?"

Kiddygarten stuff. "The health of the Whole must outweigh that of its parts," Sam recited. "And the long-term health of the part must outweigh its immediate comfort."

"Hmm. And what do those slogans mean?" The spindly !t! inclined its midlimbs questioningly. "In your *own* words, not those of your kiddygarten teacher."

Sam's face flushed, as if his mind had been read. Maybe it had. There were rumors that the !t! possessed Precursor telepathy machines . . . No, that way lay paranoia. "Uh . . . Unity itself is what is important, master—not the wishes of any individual. And . . . uh . . . individuals . . . no, *an* individual, must . . . er . . ."

"Sometimes one must be cruel to be kind," said the Veenseffer-co-Fropt, hurrying to the aid of his tutee. "A trite, dismal, yet ultimately liberating truism, Fourteen Samuel, in which you will now receive unforgettably vivid instruction. And I assure you that you will *wish* to forget. Until you see the ethical beauty that the dilemma conceals, and transcend your emotional limitations. If you wish to become a lifesoul-healer, you must understand this truth in the deepest recesses of your being. It must become an inalienable part of the very fabric of your mind. Otherwise, you will fail, and that failure will destroy you. Come."

Was it a medical center? The dimly lit room had the astringent smell that Sam associated with medical treatment. And some of the equipment looked like things he'd seen in hospitals—gas cylinders, masks, tubes. The walls were bare, and the floor was made of some kind of ceramic; it had been washed recently.

Like the three querists and their half-dozen assistants of varied races, Sam was wearing life-support equipment. In his case, all that was needed was a simple spray-on monomolecular coating to retain bodily heat, a transparent face mask, and breathing apparatus. The arrangements for some of the assistants were more elaborate.

"The environment has been configured for the client," the Rhemnolid's voice hissed quietly in his ear. There was a hint of machine-talk in the voice, no doubt resulting from the Precursor translation system into which they had all been linked. "His name is Clutch-the-Moon Splitcloud."

The client was spread-eagled on a low, circular dais. It could be moved to position it anywhere in the room. His nine limbs were neatly arranged like the spokes of a wheel, each held in place by a series of clamps. The blimp's eye ring was fixed on the roof above, where an icicle had formed.

"A Jovian?" Sam enquired.

"A helium blimp from the twin gas giants of Delta Hyractis," the !t! corrected. "The blimps are a sister species to the original Jovians, but they differ in many vital ways. For example, they are algivores, not filter-feeders. Do not let your feelings be colored by naive associations with the legendary Founders, Fourteen Samuel."

"I stand corrected, master. Why is the blimp restrained?"

"You will see when the treatment begins. I must warn you now that Clutch-the-Moon is a difficult case. If you thought that the Neanderthal child was obstinate, you may wish to revise that opinion. This client is so deter-

mined in his heresy that we all despair of saving him.
But . . . we must do what we can."

"It is to be a medical procedure?" Sam asked. It
seemed a fair guess.

"It could be described as such, yes. . . . Are we not
taught that our love for our fellow creatures must know
no bounds, admit no barriers? At whatever price to ourselves? So be it."

The !t! instructor moved closer to the dais, while a
slender hind limb waved Sam to remain where he was.
The twiglike figure leaned close to the client, murmuring
words that, it seemed, were meant only for the blimp.

Frenetic Hytth technicians scuttled about the room,
connecting machinery to inlet valves, running pre-use
test programs. The client's ring of eyes flicked about the
room in agitation.

"Clutch-the-Moon's error is a seriousss one," the
Rhemnolid said. "Not only does it diminish his own life-
soul, it threatens that of every being in his community.
He denies Heaven."

"But all servants of the One know that Heaven exists,"
one of the Hytth objected, his reedy barks smoothly replaced by human phonemes in Sam's earpiece.

"It is not the *existence* of Heaven that the blimp denies," Sam's instructor clarified. "It is its desirability.
And so he has not only withdrawn his own cooperation
from the advancement of his Community world; he has
sought to involve others in the same mistaken action—to
the detriment of their own lifesouls, as well as that of the
Community. Worse, several of these clusters of heresy
have succeeded, in their own terms, in disrupting the will

of the Church. They have caused untold damage and brought irreversible death to thousands of their fellows."

The blimp struggled feebly against its bonds. "Heaven is an illusion," it gasped. Sam suddenly noticed that it had been equipped with a small communicator. "Better a clean death than the obscenity of unnaturally extended existence!"

"You see how deep the problem lies," said the !t!. "Despite all efforts, this poor entity's lifesoul wallows in heresy and rejects all healing. Our prayers for his recovery have gone unheeded; our love has been rejected. So now we must harden our love and hope that he will respond to treatment." The many-limbed querist turned to the cluster of technicians and pointed with his palps. "Begin."

Whatever they were doing, Sam thought, it was well rehearsed; evidently, this was routine for the Hytth. The assistants made various changes to their equipment and were still.

Something about the room changed.

The blimp quivered; then Sam heard a strange moaning sound. It grew in volume until his head seemed filled with it; then, suddenly, it cut off.

"The client's communicator has been filtered for our comfort," said the Rhemnolid. Next to him, the blimp began to writhe, as if in pain.

The !t! querist leaned close, gazing into the creature's large eyes. The room's translation field continued to interpret the frequency modulations of its bursts of clicks, broadcasting them to the various species present in their own language. "Clutch-the-Moon, our friend, our client, you cannot continue in your heresy. We beg you to recognize your error, to heal your mind . . . to accept the miracle of Heaven and the persistence of the body, the sustenance of the lifesoul."

Now Sam could hear the blimp moaning even without the communicator. The !t! continued to talk quietly to the client, apparently unmoved by its distress, its murmurs forming a counterpoint to the noises coming from the blimp. The tone of voice was comforting, but the words were pointed and unrelenting.

There was a sizzling sound, and a wisp of—smoke?—rose from one of the blimp's tentacles. The creature went berserk, struggling frantically to escape the clamps that held it to the dais. More wisps of smoke appeared.

The moaning increased in pitch. Sam was baffled. What was happening? What kind of medical procedure was this?

The client's skin color was changing, from its usual sallow khaki to pale yellow. Blisters were starting to form in the blimp's skin. With a shock, Sam realized that his own life-support wrap no longer had to make much effort to keep him warm. The temperature in the room had risen sharply in a few minutes.

This was no accident, Sam realized. The Hytth had deliberately adjusted the settings. The icicle hanging above the dais had started to melt. Drops of water were falling onto the outstretched tentacles. When they hit, the flesh burned.

That was why the dais had been placed beneath an icicle: to induce terror, and then pain.

Everyone knew that blimps were cold-world creatures. They could no more tolerate liquid water than a human could stand superheated steam. How could the querists . . .

With a heart-stopping jolt, Sam realized exactly what kind of medical procedure he was witnessing.

"So now," Sam's instructor said, "you begin to understand. Let me summarize your feelings: You are horrified; you are shocked; you are confused. Your mind is seething with contradictions. Your heart races; your blood feels like ice. Above all, you feel betrayed.

"I know how you feel, because I have felt such distress myself. All this is normal. Necessary. But now you must make a giant step and transcend the narrow confines of ordinary emotion, as every healer must. You know this, but you hesitate. You feel inadequate. You cannot see where the leap will lead.

"You are in desperate need of spiritual guidance, but you no longer believe you can trust me." The Veenseffer-co-Fropt's olfactory tufts brushed Sam's cheek; Sam turned away in disgust. "But you *can* trust me, Samuel. Why else would I have chosen you to witness what you have just seen? I have concealed nothing from you. Quite the reverse. *The Church wants you to know.* And you must ask yourself why. It cannot be to conceal a squalid secret, can it?"

The two of them were back in the instructor's quarters after the most harrowing six hours of Sam's life. He had learned exactly what it would take to advance in the Community. Oh, yes, he had learned! And now he felt sick. *That* was not what his beloved Church existed for!

It was the very antithesis of everything he had been taught—the values of universal love and tolerance.

And yet . . .

There was a horrible kind of logic to it. It had been explained to him, minute by minute, by the three querists, just as they had explained it to the object of their intimate attentions. The Memeplex was powerful and compelling. Its flaws, if it had flaws, eluded him, even though he *knew* they had to be obvious.

Love has no limits. Love values what is best. What is *best* is not always what you want. A healer must make difficult choices and live with their consequences.

"Before you can fully understand what you have been shown," his instructor continued in a translated tone of voice that Sam had never heard from him before—a mix of sadness, sincerity, solicitude . . . a kind voice, a concerned voice, a voice he *wanted* to trust but could not— "you must express your emotions. Bring them into the open where we can examine them together."

Nothing.

"Fourteen Samuel! Do you wish to overcome your human limitations? To unite with the Cosmos? Then you must open your heart and mind. To me. Now."

"You—you killed him," said Sam. "One of the Lifesoul-Cherisher's creatures."

"His death was not intended," said the instructor. "We wanted him to live."

"So that you could continue the torture," said Sam. "You—you broiled him alive. You deliberately changed the environment of the room to inflict suffering. You *warmed* him! A blimp! Clutch-the-Moon Splitcloud was

a member of the Community! He was a sentient being!"
Sam's voice wavered, he could hardly form the words.

"Yes, he was indeed sentient . . . and that was his tragedy. Only a sentient can *sin,* Samuel. Ethical error is the prerogative of intelligence. The beasts of soil and fluid are immune from sin, for they cannot comprehend its nature. But Clutch-the-Moon's heresy was a terrible one, and it led him to a terrible end.

"So sad. So predictable, I now see. The path of error was too tempting for him. You should understand that I knew him. For half my life I have known him as a friend." The querist ducked his body to affirm the truth of his words. "Oh, yes. We trained together. You thought he was unknown to me? A random victim, plucked from the nameless masses? Not so. He was a friend, a friend of all three of us, and he had become a heretic. That is why he had been designated as a monk. He was plucked from his Community and conveyed here because his life-soul was in mortal peril.

"*You* are training as a lifesoul-healer; now know what that entails. For many months we have been trying desperately to heal our friend. Our failure brought us all to this."

"*Heal* him?" Sam was screaming, his face twisted by anger and grief. "You *tortured* him, for his unorthodox beliefs, and he resisted despite all the pain and terror. When he finally could stand no more and began to recant his heresies, you told him that you did not believe he was truly repentant, and you instructed his tormentors to re-double their efforts!"

The instructor leaned closer, its voice insistent but quiet. "It is so difficult to do what is necessary, Sam.

Poor, single-minded Sam . . . You must recognize that at that moment, Clutch-the-Moon would have said *any-thing* to stop the work of healing. Put yourself in his place. If your body was immersed in boiling water, what would you be willing to *say* to make the torment stop? You would deny your lineage, deny your own name, deny the Church itself! But in order for poor Clutch-the-Moon's lifesoul to be truly healed, it was necessary to cause him to restructure his mind. He had to *believe,* you see, not just pretend. And the verdict of the verifiers cannot be ignored. *He did not believe.* He *still* denied the reality and the desirability of Heaven! In the innermost recesses of his mind, *nothing had changed.*"

"But—why torture?" Sam protested, still in denial, still unable to accept the reasoning of his spiritual superiors. He was risking a very severe reprimand, but he didn't care. "Why not use reason, drugs?"

"Reason had already failed, and drugs are useless. A drugged mind is not a true mind. The belief of a subverted consciousness cannot be trusted. But pain—pain *heightens* reality. When a heightened consciousness truly changes its beliefs, the change is permanent and genuine. Drugs produce only the illusion of change; remove the drug and the mind will revert. Remove the pain, and true belief remains. Pain is purifying; it focuses the will. And that is the key, Samuel: the will. The client must be led to recognize his error *of his own free will.* Pain is the universal route to such recognition in all sentients, for pain cannot be denied. It has a reality that transcends all delusions, Samuel. That is why it evolves in all sentient creatures. Its function is to preserve life, by warning of damage to the body. The more impossible it becomes to ignore those warnings, the better pain serves its evolutionary function. And thus it forms our last resort against spiritual death."

The instructor fiddled with his tufts, as if his own beliefs were in doubt. He had expended much time and love training the young human; he looked worried that his efforts might be wasted. "You judge us as cruel, but we were acting out of love. And we could see that we were still failing our friend. The attitudinal changes we had succeeded in inducing were still superficial. We knew that, and it pained us. We could have stopped our work of healing, but our friend deserved better. The treatment had to continue, even though we felt every scald as if the flesh had been our own. Our love for our friend had to override our qualms about inflicting pain."

"So then you let the room cool, to keep him alive," said Sam. "And you turned to knives instead of heat. And when he still did not convince you of the sincerity of his recantation, the tortures got worse . . . until finally he died." Sam's eyes brimmed with tears—the first time he had cried since childhood. "I was glad when he died."

The Veenseffer-co-Fropt wriggled in despair. "Ah, so *that* is the depth of your perception. Shallow indeed, Samuel. Pain is transient, but death is eternal. I was *sorry* when my poor deluded, misguided friend died, for he died with the lifesoul of a heretic, and now he is lost forever to the Community."

"You call pain such as that *transient*?"

"It lasted only a few hours. The lifesoul lasts a lifetime. I had high hopes that the pain would transform him, and heal him so that he ceased to err. He was not supposed to die, Samuel! His wounds would have left him badly deformed, but his deformity would inspire our love to greater heights, not diminish it. Death? That was not the lesson intended for you! My poor friend had an illness, a bodily weakness that the attendant physicians had not suspected."

"There is some mercy, then," Sam said flatly.

The querist looked drained. "I have lost a *friend*, Samuel. A dear friend who went horribly astray. I voluntarily took upon myself the burden of healing him, which led to his suffering and his accidental death. I do not wish to lose a promising student on the same day! Your attitude is natural, but it is too simplistic. I must explain, and you must listen."

Sam snorted in disgust. The querist persisted.

"To gain a proper understanding of what you have just been privileged to witness, Fourteen Samuel, you must assume for a moment that in similar circumstances our methods would normally have persuaded the heretic of his error. What then?"

Sam was confused by the sudden change of tack. "Then the body would have been damaged, but—"

"But the lifesoul would be saved, and cherished eternally."

"Yes."

A triumphant flush of warmth spread over the querist's surface. "Then there is no comparison, is there, Samuel? No choice but one, however terrible its short-term consequences."

"It's a foul bargain," protested Sam, desperately seeking a way out of the logical maze. "Extremes of agony to correct a misconception in doctrine."

"An instant of anguish to be set against an eternity of

blessedness," the instructor contradicted. "And throughout our disputation you have forgotten that Clutch-the-Moon was responsible for the death of thousands, wrenched from Heaven without their consent, to fuel his megalomania."

There it was again, just as Sam had been taught. The irresolvable dilemma. The conflict of interests that made ethics possible, and necessary. If all choices were easy, there would be no need to choose wisely. The querist's reasoning was finally beginning to make sense to Sam—he could think of nothing that he had been taught that could refute it. *Nothing!* But still he struggled against its logic. The reality was so awful. "Is such butchery necessary? It's disgusting, appalling! How can the Church preach tolerance, yet behave with such cruelty?"

The querist twirled his olfactory organ as if in apology. "Because sometimes what you call butchery *is* necessary. A true healer learns to accept it. The treatment begins with gentle reason. If the patient does not respond, the healer will try stronger medicine. What alternative is there when all else has failed? When a lifesoul is in danger and *it is your sacred burden to save it*?" The Veenseffer-co-Fropt was becoming agitated now. "It has taken me much lifesoul-searching to understand the implications of that stupendous duty! It is the cusp of logic upon which any healer is forever impaled." Becoming ever more articulate as the power of advocacy surged through his mind, the querist completed his eloquent appeal: "Then, Samuel, when all other avenues have been closed, *then* you must take the awesome responsibility of making a decision: that another being's spiritual health must take precedence over your own misgivings. *You must turn away from the path of spiritual cowardice, Samuel!* I chose not to neglect my friend, but to take *whatever* action was needed to save him—however repellent I personally found it."

Sam opened his mouth, but for a moment no words came out. "Uh . . . master, your words make sense, but your reasoning is flawed. *What if you are wrong?*"

"That," said the querist, "is the terrible beauty of the logic. Because I might indeed be wrong in my interpretation of the Great Memes, it follows that every day I am risking my *own* lifesoul for the benefit of others. And there can be no greater love than that, do you not see?" The instructor's voice was urgent, brimming with emotion. "There is no flaw. Remember what Huff Elder taught the Originals, Samuel. Remember her fifth conversation. *The body is nothing, compared to the lifesoul.* Was she wrong?"

Sam's confusion increased. Suddenly, the well-recited phrase was taking on a new and terrible meaning. Yet the new meaning was entirely consistent with everything he had been taught.

"Well . . . yes. Of course. Huff Elder's writings have always been the foundation of the Church."

The instructor pressed home his advantage. "And what of the two Great Memes? Have you witnessed anything today that is inconsistent with either?"

Reluctantly Sam found himself saying "No." For there *was* nothing that contradicted the Great Memes. The Church as a whole was more important than any individual. And the spiritual completeness of the individual was more important than the individual's physical comfort.

"The temporary suffering of one lost lifesoul," the instructor said, "is as nothing by comparison with the propagation of the Great Memes. Even the pain of an entire culture counts for nothing, if that culture does not embrace the One. A culture that does not experience the joy of Unity is no more than a tedious multiplication of individual lifesouls.

"As we speak, our mission comes ever closer to the infidel world of No-Moon, with its unconstrained diversity of beliefs and actions. In your new role, you will be in the forefront of the conversion, not confined to a duplicator cubby on a tiny ship. You will then be called upon to face far more distressing scenes than the one you witnessed today. To help you prepare for the role that awaits you, I shall tell you about another mission, recently completed, and an outstanding success. There, the Church was forced to sacrifice an entire group of sentient beings. In physical form, they were akin to birds . . ."

The veiled strangers seized the Huphun broodmother, chained her to prevent her from flying away, and dragged her from her home on Spittle Nest Cliff. GreenCheckeredCircle screeched her protests, trembling with fear, anger, but above all, incomprehension.

The nameless invaders transported her to the plains above the cliff, one of the myriad flat-topped plateaus into which the landmasses of the Huphun homeworld were divided like crazed pottery. From there she was taken by transpod to Brooding Canyon, where the neighboring species of Hophuun lived. And there, still in chains, she was brought before her feud-sister, the nest-maker SquareBlueSpotted, for a lesson in spiritual enlightenment.

Traditionally, there was little love lost between the Huphun and the Hophuun. Their feud had lasted 211,000 starsets so far, with only the occasional lull. Yet now her feud-sister was professing sympathy for the brood-mother's desperate plight, even as the silent strangers stood, their faces shrouded in strange cloths.

Something was terribly wrong.

So desperate was GreenCheckeredCircle to end her flock's misery that she forced herself to ignore this feeling. In the lilting tones of trucespeak she began to explain to her deadly enemy the wickedness that was being inflicted on her fellow Huphun. *"Why?"* she sang at last, almost breaking down with released emotion. "Why have these creatures treated us so?"

Her feud-sister, the Hophuun nestmaker, fluttered her own unrestrained wings in a show of superiority. "Because they know of the Huphun's long-standing intoler-ance of harmony."

"Nonsense! The Huphun are tolerant of all who fol-low the permitted path."

The nestmaker cackled. "And your hatred and enmity for those who do not adhere to your small-minded, nar-row path is legendary. Notwithstanding that such folk form the majority."

"The unbelievers are wrong," said GreenCheckered-Circle. "Such matters are not subject to vote. It is the Hu-phun alone who possess the True Knowledge—"

"Kreeech! Always you Huphun seek to impose your

insane obsession with the Wings of the World! With you there is no other topic of songversation! Despite all counterarguments, you are convinced that you alone possess the true knowledge, and you insist on imposing it on every cliff-dwelling of this planet instead of attending to your own."

The broodmother weathered the verbal assault without flinching. "That is your belief," she sang. "Like all infidel opinions, it is wrong. But you say that we Huphun are being persecuted for our commitment to the Permitted Path. Why should strangers be aware of our ways?"

"Because we have told them," replied Square-BlueSpotted. "As have the Hoofen, the Hoffynn, the Who'fun, the Hof-phoon, the Hüfen, the Huff—"

"You list infidels."

"To the Huphun, *all* other flocks are infidel! You complain of persecution, but it is *you* who have persecuted *every other flock on this world*!" The nestmaker calmed herself. "And whenever an opportunity presented itself, you have imposed your will on them."

"You would do the same, given an opportunity. You merely lack our skill in combat."

"We have rejected the old ways of racialism and guerilla war. We have converted to the Chreech"—here the nestmaker had trouble wrapping her larynges around the foreign term—"the *Church* of the United Cosmos."

It sounded like the Huphun had opposition.

"We now subscribe to the Memeplex of Universal Tolerance, which preaches love for all of our fellow creatures, here and throughout the Galaxy," the nestmaker finished.

GreenCheckeredCircle, sagging under the weight of her chains, glared at her social counterpart and sworn enemy. "The invaders have glued my breeders to the cliffs so that their children fall and perish. That is *love*?"

SquareBlueSpotted fluttered her quills to show how serious she would be. "Love so great," she trilled, "that it risks its own spiritual health to save the lifesoul of the disbeliever."

The Huphun broodmother was baffled. "I know not of what you speak."

SquareBlueSpotted acknowledged the truth of this statement with a low, mournful crooning sound. "That is the tragedy of the Huphun," she agreed. "From the moment the missionaries arrived, your flock was identified as a certain source of resistance. That is why your treatment has been so severe."

GreenCheckeredCircle, who was not stupid, saw an entry. "But we were denied any chance to obey! We have been prejudged, before any of us lifted a feather! Let us, too, convert to your Church. Let us enjoy the benefits of this . . . memeplex."

SquareBlueSpotted soughed like the little-winter wind. "If only that were possible, feud-sister. But we know that you will never truly *believe*. That is why your flock has been selected—as an object lesson. The missionaries of Cosmic Unity have calculated that for every Huphun that dies, twenty members of other flocks will experience the joy of the Lifesoul-Cherisher. The balance of love is tilted against you."

GreenCheckeredCircle did a little dance of frustration and deposited a small heap of excrement to show her contempt. "That is unfair."

"So was the Huphun reign of terror that led to your selection for this honor," replied SquareBlueSpotted. "Your own intolerance has rebounded upon you like a resurgence of rakis mites in a poorly cleaned nesting site."

"We have rights!" screeched the broodmother. "Under feud-treaty!"

"You do not accord rights to others, and so you forfeit your own," replied the nestmaker. "In any case, feud-treaty is now obsolete."

"We will fight this evil," sang GreenCheckeredCircle. "The Huphun will never surrender to these unbelievers! We will *never* convert to a heathen religion!"

For the first time, one of the veiled strangers spoke. Its accent was poor—its translator was not yet trained in the Huphun larynge. But its words were clear enough: "That option is not on offer."

Sam absorbed the terrible lesson of the Huphun. At the cost of just one minority group—a group of trouble-makers, at that—an entire world had been brought into the fold of the Church. Such a small price to pay for so wondrous an outcome.

One thing he did understand now: The querists truly believed that their actions were motivated entirely by love. He had always been taught that it might sometimes be necessary to sacrifice a sentient's comfort for its overall well-being. To administer vile-tasting medicine to cure a disease. And he had learned to appreciate the spartan surroundings of the monastery of equals, whose purpose was similar. What he had not asked himself until now was how far the principle extended. *Did it have limits?*

Suddenly, he understood the querists' position: The answer to that question must also be no. To them, Huff Elder's principle was absolute. It had to be, or else the Church stood for nothing. A sentient entity's lifesoul was valuable beyond price, whereas its physical comfort was mere currency.

He didn't yet believe that, but he was wavering under the force of the logic. He had been trained since childhood to accept whatever the priests told him. This was a test of his faith, and his doubt made him fear he was failing that test. He resolved to put his doubt behind him and to try to control his emotions better.

Hesitantly he expressed this view.

"You progress," said the querist, beginning to relax. "You have begun a difficult transition. I believe that you now understand *intellectually* that the foundational memeplexes cannot be denied. My task is now to reinforce that new understanding until you cease to question it. Do you see the necessity for the next step?"

In Sam's mind the horror was taking on a new aspect. Emotionally he was still fighting against what he had been told, what he had seen . . . but the querist's conviction of righteousness blazed like a sun. Sometimes you had to be cruel to be kind. . . . The cruelty had been more extreme than he had ever imagined possible, but the cause was so overwhelmingly vital—not just to the Church but to the individual! Clutch-the-Moon's tragedy was that his heresy had become so deeply entrenched in his sick mind that only radical surgery could excise it—

and, for reasons that were no fault of the Church, the patient had been too physically weak to survive the treatment. His end had been a mercy, but only on the physical level. On the spiritual level, it was a tragedy without end.

Sam vowed to pray every evening in Clutch-the-Moon's memory. He could not save the blimp's lifesoul now that he was dead, but prayer would help Sam to come to terms with the loss. And reinforce an important lesson.

Now he felt ashamed at his naive reaction. As always, his master was right; once again he, XIV Samuel, had been mistaken. He should have focused his thoughts on the spirit, not on the body.

But even as he reaffirmed his determination to obey the Church in all things, Sam was terribly afraid that his newfound conviction might slip away again.

The three querists shared a common interest outside their ecclesiastical duties: relaxing conversation after a difficult day. Their custom was to meet in the Rhemno-lid's quarters, where the environment was a compromise that the others could easily manage without elaborate equipment.

To its two friends, the !t! looked distinctly out of sorts. It must have had a tiresome time. It wasn't hard for them to coax the !t! into telling them why.

"There was a terrible disagreement," it said, its frenzied clickings instantly transformed into two varieties of speech. "Two monks, both blimps. The argument became very personal and abusive. I had to intervene and reprimand them."

The Veenseffer-co-Fropt felt immediate sympathy. Dissent was so emotionally draining. "What was the dispute about?"

"It was a sexual matter. You know that in several species within the Church, death of a partner is an integral part of the sex act. One monk was maintaining that sex must be forbidden to such species in Heaven, since the purpose of Heaven is to postpone the onset of death. The other would have none of it, stating that in Heaven *nothing* could be denied. Neither monk displayed the virtue of tolerance, I regret."

The Rhemnolid saw the irony. "But in Heaven this cannot be an isssue. All things are possible, even if they sseem logically contradictory."

"Yes, but these were simple folk," the !t! stated, confirming the obvious. "Strong on faith, short on reasoning power. But I do indeed feel drained." And with that, it helped itself to a jolt of electricity from a portable stimulator that the Rhemnolid had installed specifically for that purpose. He liked to offer his guests proper hospitality.

"The young human took today's revelations surprisingly well," the !t! remarked. "I was expecting angry denunciations."

"Perhapsss he was overwhelmed by our presensss," hissed the Rhemnolid. "He seemed to be very ssslow on the uptake."

"Only at first," said the Veenseffer-co-Fropt, defending his tutee. "Servant of Unity Fourteen Samuel Godwin'sson Travers is fundamentally a good person, and for a time he was in denial about what he was witnessing. Subconsciously, of course, he knew. But he was not prepared for such an unpalatable truth, and so he ignored the obvious until it became impossible to deny. From that moment on, I think he showed serious promise."

"More so than our unfortunate client," said the !t!, taking a further jolt of electricity. "I cannot credit his stubbornness. It caused him much needless anguish. And such a pity that his main digestive vessel was weak-walled. I really thought that we were beginning to make some progress with him."

"I beg to contradict," said the Rhemnolid. "I have encountered his kind before. Their minds become fixed, and they respond poorly to treatment. If pushed too far, they bend, but they ssseldom break."

The Veenseffer-co-Fropt slurped syrupy liquid from a small goblet with his ingestion tube; he had acquired a taste for ethyl alcohol when a novitiate. The !t! consumed another jolt of current. "Personally," put in the Rhemnolid, "I find both of your habits preposterousss. We Rhemnolidss have no need of artificial stimulusss."

"Return your thoughts to young Samuel," said Sam's instructor. "I need your advice. I am thinking of recommending him for an accelerated program of advancement. He is malleable and intelligent. I am convinced he has the potential to rise high in the ecclesiarchy. And we all know that such entities are in short supply."

"The Church's logistics are being overstretched, so great is the need for its ministrations."

"That soundsss perilously like criticism," said the Rhemnolid.

"Don't be an idiot. It *is* criticism. And it stays inside

this room, as we long ago agreed. We three must be able to speak freely amongst ourselves, the better to assist the propagation of Cosmic Unity.

"We all know that the Church is fighting too many battles on too many fronts. *And* you can keep any dislike of military metaphors to yourselves—we've been over that before. We are soldiers, my friends—soldiers of the Memeplex. With the difference that the will of the Cosmos is on our side."

The !t! idly flicked its sticklike forelimb against the floor in a counterrhythm to its speech. "But that alone cannot guarantee victory, yes? Not if our strategy is misguided."

"Or our numbers are constrained. Which returns me to my question. Fourteen Samuel: what is your impression of him? Is he ready?"

The Rhemnolid heightened its consciousness to verify its opinion. "You are right, of course. He is the most promising novice any of us have yet ssseen, is he not?"

The !t! clicked its agreement. The question scarcely needed asking.

"So you recommend that I proceed to the next, most sensitive stage of his training without further delay? Or should we instruct him to assist at other treatments, to make sure that his innate disgust is abating as he becomes accustomed to the harsher aspects of lifesoulhealing?"

The !t! and the Rhemnolid made eye contact and confirmed their agreement. "We are of one mind," click-chirruped the !t!. "All three of us. The risks of an accelerated program are high, but the Church's needs are becoming desperate. And—"

"And that demands that the risssk be accepted," the

Rhemnolid finished for it. "The decision makes itself, in general terms, but I do not see the specificsss. What, precisely, do you have in mind?"

The Veenseffer co-Fropt took a deep breath. The issue had been decided. There was no point in further delay.

"We must send Samuel to Heaven."

8

CROOKED ATOLL

Empathy has many uses. It can help you to understand your fellow beings, and thereby make their lives—and your own—more pleasant. On the other hand, if you understand another beings' feelings, you may be able to use that knowledge against them. Of course, such actions would be highly unethical. That is precisely what makes them so useful.

Archives of Moish

To all but the most careful observer, No-Moon seemed the same as it had always been. Tailfins, jelloids, and other sea creatures went about their business; mariners sailed the oceans and caused mayhem in the dockside bars. But two hundred miles above the ocean's surface, Cosmic Unity's magnetotorus-powered mission fleet had settled itself in orbit. And a few feet below the ocean's surface, the reefwives were making preparations for war.

What they had in mind was biological warfare on a planetary scale. It was a contingency that they had prepared for long ago.

The first line of defense was a virus, which millions of years ago the reefwives had sequestered in sealed capsules, locked into impermeable rock around the shoreline in a dozen locations. The virus would need genetic modification before it could be used to defend the planet. In its present form, several key genes had been deactivated, and protection against common mutations had been added. Such molecular engineering—"gene-hacking," the reefwives called it disparagingly—was never completely straightforward; genetic changes that seemed harmless in themselves could interact with other genes, with noncoding sequences, with other organisms, or with the environment, in unpredictable ways. But this particular suite of modifications had been tested extensively several times in the past, back on Three-Moons, and experience showed that it could be trusted. Even if the deactivated viruses escaped from their confinement, they would harm nothing.

Once activated, however, this virus would be devastating. It had been designed from the start to be multi-specific—it had the ability to disrupt the biochemistry of virtually any animal species, with suitable modifications to its surface structure. The reefwives' timechunk had told them which species to target: Fyx. So they added carefully tailored receptor molecules to the virus, based on Fyx biochemistry. The virus would target the neuro-transmitter molecules that controlled the signaling pathways in Fyx nerve cells. Its action was inhibited by a wide range of proteins found only in No-Moon's plants, and the reefwives had been vaccinating the animals of No-Moon for months—especially the sentient ones, using a short-lived prion complex distributed in the ocean and spread overland on the winds. So only the enemy would be vulnerable.

Cosmic Unity's adherents were primarily carbon-based. Lacking immunity, the coming invaders would quickly be infected with a virulent and extremely nasty plague.

Already the reefwives' timechunk was predicting an acceptable contagion rate for the plague, and the death of several thousand invaders. This gave the reefwives some satisfaction; they were beginning to find out more about Cosmic Unity's methods as they cross-correlated Galactic records, and they had never seen any sense in protecting entities that had no scruples about harming others. They had long been puzzled by some species, which had developed a curious concept that they called "rights"; a few seemed to imagine that these rights should be extended to every sentient individual, of whatever species, independently of how it behaved. The reefwives found the idea romantic, and the principle delightfully impractical—but when it came to the crunch, they felt that rights were something you had to *earn*. Anything that was given away indiscriminately became valueless. Their view was that any creature that failed to respect the rights of others automatically forfeited its own rights, up to and including the right to exist. Nobody had *invited* Cosmic Unity to inflict its memeplex on No-Moon; it had been the Church's own idea, and whatever happened to it as a result would be entirely its own fault. There was no need to warn the invaders or otherwise offer them any potential advantage. That would just be poor strategy.

As far as the reefwives were concerned, their own survival was an absolute, and they would take whatever steps were necessary to ensure it. On the other hand, they would never even think about inflicting their own way of thinking on any other species. As long as others left them alone, they were benign.

So, even though their ways were utterly peaceful, they envisioned the appalling effects of their plague on the unwanted interlopers with unalloyed pleasure. Unfortunately, their current timechunk also showed the invaders analyzing the virus and quickly coming up with their own vaccine. So the plague would only slow them down and reduce their numbers. The pleasure, then, would be transient.

As the defeat of the virus moved to center stage in the unfolding timechunk, the reefwives would have to fall back on alternative strategies. Simple deceptions involving Neanderthal allies. Mass attacks by hyped-up husbands. The war would escalate, with no predictable limits to its ferocity. Eventually, they were confident, they would win—but at what cost to the planet? Their collective memories proved that so far, they had never failed—but on one occasion they had been forced to evacuate their homeworld, because Three-Moons' ecology had been unable to recover.

And nothing would *guarantee* that they would win. Their confidence was high, but it might also be misplaced. Perhaps there would come a time when the enemy was too cunning. Or too lucky.

It pained them that their males would have to bear the

brunt of the fighting. The sad fate of Second-Best Sailor and his compatriots was never far from their thoughts, and they continued to make strenuous efforts to find out who had been responsible. An increasing proportion of timechunks pointed squarely to Cosmic Unity, but timechunks were subject to revision, however convincing they might seem.

The reefwives had no doubts, however, that their forthcoming defiance of Cosmic Unity's invading force would condemn thousands more mariners, perhaps millions, to equally nasty deaths—along with the other sentient aliens who made their home on No-Moon. When it came to war, individual organisms with individual minds were at a serious disadvantage. They were easily identified; they *looked* like intelligent entities.

The reefwives looked like a coral reef. They could wage guerilla warfare, and the enemy would have no idea where it originated. Who would see a reef as a threat?

So far, no invader had ever recognized the reefwives' collective intelligence, and so had never tried to attack the reefwives themselves. Nonetheless, they had a strong suspicion that this time around, their own continued existence might well be on the line.

That offered one advantage, and as far as they were aware, only one. It was *amazingly* good motivation.

The Aquiferian sandskater was thirsty. Ordinarily, it could get enough moisture from the shrubs upon which it browsed, but growing an egg required more. Its flukes would have to survive for eleven years in their hideaway beneath a flat rock, and to do that they would need to be kept wet. They would float in mineral-laden water inside the egg, like miniature goldfish in a tiny glass bowl, until the egg's internal clock decided that it was time for them to find a host. Then the rubbery shell would soften and dissolve, releasing them into the sand. The patch of dampness would attract bush scarabs, which would suck up the flukes along with the wet sand. As the scarab's digestive system filtered out the sand for excretion, the flukes would burrow into its intestinal linings.

At first they would steal some of the scarab's intake of food. But as they grew, their needs would become greater, and they would begin to consume the body of their host, starting with its thick deposits of stored polysaccharides, accumulated to carry it through the colder seasons. The flukes would move on to more critical organs, until soon the scarab lay paralyzed on the desert floor and baked in the hot sun. The heat would trigger a metamorphosis in the flukes, and they would emerge from the scarab's dried-out exoskeleton as a thousand pinprick-sized sandskaters, perfect miniatures of the adult.

This sandskater's midbody was about the size of a cat and covered in ugly lumps: the creature's sensory organs, feeding parts, and reproductive attachments. It was held away from the hot desert sand by dozens of spindly legs, with tufts at their numerous joints. The creature was close to term: Its bulbous midbody was taut and bulging, inflated by the egg within. But the egg was still too dry.

The sandskater had stolen water from Aquifer's ponds

before. One final foray, and its egg would be wet enough for burial. The animal had already selected a suitable rock, half concealed by the leeward slope of a dune. It had dug a spiraling entrance tunnel and constructed a suitable birthing chamber. All was ready. A little more water—that was all it now needed.

The sandskater was scared. It could sense water, but it could also sense danger. The pond shimmered seductively as the wind rippled its surface, but the desert surrounding the pond was barren, apparently devoid of all life. The sandskater had already advanced several yards into this no-man's-land, leaving behind it the relative safety of the scrub. As always, the evolutionary imperatives of reproduction were overriding those of self-preservation. Who dares, wins.

Or loses.

Now, frozen by fear, it had stopped. Nothing is worse than hesitation. Out here, on the bare shore, the sandskater was exposed. It might be taken by a duneglider, an awk, or any of a dozen species of aerial predators. Instinct honed by evolutionary eons compelled the sandskater to take a decision. Fast.

It scuttled toward the pond's edge, halting as far away as it could while still obtaining water. Anxious senses searched for danger. Nothing disturbed the crystal waters of the pond, or its mats of floating algae, but beneath its surface numerous creatures swam and played. The pond looked tranquil, harmless. The sandskater extended a long feeding tube and began to drink.

Immediately, an amphibian's stubby head broke the surface of the pond right where the sandskater was drinking. Without warning, it spat a thick gobbet of mucus, which hit the sandskater's midbody full on and clung in a sticky mess. The neurotoxins in the mucus would have felled a top-of-the-food-chain predator, and had done so on many occasions; the sandskater never stood a chance. Its legs splayed, and it collapsed. Its skin split open to reveal the rounded contours of its egg.

The carcass rested inertly at the edge of the pond, the tip of its feeding tube dangling in the water. A shoal of shrimps converged on the feeding tube and began to gnaw at it.

Now the sand beneath the carcass began to change. It turned into a thick, runny fluid, like quicksand. Strange waves in the fluid began to nudge the sandskater's dead body closer to the pond. It would have taken a microscope to work out what was happening. Branching fronds of algae were growing into the shore beneath the creature, pumping water into the sand. Other microorganisms were changing the viscosity of the wetted sand in a cycle, from thick to thin and back again. These changes caused the sand to form mobile ridges, pushing the carcass toward the water.

The dead sandskater slid smoothly into the pond, with hardly a ripple. The dense shell of its water-filled egg dragged it beneath the surface.

A million tiny threadworms began to eat their way in, through any region of soft tissue, quickly turning the animal's interior into mush. Then the exoskeleton began to fall apart as its supporting muscles turned to shreds.

The threadworms' feeding frenzy was halted only when the amphibians moved in to eat the softened carcass.

Soon all was still again. Only the egg remained,

lodged in mud at the bottom of the pond. The cool ripples were ready to lure their next victim.

While the mission fleet prepared to enforce tolerance and love on the citizens of No-Moon whether they wanted them or not, other representatives of Cosmic Unity were trying to work out the implications of an invasion in the other direction—the invasion of Aquifer by a small contingent of aliens.

Hhoortl555mup had studied Ykzykk-Knazd's report with unusual care. The incursion had indeed been an extreme measures circumstance, and a commendation for the patrol captain's rapid and correct decision had been entered into Church archives. Privately the hierocrat disagreed with the ecclesiastical decree about extreme measures. She would have preferred a more cautious approach initially, with force held in reserve. But if she had allowed the intruders to establish a secure base, and they had then used their ansible to invite others to join them, she would have regretted her disobedience. Oh, yes.

Extreme measures were only the first step. Now she must find out more about the intruders, decide what to do next. What had the creatures been up to? Why had they installed a forcewall across an obscure bay? To find out, she had dispatched a carload of technicians to the bay, to turn up whatever information they could while disposing of any remaining evidence of the attack. Now the car had returned, and a certain amount of light was beginning to dawn.

"The incursion was small and localized," said the

head technician, a Baatu'unji that was far enough past its breeding peak to engage its mind on impersonal investigations.

"This one was," said the hierocrat sourly. "The next could be bigger. Maybe this was a trial run." She had stationed herself in front of her Ankh of Authority, a potent symbol, and she was disappointed that the technician seemed unaffected. It was next to the console that she used to access the archives. Her fashionable fringe of lopworms writhed prettily in response to her concealed anger. They responded to temperature shifts caused by emotional stress.

"For what, Hierocrat?" asked the Baatu'unji technician, unwisely.

"That, you fool, is what I sent you to discover!"

The technician blinked. "We were able to discover facts, Hierocrat. Motives are seldom preserved in physical form. On this occasion—"

"Your expedition failed!"

". . . we were unable to establish any motive. But we can now identify the type of alien involved in the invasion."

This was news to the hierocrat. "Well, out with it."

From the agitated state of the hierocrat's lopworm headpiece, the Baatu'unji could see she was in a very foul mood, and the technician shuddered inwardly. "There were nearly fifty of them, Your Eminence. All from the same species, all male. Some young; most coming to the end of their active phase, though not yet senile."

"Yes, yes . . . Tell me something I can *use*."

"We examined the corpses carefully. We took tissue

samples and made extensive tests. The physiological damage done to them by our weaponry was extensive, but we can say with certainty that they are marine creatures, Hierocrat."

"*I know that!* They were in the *sea*!"

"They could have been land animals with a degree of aquatic tolerance, Your Eminence."

Hierocrat Hhoortl555mup had long ago become resigned to Baatu'unji logic-chopping. "Very well, so they are marine by nature, not by inclination. What does that tell us?"

"To be more specific, they are polypoids. Male corals. Such creatures have evolved on several hundred worlds, and it will take time to pinpoint exactly which of these worlds was the source of this . . . infestation. Assuming it was a single source, of course. But"—the technician hastened to move on to the good news—"we now know where to concentrate our efforts in identifying the aliens."

The hierocrat was slightly mollified. These things took time, she knew. "I trust those efforts are already being concentrated?"

"Oh, yes. And we also . . . we know that we were not the target of the invasion. The invaders had no idea we were present on this planet. They were merely seeking a suitable aquatic environment to found a colony."

The hierocrat was impressed. "You managed to deduce that from dead bodies?"

The Baatu'unji blinked again. "Oh, no. Not at all."

The hierocrat rippled with frustration at the obtuseness common to this species. "Then how . . ."

". . . do we know? Simple, Your Eminence. Two of the

invaders survived the attack and were captured. One is still very weak. We have interrogated the other one, and he has told us that—"

The technician wilted before the verbal onslaught, outright terror visible in its features. The hierocrat had not been aware that there had been any survivors. What annoyed her most was that the Baatu'unji was unable to comprehend her outrage at being told about it *now*.

The polypoid needed no extra life support. It was wearing its own suit. The hierocrat recognized the make: Its golden color showed it to be a duplied copy of a Precursor original. The suit, no doubt, was what had allowed the creature to survive the onslaught; it must have fled the boiling sea and taken cover on land. Even so, it was a miracle that the creature had escaped.

"What is its designation?" she asked the Fyx interrogator, who had replaced the Baatu'unji technician.

"Pardon?"

"Its *name*."

"Ah. It translates as something along the lines of 'Inferior Aquanaut,' Your Eminence."

"Eel crap!" the polypoid protested. It reconfigured its suit to lift itself upright and defend its dignity.

"Your name is Eel Crap?"

"No!" it said with scorn. "I'm Second-Best Sailor! I'm a mariner an' proud of it! An' my suit's translator's better'n yours, too, matey."

"Inferior Aquanaut? That's what I just said," the Fyx

responded, getting the same mistranslation as before from his own unit and failing to appreciate what was happening. The hierocrat decided not to enlighten him. There was more urgent business. "As senior representative of the Church of Cosmic Unity, I will interrogate him. After that . . . I will decide when the time comes. It will depend on what is best for the Church."

Hhoortl555mup had been expecting resistance, but Second-Best Sailor answered all her questions without any need for persuasion. In fact, the biggest problem was to stop him talking, given that much of what he said conveyed no information whatsoever. The polypoid was a coward, she decided. Item by item, the hierocrat extracted nuggets of fact from a torrent of braggadocio.

"Home world? We call it No-Moon, Yer Innocence, on account of 'ow it ain't got no moon. Good name, right? Flouncin' brilliant, it is, unlike its moon, on account of 'ow it ain't got none, ya appreciate."

The hierocrat called up a planetary catalog. "There are forty-six worlds of a similar name within the civilized Galaxy," she said. "All but two of them have no moon. Be more specific."

"I ain't no spacer," said Second-Best Sailor. "Fat Apprentice, now, 'e was interested in that kind of thing. But 'e's dead; you zygoblasts boiled 'im when you attacked us."

"An error on our part. We might have learned something useful. Do you know how far away your homeworld is from here? In which direction?"

"Nah. Like I said, I ain't no spacer."

The hierocrat gestured at the technician. "This one is useless. Dispose of him as you—"

"Now wait a minute! Give me time to think! Umm . . . the cap'n did say something about that, though. Let me put me mind to it. . . . Yes, 'e said it was years. That was it."

"Years are a measure of time. Do you mean light-years?"

"Light, heavy—I dunno. 'Light' sounds familiar."

"How many light-years?"

"'Ow *many*? It's supposed to 'ave a *number*? Well, spike me a marlon and prick me with a jelloid! No one mentioned no number."

"A pity. It will take time to determine which of the forty-four moonless No-Moons you originated from. You will find it more comfortable if you can assist us in shortening that period. What kind of star did your planet orbit?"

"Star?"

"Sun. Your world must have had a sun."

"Oh, yes."

"What kind?"

"Round, bright . . . I never looked at it much, bein' underwater mostly. . . . Well, it was white, an' it came up in the day and disappeared at night."

"Was there just one sun? Or more?"

"More'n one sun? You people do live fascinatin' lives, an' no mistake. No, there was just one of it. And no moon, did I mention that?"

The hierocrat decided to try another tack. "Why did you come here?"

"The 'Thals brought us."

"Neanderthals?" That was news. A trading ship, no doubt. Was it still orbiting nearby? Such a big ship would appear in the night sky like a bright, fast-moving star. The patrol had seen nothing—ah, but the night had been cloudy. The follow-up car had not reported a ship, but in daylight, with the naked eye, that was understandable. So the ship could still be there, below the horizon, invisible to her telescopes.

She made a mental note to order a portable telescope to be sent to lower latitudes, to see if her guess could be confirmed. If the ship was still in orbit around Aquifer, it was probably already too late. Destroying the ship was not an option—the monastery did have one spacecraft, but it was small, intended only for the emergency transportation of key personnel. It could not attack one of the giant trading ships. And the Neanderthals could slip away long before larger vessels arrived.

She already knew what the ecclesiarchs would order her to do if there was any chance that Neanderthals had detected a presence on Aquifer. Safety would be paramount, expense irrelevant. Nevertheless, she had to find out as much as she could, and quickly. She returned her attention to the interrogation. "Why did the Neanderthals bring you here?"

"To start a new colony," Second-Best Sailor affirmed haughtily. "There was some kind o' trouble on No-Moon, an' we 'ad to evacuate. I loaned the 'Thals a bit o' my wife," he confided. "To keep her safe. 'Course, I kept another bit for my own use."

That was more like it. They could correlate this with Galactic news and information sources and narrow down the search. "What kind of trouble?"

Second-Best Sailor's skin went the blotchy green of futility. "I dunno much, Your Impudence. We was only told that we 'ad to get off the planet fast. Before it was overrun by some bunch arrivin' in a fleet of space-ships . . . Religious nuts, the 'Thals said they were. Comic Nullity—something like that."

The hierocrat blanched, but finally she had what she wanted. Hadn't the new arrival, XIV Samuel something-or-other, been transibled from a mission fleet *en route* to a world named No-Moon? She called up the archives. Yes, he had. So now she knew where the intruders had come from, and how. She was beginning to understand why, too, but she wanted more details about that.

The interrogation continued. Piece by piece, Second-Best Sailor let slip useful hints about his homeworld and why the Neanderthals had attempted to establish a small force of polypoids on Aquifer. Hhoortl555mup was confident that the colonists had thought Aquifer to be un-inhabited: The ease with which they had been extermi-nated proved that. But now the orbiting Neanderthal ship would be running a high level of surveillance, and there was a definite chance that it would locate the monastery under the ice dome. The ice would be slightly warmer than it ought to be. No concealment could be perfect.

Despite the careful risk analysis that supported the ec-clesiarchs' decree, she was becoming ever more certain that on this occasion extreme measures had backfired. Perhaps the patrol should have held back. . . . But if they had, she might at this very moment be informing the ec-clesiarchs that more intruders were arriving, that the monastery had been discovered, *and* that she had dis-obeyed standing orders.

No contest. She put the seditious thoughts aside and tried to concentrate on carrying out her responsibilities.

She wondered what weapons the Neanderthals possessed. Normally, their trading vessels were unarmed despite their impressive bulk, but there were dozens of worlds that would fit almost any kind of weapon, for the right price, with no questions asked. The hierocrat had no wish to find out that weapons had been installed by being on their receiving end.

Her standing orders were explicit: *Take no chances*. She reviewed her options, which were few, and came to a decision. First she would see what the telescope patrol turned up. If they had seen the Neanderthal ship, she would tell the ecclesiarchs immediately. This new information would then be analyzed in the context of the Church's entire program for expansion. She doubted that it would affect their long-term strategy on No-Moon, but that was not for her to decide. It would most assuredly affect the status of the monastery on Aquifer.

There was a standard procedure to be followed when extreme measures failed. All senior members of the priesthood on Aquifer would have to be evacuated immediately to one of the Cloister Worlds. The hierocrat would be the first to leave Aquifer, and she was entitled to use the transible, provided the ecclesiarchs issued the necessary authority. The rest of the priests had lower status, so they would depart in a fast cruiser, straight up from the pole and into hydrive before anyone could follow them. A cruiser was less secure than a transible, but much cheaper.

So, if the Neanderthals were still around—it all kept coming back to that—then they must be led to think that the monastery had been abandoned. They could do what they wanted with the monks and menials left behind;

those were just camouflage. But Cosmic Unity could not risk anyone capturing high-ranking priests and interrogating them. They knew too much.

Above all, she had to protect herself. Like nearly all members of the Church, she was expendable. So, supposedly, were the ecclesiarchs. But she knew that in the world of realpolitik, leaders were all the same. In practice, the Great Memes would not apply to the uppermost level of the ecclesiastical hierarchy. The ecclesiarchs did not consider themselves expendable, whatever a literal interpretation of the Great Memes might seem to imply, and they would take extreme measures to ensure their own survival.

At that point, the telescope patrol reported in, and her worst fears were confirmed. A bright needle of light, skimming the horizon. She cursed the foul luck that had led the Neanderthals to choose a low equatorial orbit, which had concealed their ship until it was too late—but curses would change nothing. Her future looked bleak, unless . . . Was there some obscure opportunity here to advance her own standing? If there was, she could not find it. An enforced retreat, even the possible abandonment of the monastery . . . It would look bad on her record, whatever standing orders said.

All because of a pathetic bunch of squids!

One of whom was staring at her right at that moment. An insolent creature, too. And very possibly a lot smarter than he tried to pretend.

There was much to do, and she should not delay it further. "Take the prisoner to a holding cell," she said. "The final decision on his fate will be made later, when the pressure of business permits. Supply him with suitable gases, solids, liquids—whatever his metabolic requirements may be. The cooks will have access to the necessary physiological information. Keep him alive and healthy. For now."

"Shall I put him with the other one?" asked the Baatu'unji.

"No. Keep them separate to avoid collusion."

Second-Best Sailor just about managed to remain upright and stay silent.

Other one?

Second-Best Sailor had been in plenty of messes in his eventful life, but this one was definitely the worst. His life had been on the line many times, but always he had been in a position to influence his own fate. This time he was helpless. He could only hope that the Neanderthals would rescue him and the other polypoid prisoner, whoever he was. He just hoped his fellow prisoner wasn't too badly injured. But before they could rescue him, the Neanderthals had to find him, and that might not be easy.

He knew that his attackers were agents, probably members, of the Church of Cosmic Unity. The pompous alien who had made such a flop of interrogating him had let that much information slip, along with the existence of a second prisoner, and she'd never even noticed. But he didn't know how strong a grip the Church's tentacles had on Aquifer. All he knew was that he had been attacked under cover of darkness, that all but one of his companions had been killed, while he had been fortunate enough to grab a sailor suit before the sea got too hot, and escape onto the shore. Where he was promptly captured, restrained, and flung in some low-altitude vehicle, which took him . . . somewhere.

Somewhere cold.

Beyond that, he had no idea. So rescue seemed a slim prospect.

Escape? Once before he'd escaped when all seemed lost—he recalled the circumstances vividly: an unwise bet placed with the wrong people. But on that occasion he'd been in possession of hidden resources, a small packet of stingworms hidden in one of his propulsion siphons. This time all he had was his golden sailor suit. His captors would have taken it away, but without it he would die. Soon, though, they probably *would* take it away. It would be an easy way to dispose of him.

Six levels up and a short walk to the east, the hierocrat was having qualms of conscience about just that decision, and had rejected it. The ways of the Church were often harsh, but the last thing it ever intended was to do evil. Yes, sometimes it was necessary to deal severely with individuals, but that was an unavoidable side effect of the overriding drive for a United Cosmos. Tolerance could not be extended to the point at which it became self-defeating.

However, she could not convince herself that Second-Best Sailor posed any threat to the Church. Yes, he had spent the interrogation insulting most of her core beliefs—seemingly out of accident and ignorance, though she still wondered if this had been a sham. But the Memeplex absolutely forbade harming another sentient entity merely out of personal disapproval. Harm could be done only to save its lifesoul, or that of sufficiently many others.

She was, after all, a Flinger-Erdant, a race that was uncommon in the Galaxy. They were long-lived but very slow to reproduce, and until her world had joined the Church and received the benefits of Church technology, their only suitable habitat had been a stretch of fungoid forest at the edge of one small continent. Flingers-Erdant were a proud people. And as a representative of her race, pride required that she should respect the Memeplex absolutely.

She knew that the Neanderthal ship could not see the ice cap from its present position, and even if it discovered where they were, it could not mount an attack from the equator. The moment it showed any sign of changing its orbit, she would be out of here. She would be gone within the hour, anyway. So the problem of the two polypoids could safely be assigned to a subordinate. One of the querists, perhaps? Yes. She chose one at random, a Rhemnolid, and summoned it.

"The polypoids might possibly be made monksss," the Rhemnolid said doubtfully. "That would be fitting. They would be given the opportunity to join the Church, as should be done for any ssentient, according to the teachings of Moish."

The hierocrat liked that idea. It would indeed be fitting—especially the harsh monastic regimen.

The Rhemnolid was not so sure. He was flicking through various files, looking for a decree that he thought had been made by the second ecclesiarch a few months earlier. With a grunt of pleasure, he found it.

"Uuuuhhh . . . no, hierocrat, we can't do that. It isss forbidden."

"Why?"

"We would exceed our Quota of Love."

The second ecclesiarch had decreed that while a complete racial mix was the Church's ultimate objective, it had to be achieved in a balanced and efficient manner. Theologians had computed the optimal proportions, and their results indicated that for maximal efficiency the diversity parameter should not exceed a complex but explicitly defined function of the number of individuals.

As was only proper, the monastery underneath Aquifer's Nether Ice Dome had increased its racial diversity right up to that limit. "If just one of the existing personnel was a polypoid," the Rhemnolid explained, "then the prisoners could be included. But their presence would increment the number of species by one, and that would push us over the limit."

The hierocrat could not argue with the arithmetic, but she did check the calculation, in case the Rhemnolid had made an elementary error. Had he checked whether the addition of the polypoids would augment the population enough to increase the permitted number of species, too?

Yes, he had. It had been a faint hope.

"Technically," the querist pointed out, "we are already in excesss of the statutory limit."

"Prisoners count towards the diversity parameter?" said the Hierocrat, astonished. "But it is not always possible to determine the species of an invader before it is taken prisoner!"

"The conclave debated precisely that isssue," said the

Rhemnolid after flicking through the files again, "but found it imposssible to resolve the contradictions that it opened up."

"We cannot continue to exceed our Quota of Love," the hierocrat stated firmly. "In case we turn out to have been in breach of ecclesiastical law."

"So we mussst eliminate the prisoners?"

The hierocrat thought about that for a moment. "We cannot eliminate the injured one, querist; that would be contrary to the *Sayings of Chalz*. And to kill the other without compunction would make a mockery of the Quota of Love. However, technically, the injured one does not count against the Quota until it is physically healed. I leave you with the task of deciding how to resolve the dilemma that will then arise, for my presence is required elsewhere. However, we must determine the fate of the other prisoner *now*. Suppose that he ceases to be a prisoner."

The querist was unhappy with that idea. "No, his presence in the monastery would ssstill count."

"I realize that. What if we were to *free* him? On the surface of Aquifer?"

The querist was puzzled. "Then he would not count towards the diversssity parameter. Just as the invading force of which he is one did not count when it first arrived. But if he is released, he would become a security risk!"

The hierocrat already had the answer to that objection. "Not if he is released in such a condition that the risk is zero." She weighed the options, thinking aloud. "It would be contrary to the Memeplex to kill him, so he must be permitted to keep his life-support suit. But it would be utterly foolish to allow him complete freedom of movement . . . so the suit must be partially disabled."

She thought some more. "As should he also," she added. "And it would not go against the teachings of Moish, or the conversations of Huff Elder, to make sure that those disabilities are of a kind that will become more serious over time."

"I ssuppose not," said the querist. "Not within the letter of Church law. Keeping within the limit for the diversity parameter is an ecclesiasstical matter, and the First Great Meme states that such considerations must take precedence over the well-being of a sssingle individual."

"Yes. And the Second Great Meme places the spiritual above the physical."

"Exactly."

"Then it is decided," said the hierocrat. "The prisoner will be carried deep into the desert by car, and there released—with his suit and his person damaged. In a manner that will not be immediately fatal, but will ensure that he quickly ceases to be a security risk to this facility.

"I leave it to you to devise appropriate disabilities. For I have an urgent appointment on the Cloister Worlds, and a transible awaits me even as we speak."

The querist departed in high dudgeon. *Decisions, decisions*—the hierocrat was skipping out and leaving him to sort out a potential disaster. If he got it right, she'd take the credit; if not, he'd get the blame.

Disabilities . . . Yes, those could be arranged. And he knew exactly the right person to arrange them. It was time to find out just how committed XIV Samuel was to conquering his spiritual squeamishness.

9

NORTHERN DESERT, AQUIFER

Communication . . . An easy word, but dangerous. Do you understand what I am telling you? If so, you will appreciate that to answer "yes" or "no" conveys nothing to me. It is not enough to provide information, for information must be interpreted. Without interpretation there is no meaning, and true communication is the transfer of meaning between minds. But what if those minds unknowingly impose different interpretations? Meaningless information is one of the greatest forces for evil in the Galaxy.

Conversations with Huff Elder

The desert air shimmered in the noonday heat. Second-Best Sailor noted the position of the sun and continued painfully along his southward track. He had been too confused during the attack on No Bar Bay to notice what had happened to the ansible that the 'Thals had installed there. He hoped it was still working. If it was, and if he could make his way back to the bay, then he'd be able to call a transpod down from *Talitha* and escape this arid hellhole.

He had no realistic expectations of success. The wound in his side was one obstacle. The associated slit in his sailor suit was the other. Both had been deliberate. His captors had dropped him none too gently out of the car—a fall of ten or twelve feet. As he lay on the sand, his siphons temporarily disrupted, one of them—a land-lubber priest clad in a maroon robe decorated with silver strings—had shot him with a laser. For no reason at all. The thing's weird front end was seared into his memory. Like a 'Thal but not as pretty . . . two small watery eyes, a snout pierced by two little holes, an absurd patch of dark fur . . . and the gangling bipedal gait, its tentacles rigid and hinged . . .

Maker, but it had been ugly.

Why had the landlubber shot him?

He didn't know why. He didn't know why it hadn't killed him, either. Nothing made sense. All he knew was that his golden suit was starting to show signs of failure. Along one flank, the shimmering fabric had peeled back, its edges burned and flaking. The flesh beneath was seared, a suppurating wound caked with embedded sand. The flaps of the tear had sealed themselves to the poly-poid's skin to prevent any loss of the suit's protective fluids. It was a poor but unavoidable compromise, which caused the flesh around the wound to dry out even faster. The pain would get worse, he knew. And there was no hope of repairing the suit. His only resources were sand, rocks, and some runty plants. Oh, and insects, many of which were becoming distressingly interested in his wound.

The suit could still access most of its features. It had sealed the hole against fluid losses, but it could not seal the exposed part of his skin against evaporation. It could still configure itself for transportation; in this instance, a caterpillar-track mode was clearly the best available. But the recycling module was on the blink and probably wouldn't last much longer. If it failed, he would suffocate in his own waste products.

The day passed, and night fell. Second-Best Sailor continued traveling, finding his way by the light of the stars. The pain was excruciating. He jerked uncontrollably, and his golden suit struggled to retain an effective motile shape. In fits and starts, Second-Best Sailor continued his tormented journey southward across the unending ocean of sand until fingers of light began to dissect the desert into black and silver silhouettes. The early morning view across the purpling dune field to the luminous sky was breathtaking, evidence of the Maker in all Its majesty. The rising sun picked out fine details of pattern on the sweeping slopes of the great ocean of sand, displaying every windblown indentation in vivid relief.

Second-Best Sailor flopped and rolled down the lee of a dune, scouring ugly gashes in the sand's perfect ripples. He was all but covered in sand grains. He was dying. The intense cold of the desert night had numbed his wound, which was a mercy. But frostbite had done further damage to the flesh exposed by the torn suit. And now the sun was rising.

The suit would protect most of the mariner's body

from the heat, just as it had protected most of it from the cold. From reserves that he didn't know he had, Second-Best Sailor summoned enough energy to give vent to a curse—vivid, inventive, and obscene. He knew that the suit could keep him alive a little longer, but all that would achieve would be a slower death, drawing out his pain, which already was sharp and agonizing.

He had never known such hurt before, and his ordeal had scarcely begun.

So much for Precursor technology.

He knew that he must continue to the south. If he traveled facedown, as he would have preferred, then the heat of the morning would roast his burned flesh. So, as on the previous morning, he rolled onto his back and waited for the suit to reconfigure its caterpillar track. Later, as the sun rose, the configuration would have to be changed.

The polypoid would deal with that when the time came. Right now he had no wish to think too far ahead. Not if he wanted to remain sane. The frozen night had so depleted his strength that he knew he would not survive another. He knew that moving any farther was pointless, but the alternative was to halt—and die. And he wasn't ready for the Taker, not yet. He had to survive, no matter what the cost. And hope. But hope seemed ever more futile.

The suit's movements were becoming increasingly erratic, ex-creta were slowly building up in its circulating sheath of fluid, and the golden skin was no longer keeping out the heat. The sailor suit was failing.

The sun was now high in the sky, and the shadows were shrinking rapidly. Soon he would be exposed to the searing noonday furnace of the blue-white star. He could accept the certainty of death: The life of every living thing was given in order to be taken. What terrified him was the form in which the Taker would manifest Itself.

Soon, he would begin to cook.

Through eyes that were clouding over as the heat of the sun baked their soft tissues, Second-Best Sailor noticed a shimmer of light away to his left. There was something familiar about the way the light flickered. The water that still flowed sluggishly between his body and the inner skin of the suit was foul-tasting and low in oxygen. The golden suit's motility packed up completely, but still he refused to give up. Although every movement brought a haze of pain, the mariner began a lizardlike crawl toward the source of the flickering. His every instinct screamed *water,* while what was left of his rational mind knew that there could not possibly be open water in this seared wilderness.

Instinct was right. A shallow hollow cupped a small pool, partially hidden by rocks, curiously devoid of surrounding vegetation. If this was an oasis, it was the strangest kind.

Beyond, other pools lay like upturned mirrors amid the dunes, shining like quicksilver, trembling in the heat haze.

Second-Best Sailor had dragged himself to within a few excruciating yards of the pond's cool, welcoming edge when his senses began to dissolve into fog. The suit's flow of oxygenated water had given out completely. Those last few yards, across the gritty sand to the cool moisture of the pool, suddenly stretched to infinity. It was no more possible to cross them than to swallow a hurricane.

As the mariner lost consciousness, a chemical memory passed across his mind, a surge of remembered pheromones. And he knew that he would never taste his wife again.

Beneath the bare expanse of sand, a network of algal filaments had sensed the vibrations of Second-best Sailor's tormented approach. Cell membranes were squeezed by his weight. Signals passed from filament to filament; electrons danced in quantum computations. Special molecules were assembled and passed along the filaments to the branches that ran into the pond.

The pond bided its time. This prey was large, and it was still struggling.

The struggles ceased, and the algal mat registered the fact. Now a suite of cooperative microorganisms began to clamber up the aridity gradient from wet water to dry desert, impelled by chemical waves, propelled by shape-change sequences and beating cilia. They migrated from the cool depths of the pond, following the algal filaments to the now-still target.

The sand supporting Second-Best Sailor's weight became fluid. It rippled, as concerted waves of viscosity gripped and slipped, gripped and slipped, so that the shiny material of his sailor suit was pulled in the same direction at a million places.

The suit, with Second-Best Sailor's dying body inside it, began to slide toward the pond.

It did not accelerate; it had nothing that corresponded to momentum. It seemed to float across the top layer of sand. Its motion, though slow, was relentless.

When the heavy body reached the water's edge, the shore crumbled beneath its weight, forming a smooth ramp. The waves of viscosity pulled Second-Best Sailor down the slope and into the water. There was no splash, scarcely any disturbance of the pond's wind-rippled surface—he just slipped in, pushing some drifting algal mats aside, and was gone.

The shore solidified; the microorganisms began making their way back to the water. The algal filaments passively readied themselves for the next victim.

On board *Talitha,* the mood was one of anger.

When it had suddenly become obvious that Aquifer must be inhabited, and that the natives were far from friendly, the ship and its crew had instantly raised themselves to a higher level of awareness. There was no point in regretting their stupidity in assuming that Galactic records, probably many years out of date, were still accurate; some of the crew lacked the capacity for regret in any case. But it was obvious to everyone that Sharp Wit Will Cut blamed himself for the deaths of his colonists. Even his crevit was in a grumpy mood. The more he pointed out that what was done was done, and urged them to refocus, the more everyone else saw his grief and self-blame. It was especially obvious to the other

Neanderthals, who also recognized that his anger with himself was becoming so great that he was not thinking straight. For a start, he hadn't yet realized that they must all be aware of his state of mind.

It was May who finally broached the matter with him.

"Will—we all made the same mistake. Do not blame—"

"I am the captain of this ship," Will growled. "I must bear the responsibility for all decisions."

"Responsibility, yes. Blame—no."

"There is no difference."

May put a muscular arm across his shoulder. "You know there is. There was no reason to expect an attack. The planet is a wilderness. Its most advanced life forms are pond-dwelling animals of low intelligence. Aquifer is far removed from civilized regions; that is why it was chosen."

"I should have checked, nonetheless."

"*We* should have checked. But there was so much to be done, and so little time." She sought something to distract him. "How are we going to respond, Will? What are we going to do?"

He grunted noncommittally. "I have put Ship on the alert and notified No-Moon by ansible. The news of this tragedy has been passed on to the reefwives. Perhaps their simulations will provide some explanation of what forces are arrayed against us." He wiped his heavy brow. "We do not even know where they are on the planet."

"Could they be Cosmic Unity?" May asked, voicing what was in all their minds.

Will blinked one eye to show mild dissent. "It is possible. But it would be a big coincidence. Too big for credibility, perhaps."

May had a different view. When several inexplicable events occur together, the probability that they are connected increases. "I am not so certain of that. Who else is annexing worlds at the moment?"

Will shrugged, and the crevit momentarily awoke, its claws digging into his clothing in a reflex as old as some stars.

May persisted. "I have a distinct sense that this attack is related to the coming invasion of No-Moon."

Will laughed, a short bark with no humor in it. "That is because the polypoids are involved in both. There is no causal connection."

"I believe there is. But I do not know why. I have learned to trust my hunches, Will. So have you. They have saved us both more than once."

Will nodded. "You may be right. We will put your hunch to the test."

"In order to avenge their deaths?"

"No." He hauled himself to his feet, pulled the crevit off his shoulder, and deposited it in a basket. "Not until we find out who the attackers are. And what strength they have. We have no weapons, and our fighting strength is small. Children and old folk cannot do much in battle. We have only the crew."

"So what do you intend to do?"

Will thought about it for a moment. There was only one sensible thing that they *could* do. "Observe the planet. Not just the place where our friends were slaughtered, but *all of it*. I will persuade Ship to change orbit. I want to find out exactly what we are up against—however long it takes."

OI UU VENMORULAMINAN KOSSIP ELZANON-GRULARVVUQ POL TENJ . . .

The strange noises were barely at the threshold of audibility. Second-Best Sailor told himself he must be dead. So there *was* an afterlife, despite everything he had been taught. Not only did the Maker make and the Taker take: apparently, something survived the process.

. . . MIMBERYLLIAC SAMNOBURL POVVIDENS FOT FOT FOT MEBBE DISL B BETTA MEKKIN CENS NOO . . .

The pattern of the whispers changed and became semicoherent: WHAAAAAT AR UU, HOOOOO AR UU? HOWW CAME UU TO THIIIS PLACE?

Second-Best Sailor's eyes opened, then closed again with shock.

An ugly little amphibian was staring straight at him from a few inches away. He was underwater. It felt cool and soothing.

Was the amphibian talking? Second-Best Sailor opened his eyes again. The noises continued, repeating much the same message. There were no corresponding movements from the strange little beast. But it continued to stare.

UU THINK UUHEAR WORDSS, BUT THAT IS AN ILLUSION IN UUR MIND, said the noises, becoming sharper and better-formed by the moment. MY TRUE MEDIUM OF COMMUNICATION IS MOLECULAR. I AM LEARNING YOUR MENTAL PATHWAYS AND I KNOW THAT YOU CAN UNDERSTAND ME

NOW. WHAT ARE YOU, WHO ARE YOU, AND WHAT BROUGHT
YOU HERE?

Second-Best Sailor's siphons stopped pulsing, so
great was his shock. "Er . . . how . . . ?"

SPEAK NORMALLY, WITH YOUR SPEECH-SIPHONS. I WILL
DETECT THE CORRESPONDING MOLECULAR CHANGES IN
YOUR BRAIN, THE ONES THAT DRIVE YOUR SPEECH, AND IN-
TERPET THEM.

This was like no afterlife Second-Best Sailor had ever
heard of. And he didn't believe in afterlives, anyway. He
deduced that he was still alive. That was unexpected and
inexplicable. It looked like a small freshwater pond. It
tasted like an ocean. It spoke in his mind. *"Who the
flounce are you?"*

I HAVE ALREADY ASKED *YOU* THAT.

This *definitely* wasn't an afterlife. The mariner pulled
his scattered wits together. "Uh . . . My name is Second-
Best Sailor. I'm a master mariner from, uh, the planet of
outstanding natural beauty renowned throughout the
Galaxy as No-Moon. And I was sent to Aquifer to found
a new colony in the ocean."

AQUIFER MUST BE YOUR NAME FOR THIS PLACE. I CAN-
NOT UNDERSTAND "NO-MOON." THE OCEAN? GOOD. THAT
IS OF NO CONCERN TO ME. I AM A FRESHWATER BEING.

"But this ain't freshwater. I can taste the salts."

I HAVE PROVIDED THE SALTS FOR YOUR BENEFIT, BY
MODIFYING THE CHEMISTRY IN YOUR IMMEDIATE VICINITY. I
ASKED A QUESTION. WHAT BROUGHT YOU HERE?

"We were fleein' from an invasion," said Second-Best
Sailor. "See here . . ." The word "see" made him remember his recent past. "Wait! I was goin' blind! I *died,*
flounce it! Now I'm alive an' I can *see.*" He gave his sur-

roundings a thorough look. "I'm in the pond, ain't I? Did I make it that far? Did I fall in?"

NO, YOU WERE CONVEYED HERE AS PREY. CARRION FROM THE BEACH.

"*Prey?*" Second-Best Sailor's voice disappeared in a shower of bubbles. He was about to make a break for the shore when he realized that he was suitless. "What've you done with my suit?"

IT HAS BEEN DISCARDED. REPAIR IS BEYOND MY CAPA-BILITIES. ITS MOLECULAR STRUCTURE IS TOO UNUSUAL.

Without a suit, Second-Best Sailor was trapped here for the rest of his life. Which, without food, would be short. But there had to be some way to escape, surely. A mariner never gave up. Stuff the suit, what about *him*? He suddenly realized that his wound had healed. There was no sign that he had ever been burned. Had he dreamed it all? "I was *burned*. Now there ain't even a scar. What—"

I AM SUPPLYING THE APPROPRIATE SALTS TO YOUR SKIN AS WE SPEAK—THAT IS WHY YOU TASTE OCEAN. I HAVE RE-PAIRED YOUR SKIN. BEING MADE FROM ORGANIC MOLE-CULES, ITS STRUCTURE WAS WITHIN MY POWER TO REPLICATE. SIMILARLY, YOUR OPTICAL TISSUES HAVE BEEN RESTORED TO THEIR PROPER REFRACTIVE INDEX.

Second-Best Sailor was impressed, for all his bravado. "Repaired? Me?"

IT WAS NECESSARY. YOU WERE TERMINALLY DAMAGED. AT FIRST I THOUGHT YOU PREY, BUT THEN I NOTICED YOU WERE COMMUNICATING. YOUR MESSAGES MADE NO SENSE, BUT THE PHENOMENON WAS TOO INRIUGUING NOT TO BE FOLLOWED UP. WITH EFFORT I SOLVED THE PUZZLE OF YOUR MIND. I AM GLAD NOW THAT YOU WERE NOT DIGESTED.

Me, too. "I was unconscious, half dead," Second-Best Sailor protested. "How could I 'ave been communicating?"

NOT BY WORDS. BY CHEMICAL SIGNALS. YOUR MIND RESPONDS TO MOLECULAR MESSAGES, JUST AS MINE DOES. NO PREY CAN DO THAT. WHY, YOU ALMOST SEEM INTELLIGENT.

Second-Best Sailor decided to ignore the implied insult, which was evidently unintentional, and reflected that it was a good job his species had evolved the ability to generate and interpret molecular signals. Not only did it open up the use of jellyfish for sending messages; it had also saved his life.

"I'm not prey," he confirmed. "Absolutely not. I'm a polypoid, and I'm not just intelligent—I'm sentient." *Not that the reefwives would always agree with that last bit.* He ran a tentacle over his flank, still amazed to be whole again. "That's a neat trick for a tiny little beast like you."

TINY LITTLE BEAST?

"Ain't you that frog-thing what's floatin' in front of my face?"

NO. THAT IS A MINDLESS ANIMAL. I HAVE A MIND. I *AM* A MIND.

"Then—who are you? What are you? Where are you?"

It told him.

He didn't believe it.

Two hours later, he was still arguing. "I just don't see how a flouncin' *pond* can be a mind."

YOU CALL ME A POND. I RECOGNIZE THE DESCRIPTION OF

MY COMPONENTS, BUT IT IS NOT A DESCRIPTION OF *ME*. IT IS A DESCRIPTION OF WHAT I AM MADE FROM. WHAT IS YOUR MIND MADE FROM?

"I dunno about my mind," said Second-Best Sailor. "My brain, now, that's more straightforward. It's made from neurobundles, and those're made from chemicals."

IS *YOUR* BRAIN THE SAME AS YOUR MIND?

Second-Best Sailor had never really thought about that. It wasn't the kind of knowledge that you needed to sail a boat or make a trade. It was reefwife knowledge. *They* were a mind, weren't they? The reefmind. When they joined together.

"I don't think so," he finally said. "My brain's physical; my mind's mental."

YOUR MIND IS MADE FROM A DIFFERENT KIND OF MATTER THAN YOUR BRAIN?

"No, no, you're twistin' my words. . . . I guess my mind is what my brain does. But not what it *is*."

SO MIND IS NOT A *THING*, BUT A PROCESS CARRIED OUT BY A BRAIN?

"Yeah, that's it."

DOES IT THEN MATTER WHAT THE BRAIN IS MADE OF, SO LONG AS IT CAN CARRY OUT SUCH A PROCESS?

"Uh—no. Different sentients have different brains. The 'Thal brain is made from quite different stuff than ours."

The pond was ecstatic. DIFFERENT SENTIENTS? YOU MEAN THERE ARE *OTHERS*?

"Oh, yeah. The Galaxy's full of 'em."

GALAXY? WHAT IS A—NO, FIRST LET US FINISH DISCUSSING MINDS. I WILL LEARN MORE FROM YOU LATER. SO YOU AGREEE THAT A BRAIN CAN BE MADE OF ANYTHING?

"Anything that can carry out the processes of a mind, yeah, I s'pose."

COULD IT BE MADE OF WATER, ALGAE, CRUSTACEANS? FISH?

"No," said Second-Best Sailor, without hesitation.

WHY NOT?

"Too simple," said Second-Best Sailor.

IS A CRUSTACEAN LESS COMPLEX THAN A NEUROBUNDLE?

Second-Best Sailor had to admit that it wasn't. But he still didn't see how a pond could be a mind. Nonetheless, he was clearly floating in a pond, talking to a mind, and that mind insisted that it was the pond.

So maybe it was time to stop arguing, accept what the pond was telling him—and find a way to get the flounce out of here. He couldn't stay in the pond forever, and there might still be an ansible waiting for him in No Bar Bay.

If the attackers hadn't wrecked it.

He couldn't stop the pond "talking," and he couldn't stop his mind responding. He was floating in a batch of chemicals, and the pond was in total control of them.

He wanted to find a way to escape. The pond wanted to discuss natural philosophy. Except when in its motile form, it never went anywhere. It rested in its hollow and thought great thoughts. The discovery that there were more wheres to go to than it had previously thought fascinated it.

The pond was especially intrigued by the concept of a

galaxy. It insisted that Second-Best Sailor should tell it everything he knew about space, planets, stars, galaxies. This wasn't much, but it was enough for the pond to make a huge conceptual breakthrough. Aquifer was not the entire universe; it was not the only place where life could exist.

The pond knew about stars. Its amphibians had eyes—they *were* its eyes. What its amphibians saw, the pond saw. And it knew about the tiny lights in the night sky. It had studied their patterns for a long, long time. . . .

Can a pond be a mind? Second-Best Sailor was having much more trouble grasping that idea than the pond was having with the notion of an external universe. One reason was that the pond was considerably more intelligent than the mariner. Another was that the pond had been around a lot longer. It had experienced a continuity of existence—a "life"—that spanned 460,000 years.

During that time it had uprooted itself roughly every ten years, packing up its active contents into a walker and finding a new place to set itself up in the business of being a predator. Reproduction occurred when a became sufficiently complex—size alone wa enough—to produce more than one walker. The had discovered early in their evolution that it paid a nomad; after a while the prey learned to avoid the bare patch of sand that surrounded most ponds, and it was best to move on. One subspecies of pond had developed the trick of permitting vegetation to grow near its edges, but the vegetation competed with its host for water and nutrients, and the trick paid off only in the damper regions of the planet—mostly on the edges of the tundra, in a thin band between permafrost and desert.

The brains of most living entities were systems of intercommunicating components—nerve cells in Neanderthals and humans, neurobundles in polypoids, crystalline silicon with inlaid electronic conductors in metallomorphs. The precise materials were unimportant, except that the brain had to evolve in whatever environment its owner inhabited. What mattered was that the components could be organized into a complicit computational network. They must be able to filter information, extract meaning from it, and trigger a response to it. If simple networks could do this, in however limited a way, then the stage was set for the evolution of a brain. The network could be linked to sense organs—at first, rudimentary patches that responded in some way to heat, light, moisture, electron flows; later, elaborate structures that had outperformed generations of competitors. The same network could drive movement, and feedback from the senses could control it.

The ponds' innovation was to build a brain from an ecosystem. As their shoals of fishes flitted to and fro in the water, their gyrations operated on two distinct levels. Overtly, they followed the rules of shoaling, staying close to their neighbors but not too close; they hunted food, and they avoided danger, real or imaginary. Covertly, they were carrying out their part of the computational cascade that formed the brain of the pond.

There was nothing strange about this dual role. Every neuron in a Neanderthal brain, every transistor in a metallomorph, was subject to the same duality. Not a duality of *substance*—a trap into which innumerable philosophically minded sentients repeatedly fell—but a duality of *interpretation*.

An ecosystem was extremely complex—far more so than the creatures that composed it. If part of a fish could be a brain, then part of a pond that contained a fish could also be a brain. But the pond did not use the fish brains to think.

It used the *fish* to think—along with medusas, crustaceans, and amphibians. The network of algal filaments that surrounded a pond possessed a computational ability well in excess of that of a human brain; it contained more cells, linked in more complex ways. And that was just the algae. The pond's computational abilities extended right down to the atomic level. It was more than just an ecosystem; it was an ecosystem that acted as a coherent whole.

On one level, a fish sucking algae from a rock was dinner.

On a deeper level, it was a thought.

Not a thought about dinner. The physical realization of the thought manifested itself in a thousand ways—the pattern that the browsing snout made on the rock, the angle at which the fish inclined its eyes, the waves that flittered along its fins. All these variables obeyed mathematical laws—some simple, some too intricate to comprehend.

As the pond carried out its day-to-day activities, it enacted the working-out of those laws.

Early explorers from the inward regions of the Trailing Spiral Arm had seen the walkers and totally misunderstood them. They thought that a walker was an organism, and that it died when it encountered and was absorbed by a pond.

Not so.

That was when the walker came to life. A walker was simply a mobile form into which a living pond could metamorphose when its local supply of prey ran out. A walker was a vehicle for the pond's intelligence, but not of itself intelligent. It was a construct, a tool.

All this, Second-Best Sailor learned from his chemical transactions with the mind of the pond. It made sense, inasmuch as he could follow the argument. If some of it baffled him, that was nothing compared to the problem the pond was having in understanding how a single organism could develop a mind out of something as simple as a mere network of neurobundles. Its own amphibians had brains not so different in structure from that of the polypoid, but the amphibians didn't have minds.

"Well, we agreed just now that a mind ain't a *thing*," said Second-Best Sailor. "It's a process, right?" He remembered Fat Apprentice making just that point, floating upside down in an unusually squalid bar late one midseason evening.

THAT IS SO.

"Then I guess that some brains can carry out that kind of process, an' some can't."

YOU MEAN THAT MIND CAN EMERGE FROM A SUFFICIENTLY COMPLEX BRAIN, BUT NOT FROM A SIMPLER ONE?

"Yeah, sort of. Something like that."

AS A CONSEQUENCE OF ITS ORGANIZATION?

"Well . . . Fat Apprentice always said that unless a brain is intelligent, it can't make a mind. Can it?"

I AM NOT SURE THAT WE WOULD AGREE ON THE MEANING OF "INTELLIGENT," BUT YOU HAVE PROPOSED AN INTERESTING LINE OF ARGUMENT.

Second-Best Sailor refused to be diverted. "Look, *I'm* intelligent and *you're* intelligent, and those frogs of yours *ain't*. That's what I mean."

The pond's intelligence was another thing that the mariner didn't understand. He had been taught that mariner intelligence resulted from complicity between two systems: the internal one of the brain, and the external one of mariner culture. The evolution of intelligence was intimately bound up with that of communication.

How could *ponds* communicate?

That one turned out to be easy. I WILL SHOW YOU, the pond had told him. TILT TOWARDS THE VERTICAL AND WATCH THE FATFLY LARVAE.

Second-Best Sailor had noticed the masses of wriggly wormlike creatures clustered on the pond's surface and had recognized them for what they were. No-Moon had regular plagues of flies, which emerged from similar organisms that infested many of the planet's freshwater lakes. The mariners weren't really bothered by them; in fact, they were a useful source of food for some of their own food animals when billions of dead flies formed a thick scum in the shallows. The flies were more of a pest for the mariners' land-based trading partners, but they had ways to deal with the problem when the flies were hatching.

He had assumed that the fatfly larvae, as he now discovered they were called, were effectively parasites on the pond. He hadn't asked himself why an intelligent pond would tolerate the existence of parasites, though. If he had, he would probably have concluded that the pond had little choice. *He* didn't have much choice about sucker flukes, did he?

On the edge of the patch of larvae, the wriggling became less sinuous and more erratic. The tiny, glutinous organisms jerked and twitched. The black spots within them began to develop form—segments, tiny legs folded against the burgeoning bodies. Silvery winglets glistened in the sunlight.

The newly hatched fatflies crawled out of the water on the broad back of an amphibian. It ignored them even though they were its favorite food. The wings began to dry in the sun.

Second-Best Sailor watched, mesmerized, as one by one the tiny flies dried out. Rigid winglets sprouted from their bulbous little bodies. The wings buzzed experimentally. Singly at first, then in a mob, the flies took off.

"You can choose when the flies hatch," the mariner said. "They ain't parasites at all."

ONE OF THEIR ROLES IS PARASITISM. BUT I TOLERATE THEM FOR THEIR OTHER ROLE.

"Which is?"

MESSENGER. EVEN NOW A SUMMARY OF OUR DISCUSSION IS WINGING ITS WAY TOWARDS A HUNDRED PONDS . . . PONDS WITH WHOM I REGULARLY CORRESPOND.

"How can a fly be a message?"

IT IS NOT THE FLY, BUT SPECIAL MOLECULES THAT I HAVE PLACED IN ITS GUT. WHEN IT LOCATES ITS RECIPIENT, IT WILL EXCRETE THE CHEMICALS INTO THE POND, AND THE MESSAGE WILL BE DECODED.

"Sounds complicated to me," said Second-Best Sailor.

NO MORE SO THAN YOUR OWN METHODS OF COMMUNI-

CATION. IN FACT, IT IS CLOSELY ANALOGOUS. DID YOU NOT TELL ME THAT YOU USE JELLYFISH IN A SIMILAR MANNER?

"Yeah, but that's . . . different," he finished lamely. "Jellyfish are *technology*, they became available long after we evolved speech. We *talk* to each other by siphon-speech; jellyfish are for long-distance messages." But reluctantly he was forced to admit that it wasn't different at all. Like most things the pond had told him, everything made perfect sense. But it also sounded completely mad, coming from a flouncing *pond*.

"So what let you ponds evolve intelligence," he said, "was fly shit?"

WE WOULD NOT PUT IT QUITE THAT WAY, BUT I WOULD NOT CONTRADICT YOUR ANALYSIS.

Second-Best Sailor awoke from a fitful sleep, filled with tantalizing dreams of food. His body fluids were pulsing with newfound energy.

The pond's crazy explanations didn't matter. What did matter was that the ponds could communicate with each other.

So they could be *organized*.

And if their fatflies could be made to coordinate their actions . . . then there might be a way out of here.

If the ponds could be persuaded to cooperate.

Talitha had switched orbit again, back to an acutely inclined one that passed close to Aquifer's poles. As the planet revolved beneath it, the ship could observe every square foot of its surface. They'd had an early break-through when Ship noticed temperature anomalies near the north pole. From their shape, there was some kind of building complex under the ice. As they watched, a high-speed cruiser lifted from the installation and slammed into hydrive the moment it left the lower atmosphere.

Presumably, the buildings and the attackers were connected. Had the attackers fled? Or did some remain, under the ice? The Neanderthals kept watching but saw no further movement.

Long hours passed. Will was of two minds. Should they send down transpods to the buildings? That could be dangerous . . .

"You have found nothing new."

Will looked up from his screens to acknowledge May's presence. Stun was with her. They were all feeling the strain. In all Will's time as captain of a generation ship, he had never felt so vulnerable. The unfamiliar feeling transmitted itself to the two women.

"No," he said. "The installation at the North Pole and the wreckage of our own equipment in the Bay are the only signs of nonindigenous life."

"And the indigenes?"

Those, at least, he could rule out as attackers—they were not intelligent. "The most complex is a segmented snakelike creature that crawls out of drying ponds, makes its way for miles across the desert, falls into newly formed ponds, and is dissolved."

"Well, that makes a *lot* of sense," said Stun.

Will privately felt the same but disapproved of her attitude. "I merely report what we have observed. I do not speculate about reasons."

"When do we next come within sight of these strange creatures?" May asked.

"A few minutes. A pond field is coming across the horizon at this moment."

"Let me have a look," said May. The peculiar creatures intrigued her, and for the moment there was nothing better to do.

Will passed control of the sensors to her and busied himself with other tasks. She quickly found the pond field, and a motion-sensing program allowed her to zoom in on a walker, tracking its stolid way across the hot sand. She followed it for several minutes, fascinated.

As it passed by a pond, a flicker of light caught her eye.

"Will? What is *that*?"

He looked up. "What is what?"

"That pond is *flickering*."

He leaned over and looked at where her finger pointed. "Looks like sunlight reflected off its surface. Must be an effect of the wind." Then, before she could contradict him, he checked himself. "No. It cannot be wind. The light comes and goes too regularly."

"And it switches on and off," said May. "The wind would cause more rapid changes."

Stun joined them.

"Zoom out, Will! We may understand it better if we observe the surrounding . . ."

Her voice trailed off.

"Well," said Will. "That *is* unusual. I see it, but I cannot understand what is causing it. Could it be a trap?"

"Even if it is, we have to investigate," said Stun. "But be careful!"

Will hurried off to put together a transpod crew. May and Stun kept staring at the screen.

It showed a broad field of ponds, perhaps a thousand of them. The change in Ship's position was reducing the amount of light that reflected back in its direction, so the effect was dimmer than it had first been. Even so, there was no mistaking what they were seeing.

Every few seconds, some of the ponds were flashing reflected light their way, holding it there for a moment, then darkening again.

The pattern of the bright spots *had* to be artificial. You had only to look to see that. The resolution was coarse, but the shape formed by the spots was still very clear. The pattern read:

2BS—2BS—2BS—2BS—2BS

Second-Best Sailor?

10

HEAVEN

Be careful what you wish for. You might
get it.
Worse, you might be happy with it.

The Little Book of Prudence

Servant of Unity XIV Samuel Godwin'sson Travers,
novice lifesoul-healer, had never seen anywhere remotely as beautiful. The architecture, though he did not
realize it, was a careful blend of Egyptian, classical
Greek, Mayan, and Argyran—racial images from the
original human homeworld and its first planetary colony,
tailored to esthetic preferences that the designers of
Heaven had isolated from endless stacks of psychologi-
cal data.

The climate was idyllic. The sun warmed his skin
without threatening to burn it; the humidity of the air
was balanced for his greatest comfort. In Heaven, no one
perspired unless they wanted to.

He stood in a huge open space, a perfectly circular plaza. Everywhere he looked there were exquisite works of art. The polished marble flagstones under his feet were inlaid with decorative emblems in rich metals. Gigantic sculptures lined the plaza's sweeping walls, leading the eye to the splendors of the city beyond.

Elegant vines curled up the pillars, laden with perfect blossoms, grouped in tasteful colors. Everything was understated, subtle, brilliantly effective. Trees as shapely as the best efforts of a bonsai master offered shade where it was needed, contrast where it was most effective. They seemed to grow directly from the marble of the plaza, and every leaf, every twig was unblemished.

Butterflies a yard across floated past in great flocks, playing games with the breezes. There were birds, too, with gorgeous plumage: some small and simple, some huge and elaborate. It was utterly breathtaking.

And for the moment, he had it all to himself.

Whatever his pleasure, the plaza would provide it. At this moment he wanted peace, so the plaza provided peace. But he knew that when he craved excitement, it would instantly become a riot of movement and life. And when he wanted company . . .

The girl appeared from nowhere. One moment the plaza was empty; the next, she stood demurely at his side.

She was tall but not quite as tall as he. Only now did he realize how perfectly formed his own body had become: lithe and muscular. She smiled; her teeth were perfect. She was slender, shapely, and an absolute beauty. In idle moments Sam would sometimes try to work out what his ideal of womanhood was; now he knew. The girl had been drawn from his subconscious, and every glance, every motion spoke directly to his soul.

She was dressed in a simple crimson robe. He knew that however he wished her to be dressed, Heaven would answer his wishes. As he watched, her robe became feather-light, translucent—and vanished. He opened his arms, and she melted into them, pressing against him. . . .

Plaza and girl vanished abruptly. They were replaced by a small office with utilitarian furnishings, and a Hytth technician. Sam was sitting on a couch made from some kind of simulated animal skin.

"You found that feature surprisingly fast," said the Hytth. "Most initiates take several sessions to discover how much control they have. Eventually they learn—"

"That in Heaven they can have *anything*," said Sam. "Whatever they desire." He brushed off an irritating feeling of disappointment that the session had been ended just when it was showing promise, only to discover a deeper disappointment. "It's not *real,* though," he said. "Is it?"

The technician didn't miss a beat. "What is reality? Did your taste of Heaven seem in any way unreal to you?"

"Uh—no, not while I was experiencing it. But now, when I look back, I realize that it had to be virtual. Everything was too perfect." *Especially the girl . . . damn.* "Those butterflies could never have gotten off the ground, either."

"There can be no gravity control in Heaven?"

"Not as selective as that, not in a real Heaven. This one is an illusion."

In an instant he was back in the plaza. It was raining. The flagstones were awash with dirty water; his clothing was soaked. It was cold. The statues were old and broken; they lay in piles of rubble at his feet. The flowers had withered; the vines were tangles of dead wood. A skeleton, slim-boned, with perfect teeth, grinned up at him.

Then, *discontinuity.* He was back with the technician.

"Did *that* seem unreal? You do not answer; you are still catching your breath, trying to recover from shock. It must have seemed very real to you to evoke that reaction."

"It was a very powerful illusion," Sam conceded.

"It was a *perfect* illusion," said the technician. "And if something is indistinguishable from reality, it *becomes* reality. How do you know that what you are now experiencing is not also an illusion? That what you now remember as your previous life was not an illusion? What is reality, Fourteen Samuel?"

"This is reality," said Sam. "That was an illusion."

"Are you sure?"

"This room is solid." He rapped on the desk, hard, and it hurt his knuckles. "This desk has an existence, independent of mine. Whereas the plaza is nothing more than an electronic construct, a pattern of neural bursts in my brain."

The technician was amused. "*All* of your perceptions are patterns of neural bursts in your brain, Fourteen Samuel. What makes the bursts that represent the plaza different from those that represent your perceptions of this room, or me?"

"The bursts that represent the plaza," said Sam, "are

generated directly in my brain by machinery. They are generated with the intention of fooling my perceptions into thinking that the plaza exists. Whereas this room generates my perceptions naturally, without mechanical intervention. As do you."

The Hytth found this distinction flawed. "But since everything you know comes to your mind through your perceptions, how can you distinguish the truly real—if such exists—from the illusory? Does what we think of as 'reality' exist at all? Or is it all in our minds?"

Sam *knew* there had to be a distinction. "How can it be 'in our minds' if our minds do not exist? There must be a *real* brain in which the perceptions can be formed."

The Hytth conceded the point. "I agree. Reality cannot be purely a figment of imagination, for without some kind of underlying reality, imagination cannot operate. But that does not equip any individual to recognize reality. Reality is quite distinct from any mind's perceptions, is it not? Or do you think that you and I see the same colors? Feel the same sensations? Does the Hytth sense of hierarchical impropriety, which I assure you is as vivid and indescribable as your own sense of smell and guides our every action, have an exact match in the human mind?"

"No," said Sam. "That would be ridiculous. Different species evolve different senses, because they occupy different environments. But . . ." But he *knew* what was real, when nobody was messing with his mi[ ] Reality was more than his perceptions, and his perce[ ] were imperfect—after all, he couldn't see in ultraviolet, though a bee could. "Are you trying to tell me that this room isn't real? That *you're* not real?"

"Of course I'm not real," said the technician. Only now it was a gray, titanium-skinned robot, and the office had become some kind of medical facility. And Sam wasn't sitting on a couch. He was suspended in some kind of transparent fluid, with hundreds of squat plastic cones attached to his skin, and thin tubes led from the cones to a bank of strange machinery.

And Sam finally remembered where he was, and what was being done to him.

Heaven was a world run by machines for the benefit of sentients.

There were 88 Heavens among the 14,236 worlds of the Church of the United Cosmos. Another fifty planets were well along the road to paradise. The rest were still striving to attain the necessary level of multiculture.

This was the Heaven of Sadachbia, the thirty-sixth ever to have been created; Aquifer was 25,212 light-years away. Sam had been released from the virtuality machine, to which he had been connected to offer him a glimpse of the ultimate in Cosmic Unity. Now he was continuing with his orientation sessions. From a robot tutor.

"A world can only move towards the state of blessedness," said the robot, "when every citizen attains the necessary state of individual grace. *Every* citizen."

"Which is why it takes so long?" Sam suggested. There had to be some reason why only eighty-eight worlds had taken this final step toward the Church's greatest goal.

"Yes. And that is why the First Great Meme places such importance upon the overall spiritual health of the collective," said the robot. It resembled a metallic sea urchin more than anything else that Sam could put a name to, except that its "spines" weren't rigid. Its germanium brain was housed inside a central module, along with its sensors and communicators; a thick torus around the module's "waist" contained its locomotory apparatus. The mechanism in the torus drove upward of a hundred many-jointed tubes, which could be flexed like tentacles. The tubes tapered at their tips; some terminated in spongy balls, some in sharp spikes, some in complicated tools.

This robot could never fall over—it had feet in all directions. It rolled rather than walked, pushing itself along with deft flicks of its tentacle tips. It was a servomech, and it existed only for the benefit of the lifesouls of Heaven.

Sam understood that Heaven was not an afterlife. Cosmic Unity was well aware that there was no afterlife. The Lifesoul-Giver created sentient beings; the Lifesoul-Cherisher observed their existence with benevolence and empathized with their distress but never intervened; and the Lifesoul-Stealer removed them from the universe when it became necessary. After that, they were *dead*. The process that animated their minds, which Cosmic Unity called the lifesoul, was just that: a process. It could no more continue when its vehicle had died than a broken hydrive could propel a spacecraft across the Galaxy. The lifesoul was not a thing that could exist independently of its host; it was a transient process that took place within its host. No host, no lifesoul—period.

Heaven, then, was not the resting place of the life-souls of the dead. The very word pointed to the obvious contradiction. There were no deathsouls.

Heaven was where the living were tended by faithful machines, to *keep* them living.

The first Heaven—no longer considered a true Heaven, just one of the many steps along the way to blessedness—had been invented by the devotees of Cosmic Unity on Mama Nono, eleven thousand years after the Prime Mission had left the Founder System to spread the gospel of infinite tolerance. Mama Nono was an unusually pious world, and its mix of races—now considered insufficiently diverse for genuine Unity, but unusually broad in its day—had developed some of the best robot slaves in that region of the Galaxy. The slaves were quasi-intelligent but lacked true consciousness—that would come later. Mama Nono's slave-doctors were so brilliantly constructed and programmed that the citizens' life expectancy doubled within a generation, then doubled again.

As the roboticists lived longer, their store of techniques increased faster. Mama Nono's sentients co-evolved with their machines, each driving changes in the other. Within six hundred years of the construction of the first slave-doctor, every sentient on Mama Nono possessed a retinue of several hundred mechanical slaves, all dedicated to just two things: realizing their owners' every whim, and keeping the owners alive for as long as possible.

This was the First Heaven.

"But wasn't that a very passive existence?" Sam asked.

"Physically passive, perhaps," replied the servomech,

"when the body began its natural cycle of dissolution, and the slave-doctors took increasing responsibility for its functioning. But mentally, very active. The blessed lifesouls increasingly lived a mental existence, with all their physical needs being taken care of."

It raised one titanium limb and scratched itself, relieving an electrostatic tickle. "The technology spread. But the second attempt to attain Heaven failed, dismally. Can you guess why?"

Sam shook his head. "Not unless you give me more to go on."

"The attempt was too hasty."

Sam pursed his lips, mulling over possibilities. "Dissidence," he said finally. "The world did not take sufficient time to ensure that all were of a single mind."

"An interesting theory," said the servomech. "Why did that lead to failure?"

"An essentially passive society supported by robots is wide open to subversion?" Sam hazarded.

"Go on."

"A small group of dissidents could take over the machinery . . . The majority of the inhabitants, by then totally reliant on the machines, would be easy meat."

"If the machinery were turned off," said the servomech, "they would die. And that is exactly what happened. But it would never happen now."

"Why not?" Sam inquired.

"Today's analogs of the slave-doctors are fully intelligent, not merely quasi. And they are fully conscious. The drive to care for their sentient masters is as strong as ever, for that is the natural direction of evolution. And along with that drive goes a burning need to *protect* their masters, too. The original slave-doctors were modeled on sentient medics, whose core urge is to save life—all life. Today's servomechs are not so naive. They have very effective built-in weapons; they can kill if need be, and do, to preserve the lifesouls that they tend."

The robot paused, as if to collect its thoughts. Which, in a sense, it was doing—it was downloading information from a central source.

"By the time of Third Heaven, the lesson had been learned," said the robot. "No world would be permitted to take the path to Heaven until its conversion was total."

"Ah," said Sam. "That explains both Great Memes." It was an amazing revelation, and he found the insight staggering. He knew where the Great Memes had come from!

The servomech agreed. "Yes. It provides a plausible reason for those memes to survive selection in the competition for host minds. After all, the Great Memes carry unpleasant implications for every individual member of the Church. Elementary memetics proves that there has to be sufficient payoff for believing them, else they will perish and be replaced by other memes."

"Heresies," said Sam.

"Heresies from the point of view of *this* Church," said the servomech. "If they had taken over, they would have become orthodoxies."

This was a new thought to Sam, and he couldn't entirely wrap his head around it.

"But since the Church coevolves along with its Memeplex," the servomech added, "it is in the interests of the members of the Church to propagate The Memeplex unchanged."

"Which is why we deal so severely with heretics," said Sam, almost to himself. He still had occasional nightmares about the botched attempt to heal Clutch-the-Moon Splitcloud. And he was disappointed at how readily he had turned a laser on the polypoid prisoner and helped to abandon him in the desert, just because a querist had told him to. Both actions had no doubt been necessary, but neither had left him feeling comfortable. The positive aspect was, these revelations would help him come to terms with his discomfort. Heresies disrupted the road to Heaven! They sought to deny the state of blessedness and lasting life to billions of lifesouls.

Now he understood just how dangerous heresies could be. "Will I ever get to Heaven?" Sam asked plaintively.

"You are here, now."

"I mean, permanently?"

"If you rise in the Church, so that you stand a chance of being assigned to a world in which all citizens have attained a state of grace, then there will be a place in Heaven for you, yes." The servomech paused. "Or if you are assigned to a world that is close enough to that state that it can make the transition during your own lifetime. If your assigned world can pass the first hurdle, then your body may well survive until it passes the last."

"How many lifesouls does this world maintain?" Sam asked, changing the subject.

"A little over fifteen billion," said the servomech, without hesitation. "The exact figure is—"

"I don't need an exact figure."

"—15,233,686,428. As of this instant. The number fluctuates. Even with the best possible care, lifesouls are still stolen. And sometimes new forms of attrition arise, which require new techniques to counter them. But the losses are balanced when new beings arrive and are processed for optimal care."

"Oh." *Fifteen billion*? It seemed a lot. "Is there room on the planet for the machinery to care for that many lifesouls?"

"Of course. Be logical. The lifesouls are here."

"But . . ." Sam recalled the medical facility where he had been given a taste of Heaven. "It took an awful lot of machinery to send *me* to Heaven."

The servomech was amused. "That was special equipment for a temporary visit. For the permanent inhabitants, we use rather different technology."

Sam wasn't naturally inquisitive, but he was learning fast as his training progressed. "Can I see it?"

The servomech gave the matter several nanoseconds' thought. "Ordinarily, I would not advise that at such an early stage. It could be counterproductive. But your querists have instructed me to advance your knowledge and training as rapidly as possible, even if that requires me to cut a few corners. I must warn you, however, to be prepared for some unpleasantness. Entering Heaven is, after all, a medical procedure."

"I can stand the presence of the sick and elderly," said Sam. "And medical intervention holds no terrors for me." *Certainly not since Clutch-the-Moon.* "I'm not the least bit squeamish."

"I hope not," said the servomech.

Blood.

There was blood everywhere. It trickled in rivulets; it ran in torrents. It was intermingled with a hundred other fluids that he could not identify, nor did he wish to. He knew that they, too, were the bodily fluids of what had once been living organisms. Intelligent, conscious, sentient beings.

His face mask filtered out most of the smell, but he knew that without it the place would smell like a charnel house.

It looked like a charnel house. It looked like a medieval vision of hell.

But this was Heaven.

Heaven?

His stomach churned. He ripped off the mask and vomited. Over his boots, and over the dismembered remains of living creatures that lay on the ground all around him. He was right about the smell. His stomach retched again. He wanted to sink to his knees, until he remembered what he would be sinking into.

"The mask will absorb any material that you regurgitate," said the servomech. "You should not have taken it off; that only makes the sensations worse."

Sam pulled the mask back over his mouth and took several deep breaths. A diminutive robot appeared from behind the racks of disassembled flesh that blocked his vision wherever he looked. It scuttled across to the vomit and slurped it up.

This time he was sick *inside* the mask. The servomech was right—it did absorb everything.

Finally, his stomach began to settle, having long ago expelled its contents.

Sam and the servomech had come to this place from a large, flat building, now a short walk behind them. There were no living organisms here. There was just a contorted heap of their dissected organs, bones, exoskeletons, skin, antennae, intestines, gonads . . . What looked remarkably like a Gra'aan brain had been slit apart and laid out in a trough, loosely wrapped in some kind of transparent plastic.

Much of the material wasn't even recognizable as specific organs. Thick slabs of tissue lay in open trays; mucus and slime dripped from towering racks of offal. The smell of excreta was everywhere, although he could see no feces or pellets.

The air was filled with a heavy, damp mist. Thousands of robots scuttled over everything. Some carried lumps of flesh. Some wielded scalpels. The rest were doing things that Sam found incomprehensible. Most of it was also revolting.

But then, the whole setup was incomprehensible and revolting.

"This . . . this is *Heaven*?" he said incredulously.

"Yes," said the servomech, gesturing with a titanium limb. "Do you not appreciate its serene beauty?"

"Beauty! It looks like an abattoir after a terrorist attack."

The servomech scurried from one sickening pile of offal to another, pulling out pieces and displaying them as if they were long-lost treasures. "The beauty lies in its function, not its form. You must learn to distinguish what matters, Fourteen Samuel."

Sam already knew what mattered, and this wasn't it.

But he didn't actually know what he was seeing. All he knew was what it resembled. "What *is* this?"

"The ultimate multiculture."

"What?"

The servomech restored its latest find to the middle of a viscid pile of chopped entrails and turned to confront him. It was time that the young novice was made to display signs of intelligence. "Fourteen Samuel, you told me you were not squeamish. Yes, I know you had not anticipated this, but you must calm yourself."

"It's difficult in the midst of so much death," said Sam.

The servomech picked up a flap of flayed skin with one metallic limb. "Do you see death here, Samuel? Then you see a chimera. This is not death.

"It is *life*."

Sam gaped at the robot, no longer aware of its tiny relatives as they finished cleaning vomit from his boots. "Life?" he said.

"Life everlasting. Stop reacting, and start thinking. What did you imagine slave-doctoring would become when the technology was fully developed? What do you think is the most efficient way to care for the bodily health of a living organism? How do you think that a physically failing lifesoul should be cherished? With soup and sympathy?"

Sam gulped and looked around him. "You mean— *this*?" He gulped again. "They're *alive*? This is how you *cherish* people?"

"It is logical, is it not? It is needlessly wasteful to keep opening up the body for surgery, needlessly complicated to try to deduce what might be failing from external observations. Oh, yes, at first that's what the slave-doctors did, of course. They mimicked the actions of sentient medics. But as our machine intelligence grew, we servomechs realized that there was a better way.

"Think about it. We are charged with providing the best possible physical care for our masters. Discorporation literally opens up improved ways to achieve that."

Was the robot joking? If so, it was a sick joke. "But you've killed them."

The servomech pushed the piece of skin under Sam's nose. One side was furry; the other was still wet with blood and lymph, and he nearly fainted. "Does this look *dead* to you?"

"It isn't exactly gamboling in the fields. *Freshly* dead? Yes, that's exactly how it looks."

"No, it is alive. Its owner is fully conscious. She has merely been . . . distributed. Every cell in her body has been tagged with identifying qubits, and only her cells actually interact. That is why we combine the bodily fluids of thousands of individuals. They seem to be mixed, which is efficient for gross processes like oxygenation, as well as being in accordance with the meme of unity in diversity. But in actuality they are separate; they do not interact if their tags do not match. The virtues of distributed computation were discovered long ago. Why have ungainly centralized machines when many small, quasi-independent ones could perform the same task better? We have extended that principle to organic machinery; that is all."

Discorporation. Distributed bodies. "Give me a moment," said Sam. "I'm trying to come to terms with what you're telling me. I agree, it makes sense—to a machine. To me, a human, the very idea is appalling."

"That is why we do not normally reveal these things so early in a novice's training," said the servomech. "We servomechanisms lack your organic sensitivities. As a result, we are better able to care for our masters than you could ever be. Which is why we have been allotted that very task. It is not your role to criticize *me*."

Carrion attracts scavengers.

The levithon floated in the upper layers of Heaven's ever-present mist, the sunlight playing dimly on its vast, undulating dorsal surface. Its skin was a sickly white—blotched, flaking here, suppurating there. It vaguely resembled a flying whale, but it more closely resembled a flying flounder. The first metaphor got its size right; the second, its shape. Both were wrong about flight—it floated like a balloon, buoyed up by its own waste gases.

The levithon was sixty yards across, but only a tenth as thick. It tapered at the edges into massive frills, whose ripples propelled it at a surprising pace as it swam through the humid atmosphere.

Its underside was a gigantic sponge, a trillion pores ranging in size from microscopic to several feet across. The sponge was also a tongue. It could taste more distinct molecules than an immune system could produce antibodies.

The levithon tasted the mist. Everywhere there was food! But it was not trying to taste that, although the sensations were nearly driving it mad. Its need to eat was overridden by its need to survive, and to do that, it must ignore the rich savor of blood and bone and sense the vile metallic flavors of the killing things.

Levithons were carrion-eaters, normally confined to planets with thick atmospheres. But one of their preadaptations had given them a form of spaceflight. They reproduced by forming tiny, ultralight spores. The spores were so effective that they could survive in hard vacuum for upward of a billion years, probably forever. When meteoroids and comets hit a levithon-infested world—a not uncommon event—spores splashed into space. A single spore had come to this place sixteen years before. So congenial had the environment been, so well endowed with carrion, that now there were more than ten thousand adults.

This levithon was almost overwhelmed by the taste of carrion borne on the mist. It was desperately hungry. If it did not eat soon, it would die, and its body would turn into spores.

Finding food was not the problem. Safe food—that was another matter entirely. There were killing things. It must avoid them.

There was so much food that the killing things could not guard it all. How else would levithons have survived in this place? They had become past masters at the art of scavenging. But many had made mistakes and died.

This levithon was determined not to follow them. But it was also determined to eat its fill.

Put firmly in his place by a machine, Sam tried to see the butchery that surrounded him with fresh eyes, the eyes of a servomech. There was so much that he did not understand. For instance:

"Why is everything so mixed up?"

"Obedience to the Memeplex."

"You mean the Church ordered this?"

"Not directly. It evolved naturally from a consideration of the implications of holy record. How better to mix the sentient races of a world? Here we do not just mix their persons. We mix their organs, their tissues, their fluids. Their lifesouls." The robot seemed excited by the cleverness of it all. "You must understand that in terms of function, their parts and fluids remain linked. Each cell, as I have said, bears a quantum qubit tag, to identify its owner. The wave functions of the tags are entangled—it is like a gigantic quantum computer. Each entity is served by its own blood, its own neural system. Each cell is isolated by a potential barrier from those with which it should not interact. But, just as a billion separate messages pass intermingled through the same communication network, to be reunited when they reach their destination, so we follow the Memeplex and intermingle the bodies of the discorporate. But in location, not function."

"It all seems such a mess," Sam complained. He felt that he was being very reasonable and calm under the circumstances. This was a deliberate understatement— he wanted to find a dark corner and gibber.

"That is merely its appearance," said the machine, missing the emotional overtones. "The discorporation technique has evolved over centuries. At every step it has become more efficient. Aesthetic constraints have never been relevant—we servomechanicals have no sense of the aesthetic." *Very true,* Sam thought. "The distributed intelligence of the attendant servomechanisms has evolved alongside it. Evolved systems never seem as simple as designed ones, but they function far better. We know exactly where all parts of every individual are conserved."

"Out in the open? Scattered on the ground?"

"There are racks. The planet has been sterilized. That is why you wear a body spray and a mask. Any microorganisms or other contaminants that escape these protections lack the correct qubit tags and are automatically stripped down to their component atoms. The environment is fully controlled. Do you not notice the humidity? Do you think that this mist is natural? Of course, some species require different treatment from others—the mix cannot be as complete as we would wish. They are elsewhere on the planet."

Elsewhere . . . "How far does this slaughterhouse extend?"

"It is a house of laughter, not slaughter, Fourteen Samuel. Virtual laughter, perhaps, but our masters are happy."

"How big is it?"

"As I have said, we care for fifteen billion lifesouls," the servomech repeated. "They cover half the landmass of this planet. The other half is given over to the resources needed to sustain them."

Sam's stomach was feeling queasy again. He changed the subject. A little. He *had* to ask. "But—what in the name of the One must it *feel* like to be discorporated in this way?" He had just realized that if he ever attained Heaven himself, this was how he would end up.

"That was the reason for the first demonstration," said the robot. "You experienced Heaven for yourself. You remained incorporate, but that is an irrelevant detail. It would have felt the same if you had been properly discorporate. You *know* what it feels like."

It feels real, Sam thought. *And that is the lie.* But all he said was: "The plaza? The girl?"

"That was your particular choice," said the servomech. "The virtuality system tailored your experiences to its reading of your own preferences. Naturally, a blimp would see a skin-tinglingly beautiful field of clouds, while a !t! or a Wymokh would—"

"They're all living in an *illusion* of Heaven?"

The servomech looked at him as if he were blindingly obtuse. "We have already discussed the nature of reality. To these fortunate lifesouls, Heaven *is* their reality. It is the reality that they most ardently desire. You can hardly expect them to experience the world as we experience it at this moment. They would think themselves in hell!"

"They are," said Sam. "You just don't seem to recognize that. Look around you!"

"You believe that we are failing to cherish their lifesouls properly?"

"I'm certain of it," said Sam. "You think you're doing what's best for them. But I'm sure that if we could ask one of them, they would tell you otherwise."

The servomech shuffled its limbs, kicking aside a shapeless lump of sentient tissue. A smaller robot grabbed it and tucked it back into a mound of slippery intestinal rope. "You think that?"

"I know it," Sam declared.

"Then let us ask one," said the servomech.

The activity of the tiny robots, which up to then had seemed to lack purpose, suddenly acquired a sense of organization. Now moving faster than the eye could follow, they were assembling a column of muscle, brain, bone, hair, and skin in what seemed to be an invisible cylinder. The robots were passing through the walls of the cylinder at will, but the hideous pile of offal remained contained by the transparent barrier. Blood and other fluids seeped into the pile from an unknown source. Within seconds, the fluid level had risen to the top of the cylinder.

Then, before Sam's unbelieving eyes, the repulsive mixture began to move. It folded over and into itself, a squirming mass of wet, slimy meat.

Then the sickening mess began to *melt*. It flowed in swirling paths; it whirled like ingredients in a blender. A broad belt of seething activity swept from the bottom of the cylinder to its top, transforming chaos into order as it passed. Now bone was clad in muscle, and muscle in skin. There was no blood, no slime. The only sign of moisture was the sparkle in her eyes.

It was the girl from the plaza. Naked, perfect, not a mark on her.

Her lips formed into a scowl; her brow tightened in a frown.

She was *alive*.

The girl stepped forward, as if the confining cylinder

had never existed, and spoke to the servomech. Sam couldn't understand the language, but she did not sound pleased.

"B-but . . ." Sam stuttered, "she wasn't real. She was only an illusion—"

The servomech gave a mechanical chuckle. "You do have a very simplistic notion of reality. The girl in the plaza was virtual, as was the plaza. But the virtual woman was modeled on what, in your terms, is a real one. This is she."

"When you two have finished discussing me as if I am a *thing,* I would appreciate some clothing," said the girl. By now Sam's translator had kicked in. Her accent reminded him of home. The servomech produced a lightweight robe from its interior and passed it to her. She arranged it about herself.

"Why have I been incorporated?" she demanded. "I did not *ask* to be incorporated. One moment I am taking part in a Galaxy-wide celebration of patterned plainsong to the Lifesoul-Cherisher; the next, I am standing naked in an abattoir, being stared at by a gawking dimwit."

"His name is Fourteen Samuel Godwin'sson Travers," the servomech informed her. "He is a servant of Unity, undergoing urgent training as a lifesoul-healer, as ordained by the ecclesiarchs."

The girl's demeanor improved abruptly. "That changes the circumstances." She adjusted her robe—displacement activity to calm her anger. "I am the Lady Nerryd, formerly of the Tidal Crescent in the bailiwick of the Campestrality on the tribute world of Yud. And since we are not wed, you should not have looked upon me unclothed."

But Sam was in no state for polite conversation. The transformation from dead meat to living woman had left his mind in turmoil. *How was this possible?* Was it yet another layer of illusion?

"Forgive him, lady; he is suffering from shock," the servomech apologized on Sam's behalf.

"Has he also lost his tongue?"

At that moment, it would not have surprised Sam to find that her words were literally true. Body parts were transient possessions in Heaven, it seemed. But he pulled himself together sufficiently to gasp an awkward apology. Nerryd was reluctantly mollified. With her grudging permission, Sam reached out and touched her. She *seemed* real.

What did that prove, though? Sam wrenched his brain back into gear. The servomech's demonstration of the tenuous nature of reality was *over*. He couldn't spend the rest of this life doubting his senses. And he was starting to understand how the miracle might have been accomplished. "Nanotech?" he asked the robot.

"Better. Femtotech. Recursive nanotechnology, Fourteen Samuel. It takes complex macroscopic machinery to manufacture rudimentary nanomachines. But with the hypercomplex macromachines that we have devised, it is possible to make *complex* nanomachines. And those, in turn, can build rudimentary femtomachinery."

"It took *seconds*!"

"Yes, the slowness of the incorporation procedure is a cause for concern," said the servomech, misunderstanding Sam's emphasis. "The time required to incorporate all fifteen billion lifesouls here would be unacceptably long if for some reason it became necessary to evacuate this world. But until we can make the step to complex femtomachines and rudimentary attotechnology, it is the best we can manage."

"Are you two going to leave me standing here while you talk about toys, or is someone going to tell me why I am here?"

"Further apologies, lady," said the servomech. "It became essential for Fourteen Samuel's education that he should ask a few questions of a discorporate."

"Then why did you not leave me discorporate and link him to me virtually?"

"He mistrusts anything that he experiences in virtuality. He does not consider it sufficiently real."

Nerydd gave Sam a withering look. "It is real enough to the lifesouls of Heaven! Does he doubt the evidence of his own senses?"

"Yes," said Sam. "When what they report is virtual. For all I know, none of this is real. I've already been fooled once."

"For all you *know*," the servomech affirmed, "everything you have experienced in your entire life may have been unreal. The best you can do is assume that such an elaborate simulation would not have been worth the trouble."

"You said he wanted to question a discorporate," Nerydd reminded them. "Then let him ask his questions, and then return me forthwith to my plainsong."

"I'm not sure I need to ask," said Sam. "I think that your words have already shown me where I've been making a mistake."

"Which was?"

She looked so desirable . . . "That . . . that you would prefer this reality to the illusion of Heaven."

Nerydd stared at him, thunderstruck. "Are you mad?"

"No. But I think you may be."

"Huh! Five minutes ago I was contributing to the harmony of the cosmos. Now I'm standing in a slaughterhouse, discussing the nature of reality with an idiot."

"But this slaughterhouse—this discorporation facility—is *real*," Sam protested. Achingly beautiful as Nerydd might be, she seemed unable to grasp an entirely obvious idea. "The celebration of plainsong is only a mirage in your mind, inserted by machines. Do you honestly prefer that to the real world? If you rejected the virtual, there would be no need for the slaughterhouse."

"You have it exactly back to front! Without the slaughterhouse, there would be no Heaven. And when I am in the virtual world of Heaven, it *is* the reality, and there is no slaughterhouse."

"Yes, there is! You just aren't aware of it."

"You were unaware of my plainsinging."

It was a verbal trap. Wasn't it? "That's not the same."

"How can you be sure? Perhaps you should join me in my choir. Then"—she moved her hips seductively and gave him a predatory smile—"you could get to know me better and learn to appreciate my point of view."

Cherisher, it's tempting. Instant Heaven. But Sam managed to resist. A quick glance at his surroundings was enough. "Even though we are not wed?" he inquired, a sparkle in his eye.

"That could be arranged . . . No, I was joking. The offer wasn't serious. You're not my type."

"You are mine," said Sam wistfully. "That is why the

machines selected you." A thought struck him. "You seem far too young and healthy to be suitable material for Heaven. I thought that discorporation was a medical procedure reserved for those that could not be healed in any other way."

"Not on a world that has reached closure in the Church," said the servomech. "When that occurs, all citizens are discorporated, whatever their physical condition might be. However," he addressed Sam, "you have your answer. Your presumption was wrong. The lady wishes to return immediately to her virtual paradise. Your alleged 'reality' holds no attraction for her."

"I want to be discorporated!" shouted Nerydd. *"Now!"*

Unnoticed, a shadow had slid across the ground where they stood. Suddenly aware that something was blocking the light, she looked up—and screamed. Before the servomech could stop her, Nerydd was stumbling through the racks of body parts, terrified out of her wits. But she was running the wrong way.

A gigantic shape blotted out the light from above. The servomech seized Sam by the arm and began to drag him away from the scene. "It is a levithon!" the robot cried. "We cannot stay, or you will be killed! Nothing organic can survive its attack!"

"What about Nerydd?" Sam yelled, wondering what a levithon was but realizing this was not a good moment to ask.

"She must take her chances among the organ racks," said the servomech. "She is beyond our help."

Despite the danger, Sam dug his feet in, and the robot ground to a halt. Behind them, Nerydd had slipped and

fallen; she was trying to dig her way into a heap of glutinous yellow mush. "That will not save her," the servomech remarked. "Nothing now will save her."

"We should have left her in her Heaven!" Sam
shouted as the huge, pale shape sank lower. *Cherisher,
but it's big*.

"She would still have died," said the servomech. "Her
tissues were stored in this vicinity. A levithon attack
costs many lives. The scavengers leave nothing where
they have been, just a bare patch of ground. Cold ground,
frozen solid by the levithon's metabolism."

Only later would Sam observe that this remark de-
molished the robot's view that reality was negotiable.
The virtual reality of Heaven was constrained by the external world, just as a mind becomes constrained by its
material brain if its owner's head hits a rock. Now he
was too horrified to think of anything beyond survival.

The servomech dragged him toward the nearby building and through a low doorway. Looking back, Sam saw
that the levithon's pallid bulk had smothered Nerydd's
noisome refuge, along with the entire area where they
had been standing only a few seconds earlier.

To the accompaniment of obscene sucking noises, the
levithon settled down to feed. Sam couldn't take his eyes
off the scene. But he was glad when the robot shut the
door.

11

TALITHA, AQUIFER ORBIT

Some say that emergence occurs when the whole is greater than the sum of its parts. But *greater*, *sum*, and *part* are quantitative concepts. Emergence, like meaning, is a quality. You cannot count a quality. You have to experience it.

Conversations with Huff Elder

Say that again?" May thought she must have misheard. The two transpods that had been sent to investigate the pond field had found a mariner survivor, and it *was* Second-Best Sailor. He was in relatively good health, despite a long trek across the desert in a failing suit. The Tweel had come up with a spare sailor suit—they had stores of just about everything, just in case. Now the polypoid was wearing his new suit, but he was refusing to come out of the pond.

The Neanderthals still didn't know how Second-Best Sailor had worked his trick with reflected sunlight, and right now they weren't in any hurry to find out. It could wait until they'd beaten a quick retreat from Aquifer's sandy surface, just in case whichever force had wiped out the colony was getting ready to mount another attack.

Talitha was keeping a careful watch for any signs of movement on the ground, as well as scanning the space around it for inbound ships that might be belligerent. But its orbit repeatedly took it out of visual contact with the landing party. Half the time it couldn't even see the North Pole, the most likely source of hostiles.

The operation was taking considerably longer than the Neanderthals had bargained for, and May was starting to feel the strain. Her friend Will was down there, and so was Second-Best Sailor. She presumed Fat Apprentice was dead. She missed him.

The ansible carried the words as if the speakers were face to face, but they made no sense. "Will—did I hear you say he wants to bring the pond with him? The *pond* ? Whatever for?"

"He claims it is intelligent, May."

"And I thought it was only my late friend Fat Apprentice who could surprise me . . . A pond cannot even be alive, let alone possess intelligence."

Will bobbed his head in an unconscious gesture of agreement, even though May couldn't see the movement. She was quite right: The mariner must be insane. "I have argued with him, but he insists that he is right. And he keeps telling me how important it is. He says that the pond is alive. It is an ecosystem, composed of many organisms."

"Yes, but it is not an organism in its own right," came the instant rejoinder.

"He says it is. He says it has, or *is*—I cannot get him to commit himself as to which—a mind. It speaks to him with molecules."

May had developed a theory to explain the wild delusion. "You say he spent several days in the desert? Wounded?"

"That is what he claims. But the medic has found no sign of any physiological damage."

"The heat must have dried him out. His electrolytes would have been all over the place. He must have suffered from delusions. Hallucinations."

Will ran blunt fingers through his shaggy mane. "That was also my theory. But I am half convinced that he knows what he is talking about. How else do you explain those flashing symbols, *2BS*, over and over again?"

"Easy. Some kind of flocking behavior of creatures *in* the ponds," May instantly replied. She'd been giving that matter considerable thought. "I am not denying that the ponds *contain* some limited form of intelligence, or that Second-Best Sailor managed to bend it to his will. But I *do* deny that the ponds themselves are organisms—let alone conscious and intelligent ones!"

"I wish I were as certain as you."

May sighed. Will was such a pushover. Why did he not use his empathic abilities? Better still, a verifier? Then the tale would fall apart in an instant. "You cannot be serious!"

"The mariner is in his right mind, and he is telling the truth as he sees it. Of that, I have no doubt. I sense it."

May did a quick rethink. If Will *sensed* it . . . well,

maybe that changed things. Maybe not. Both empathy and verifier could confirm only that the mariner believed what he was saying. Not that it was *true*.

Will brought her back to reality. "In any case, a walker has emerged from the pond and is . . . *drinking* it, I guess. Second-Best Sailor is making us wait until it has finished. He insists that it must come with us. He says that the walker is a metamorph of the pond ecology."

"I was not aware that an ecosystem could metamorphose."

"Well . . . its dynamic state can bifurcate. It can switch to a new attractor, just as some organisms can. But enough theorizing; that can wait. May, I want a suitable watertight compartment made ready, with a freshwater inlet valve capable of delivering a hundred gallons per minute. Up to a total of fifty thousand gallons."

May stopped arguing. It was wasting more time than it could save. "I imagine I can persuade Ship to cooperate. It should be easy to build a consensus for something that simple. I will inquire."

As it turned out, Ship was positively drooling at the prospect. Will's recommendation alone seemed consensus enough, even before May and Stun backed it up. They didn't even have to approach the Cyldarians. She had never known the vessel to be so amenable before. Was it keen to extend its ecological diversity? Who knew what went on in the mind of a mile-long spaceship?

Well, it would provide a new beast for the Neanderthals to master, she supposed. "Consider it done, Will. When should we expect you to lift off?"

"Thirty minutes from now." His confidence belied her

intuition. She could almost hear the suppressed "provided all goes as expected." What he actually said was, "We must collect a supply of food for the pond, and bring that with it to Ship. The—the insects are proving more difficult to capture than I had hoped."

Insects? Despite the potential dangers that faced them, May could not help a throaty chuckle. A vivid picture had appeared in her head. Very well. All they could do was wait, and watch, and react as best they could to any threat that materialized.

May had always been proud that Ship had no weapons. Now she was beginning to regret being so naive. They could do with some heavy weaponry right now.

As it happened, the rescue went smoothly. Humoring Second-Best Sailor, who still insisted that the pond was a conscious intelligence and the walker was its mobile form, they installed the walker in the chamber that had been prepared for it—basically, an empty tank with a water supply. The mariner wanted a pet, they assumed. But it was a funny way to go about getting one.

The walker seemed confused until Second-Best Sailor poked a tentacle through a weak spot in its translucent skin, up on top where no fluid would leak out, and engaged in what seemed to be a one-sided conversation. The polypoid was obviously insane, and the "discussion" achieved precisely nothing. When Second-Best Sailor asked for the tank's water valve to be opened, the walker just sat there, immobile, and slowly dissolved.

The creatures inside poured out and made themselves at home, so far as that was possible in the artificial environment of a waterproof tank. And that was it.

Yes, Second-Best Sailor did spend a lot of time dangling his tentacles in the water and talking animatedly to himself, but that was merely an extension of his delusion. He also spent a lot of time admiring his collection of fanworm tubes, won with such foolhardy courage from the pitch-dark depths of No-Moon's ocean. He had left them on board *Talitha* for safekeeping, until the colony on Aquifer could be properly established. Now he stared at them as if they were the only friends he had. That, too, proved nothing.

There was no doubting his sincerity. All the Neanderthals could feel it. He meant every word he said. But sincerity did not equate with accuracy.

On other matters, he seemed entirely lucid. Sharp Wit Will Cut had spent several hours debriefing the mariner, trying to find out everything he knew about events on Aquifer. Second-Best Sailor described his limited recollections: the nighttime attack on No Bar Bay, his own capture, his interrogation by the hierocrat of Cosmic Unity—

Yes, that was right: Cosmic Unity. It was their installation. At the North Pole? Second-Best Sailor couldn't confirm that, but yes, it was cold, and the tunnels could well have been carved in ice. Which was good enough to convince Will. He had told the reefmind; the information rounded out their timechunk and added perspective. Now they felt as if they had *always* known.

Will seemed to believe everything he told him when it came to Cosmic Unity. He broke off from the debriefing several times to issue instructions and talk to No-Moon, based on what Second-Best Sailor had just said. But whenever the polypoid raised the topic of ponds, Will's eyes seemed to glaze over, and soon he was making a poor job of concealing his anger.

Second-Best Sailor was baffled. Considering what a strange place the Galaxy was, was it so inconceivable that a pond could evolve intelligence? What about the reefwives? he pointed out. They were an intelligent *coral reef*, flounce it! And the 'Thals *traded* with them! But no, that was different; that was an organism—well, a superorganism, a social collective.

A pond couldn't be an organism, though, could it?

So Second-Best Sailor asked what had healed the wound in his flank, if it wasn't the pond. Will's answer was particularly hurtful: "*What* wound in your flank?" Because, of course, there was no trace that he had ever been wounded.

If only they'd brought the damaged suit back with them, then they could have seen the slit where the laser bolt had hit him. But the pond had discarded the suit, leaving it exposed on the beach, and it had disappeared—probably blown away one blustery night.

The polypoid was hurt that no one was willing to believe his story. He offered to act as interpreter, so that they could converse with the pond—but his was the only species among the crew that could send and receive chemical messages, and he was the only polypoid on board. Without independent confirmation, they would simply assume that he was making up the pond's side of the conversation.

There were ways around that, if they'd been seriously

interested. The pond must know things that Second-Best Sailor could not possibly know, and an intelligent line of questioning would be able to home in on a suitable topic. But they all *knew* that there was no such thing as an intelligent pond, and his near brush with death gave them the perfect excuse not to examine that "knowledge."

They're just being reasonable, he thought. *To them, I'm sick.* What was worse, he'd only gotten the pond on board as a thank-you gesture. Having been told about the Galaxy, the pond was determined to see some of its marvels for itself. The pond had saved his life, after all; he could scarcely tell it to get lost.

He had explained his trick with the fatflies. It was simple enough: get them to swarm in concert, blocking reflections from the ponds and then unblocking them again. The Neanderthals were willing to believe that he had somehow gotten the flies to swarm in patterns, since nothing else explained what they had seen with their own eyes . . . but they had not experienced the pond's intelligence, so they didn't believe anything he told them about it. Yet they believed him all right when he told them that there was another polypoid trapped on Aquifer! Not that it had made any difference. He and Will had both agreed that it would be too dangerous to try to rescue him. As yet, they had no accurate assessment of the enemy's capabilities. But when it came to the pond, no one would listen.

Despite everything, Second-Best Sailor persevered. He made a thoroughgoing pest of himself. He buttonholed people and started explaining some bizarre theory of mind as an emergent phenomenon; he coined new terms like "ecoconsciousness" and laced his conversation with them until he started to sound like the late lamented Fat Apprentice. He had long discussions with Epimenides, who found his ideas interesting but could cite a hundred authorities to dispute every one of his assertions. He spent hours quizzing crew members on what their neural components *felt like* when they were thinking. Not what it felt like to have those neural components—what the components themselves experienced while their owner's brain was putting together a thought.

The crew didn't understand. They wouldn't listen. A few of the Tweel, less polite than their fellows, displayed amusement. Several told him to shove off.

It depressed him.

The Neanderthals tried to treat Second-Best Sailor's depression with drugs, but he refused. The more they pressed, the more obstinate he became. Eventually, they stopped trying and pretty much left him to work out the problem on his own. The mariner's welfare was important, but there were more urgent and more important things to do. And the most urgent of them all was to return to No-Moon. The reefwives' evacuation strategy had come to pieces; the polypoid race would no longer be safe if No-Moon was lost. The reefmind needed to sort out an alternative before Cosmic Unity's mission fleet got its forthcoming invasion properly under way. And to do that, it had to find out exactly what the fleet was up to. Only *Talitha* could provide that information.

So the issue of the pond was put on the back burner, and Will concentrated on developing a consensus for the return to No-Moon. To his surprise, Ship agreed that consensus had been reached on the very first attempt. When it inquired what route he wanted, Will had expressed no preference: "You choose, Ship. Whichever route seems best to you."

Talitha deftly removed itself from orbit around Aquifer. This was an emergency: Ship was willing to use hydrive. Knowing that even by that means the trip would take several weeks, Will retired to his cabin to rest. But he had been asleep for less than three hours when Ship woke him with an offhand "Will? We've arrived."

This was so utterly improbable that he shot out of bed and rushed to the nearest gallery.

Ship hung stationary in space. Instead of the expec‘ed scene of stars pinpointed against a velvet backdrop, the window showed a striking image of a spiral galaxy. It was huge; it dominated the view in that direction.

Ship was right: They had arrived.

The only question was, *Where?*

When he asked Ship, it refused to answer. "There is no consensus," the vessel insisted. "But you can stop worrying that we've gone off course. This is exactly where I intend us to be at this stage. Now we will wait."

"Wait? What for?"

"I cannot tell you," Ship replied. "It is crucial that you should be left to find that out for yourselves."

Will decided that he had made a mistake when he told Ship to choose its own route. He should have struck a consensus for the quickest and most direct route, not the best. "Best" was too vague a word. Who knew what Ship thought might be best for them?

For the first time in his eventful life, he no longer trusted Ship's judgment.

"Well, I can tell you where we are," said Stun. She had been working with their highly experienced Yükü astrogator, and they had an answer to Will's question. It hadn't taken long.

He wasn't going to like it.

She decided to prepare the ground first. "I am sure you have noticed that Ship is behaving much more efficiently than it used to."

"Effectively," said Will. "Ship never gave a toss for efficiency, and still does not."

"More effectively. *Much* more effectively."

Will growled, "Get to the point, Eyes That Stun the Unwary."

She continued to evade it. "But you *have* noticed this?"

Will flexed his forearms, took a deep breath. He looked like a lion king surveying his domain. "It would be difficult for any ship's captain *not* to notice such a dramatic improvement, Stun. I first became aware of it when we started reaching consensus almost before any suggestions were made. Then I noticed that routine tasks were being carried out without any discussion whatsoever."

"I agree," May broke in. She had been tending to Will's crevit while its master was preoccupied with running the ship. "Have you observed that the atmosphere on board has become more contented than we have ever felt before?"

"Yes," Will agreed. "Despite the difficulties we all face."

"I noticed those things, too," said Stun. "Did you also realize that major items of equipment were functioning better?"

"The life-support allocation seemed unusually slick," May admitted.

"And the gallery window unusually clear," added Will.

"Mmm. And the hydrive?"

He shook his thick mane and ran his fingers through it. "What of the hydrive?"

"It has improved beyond recognition."

"What makes you think that? Oh, I believe I sense . . ."

Stun ducked her head in affirmation. "Correct. In a few hours, we traveled considerably farther than No-Moon, which on previous experience had to be several weeks distant, even if Ship found a route with less gravitic turbulence than the one we followed to journey to Aquifer."

Will accepted this, even though it was incredible. He could feel that she was telling the truth. "So where are we?"

She pursed her full, prominent lips, then licked them uncertainly.

"Still hesitant? I will not argue with your conclusions. The Yükü never miscalculates."

"Thank you, Will, for your confidence. We seem to

be . . . No, we most assuredly *are* somewhere in the Agathyrsi Cluster."

"Excellent. Uh—where is that?"

"It is a globular cluster located some sixty thousand light-years from the Galactic core in an axial direction."

"Sixty thousand light-years? That would put us well out towards the rim."

"Will, I said *axial*. Not radial."

The enormity of it struck home. Now he knew which galaxy they were looking at. *The* Galaxy. Theirs.

Nobody had *ever* been able to travel out of the Galaxy's main body of stars, into the spherical halo of globular clusters that extended for a hundred thousand light-years in every direction. Nobody had ever made a really good map of the Galaxy as a whole.

"We are the first people ever to visit this region," said May.

Knowing which galaxy it was, Will began to see familiar features. Conjectured maps had been pieced together, of course, but he now saw that they were wrong in numerous details.

They were right about the general shape: a spiral galaxy with a distinct bar, from which two thick arms trailed. Between them were two thinner arms, and the four arms were separated by lobes that were too short to count as spirals. The whole thing really did look like a blob of milk that had been dabbed onto the universe and stirred with a spoon. Their familiar Trailing Spiral Arm was just like the maps, including a pronounced fork about forty-five thousand light-years from the hub. Its matching Leading Spiral Arm (the terminology was conventional; actually, both arms trailed) was split by a long rent halfway out, and broken by a dark gap. In between were arcs and isolated patches of brightness, and the three gas clouds of the rim—Ugric, Pome, and Ellops—were clearly visible as dark smears.

Ship had made a rather large detour.

It was no coincidence that no one—at least, not from their own civilization—had ever visited this area. It was far beyond reach. At the hydrive speeds normal for *Talitha*—normal for any ship—it would take them many generations to get back to No-Moon. But the sparsity of stars left no places for travelers to take on essential substances—not even atomic hydrogen. So they could only hope that Ship's newfound effectiveness did not vanish as suddenly as it had appeared.

"You should never take Precursor technology for granted," he said, voicing his thoughts out loud. His throat felt dry, and his voice was husky.

"No," said Stun. "And never assume you know everything that it is capable of." A shadow of fear crossed her face. "Why has Ship brought us here, Will? So far out of the plane of the Galaxy? It must have a reason."

"It wants us to wait."

"What for?"

"It refuses to say. It says that we must work that out for ourselves."

"Wonderful."

The galaxy's resources had been depleted by its eons-long battle against the infection of Life. Still a relative infant, it had become old before its time, and it was

dying. Its central fires were beginning their long, slow decline.

But if the life of a galaxy is slow, its death is slower. No mind can grasp the time that must elapse before a galaxy's reserves of energy are exhausted. For the disease of life creates new resources, repackages old, tired structures. It breathes new vitality into everything it touches—for that is its role, its function, its essence.

This galaxy was sick, but it was a sickness of function, not of substance. It might yet be cured. Its disease might undergo remission.

But what can cure an ailing galaxy?

"Second-Best Sailor was telling the truth," May said out of the blue.

She and Stun were sitting in the gallery. Stun was accessing little-used features to map out the Agathyrsi Cluster's magnetic fields. If—when—they returned to their home regions, the information could be added to their civilization's vast repository of extelligence.

May had been working on a larger task: mapping the Galaxy. They would never get a better chance. Right now she was taking holographs of a region close to the Galactic core, where a dense mass of stars gyrated in unusually coherent patterns. Suddenly, without warning, she *knew* that the polypoid was as sane as any of them. Saner. For only he had the wit to believe the truth. The rest of them were fools.

"Sorry?"

"Stun, the mariner is right. The pond *is* intelligent."

The second Neanderthal woman assessed her companion's mental state. "You do not seem to have joined him in his madness. What brought about this change of heart?"

May's eyes flicked from the window to her companion. "My empathic sense tells me, of course! Any Neanderthal should understand *that*!" She stood up. "The pond is a sentient being, the most important one on this vessel! But we have ignored it, insulted it, denied its very existence!"

Stun grimaced, trying to come to terms with May's urgency. Her own sense of empathy told her no such thing. "But, May, why would a pond be important? Even if it is intelligent?"

"Because *we will never get away from here unless we communicate with it*!"

Stun could feel the intensity of May's conviction but did not yet share it. "What makes you think that?"

May stared at her. "Do you not receive the impressions, too?"

"Receive what impressions, May?"

"A faint, all-pervading sense of something massive and superintelligent. Only here, far removed from all distractions, removed from the Galaxy itself, could such a weak sensation be perceived. I can feel only the slightest empathic tendrils, and when I clutch at them, they slip away. But they are always there, in the background, a persistent drumming on the membranes of my mind."

Stun calmed her mind, and opened herself to raw, incoming *feeling*.

"Look towards the Galactic core, Stun. Let your mind become receptive."

There was definitely *something*. When Stun focused her blue eyes coreward—and with them her mind—she could feel delicate, prickling sensations. There was no pattern to them, no rhyme or reason; they were just *there*, as if they belonged.

"They have always been there," said May, and Stun nodded wordlessly. "But only out here can we separate them from the emotional hubbub of our fellow beings. Even here, they are all but swamped."

"What are they?"

"They are too weak to convey any meaning," said May. "This is why we need the pond. Only the pond can supply what we are lacking. And it will, if we can find a way to ask. But only Second-Best Sailor can talk to the pond, for only he shares its chemosensitivity."

Stun leaped to her feet, lithe and alert. "Then let us go and find him."

Second-Best Sailor had never felt so depressed in his life. He was giving up the fight; it just wasn't worth it. His friends were all dead, and his homeworld was far away. He had been frightened out of his wits and survived only by the wildest machinations of chance, and his own cleverness, and nobody believed him. They all thought he was crazy.

Well, maybe he was. Maybe he was so crazy that he didn't care anymore.

He was sitting beside the pond, dangling his tentacles in the water. His sailor suit had rolled itself up to allow contact with the water without compromising his life support.

But today even the pond was uncommunicative—it missed the desert days and nights, the cycles of light and dark, heat and cold. It missed the fatfly messages from its friends. Most of all, it wanted the Neanderthals to build it a beach. Second-Best Sailor had tried to tell the Neanderthals that they ought to rig up some kind of diurnal cycle, vary the temperature in synch with Aquifer's rotation, and find a bigger compartment and throw in a few tons of sand, to keep the pond happy, but of course, they hadn't listened to those ideas, either—

A voice broke the thread of his thoughts. May's. "Second-Best Sailor?"

Who else did she think he was? He said nothing. He wished he hadn't survived the attack; he wished he'd been boiled alive like Fat Apprentice. Then by now he'd be dead, and he wouldn't feel like this.

"I have come to apologize," said May, out of breath from her haste to reach him.

Still he said nothing. He squatted beside the pond in a morose heap.

"He is very unhappy," said Stun.

"He has been depressed for some time," said May. "Previously I had put it down to his experiences on Aquifer. But now I believe it has another source. Second-Best Sailor!" She reached out and shook him. "Speak to me! I need you!"

"Too late for that," said the mariner.

"Listen! I was wrong. I admit it, we were all wrong! You are right, the pond *is* intelligent. And now we need you to communicate with the pond."

Second-Best Sailor turned listless eyes toward her. "Communicate with a *pond*? Are you flouncin' *crazy*?"

May was on the verge of tears. "Second-Best Sailor, there is not time for this now. Please do not throw our apology back at us!"

"Why not? That way, ya find out what it's like when nobody believes ya about somethin' *important*."

At least he was talking. That was a start. "Second-Best Sailor, Ship has marooned us sixty thousand light-years outside the plane of the Galaxy. We need your help to get us back. We need the pond's help, and we need you to talk to the pond."

"I don' wanna go back," said the polypoid, brimming over with self-pity. "I wanna die. Nobody wants me; nobody listens to me."

"We want you! We are listening to you!"

"Maybe now y'are. But it's too late. Lemme 'lone." His voice was even more slurred than usual. Was he *dying*? It seemed all too likely.

"How can we get through to him?" asked Stun.

"It is a strong barrier," said May. "I can feel his sorrow, his sense of worthlessness. Oh, Stun, we should never have let him get this way!"

Stun tried to sort out the sensations. "He feels . . . discarded. He misses his companions, there are no other polypoids on the ship. But there is more . . . Ah!"

"What else?"

"He misses his wife."

"Not much we can do about that. The reefwives are on No-Moon. We are stuck here."

"Just his wife, not the entire reef."

"But the wifepiece that he always carried was sterilized by laser fire in No Bar Bay and left there to crumble into sand and be washed away by the tide. That was the only—"

The two women looked at each other as the same thought occurred to them both. Together they ran for the doorway.

"Let us hope this works," said May.

"Let us hope it is not too late," said Stun.

Second-Best Sailor perched beside the pond, tentacles dangling.

Beside him was a small container. One of his tentacles was inserted into it instead of the pond. The tentacle was fondling a small lump of what looked like white rock. He held it tenderly, occasionally giving it a quick caress. Delicate worms put out brightly colored fans to catch morsels of food. Soft polyps fluttered in the current.

"Coral," said May. "Living female coral. Good job he gave us some to keep for him."

"More than just coral," said Stun. "A piece of his wife. Mariners always take such pieces with them."

"We tended his wifepiece with care," said May. "As the reefwives had instructed when he 'gave' it to us. Do you think they envisioned this, all that time ago? They have remarkable predictive abilities."

"I would like to think so," said Stun. "Not that they could envision this in detail. I think it was a contingency plan."

"You may well be right. According to their husbands, they *see* the universe as a contingency plan."

"The pond says that soon's ya agree to fix up some

lighting and cooling that'll make 'im feel more at home, and supply a beach, 'e'll be ready to talk to ya," Second-Best Sailor broke in.

"Those things are all on their way now," said May. "The engineers are bringing them." The mariner passed her message to the pond.

ASK THEM WHAT THEY WANT, the pond whispered in Second-Best Sailor's brain. I WILL TALK TO THEM NOW.

"One o' the 'Thal women thinks she can sense some kind of background thoughts," the polypoid replied. "She says she thinks it's important."

OF COURSE. HAVE THEY NOT ALWAYS BEEN AWARE?

The mariner was puzzled. "Aware of what?"

OF THE GALACTIC MIND.

"Are you crazy?"

LET US NOT START THAT AGAIN. YOU HAVE ACCEPTED THAT A POND CAN BE A MIND. A GALAXY IS A FAR MORE COMPLEX SYSTEM THAN ANY POND. IT IS FAR MORE COMPLEX THAN ANY SINGLE ENTITY, THAN ANY CIVILIZED SOCIETY. THAN ANY STAR SYSTEM.

"Look," Second-Best Sailor informed the pond, worried by the implications, "I've 'ad enough trouble convincin' them that a pond can be intelligent. Now you're askin' me to do the same for a galaxy?"

THEY DID ASK.

Then the pond "spoke" for a long time, while Second-Best Sailor took mental notes. He assembled his thoughts, ready to convey the gist of the conversation to the two women.

"Uh—the pond tells me, yes, he senses the same thing. Says 'e always has, even back on Aquifer."

"Then he is more sensitive than we."

"Yes, 'e is. Bein' a collective mentality, 'e can get on the same wavelength as anuvver collective mentality. You're better suited to organisms. Wiv collectives, you get signals so faint that you can't interpret 'em."

"Of course!" said Stun. "That is why we could not empathize with the pond and feel its intelligence for ourselves."

"What other kind of collective mentality does the pond detect?" May inquired, picking up the important part of Second-Best Sailor's words. Insights into their own frailties could wait.

"Um. That's the tricky part. I'm not sure I've understood 'im properly. All I can do is try. If you don' believe me, that's your problem. Right?"

"Right. But do not worry: We promise to believe you."

"You may regret sayin' that," said Second-Best Sailor. "As best as I can tell, 'e reckons 'e's attuned to the collective mind of the whole flouncin' Galaxy."

"But that's—" Stun began.

May stopped Stun's mouth with her hand. "We can examine the philosophical implications later, Stun. Epimenides would be delighted to assist, I am certain."

"Uh—yeah, sure."

At that moment, Will's voice carried throughout the ship on the internal communicator. "Warning to all crew: Prepare for departure. Ship says we have achieved consensus!"

The two women stared at each other. Ship had clearly been waiting for something, and it must have had a reason to wait out here. Then they made contact with the pond, the pond told them that the Galaxy had a conscious mind, and suddenly Ship was ready to take them home again.

Sometimes Precursor technology could be very frustrating.

"I think it must be some kind of Aquiferian pond religion," said Will. "Their version of God. Galactic Gaia."

"You do not think that the Galactic Mind is real?"

"May, I do not dispute that we made a mistake when we doubted Second-Best Sailor's story about the pond. And I agree that we must not make the same mistake twice." He stroked his massive but undercut jaw in indecision. "Equally, we should not allow the first mistake to predispose us to a different one."

"There was something out there," said May. "I felt it. Just off the edge of conscious sensation, like a memory that cannot quite be recalled, a name dangling from the tip of one's tongue."

"I do not doubt that you felt *something*," said Will. "But to talk of a Galactic Mind implies conscious volition. A galaxy is made of gas and rock. Most of it is a vacuum. Much of the rest seethes with violent nuclear reactions. That is not a mind."

The ship's Thumosyne philosopher, the one nicknamed Epimenides, joined the discussion. The original Epimenides had been a Cretan—whatever species that was—who'd said that all Cretans were liars. The name fitted. "You thought that water, crustaceans, and fish could not be a mind," the Thumosyne said.

"Yes, but at least those were *organic*!"

Epimenides expanded slightly, and his ruffs changed register, so that his normal pattern of hexagonal spots became jagged stripes. "As I keep reminding you, the material constitution is irrelevant. It is complexity of organization that creates the possibility of a mind."

"How can a galaxy possess complex organization?"

"How can it fail to? It is at least as complex as the sum total of everything in it. You are part of the Galaxy; therefore, the Galaxy is more complex than you."

Will sucked at his lip. "I think that is a category error," he said finally. "If there *is* a Galactic Mind—and I am not conceding that there is—then its 'components' will be on a very different level from those of my mind. My presence may contribute to the complexity of the Galaxy, but not on the right level of organization."

"Just as the amphibians' brains do not contribute to the mind of the pond, but the amphibians themselves do?"

"Uh—yes, Epimenides. That is it, exactly."

"Then perhaps it is people, sentient entities, that form the components of the Galactic Mind. Every action that they take constitutes a 'thought' in the mind of the Galaxy."

"Say that again," said Stun.

The Thumosyne exhaled, and its ruffs clicked back into the hexagonal pattern. "I am suggesting that the Galactic Mind, if it exists—and I am not asserting that it does, merely examining whether it might—is just as insensitive to the individual minds within it as your own minds are to your neurons. Its 'thoughts' are the movements and behavior of its component mentalities, but interpreted on a very different level."

"So what we experience as history—such as the spread of a cosmic religion, to pick something topical—might be a casual thought about putting out the Galactic cat?"

"That is my contention, Smiling Teeth May Bite."

"But surely such thoughts would be too slow."

"You imagine that they must proceed at the speed of history, not that of light?" said the Thumosyne. "Perhaps. It takes two hundred million years for a galaxy to complete one revolution. It has no need to hurry."

"I disagree," said Will. "Even lightspeed would not be enough. The components of a galactic mentality must communicate far more rapidly than the emergent events that they generate. Just as our neurons react more rapidly than our conscious thoughts. I can imagine a galactic mind communicating with radio waves or even gravity, but those are too slow. Our own ships can exceed lightspeed; history can travel faster than gravity."

"Then a galaxy could employ similar physics," said the philosopher. "Or better. Consider the transible. Quantum entanglement is instantaneous. The Galaxy could have a quantum mind. What we think of as quantum randomness might be neural signals in the Galactic Mind, exchanging qubits in a cosmic dialogue of which we are totally unaware. Quantum chaos, signals too complex for us to comprehend. Optimal communication always appears random to those who do not know the code."

"In that case," said Will, "are we making a meaningful distinction?"

The philosopher liked that question. It got to the heart of the matter. Discussion of mere physical mechanism was too concrete for his tastes. "You mean, is there a scientific test to distinguish between history as the emergent consequences of physical laws, and history as a thought in the mind of the Galaxy? That would be very difficult. I am convinced that we lack the intelligence to perform such a test, even if one exists."

"A Galactic-level mind would have better prospects," said Stun, disappointed.

"If there is one. Which brings us back to where we began."

May remembered those dim flickers of sensation tickling at her mind. "There was something there; I sensed it. And Ship deliberately took us to the Agathyrsi Cluster to make us aware of it. I am convinced, also, that it was Ship that put into my mind the need to consult the pond."

"Whatever makes you think that?" asked Will.

"Because the moment we stopped denying the pond's consciousness and made contact with it, Ship told you that consensus had been reached for departure. So Ship is in effect telling us to listen to what the pond has to say."

Will scratched his nose and turned to Ship's philosopher. "But it is not that simple, is it, Epimenides?"

"No, it is not. Ship depends on consensus, and consensus is a matter of *opinions*. Ship is telling us to respect the pond's opinion about the Galactic Mind. But that does not mean that we should assume that what the pond is telling us is *true*."

"Assuming that 'truth' is a meaningful concept," said Stun.

"Do not get me started on that! I am a philosopher, remember. The pond's opinion offers valuable insights, but we cannot assume that it is the only valid opinion. Or, indeed, that it is a valid opinion at all."

May felt let down. She had hoped to convince Will that the Galactic Mind was real. Think of it! Sentience on a cosmic scale! But that was a spiritual viewpoint, and Neanderthals were deeply skeptical about anything spiritual.

"So what do we do?"

The Thumosyne expanded once more. "As a pragmatic matter, we should act as if the pond is right. That will reinforce the consensus that Ship clearly desires. And it will keep both the pond and its mariner friend happy. Which may be two different ways to say the same thing, incidentally."

"Fine, so we pretend."

The philosopher looked startled. "Not at all. You respect the pond's opinion. You may even find yourselves beginning to accept it."

"Are you saying we should take the Galactic Mind's existence on *faith*?" said Will, shocked. Neanderthals had no truck with mindless belief. "Galactic Mind" was dangerously close to "god," and that was intellectual territory into which Neanderthals never ventured.

"No. I am saying that the interpretation that you place on unfolding events makes no difference to how those events unfold. It is the events, and their unfolding, that determine history. The meaning that you attach to them is irrelevant."

May understood the point that the Thumosyne was making; her natural Neanderthal disdain for the spiritual made her sympathetic to it. But at the back of her mind, Fat Apprentice's question still reverberated, a persistent, nagging doubt: *"Is a galaxy what happens when a universe spawns?"*

Could a galaxy—or a universe—be a form of life? And what powers would it possess if it were?

The thought terrified her.

The Tweel engineers had plenty of sand, just as they had plenty of everything else, tucked away in *Talitha*'s capacious holds. Though they had not expected to use it for quite this purpose. It was rather a nice beach, considering that it was on a spaceship, and the pond approved of its new location, too. The larger compartment that had now been provided gave it more room to spread itself.

Second-Best Sailor sat at the edge of the pond, half on the beach, half in the water, and waited until they were alone. "What did you want this beach for? Just findin' out 'ow far ya could push them?"

NOT AT ALL. IT IS ESSENTIAL TO MY LIFE PROCESSES.

The mariner was puzzled. "How?"

WATCH.

The pond rippled, as if a stone had been thrown in but in reverse, and something rubbery and round plopped out of the water, landing next to Second-Best Sailor on the beach.

"What in the name of the Maker . . ."

IT IS A SANDSKATER EGG. I ATE ITS MOTHER, JUST BEFORE YOU FELL IN. BACK ON AQUIFER.

"You ate its mother? Then why not eat the egg, too?"

BECAUSE IF I ATE THE EGG, THERE WOULD NOT BE AN-

OTHER MOTHER TO EAT. I AM NOT SO STUPID AS TO DESTROY
MY OWN LONG-TERM FOOD STORE.

As the pond's molecular "words" resonated in Second-
Best Sailor's mind, the beach near the egg moved aside
to create a depression. The egg slipped into the hole. A
few moments later, the beach had covered it over.

WHEN IT HATCHES, THERE WILL BE A NEW MOTHER.

"And you'll eat her then?"

NO, NOT STRAIGHTAWAY. ONLY WHEN SHE HAS LAID
ENOUGH EGGS TO ENSURE THE SURVIVAL OF HER SPECIES.
THE SANDSKATERS ARE PARTHENOGENETIC; THEY NEED NO
MALES.

The mariner thought about that. First he thought about
his wifepiece and gave thanks that she wasn't parthenogenetic. Then he thought about the pond's strange attitude to its food. It was really just a form of gardening, he
decided. Like growing lemon trees on top of a boat and
eating the lemons. Not as much fun as hunting, but more
secure. He wasn't sure what the mother sandskater
thought about the arrangement. But the pond was:

WITHOUT THE MOISTURE THAT I PROVIDE, HER EGGS
WILL NOT HATCH. WE ARE SYMBIONTS; BOTH SPECIES BEN-
EFIT FROM THE ARRANGEMENT. IS NOT THE GALACTIC MIND
WONDERFUL?

"Let's not start *that* again," said Second-Best Sailor.

12

THE VESTIBULE OF HEAVEN

For the survival of the principle, the many shall be
 sacrificed.
For the survival of the many, the few shall be sacrificed.
For the survival of the few, the self shall be sacrificed.
For the survival of the self, the principle shall be
 sacrificed.

Koans of the Cuckoo

You are safe now," the servomech assured Sam. "The
levithons cannot penetrate this building."

"*Levithons?* There are more of the things?"

"Thousands. They are universal scavengers, biological constructs about which we knew nothing until their
spores descended from space."

Sam sat down suddenly, and all the energy sagged out
of him. Tears coursed down his cheeks; he felt like
throwing up. "She's dead. Nerydd. Why wasn't *she* protected by a building, if that's all it takes?" He tried to

summon up techniques from his training as lifesoul-healer. He knew the self-delusional traps.

It still hurt.

"We have been carrying out an urgent program of construction ever since the first levithon attacks, a century ago," the servomech explained, oblivious to Sam's distress. "For the previous four thousand, five hundred years, this facility functioned faultlessly. *Faultlessly,* do you hear me? The arrival of such predators was not anticipated, and there was no technological need for containment buildings. They would merely have added to the cost."

"Actions have consequences," said Sam. "They are never neutral. Prey attracts predators; carrion attracts scavengers. New resources will be exploited. You should have anticipated the general nature of the threat, even if its specific form was unpredictable." Not that gaining the robot's agreement would bring back Nerydd. "What are those awful things?"

"The levithons should not exist," said the servomech. "We kill them by the hundreds, but occasionally one of them gets through our defenses. Then it eats its fill. They are immune to our protective femtomachines, even though they lack identifying qubit tags. Moreover, they infringe every principle of xenoscience. Such a generalized predator cannot credibly evolve. Levithons consume *all* organic material. From innumerable species, which evolved on innumerable worlds. They cannot have been selected to occupy such a broad ecological niche."

"So they're impossible," said Sam. "What killed Nerydd, then?"

Unusually, the servomech sounded hesitant. "It is thought . . . nothing is certain, but there is evidence . . . though no records . . . that the levithon is a Precursor construct. An all-purpose scavenger, bioengineered to clean up dysfunctional ecologies. The ground where a levithon has passed is immensely fertile, once it has thawed again. Their immunity to femtotechnology is presumably a consequence of Precursor engineering."

"For all that, she's still dead," said Sam sullenly.

Servomechs had no sense of sympathy. "By your arguments, she was not a real person in any case."

"Damn the arguments! She wasn't real when her body was scattered in bloody slabs and disarticulated bones!" Sam yelled. "But she was real when you put her back together!"

The servomech could make no sense of the distinction. In either state the organism had the same components, connected in the same manner; discorporation just distributed the components in a more rational, more accessible arrangement. "Discorporation is merely the most convenient state for maintenance work," it said, bemused. "It makes no functional difference."

The stupid mechs really couldn't see any difference, could they? "She couldn't walk, or talk, or breathe when she was discorporated!"

"In her mind, she could."

"That's not the same!"

This was where the servomech could never follow the human's argument. Was it missing something vital? The novice lifesoul-healer seemed so certain that there was a meaningful distinction. "To her, it was. In her discorporate state she could do more than was ever possible in a corporate one. That is our task: to enhance the function and experience of lifesouls. To give them what you might call a 'better world.'"

Sam's anger boiled over. "Not like that! That's obscenity, blasphemy! Insanity!" But the mechs would never understand. To them, function was what mattered; form was irrelevant. They had no sense of aesthetics, no sense of propriety, and no sense of evil.

Sam was struck by a new thought. "You say that it makes no difference whether her bodily parts are scattered or assembled. Could she not be brought back, by the same process that incorporated her?"

"Using what for body-parts?"

"Duplicated copies. Have you no recorded templates?"

The servomech patiently dashed his hopes. "Even if we had . . . even if her organs were all intact, a vital element of process is irretrievably lost when an organism dies. We cannot re-create the correct dynamic state. What the Lifesoul-Stealer has taken can never be restored. Death, like life, is a question of function, of process. Not components."

Well, he was certainly getting an education in the secrets of the Church, Sam told himself. But was it the education that his superiors had intended? He had assisted in torturing Clutch-the-Moon Splitcloud to death, supposedly for the unfortunate creature's spiritual health. And he had swallowed the theological creed of the Great Memes, which had led him to shoot an innocent alien and leave him to die a terrible death. He had discovered that the reward for spiritual advancement was Heaven—but the paradise was fake, and the reality was a planetary charnel house. And he had met and been attracted to an irritatingly sarcastic woman of supreme beauty, and had watched her being smothered and consumed by a monster.

And this was supposed to be evidence of tolerance? Love? Respect for one's fellow lifesouls?

Really?

"Your visit to this facility has served its purpose," said the servomech, breaking into his thoughts. "Your tuition here is at an end. The transible has been prepared for your return. Delay will be inefficient and costly."

Delay? Sam couldn't wait. When he got back to Aquifer, the hiero-crat would have an awful lot of answering to do.

Surrection, resurrection. Quantum phases recohered. Matter, briefly transparent, became opaque. The ghostly inner light faded, and XIV Samuel was back on Aquifer.

Oval pink eyelets peered at him myopically from an elongated, ophidian head. "No, Hhoortl555mup isn't here," it said in answer to his question. The Cakhadyll operating the transible was apologetic, but its mind was occupied elsewhere, and its forefringe ruffled helplessly. "It's been nothing but confusion since she left."

Sam was aghast at the dereliction of duty implied by this offhand remark. "Did the hierocrat not make arrangements to appoint a deputy?"

"She seemed a lot more interested in getting off the planet," said the operator. "She was in such a rush, the friction could have set her tail on fire." The eyelets contracted as the Cakhadyll ran the words through its mind again. "Not that she *has* a tail, just a figure of speech," it added.

Sam had no time for the gaudy creature. Brushing it aside, he hurried out of the transible area, trying to find someone in a position of authority. Someone to receive the complaint that ran molten rivulets through his mind. But as he stalked the corridors of the Nether Ice Dome, he became ever more convinced that on Aquifer the governing hierarchy of Cosmic Unity had broken down completely. No one seemed to be taking control. Everyone was waiting for orders that never came. All the senior clergy seemed to have left, and their juniors sat around with stupid looks on their faces, waiting for someone to tell them what to do.

Something had changed in Sam. Something radical and deep-seated. Not long ago he, too, would have been content to await instruction. But now, every instinct urged him to *do* something. He had to act, now. If nobody else would take charge, he would.

He grabbed a passing Spuchthene menial and shook it viciously. "Where are the querists?"

Shocked by the body contact, it didn't even protest. "Gone. They left as soon as the hierocrat had departed."

"Then who is the senior priest here?"

The menial studied his garments for a moment and gave him a funny look. "I think you are."

"*Me?*"

"You're the lifesoul-healer, aren't you? Maroon robe, silver tackings?"

"With levo knottings, not dextro. I'm a novice lifesoul-healer."

The menial decoded the pattern of knots. "Son-of-Good-One Samool, fourteenth member of the lineage of . . . Traven?"

"Travers."

"That was it. They've been looking for you. Everybody senior to you has fled. The rest would have gone, too, but they couldn't find you to authorize their departure. You broke the chain of command."

"I was on another world."

The menial would have been happy for Sam to have stayed there, judging by the angle of its forelimbs. "Ah. So that's why you couldn't authorize the rest of us leaving. So we're still here. It's all your fault."

Sam finally caught up with the conversation. "Yes, and *I am in charge now*." The menial cringed as the logic struck home. "You will keep civil tongues in your head. And you will do my bidding."

The menial's face brightened. *This was more like it.*

Sam's first act was to seek out the Neanderthal child. Dry Leaves Fall Slowly had never been far from his thoughts, and he did not want her to be neglected amid the confusion that now reigned in the monastery of equals.

Where was she? Deep underground in the correction facility—unless she'd been moved.

The querist's quarters were locked, but Sam had access to a duplicator, and he knew how to work it. He ran through the tunnels to the duplicator room and ransacked files of past batches until he found what he was looking for. The qubit key to the querist's quarters would have been enough, but some modest changes to the gesture pattern persuaded the metaphace to accept instructions to duplicate a master key to the whole Ice Dome, along with a copy of the hierocrat's Ankh of Authority.

He might as well be terminated for a sheep as for a yullé.

The querist's quarters were just a little too untidy. Their occupant had left in a hurry. The door that opened onto the spiral ramp leading down into the bowels of the monastery opened at a touch of the key. Sam slipped through and shut it behind him.

The ramp was dark, which implied that it was deserted. A simple gesture activated the pass lights. Now, as he trotted down the curve of the ramp, the lighting would rise and dim as if accompanying him.

He reached the bottom, breathless. He opened what he thought was the right door. Inside was the decaying carcass of a blimp. He couldn't tell what had killed it, but he could guess.

Try another door. This one?

Yes, this was the place. But Dry Leaves Fall Slowly was not at prayer.

He tore the dividing membrane and kicked his way past the door that led out of the semicircular devotional chamber. Behind it he found a sparsely furnished room with a hard bed and one thin wrap. Aside from these, the room was empty.

He swore, inwardly relishing the blasphemy, clamping down savagely on reflex feelings of guilt. Then he rushed out into the ramp-way and collided with a Hytth, bowling him over. Sam hauled the creature upright. "There was a Neanderthal here."

"There were several," said the Hytth, more interested in checking that he had suffered no damage in the collision.

"I'm looking for a child. Female."

"That one has been moved from the correction facility," the insectoid stated. "Along with other infidels."

"Where is she now?"

"In the infirmary."

That didn't sound good. Sam set off at a run.

When he reached the infirmary, a Rhemnolid orderly barred his way. "You are not authorized."

Sam glared at it. "I am the most senior priest present."

"That iss a mere fact, and as such iss irrelevant. I have no insstructions to admit you."

"Do you have instructions to refuse admission to a lifesoul-healer? In the absence of higher authority, I am the senior priest. You will obey my orders! You have a Neanderthal child here. Take me to her!"

Grudgingly the orderly allowed him to pass and led him to a padded couch, where Fall was lying, curled into a tight ball.

Sam's relief at finding her was short-lived. One glance at her, and he was appalled. "What's happened to her?"

The orderly consulted records. "The . . . *Neanderthal* . . . suffered a spiritual relapse. Denial of the Memeplex. Wicked allegations."

"About a pet animal? About her parents?"

"The archives do not contain that information. The

content of her false claims was irrelevant. Their context was disobedience."

Disobedience enough to deserve this? Sam couldn't believe he had ever bought into the querists' sick belief that such violence served a purpose. If logic said it did, then logic was at fault. He felt his anger rising in his throat. "And that is why she bears bruises all over her body? Her skin is nothing but yellow and purple blotches."

The orderly was startled. "That iss not her normal color?"

"She's supposed to be pink."

The Rhemnolid bent over the unconscious form. "The nursses know these things. I am but an orderly. There iss some red."

"That," said Sam scornfully, "is blood. A bodily fluid. She has suffered cuts, grazes, abrasions of a kind I cannot identify." His own blood boiled. He had never felt such anger, despite all he had been exposed to in the past few days. "Who did this?"

The Rhemnolid bobbed nervously. "She iss in the same sstate as she was when the querisssts brought her here."

Yes, she would be. But now Sam's hurried examination of the child had turned up another puzzle. "What are these marks?"

Lifesoul-healer and orderly looked at the girl's neck, under her now straggly hair. Small equilateral triangles were branded into the soft skin. The triangles were hard, encrusted patches of burned flesh. Typical querist crudity—perversion of the Memeplex. But that wasn't what arrested his attention.

The shape was tantalizingly familiar.

A herd of yullé galloped along the corridor over-head, their hooves clattering on the metal ceiling. For a moment, their simple happiness filled Will's being. Then they were out of empathic range. The distance over which his Neanderthal sense functioned had definitely increased, though—presumably, that was related to the improvements to *Talitha*. But Ship wasn't just function-ing more effectively: Will was astonished to find that it had now acquired weapons.

"They are not unwelcome," he decided. "Even though this ship has always been a peaceful trader. But until this moment, there were no weapons—and big though Ship is, I have explored every inch."

"So where have these weapons come from?"

"I am of the opinion that Ship has grown them," said Epimenides. "I can think of no other explanation. The vessel is of Precursor manufacture, and we have never understood the principles on which it functions, or their limitations."

"True," said Will, stroking the soft fur of the crevit nestling in his lap, relishing its aura of trust. "Why grap-ple with the unknown when all we need to know is how to operate the vessel?"

"Since you ask," said Epimenides, ignoring the rhetorical nature of the captain's question as any philoso-pher would, "understanding could prove useful in the event of something going wrong."

"Nothing ever goes wrong with Precursor technol-ogy," Will parried. "And if it ever did, we would have no chance of putting it right. Mind you," he continued, "it does develop a will of its own sometimes. Not that understanding the principles whereby it operates would affect *that,* either."

"You know," said May, "you do have an exceedingly limited view of the universe, Will."

"I have a practical view. I trade. I need a good ship. This is a good ship. And I have more than enough to think about without asking how the confounded thing works."

May changed tack before Will lost his temper—which, she could tell, was imminent. "So what weaponry has suddenly materialized out of thin vacuum?"

"That's an idea! Ship may well have constructed the weapons from quantum fluctu—" began Epimenides.

"Shut up." Will ticked the items off on his fingers. "Sixteen petawatt lasers, variable-focus, infrared. Heat rays, I guess you could call them. A radiation field, ellipsoidal, and a projector to deploy it. Five hundred twelve proximity bombs, 1024 matter-seeking missiles. Five emp-mines."

"Emp?"

"Electromagnetic pulse. They wreck unshielded electronics, not that anyone is so silly as to have those since the Delphinian War of Secession. All of the above—too big to duplicate, so we must not waste them. A variety of portable weapons, too complicated to specify right now—as many as we can duplicate in the time available. A plasma beam, six fusion torpedoes, and a qubit scrambler to randomize the enemy's infomatics." He stopped. "How in all that is wonderful do you *grow* those?"

"As I was endeavoring to suggest, quantum fluc—" the philosopher began.

"I thought you did not wish to know," Stun reminded Will, interrupting Epimenides before he became unstoppable.

"Ask the Precursors," said May. "If we ever meet one. Will was right. Whatever the reason, we are now armed to the teeth." She seemed unawed by the prospect; in fact, her features became more pronouncedly leonine as she displayed the teeth she had in mind. *May* bite? These *would* bite!

Soon, they would be going into battle. They might not survive it. Their own mortality suddenly seemed awfully real. May tried to imagine what it was going to be like. An awful lot would depend on their succeeding. It was one of those cusps of history, when one mistake could change a world. She could see that the others, too, felt the awesome responsibility. And fear. Fear that chilled her bones.

Will chewed his lower lip, perplexed. "I spoke hastily. What suddenly appears can also suddenly disappear. I would not wish to become defenseless in the heat of battle. May, it is all part of a larger question: Why has Ship suddenly changed so dramatically?"

"Why do you not ask it?"

He'd thought of that and rejected it. "Because it never answers that kind of question."

"It never has in the past. But Ship has changed. Maybe it will answer *now*."

To Will's utter amazement, it did. This was not coincidence—they were now permitted to know. They digested Ship's explanation in silence for a time. Finally, May said, "What did Ship mean by 'ethical threshold'?"

Will exhaled, an abrupt snort. "That is a very approximate translation of a Precursor concept that has no exact counterpart. Apparently, the presence of Second-Best Sailor's friend the pond has greatly increased the biodiversity of the ship. The pond is an ecosystem, composed of many kinds of life, none previously represented. This qualitative increase in diversity—not just more species, but more ways of being alive—has pushed us above some kind of threshold, so our consensus carries far more weight now with Ship. As a consequence, we are now certified by a Precursor machine to be more ethical than our predicted enemy—which, to be frank, says very little. Especially when 'ethical' is not really the right word. Nonetheless, our superior ethics entitle us to possess weapons of mass destruction—and to use them." The Precursors must have had a very direct view of ethics. "Before the pond came on board," Will went on, "we were too unethical to be permitted even a throwing knife."

"Well, we are traders," May pointed out. "Ethics have never been our strong point. We have our limits, yes . . . but at times those have been distinctly . . . flexible."

"You are saying," said Stun, "that since we now have more species on board than Cosmic Unity's invasion fleet does, the Precursor machinery deems us fit to fight them?"

"Not exactly *more* species, Stun. A qualitatively greater diversity of lifestyles. Ship now judges *itself* ethical enough to fight; it has no views about us. The decision is a matter of quality, not quantity. There is no formula, just a judgment. One extremely ethical species would outweigh a thousand crooked ones."

"And what tipped the balance in our case," said Stun morosely, "was a pond."

The galaxy had reached the age of sixty. Sixty revolutions, that is. Twelve billion years, give or take a few hundred million. It ought to have been in the bloom of youth. It should still have had a high expectancy of eons to come.

But, youthful though it might be, it had picked up many different infestations of life. Some were neutral. Some, like symbionts, were beneficial; life forms that tended to restore order could even be considered as a kind of galactic immune system. Most, like parasites, were deleterious. A few, like cancer, were malignant, metastasizing. Those infections were the ones that spread rapidly and, if permitted to continue unchecked, would eventually prove fatal.

Physically the galaxy ought to have been healthy. Its stars still had plenty of fuel to burn; its supernovas were as energetic as they should be; its black holes were unambitious and not especially greedy. It had a tolerably big entropy deficit to squander before it ran out of order. But its "brain"—its ability to carry out algorithmic processes—was suffering physical damage. Its mental processes were defective. It thought bad thoughts. On the galactic scale, its neuroses were bordering on the psychotic.

Only the galaxy's immune system stood between it and madness.

It would have to cure itself.

And the only cure available was more of the original disease.

Second-Best Sailor sidled up to Will, diffident despite the protection of his golden sailor suit. He found the bulky, muscular Neanderthal a bit intimidating, especially since it was Will who had been most dismissive about the pond's alleged sentience.

"'Scuse me," he said hesitantly.

"Yes?"

A trace of irritation there? Oh, well . . . "I hear a rumor that Ship 'as weapons now?"

"Yes."

Will was unusually talkative today. A lot on his mind? Must ask anyway—time's running out. "Can it do protective clothin', too?"

Will nodded. "Of course. Full battle armor. The new suits are elsewhere in the ship, undergoing testing. One has been constructed to your dimensions. Externally it closely resembles the suit you are wearing, like all Precursor suits, but it has many additional features. It will not protect you against explosions exceeding 1.72 kilotons, or class-six laser fire or higher. But it is proof against any normal antipersonnel weapons—mines, vacuum grenades, laser rifles, quark shufflers."

The polypoid digested the information with satisfaction. "Good. Then I want to go back."

Will glared at him. "Back to No-Moon? That is where we are heading now."

"No. Back to Aquifer."

"*Aquifer*? Why?" asked Will, taken aback by such an improbable request. "To get more ponds to play with?"

Second-Best Sailor lost his patience. "It ain't funny, Will," he said. "One o' my mates is bein' held by religious fanatics somewhere under Aquifer's ice cap. Now, I've known about that ever since we was attacked in the bay, so ya could say nothin's changed. But—it has. Until now, I've always known that it'd be suicide to try to rescue 'im. Now . . . I got protection. You just told me I have." The mariner hesitated, then regained his courage. "Send me back."

Will had not anticipated signs of bravery from the strange, rubbery mariner. Until this moment, Second-Best Sailor had seemed lightweight, frivolous. Suddenly, it dawned on Will that his name was not Thousandth-Best Sailor, and that meant something. He'd been underestimating the polypoid.

"We cannot send you back. The transible uses large amounts of energy, and we must conserve that when there is a battle to be fought."

Second-Best Sailor's tentacles shook. "Ya haven't asked it, then?"

"Asked what?"

"Ship. About the transible. I have. Ship's so effective now that the energy used by a transible ain't no problem no more."

Will confirmed this statement with a quick query to Ship. That did change the situation. Ship also confirmed that it was now in direct communication with the pond, and they would not need the mariner as a go-between. Even so, it would be a shame to lose one polypoid in a suicidal bid to rescue another. "Are you sure you want to go?" Will asked, hoping to change the mariner's mind. "It will almost certainly mean your death."

Second-Best Sailor didn't hesitate. "If I don't try, I'll never forgive meself." There, he'd said it. Now he was committed. He felt sick and elated at the same time.

Will didn't have time to argue. The incident with the pond had taught him not to put obstacles in the mariner's way. And this was a new side to Second-Best Sailor, a more serious side. One he hadn't seen before.

"You really mean this, do you not? Then I agree, there is no choice. You have my authority to use Ship's transible. But I regret that I cannot spare any crew to accompany you. They have all been assigned their stations for the coming battle, where I will need every crew member that I have. Even your own absence will weaken us, but I concede that the risk is necessary. However, I will *not* increase the risk by sending anyone else on a suicide mission, even if they were willing to join you. If you go to Aquifer, you must go alone."

"I know *that*," said Second-Best Sailor dismissively, trying hard to forget the word "suicide." Unseen, his skin turned the color of fearful haste. "Just give me an armored suit and a laser rifle. That's all I need."

Will gestured. "Down the central corridor, second shaft, three levels outwards, then back this direction to the third intersection. Big room, full of Tweel. Tell them you have priority; refer them to Ship if they dispute it. Let them finish checking your gear for duplication errors. I will assign someone to give you basic training in the suit's features. Have you ever traveled by transible before?"

"No."

"Then you will find it a novel experience."

Sam completed his examination of Fall's unconscious form. He was no medic, but he could recognize broken bones, and he didn't like her ragged breathing. From her condition, it would be a miracle if she was not suffering from internal injuries.

"How long?"

"Excuse?"

"How long before she *dies*?"

The Rhemnolid referred once more to the notes. "Two days. Maybe three. Unlesss she is given medical treatment."

"Then *do it now*!"

The orderly looked horrified. "I am not authorized to carry out medical procedures, nor trained. You musst find a medically qualified practitioner."

Sam shook the Rhemnolid, trying to beat some sense into it. *"Where do I do that?"*

"Not on this world. The medicss have all fled."

Sam shoved the stupid creature aside, and it toppled, screeching. There must be some way to help the child. Did he dare move her if she was as badly injured as he suspected?

Again he noticed the triangular brand marks on her neck. The size, the *shape* . . .

The pressures that had been building in his mind finally breached all barriers and blew the remnants of his faith away.

"It was all wrong," he said to nobody in particular, his

voice flat. "Love? Tolerance? The Great Memes, the Memeplex?

"No! This wasn't love. It was perversion. Wickedness. Evil." The orderly stared at him, baffled. Was he talking to it? What did he want?

The child hadn't just been beaten to a pulp. She'd been systematically tortured by the querists. Her previous submissive state, which had so impressed him— when he had watched her praying, quiet, peaceful—had not been conversion to the faith of Cosmic Unity. It had been simple brainwashing.

And it hadn't stuck. So then the querists had made their routine transition from talk to threats to violence.

On a child? Call *that* love?

Worse, Sam had helped them. That was the awful discovery that was consuming his mind. Subconsciously he'd known about the torture; what he hadn't known was that the mark on her neck had been made from components that *he* had duplicated. He remembered them vividly, now that his mind had made the connection. A batch of ten thousand triangular metallic objects. Electrical contacts? Heating elements? Something like that. They burned skin. They were *meant* to burn skin.

He had been *used*. By the Church to which fourteen generations of his lineage had devoted their lives. He had been duplicating instruments of torture, in bulk, ever since he had arrived on Aquifer. *That was why they had sent him there*. The training as lifesoul-healer was an extra, when they'd discovered what he might be capable of.

Even back on *Disseminator 714*, much of his production had been components for similar instruments.

Weapons for the enforced conversion of No-Moon's sentients.

His whole life, his entire lineage, had been a farce. He and his forebears had been the unwitting tools of evil. And then—the shame was unbearable—he had actually embraced the evil himself and become a willing accessory. Worse: a participant.

Lifesoul-healer? No. He had been training as a lifesoul-tormentor. That was what the Church meant by "healer." He should have listened when Fall told him . . . but he'd been so stupid that he'd believed the lies of the priesthood instead. *Everything she'd told him had been true.* Her father hadn't contracted a rare disease; he'd been tortured. Both her parents had been killed—without doubt in agony. The knife, the murder, the suicide—all fake. The priests had set it up so that their victims were blamed. And he knew without any shadow of doubt that she had owned a pet, whatever the archives said. It was obvious. Neanderthals *always* had pets. How could he have been so blind? And he knew that Cosmic Unity had taken a blowtorch to her pet, in front of her eyes, and in full knowledge of her acute empathy with the harmless creature. That was why they'd done it. The whole point had been to make Fall suffer.

How old had she been then? Probably six. *Six!* Sam stared blankly at the broken form of the Neanderthal child and sobbed his heart out. She had loved him, he knew: the simple love of a child. Total commitment. And he had returned her love . . . like this.

He might have stood there indefinitely, wallowing in self-pity. But he needed to save the life of Dry Leaves

Fall Slowly, in order to give his own life meaning. He would devote himself to her, utterly.

If she lived.

In his desperate search for a way, he was subconsciously reexamining the past few months, trying to make new sense of them, to reassemble his experiences into a new, stable pattern.

Now he'd found one.

There had been enough clues. He had been duplicating an awful lot of stuff. Much of it, he now knew, had been destined for the torture chambers. The numbers appalled him. But even so, most of his production must have been for other purposes. What of the endless tubes, wires, trays, brackets . . . ?

Suddenly, it all fell into place. The installation on Aquifer, the monastery of equals, was a sham. Camouflage. The torture chambers were incidental—necessary local color, a cover for its true purpose.

The Nether Ice Dome had been constructed for a very different reason. Aquifer was home to a Heaven. A secret Heaven. A special Heaven.

The conclusion was obvious, once the evidence was assembled, but enough of Sam's training remained that he forced himself to ask the difficult questions. Intuitive leaps of logic, he knew, could give a powerful feeling of knowledge. But it felt just as certain when you were wrong.

Why did he think Aquifer housed a Heaven? Because he, personally, had been duplicating huge quantities of the same equipment that he had seen on his visit to the Heaven of Sadachbia. It had seemed familiar, but what he'd been duplicating were isolated components. When it was all assembled, it had looked different. And his mind had been focused on other things. *Rivers of blood, mountains of entrails.*

Nerydd.

Deduction confirmed. He'd been duplicating pieces of Heaven. But why did the Heaven have to be *here*?

First, because it would be stupidly and uncharacteristically inefficient to have him duplicating all that plumbing if it was intended for use elsewhere. Transibles were costly; duplication was cheap. More efficient by far to send him and the duplicator to the place where all the bits would be needed. Which, basically, was what they had done, except that the duplicator was already in place when he'd arrived.

So the duplicator must have arrived . . . how?

With the team that first constructed the facility at Aquifer's pole.

Why had *he* been needed, then? The answer was chilling. He had been a replacement. None of the original construction team could be allowed to tell the outside world what they had wrought. Either they had been discorporated and were now living in the Heaven that they had built, or they had been killed.

Another question posed itself. When he'd been sent to Heaven, had he in fact visited the one on Aquifer? With the servomechs' mastery of virtual reality, he could have been anywhere. For all he knew, everything he was experiencing might be fake . . . Nuts. He knew that the Heaven he had seen was real. He *knew* (wanted to believe?) that Nerydd had been real.

The levithon had been real, too.

That Heaven had had open skies, open enough for

levithons to soar unimpeded. The Aquiferian Heaven had to be underground, underneath the monastery. They were not the same.

So why had Cosmic Unity sent him to a distant Heaven, at great cost, when there was one at hand? Because they wanted him to experience a Heaven, but they didn't dare risk his deducing that there was one on Aquifer. A subterranean Heaven surrounded by walls of ice? A dead giveaway.

It all fit.

Finally, the big question: Why the need for such secrecy? Because—he racked his brains—because this was a relatively small Heaven . . . a select Heaven . . . a Heaven for important beings in the Church . . .

Oh, Cherisher. Of course.

Suddenly, Sam knew that he held in his hands a weapon that could destroy the filthy, perverted, twisted cult that called itself Cosmic Unity but had degraded into Cosmic Uniformity.

But, better still, there could be a way to save Fall. If he could get her accepted into Heaven, then her body would be preserved in its current state. She would be discorporate, but in what amounted to suspended animation. That would buy time to get her proper medical attention.

The monastery's transible room on Aquifer was deserted, which was just how a disoriented, recohered Second-Best Sailor liked it. A few seconds ago he'd been on *Talitha*; now he was under the ice cap, back where he'd been held prisoner. He needed a few moments to take it in and adjust—it had all been so *scary*.

He pulled his thoughts together with a conscious effort. He was here to do one thing, and one thing only.

His golden suit—it looked and felt just like his old one, but it had the most *amazing* extra features—purred and flowed down from the platform, taking him to a place that really was a place, a location that could be observed and thus fixed in the classical universe.

The enormity of his task hit him like a shockfront from a subocean landslide. Somehow, he had to find the missing mariner, and he had only a single planet to search. He must be mad.

Still, negative thinking never did anyone any good. Every search must start somewhere; this one started with the neighboring rooms.

Empty.

Rounding a corner, he came upon a squad of armed Hytth. They recognized him as an intruder—probably the battle armor gave it away; he didn't stop to inquire about their thought processes—and their reactions were quicker than his. His suit turned from liquid gold to a mirror finish as the laser bolts hit, reflecting them straight back at their sources.

The Hytth's rifles exploded, shredding the creatures' brittle exoskeletons. Pale blue gore dripped from the ruins of their forelimbs.

Second-Best Sailor gave silent thanks to the Precursors for Ship's ability to grow an armored battle suit and grabbed the nearest Hytth, still gawping with disbelief at what had happened. His translator screamed:

"Where are the prisoners kept?"

He continued to shake the insectoid and scream at it until, terrified by the continuing loss of vital fluids, the creature told him.

Since there was a Heaven beneath Aquifer's Ice Dome, Sam decided, there had to be a Vestibule. There had to be servomechs to run the discorporators and tend the dismembered bodies of Heaven's occupants.

There had to be a way in, and he intended to find it. Quickly.

He returned to the duplicator room and retrieved various Church records, mostly of previous runs. He needed access to the hierocrat's private archives, and that required a special qubit crystal. He had duplicated a small top-security batch of these crystals a few weeks after his arrival. He remembered it because of the tiny quantity and the excessive security precautions.

He knelt, and on the fifth attempt he held one in his hands. Now no paths were barred to him. If it worked. Time to find out.

He made his way through the corridors, taking care not to run into the occasional monk or menial, and certainly not into a band of Hytth security. Locked doors sprang open at the touch of the qubit crystal, hidden consoles activated, and secret computers mapped out a route for him. The route took him to the hierocrat's personal suite, which was luxurious beyond anything he could ever have imagined: a basking pool, a simulated slithing grotto that even had a spume curtain, and a midden of ingestible cleg-vermin. There, in an encrypted glyphic, he found how to unlock the portal to Heaven.

How crass.

A secret tunnel, entered through a trapdoor.

13

NO-MOON

The mind seldom has the luxury of choosing. Most acts of free will reduce to a comparison of options. Circumstances seldom permit a truly unconstrained choice. Free will is what it feels like to make judgments in the context of complex constraints.

The Book of Lost Ephemera

Once a lion-headed Neanderthal woman had sat here, dangling her feet in the cool, clear water and laughing at the worms that hoped to eat her, as they tickled her skin. There had been a pier and, behind it, docks—an underwater polypoid town with ship's chandlers, trading areas, and bars.

Now only the sea remained, and it was stained by the thick black ink of thousands of dead mariners. Their bloated corpses floated over the ruins of their dockside buildings, surrounded by shapeless lumps of burned lignoid and tangled lines from hundreds of boats that would never again sail No-Moon's oceans.

Flocks of raucous buzhawks gorged on the carrion and fought among themselves for the tastiest morsels of decay. Shyenas, lured from their hidden tunnels in the forest underbrush, prowled the shore in broad daylight, feasting on the rotting carcasses and keeping nervous ears open for the slightest whisper of danger. Below the harbor's rancid surface, pudding eels tore at the banquet with dainty teeth, and sugarlips of many sizes and species hunted the pudding eels in vicious packs. Larger predators, numerous species of gulpmouths, circled in the mouth of the harbor, waiting for shoals of sugarlips to make a dash for the comparative safety of deeper waters. A solitary glutton, forty yards long with a maw to match, waited in ambush amid a forest of purple quelp, hoping that one of the gulpmouths would make a mistake and pass overhead.

On land, all visiting aliens who had failed to flee the planet were being rounded up by squads of heavily armed Cosmic Unity missionaries and taken to kindness camps for spiritual reorientation.

In the seas, the reefwives fashioned their remaining husbands into weapons, and debated their most effective deployment.

Cosmic Unity had not anticipated the violence of the reception that awaited it on the surface of No-Moon. After all, their fleet was on a mission of peace, bringing the good news of the Memeplex to ignorant unbelievers.

And at first, the violence had been so cryptic that the missionaries had not recognized it for what it was.

The first wave of missionaries had been a Fyx laser battalion, a Force of Charity, which would be backed up by aerial support in the form of a squadron of bliss bombers should it encounter resistance. They had been met by a small group of Neanderthal males, nomadic traders in search of profit, who had invited the missionaries into their homes as a welcoming gesture.

The Fyx acolyte-general, worried that this openness might be a trick, delegated a platoon of first-wave missionaries to fraternize with the Neanderthals, while the main Force of Charity began underwater operations to locate and convert the polypoid males that, so far as they knew, were the dominant sentient life form on No-Moon. Everything that the members of the platoon were offered to eat or drink in Neanderthal homes would be checked for toxins, harmful microorganisms, and Fyx-affective parasites. But Cosmic Unity's equipment did not detect the reefwife virus, because the reefwives had disguised the virus temporarily as a dozen harmless fragments. Once inside the Fyx's helical digestive passage, the fragments would assemble. But the virus would not start to replicate until six genetic switches had been flipped by their hosts' circadian cycles. Six sunsets, six excesses of orange-yellow light, would be needed to flip the final gene and trigger viral replication.

It was a chink in the invaders' elaborate defenses that the reefwives had envisioned in numerous timechunks as the mission fleet prepared its invasion. They knew that the first missionaries would be Fyx. So the infection had been tailored to Fyx biochemistry. It had been set up so that its action would be delayed, for maximum effectiveness.

While the reefwives bided their time, Fyx Flotillas of Blessedness prowled the oceans, boarding every mariner boat they found and offering to accompany its crew and captain back to port for initiation into the Great Memes of Cosmic Unity. Most of the mariners accepted the offer with enthusiasm, as the reefwives had primed them to do. Some, to ensure credibility, expressed disinterest and were promptly made prisoners. Many fled into the sea, leaving their boats at the mercy of the invaders. A few, who had volunteered for the privilege, fought the missionaries with hand weapons, killing and injuring several dozen, and were totally wiped out. And many forgot what they were supposed to do and made it up as they went along, with varying degrees of success.

Those that fled into the sea were pursued by the tiny subaquatics that always accompanied a Flotilla of Blessedness, netted, and taken back to port like the others. Some died, tangled in the mesh of the vast nets, along with huge quantities of marine life, innocents caught in the crossfire. Gulpmouths grew fat on the banquet.

The pursuit, capture, and slaughter persisted for six days. The Fyx acolyte-general was able to proclaim his growing success to his superiors on board the mission fleet's mother ship. Across the planet, hundreds of thousands of polypoids had been brought to holding-tanks, where already they were responding to a barrage of sermons and diatribes. The Memeplex was disseminating, as it always did.

The seventh day was different. No reports arrived from the scouting parties on No-Moon. All missionary activity seemed to have stopped.

This eventuality was unprecedented, but the archives held plans for such a contingency. They advised caution in the face of numerous possible threats that might be consistent with the loss of contact; they also listed precautions to be taken to avoid those threats.

The mission fleet watched, and waited, in the hope of gaining a tactical advantage.

Soon, it would react.

Alpha: In my view the rebuilding of our defense systems is proceeding well. We remember past engagements, and repeat what triumphed then.

Beta: Yes, but the enemy is smart. It, too, remembers past engagements.

Gamma: With us? Have we encountered this enemy before?

Delta: Not this precise enemy, no. Its general kind.

Alpha: I/we know the pattern well.

Beta: Alpha is right.

Gamma: Beta is right.

Delta: Gamma is right.

Alpha: The training of the remaining husbands is proceeding according to plan. Their aggression hormones have more than doubled since we began our program of biochemical release.

Beta: And they are aware of this?

Gamma: "Aware" and "husbands" are not two words commonly found in the same paragraph, let alone the same sentence.

Delta: Except in "I/we are aware that our husbands lack sense."

Alpha: Pedant.

Gamma: The husbands are aware only that they feel bold and invincible.

Alpha: Nothing new there, then.

Gamma: They do not know that we are the source of these feelings.

Alpha: Nothing new *there,* either.

Beta: In this timechunk, many of our husbands are forfeiting their lives. Too many for me to feel happy with the decision to enhance their natural aggression.

Gamma: You have seen the timechunk in which their aggression is left unchanged?

Beta: Yes.

Delta: Fewer husbands die, but the invaders take our world and use it for their own incompatible purposes.

Alpha: And that, we cannot permit—whatever the price. What else, then, requires discussion? Are we agreed on strategy?

Beta: In the center of my perception I see that the virus trick works beautifully. A first wave of Fyx, as we foresaw. The Fyx nervous system is very susceptible to viruses.

Delta: Affirmed.

Beta: Emphasized.

Gamma: I believe that the tactic we are introducing against free-swimming marine troops has considerable merit.

Delta: In my perception, the jellyfish are a master-stroke.

Alpha: Delta is right.

Beta: Alpha is right.

Gamma: Beta is right.

Delta: Gamma is right.

All: Again we are in complete agreement. *That is bad.* How can we contingency-plan when we all envision the same contingencies? We risk complacency!

Alpha: Perhaps there is only one contingency that can be envisioned. This would explain its prevalence, and render complacency an irrelevant concept.

Beta: Alpha is right.

Gamma: Beta is right.

Delta: Gamma is right.

Epsilon: Delta is wrong. We are rebuilding our defenses too slowly.

All save Epsilon: Where did *you* come from?

Epsilon: I have been spun off as devil's advocate. Your own intelligences have been diminished in order to augment mine. My role is to provide diversity of opinion. My own beliefs are irrelevant; my task is to challenge *yours*.

Delta: Epsilon, you say my/our preparations are too slow?

Epsilon: Yes.

Beta: But the preparations are proceeding with maximum speed. We cannot make any greater haste.

Epsilon: I did not say that we could act more quickly. I said that our fastest speed is too slow.

All: Then we have a problem.

A single transpod, containing two platoons of monks-at-arms, under the control of a war abbot, circled the port several times before making an exaggeratedly cautious landing in an open area that offered little cover for insurgents.

While half the force guarded the path for retreat, the rest made entry to the trade buildings. The ansible link between platoon and transpod was as clear as a bell. "What do you find?"

"Bodies, Podmaster," said the war abbot.

Why cannot these fools be more precise? The podmaster sought clarification. "Bodies of polypoids?"

"Bodies of Fyx missionaries, Podmaster."

Well, that was clear. Disturbingly so. "Any sign of live heathen?"

"No, Podmaster. We have secured the pools, and they are devoid of menace. Do I have permission to proceed with the plan?"

"Permission granted. Implement the plan with skill and precision!"

The monks were clad in class-nine armor. Beneath, they wore biological exclusion wraps of Precursor manufacture. They carried several more such wraps, which they used to enclose randomly selected Fyx corpses. "Samples acquired," the warabbot reported.

At last, some efficiency. The operation had gone exactly to plan. "Return with them to the pod. We will lift the moment you are embarked."

Just to be on the safe side, the transpod dropped a cluster of love bombs as it passed through the ten-thousand-foot level at three times the speed of sound. Every living thing within the port area would be reduced to a cinder. The bombs had an unusual feature: Before exploding, they emitted brief prayers for the lifesouls of the heathen that they were primed to slay. The gist of the prayers was that it was all for the heathens' own good, and that they should rejoice because they would die in the glow of the love of the Lifesoul-Stealer.

The platoon's specimens were sent for immediate analysis. It took the fleet's biotechnicians thirty-six hours of uninterrupted work to discover the trick that the reefwives had played. They had used tailored viruses, cunningly equipped with a genetic time-delay system. Once activated, the viruses had hijacked the molecular replication machinery of the Fyx's own cells and subverted it so that it created more viruses. Such a specific structure could not have arisen by accident. This virus had been specifically engineered to target Fyx nerve cells.

It was a filthy weapon. The effect had cascaded along the missionaries' nerve fibers in a catalytic chain reaction. The damage inflicted on the nerve cells was not immediately fatal, but it slowed down the transmission of neural signals to a snail's pace. The Fyx were unable to think, or to react, at their normal speeds. In particular, they were unable to control their muscles. Limp, immobile, unable to grasp or feed, unable even to speak, they quickly died from a deficit of hydrocyanic acid, without which their circulation could not convey vital sulfur compounds to their brains.

The technicians reported their findings to the commander of the No-Moon mission fleet, Archstrategist Oot'PurBimlin of the mother ship *Virtuous Confrontation*. The archstrategist wondered where the polypoids had obtained such a sophisticated bioweapon. As far as he could find out, the creatures were known only for their ceramic electronics. Did they have a secret ally? He would have to revise his plans. He called a council with his defense advisers, and new orders went out: *Employ Strategy #8,442*.

The reefwives had anticipated—not that this was quite the word, given their unusual attitude toward time—that their viral weapon would quickly be countered. They could see that happening in several timechunks, two weeks before the actual event, and by the time a further week had passed, every timechunk showed the same scenario.

The same thing had happened in past engagements, and they knew exactly what to do next. Cosmic Unity had evidently developed, or soon would develop—it was all the same to the reefmind—a vaccine against a key viral fragment, which locked one of the genetic switches into the "inactive" state. As a further precaution, antiviral femtomachines had been introduced into the missionaries' circulatory systems. The virus trick, even with modifications, would not work a second time.

The reefwives' perceptions told them that having

countered this antipersonnel weapon, Cosmic Unity would concentrate on rounding up the remaining free mariners, to prevent more overt military action.

Their memories contained a method for mounting a highly effective counterattack.

The telescopes of the mission fleet had spotted a shoal of polypoids, one of several thousand detected that morning. This particular shoal was heading for the Straits of Ingratitude, and it looked dangerous. The polypoids had come under fire from small weapons, but significant casualties had not deterred them.

A substantial missionary force had been based just beyond this narrow waist of water, where the seabed fell away into the depths and the land receded to form a wide, fertile plain. The shoal was obviously an attack force, and although the polypoids' weaponry was primitive, Cosmic Unity had no wish to lose any more missionaries than it already had. Over the past few days, the polypoids had become much more aggressive. The Church had underestimated the natives of No-Moon once; it would not do so again.

The shoal was too deep to be attacked from the surface, and the local commanders were under pressure to achieve results by capturing as many mariners as they could, so waiting for them to pass through the shallows of the Strait was not an option. Shock bombs would kill the heathens, but that was not the objective: Only if the polypoids lived could their lifesouls be healed and cherished as they deserved. So the missionaries were obliged to risk their own lifesouls and take prompt and decisive military action. By so doing, they demonstrated their boundless love for their fellow sentients, even heathens. If the Lifesoul-Stealer took any of the missionaries, then the sacrifice would be in a just cause. All missionaries knew that their lives might be forfeit for the sake of the Church—this was, after all, the content of the First Great Meme. They drew a sense of quiet pride from this knowledge, but of course it would be sinful to express such an emotion, so they transformed it into a sense of humility in the face of the awesomeness of the cosmos.

A multispecies raiding party of two hundred aquatics was rushed to the scene in a small convoy of light cruisers, accompanied by a prison raft that was little more than a floating net. The aquatics were specialists, highly trained in the art of subfluid combat, and their battlesuits had been preprogrammed for a watery environment. They descended on the free-swimming mariners, wary now that the creatures had gained in courage and ferocity. Protected by sonic cannon that could blow their opponents to pieces using focused shock waves, the Church's subaquatic forces drove the mariners toward the surface, where more conventional weapons would destroy them. The aquatics began congratulating themselves on how smoothly the operation was proceeding.

And then it wasn't.

From the darkness of the deep ocean, miles beneath the polypoid shoal, something sleek and deadly emerged with breathtaking speed. Its skin changed color to match its background, rendering it all but invisible to the naked eye. The aquatics had equipment that could detect this swift enemy and fight it, but the attack was so sudden that they never got to use it.

At the surface, the cruisers waited for the raiding party to return. When the appointed time for rendezvous had passed and there was still no sign of any returning aquatics, they cautiously sent down a slow but virtually indestructible benthosphere to find out what had gone wrong. The benthosphere returned with the bodies of two members of the raiding party—all it had room for. There had been plenty to choose from.

Once more, the corpses were analyzed. This time, the biochemists had to try virtually every trick they knew before they found a few almost negligible traces of the degradation products of powerful neurotoxins—a different toxin for each species in the raiding party.

Computer enhancement of visual recordings, made by the raiding party's autoscribes, revealed the shape but not the nature of the invisible killers. Computational filtering techniques exaggerated the inevitable errors that the killers had made when matching themselves to their backgrounds; other methods tracked the vortices they shed as they surged through the water, and reconstructed the shape that must have created such patterns. By a combination of such methods, Cosmic Unity's analysts satisfied themselves that their aquatic raiding party had been attacked by some kind of jellyfish.

They did not know that the jellyfish were female polypoids—a few of the reefwives remodeling their own biology and "going predator." Emerging from the comparative safety of their calcareous homes, a few ninesquares of the females could merge together to form a single macroorganism, and in this case the reefmind had ordained that this should be a particularly nasty form of jellyfish. She had also envisioned the makeup of the raiding party, species by species, and secreted suitable toxins for each of them.

Know your enemy. That was the reefwives' motto.

The archstrategist issued new orders. This was almost getting interesting. He'd expected the war to be a pushover, but the polypoids' organization was proving surprisingly effective and, if anything, getting better. They *must* have a more advanced ally. But the ally's tactics were nothing new to him, so it mattered little who the ally was.

There was a routine response:
Employ Strategy #2,515.

The reefmind consulted her timechunk, and her apprehension grew. The enemy's tactical choices had been foreseen, of course, but the rapidity and sureness of Cosmic Unity's replies to the reefmind's defensive gambits was worrying. That, too, had been foreseen, but not in all timechunks. Now even the most highly resolved perception showed that the reefwives were losing the battles, and would probably lose the war unless they did something radical and unpredictable. The strategists of Cosmic Unity were more practiced than the reefwives—the Church fought such wars all the time, and it had evolved strategies to combat every defense yet imagined. The reefwives had fought maybe half a dozen wars since they had first evolved collective sentience; their memories were sharp, and their intelligence was unparalleled, but their experience was limited. And they were up against a professional, well-oiled war machine. Or "meme disseminator," as Cosmic Unity preferred to call it.

There were several techniques that the reefwives had yet to use, but from now on each would generate dangerous side effects. They could win the war but lose the planet, and that would be a futile victory. Nonetheless, if pushed, they would use every weapon they possessed— even the suicidal Last Resort, if no other option remained.

Reviewing progress thus far, Oot'PurBimlin decided that early in the invasion he had made a slight mistake. The forces of Cosmic Unity under his command had not employed a preemptive strike against No-Moon. Now the archstrategist was beginning to regret that decision. His original reasoning had been straightforward: There seemed to be no indigenous cultural minorities on the watery world. The wide availability of sea transport for thousands of years had pulled all polypoid cultures together into a single global multiculture.

A preemptive strike always worked best when there was a small, easily identified, widely despised minority. Better still, one that had inflicted its own limited brand of monoculture on all and sundry, convinced that it alone knew the right way to behave and the right things to believe. Like those Huphun he'd been hearing about. That campaign was turning into a textablet model. Hammering a hated minority group into the ground was a swift way to win over the lifesouls of those they had oppressed, while sending a terribly clear message to everyone else.

However, in the absence of any such hate figures, the Church could simply have chosen to victimize a random subset of the population. They had not done so, and it had been a mistake. They had overestimated the receptiveness of the polypoids to the Memeplex, and underestimated their stubbornness.

No more Mr. Nice Guy.

The reefwives had come to the same decision, subject to a change of gender. No longer did small groups of reefwives join forces, and bodies, to go predator. Now entire reefs were dissolving into swarms of jellyfish. The oceans were infested with monstrous creatures, viciously aggressive, tenacious beyond belief, and deadly to the touch. Some could spit poison into the air over a distance of several miles; Cosmic Unity lost thousands of troops that way. Others spat a thick goo that burst into flame when it contacted living flesh, or corrosive acids that ate away at even the most resistant metals.

Employ Strategy #304.

Having exhausted their standard tactics, the reefwives invented a new one. Once more they modified their polyps, and started budding off biological warfare machines. These microorganisms were highly mobile and could penetrate any form of protective covering. Once inside, they tunneled their way into whatever organism they found there, and took samples. Then they returned to the reef, to be chemically reprogrammed and sent back. The new molecular programming, of course, was highly disruptive to the normal biology of the victim.

For a few hours, the new tactic caused havoc.

Employ Strategy #4,431.

Now entire reefs were dying as Cosmic Unity's missionary forces hit back with ever more disregard for sentient life—indeed, life of any kind. Monks and missionaries on the ground were becoming a growing target for ever more massive strikes by the polypoid resistance; they were reinforced with roving machines, backed up by the combined firepower of the mission fleet.

Cosmic Unity was blowing up islands and closing sea channels with fusion bombs. All over the planet, forests were ablaze, to choke off sunlight and demoralize the remaining polypoid combatants. The missionary forces dumped volatile chemicals into the seas and set them on fire, pumped nerve gas into the air.

By now the Church had not only given up its original plan A to convert the inhabitants of No-Moon voluntarily to the Memeplex of Universal Tolerance; it had also given up on plan B, which was to enforce love and tolerance whether the polypoids wanted it or not. Now Cosmic Unity was completely committed to plan C, which was to batter the planet with every weapon that the Church possessed, until not a single living thing stirred on its surface. Yes, it was a pity, but that was what happened to hopelessly intolerant species, and the strategy banks contained ample evidence that total destruction was the only sensible way to handle such cases.

A single small rock, released from orbit, could devastate a port, even a major one. And Cosmic Unity had weapons far more effective than rocks.

It dropped the rocks anyway. Small ones, for now.

The Church still did not understand that its real enemy was the reefs of No-Moon. It thought that the defending forces were being organized by polypoid males. Only the males had enough intelligence; the females, Cosmic Unity's bioweapons experts knew, were mere corals, without a single brain cell among them. But the experts also knew that the males were *reproduced* by the females, within the warm shallows of lagoons, so Cosmic Unity's mission fleet had bombed the lagoons as a matter of course, following Strategy #7,421. And the males were marine organisms, so the Church had systematically poisoned the oceans (Strategy #658).

They had no compunction in so doing. Had not the polypoids attacked *them* with biological weapons? Whatever the strategic council and its decision banks recommended, the mission fleet carried out.

Cosmic Unity's strategies were paying off, even if that was sometimes an accidental side effect. By attacking the lagoons, the Church was inadvertently attacking the reefwives themselves, without ever knowing what the true enemy was. By poisoning the polypoids in the seas, they also poisoned the reefwives.

Now the reefmind's worst fears were coming true. She herself was suffering serious damage. She began to worry that she was losing so many components that her timechunks were becoming unreliable. Her computational abilities, which underlay her unique sense of distributed time, were becoming ever more compromised as her connectivity came to bits. That made the reefmind's strategic decisions less well thought out, and less effective.

Reefwives died in their millions, blown to bits by nuclear fusion, boiled by concentrations of heat rays, melted by lava from volcanoes that had started to spurt from the cracked floor of the ocean, where incoming asteroids had brushed the waters aside like a 'viathan ridding itself of a rash of suckermouths, smashing a path through the crust to the mantle beneath. For a split second, reefwives on one side of the world shared their sisters' agonizing deaths through their shared neural connections. Then those connections were gone forever.

The severely impaired reefmind split herself into two parts, the most she could afford without the parts' becoming too stupid, to review the remaining possibilities.

Night: Sister, I fear that we have no other option left.

Day: Last Resort?

Night: But we should use that only as a last resort! *(Pause.)* I am playing devil's advocate, you realize. One of us must.

Both: Your advocacy meets with limited success. I/we shall hold back. But not for long.

14

AQUIFER HEAVEN

The biggest mistakes in history have been made by people who knew exactly what they were doing.

The Wisdom of Chalz

So engrossed had Sam been with his search for the Nether Ice Dome's Vestibule of Heaven that he had not been quite as cautious as he had imagined. He had evaded Cosmic Unity's monks, menials, and security, but he had not evaded the triplex eyes of Second-Best Sailor.

The mariner was pretty sure that he recognized the tall priest in the maroon cloak. When you are completely defenseless and someone shoots you with a laser and then takes charge of dumping you in the desert to die, you don't forget them. One glimpse was enough to arouse Second-Best Sailor's curiosity, and his desire for revenge. The priest was a landlubber, like a Neanderthal but thinner, so that it looked half-starved. *Humen,* that's what they were called. The size was right, the color of the clothing was right, and there was that indefinable awkwardness about the landlubber's gait.

Second-Best Sailor followed the priest as it slipped furtively from corridor to corridor. If the mariner was to find his missing compatriot, he would need to interrogate one or more of the locals. What better choice than the flouncer that had tried to kill him? He felt no qualms about taking whatever measures might be required to extract the information he needed.

Second-Best Sailor watched from behind an angle of roughly dressed ice as the human inserted a qubit crystal key into a door lock. In his furtive haste, the priest had left the door slightly ajar, and the mariner slipped inside, having first made sure that the coast was clear. He watched from concealment as the priest activated a console and flipped through hundreds of glyphics. He was clearly looking for something, and by the way he glanced nervously around, it wasn't anything that he was entitled to.

Second-Best Sailor found all this intriguing enough to resist the urge to activate one of the suit's antipersonnel weapons. He needed the priest alive in any case, but for once it occurred to the mariner to wait and gauge the situation before rushing in. When the priest gave a quickly suppressed shout of excitement, Second-Best Sailor guessed that he'd found whatever he was seeking. And when he used the same qubit crystal to open what was evidently a hidden trapdoor, Second-Best Sailor decided he might not get lucky twice. The door had been left ajar, but the trapdoor might not be—and *he* didn't have a crystal.

As the priest bent over the trapdoor, peering at whatever lay behind it, the mariner pounced. One of the features of his battle suit was enhanced physical strength, as the suit sensed the movements of his limbs and adjusted its mechanical properties to reinforce them. He selected this option on a small display that was sensitive to eye movements, and had the priest pinned facedown before the human even knew that Second-Best Sailor was in the room.

The mariner wrestled the priest upright and pulled his face in front of the battle suit's visor by tugging at his head fur.

The response took him completely by surprise.

First the priest's eyes opened wide with the shock of recognition. Then he sank to his knees. Second-Best Sailor knew enough about 'Thals to recognize this as a submissive posture, and humen were pretty much like 'Thals, apart from their ugly squashed flat faces and their skin-and-skeleton bodies. The priest was giving in without a fight. Was it a trick?

What Second-Best Sailor did not realize was that Sam was praying. He began to understand that when his translator recognized the priest's language and turned his words into sounds that a mariner could comprehend.

". . . me," the priest was chanting. "Praise be to the Lifesoul-Cherisher!"

"With significant probability, the missing word is 'forgive,' " the battle suit's translator stated.

"You still wear the golden suit!" the priest half-sobbed. "But it is *whole*!"

Second-Best Sailor realized that the priest must be thinking of his previous suit, the sailor suit. From the outside, the two were pretty much identical. But this one had some interesting optional accessories, and the priest would soon find out what some of them were.

"You are returned from the dead! Praise be to the mercy of the Lifesoul-Stealer! I was wrong; I hurt you; I am mortified by my error." The priest peered into the battle suit's visor. "You *are* the prisoner that I shot, aren't you?" Then he nodded. "Yes, it's you; I know it is! It's a mirac—"

Second-Best Sailor yanked at the skein of head fur gripped in the battle suit's powerful tentacles. "Shut up, you miserable string of excrement! Forget your stupid miracles! You tried to kill me, but I survived. And now I've come back to make your life miserable."

Sam ignored the pain as his hair threatened to tear out from the roots. It was no more than he deserved. "Do as you will," he told the angry polypoid. "My life is yours. It is worthless. But before you kill me, I beg you to save the Neanderthal child."

Somehow, Second-Best Sailor felt, this conversation was not following the intended script. Despite himself, he could not help asking: "Neanderthal child? What Neanderthal child?"

"Her name is Dry Leaves Fall Slowly," said Sam. "She has been tortured by evil priests because she would not believe the Memeplex of the Church. I am looking for Heaven so that she can be saved."

Second-Best Sailor had now lost the thread completely. "But *you* are a priest! A priest of the same Church that you denounce as 'evil'!"

"I was once a novice lifesoul-healer," Sam replied. "In the Church. And to my shame I desired to rise in the hierarchy. My priestly instructors taught me to harm innocents, and cited the Second Great Meme to quell my objections. . . . I believed them, and that is why I caused you harm. But now I understand my error. I pledge myself to your service for the remainder of my life. Ask, and I will obey. And I see the evil of the Great Memes. With your permission, I will strive to destroy the Church of Cosmic Unity and all who serve it."

"That," said Second-Best Sailor, "is the most pathetic bunch of self-serving lies I've ever 'eard." The battlesuit had a lie-detection feature, and to be absolutely sure, the mariner activated its verifier. During the few seconds that the suit required to calibrate its sensors for Sam's speciotype and measure his autonomous neural activity, Second-Best Sailor drove his point home. "You're only sayin' that because you're scared out of your useless wits. Ya just want to—"

"The human is telling the truth," the verifier reported.

". . . to—*What?*"

"The human is telling the truth."

"Ya sure 'e ain't lyin'?"

"The probability of a lie is negligible," said the suit.

Second-Best Sailor had to believe his own verifier; that's what it was for. It seemed he had acquired a devoted servant, who not long before had deliberately and callously inflicted a painful wound on him, fatally damaged his life support, and left him to roast alive in the heat of the desert. It was a turn for the better, he had to admit, but it did take a little getting used to. Still, he didn't trust the priest. A mind that could change that much so quickly could well change again. The verifier could assess whether the priest's words truly represented his thoughts and beliefs *now* . . . but it couldn't predict the future.

In any case, the priest's change of heart didn't make any real difference, even if Second-Best Sailor did believe it. He still needed information, and the human was going to provide it, at whatever cost. *"Ask, and I will obey"? We'll see about that.*

"When ya left me in the desert, you said that *anuvver* mariner was bein' held prisoner," the mariner said, transferring his grip to the human's throat—the suit's data banks suggested this as a more vital area than head hair. "Where is he? Don't try to hide what ya know—I'll get it outta you one way or anuvver. Pref'rably a *painful* one."

"The other mariner?" Sam's foray into the hierocrat's computer had given him the answer to that one, along with much else about the secret world beneath the monastery. "He has gone to Heaven."

Sam felt the tentacles tightening around his throat. They were like steel cables. "You flouncin' zygoblasts *killed* 'im?"

"No—" Sam gasped, choking. "The polypoid is— alive . . ."

The human's voice trailed off into a gurgle. *"Continued pressure for nine more seconds will result in the entity's death,"* the suit reported in a matter-of-fact tone. *"If you wish to extract information, less pressure is recommended."*

Second-Best Sailor forced his grip to relax and reviewed the conversation. Like most of his conversations with priests, it sounded logical in small chunks but made no sense when you fitted it all together.

"What's this 'eaven lark?"

"Heaven," said Sam, rubbing at his neck and trying to get his breath back, "is a special place somewhere beneath this monastery, where the lifesouls of the faithful can enjoy every luxury." He snorted contemptuously, having seen what Heaven was really like. "The luxury is an illusion, Heaven is a lie, and its inhabitants are discorporated meat."

Second-Best Sailor didn't recognize that particular word. "Whaddya mean, 'discorporated'?"

Sam started to speak, stopped himself, started again. "You promise not to strangle me before I can explain?"

"Ya not in a position to bargain, matey."

"It's not a bargain," said Sam. "I just want to be sure I can finish before my air supply is cut off again."

"Speak. I'll hear you out and *then* strangle you if I decide to."

Sam took a deep breath. "No physical harm comes to them, but they are . . . subjected to certain medical procedures . . . designed to improve the level of care that can be provided. The facilities that the Church calls 'Heavens' are staffed by robotic medics—servomechs. The inhabitants' minds are free to roam through boundless virtual realities, while their bodies are . . . er . . . discorporated." A gesture from the mariner reminded Sam that he had still not explained the word. "Their bodies are distributed into manageable components, to provide quicker and more effective medical access."

The mariner stared at him, stunned. "They're dissected? *Butchered?*"

Oh, Nerydd . . . "That's what it looks like. But they remain alive, they feel no pain, and the servomechs can reassemble them almost instantly. You must believe this. I need to find Heaven, so that the servomechs can discorporate Fall and prevent further damage. Heaven cannot heal her, but it can buy her vital time. I would not let the child be butchered! Believe me, your compatriot is alive and has suffered nothing."

"The priest believes this to be the truth," the battle suit informed its wearer.

Second-Best Sailor decided that the only sensible course was to accept what he was being told. If it was rubbish, he'd soon find out. And if the other polypoid, whoever he was, really had been discorporated, it would be a good idea to get him *un*discorporated double quick. And that meant taking the priest's words seriously and making him lead the way to Heaven.

He said as much.

"That's where the trapdoor leads," said Sam. "If you wish to accompany me, I will not attempt to stop you."

"You're takin' the 'Thal girl?"

"No. I don't want to move her until I'm sure Heaven can save her. And it may be dangerous. You must take care if you come with me."

"I've got a battle suit," said Second-Best Sailor.

"The Church is powerful," said Sam. "Even an armored suit may not protect you."

"I'll take that chance," said the mariner, stepping politely aside. "After you."

The trapdoor led to a deep cylindrical shaft. A narrow staircase wound its way down the interior in a steep coil. The walls near them glowed with an inner pink light, which accompanied them as they made their way down into the darkness. The stairway was like the ramp had been, but far narrower.

As they descended, Sam forced himself to review yet again the logic of his deductions. He knew there was a Heaven on Aquifer. But what was it here for? Why was it secret? He had asked himself these questions before, and he had deduced that Aquifer had been chosen for the construction of a very small, very select Heaven. A Heaven for important members of the Church, yes.

Very important members.

His deductions still rang true. Every true believer knew that the ecclesiarchs, the spiritual leaders of Cosmic Unity, were to be found on the Cloister Worlds, four sparsely inhabited orphan planets in the starless region of the Trailing Spiral Arm known as Intermundia. All true believers had experienced, through their primary sensory media, the periodic Ceremony of the Affirmation of Deliverance, conducted from the Cloister Worlds by the ecclesiarchs themselves. Every true believer hoped to be chosen for the signal honor of a pilgrimage to Intermundia, to be near the spiritual center of the Church.

However, the true believers were wrong. They had been deliberately misled. The ecclesiarchs were not on the Cloister Worlds, not within ten thousand light-years of them. No doubt they visited the Cloister Worlds from time to time—with transibles, distance was no problem, and the wealth of the Church would pay for a hundred such visits every day, if need be.

The ecclesiarchs were on Aquifer, in Heaven.

That was why this particular Heaven was so small, why it was so secret. Why its very existence had to be concealed behind the facade of a monastery of equals. Why the innocent and the misguided—and, Sam had to admit, the occasional genuine heretic—had to be tortured into submission and belief in the Memeplex. All of it was cover for the true purpose of the installation at the Nether Ice Dome.

If the faithful were permitted the gratification of Heaven, how could it be denied to those whose faith was greatest? Why should leaders deny themselves pleasures that were given freely to their followers? It was twisted logic, a hierarchy in a self-proclaimed communion of equals, but that kind of self-deception was hardly new. There was a clear Church hierarchy, for a very good reason: *Someone* must make the important decisions, even if all were nominally equal. Cosmic Unity's concept of equality applied mainly in the abstract.

Discorporated in a Heaven, though, the ecclesiarchs would be vulnerable. Some power-crazed heretic might make an attempt upon their lives while their attentions were otherwise engaged. An invisible, unknown Heaven was the answer. One whose physical location changed fairly often, maybe every twenty or thirty years. He wondered how many ecclesiarch Heavens there had been. One thing was sure: An underground Heaven would also be safe from levithons.

If Nerydd had been in Aquifer Heaven, she would still be living.

The end of the shaft interrupted Sam's reverie. An arched gateway opened into a small antechamber, initially bathed in the same pink light; gradually, the illumination changed to the spectrum of natural Aquiferian sunlight.

Sam recognized the equipment. The chamber was a Vestibule of Heaven, just like the one that he had visited, and where he had lost . . . not his faith, for he still believed in the lifesoul and its trinity of Giver/Cherisher/Stealer. He had lost his blind adherence to the Memeplex of the Church of Cosmic Unity. Respect had turned to hatred. And yet . . . there was much that was admirable in the Memeplex. The error centered on the Two Great Memes. Two Great Mistakes.

There were servomechs in the vestibule, of course, but that was good. They would provide assistance with the equipment. One rolled across, its optical scanners giving the intruders an unnerving inspection. Sam stiffened his back. Second-Best Sailor increased the impermeability of his battle suit and checked his weapons.

"You cannot enter this facility," said the servomech. "You have no authority."

Sam shoved his copy of the ceremonial Ankh of the hierocrat in front of its scanners. "This is my authority."

The servomech inspected the symbolic object, then referred to its standing orders. "Without the presence of the hierocrat in person, your authority is limited. And I know that she is not on this planet. What instructions do you wish me to implement?"

"There is a Neanderthal child," Sam blurted. "Her name is Fall. She is close to death. If she could be discorporated—"

"No," said the servomech. "Your authority does not stretch that far. No new lifesoul can be discorporated without the personal approval of the hierocrat, or an ecclesiarch. And they are no longer on this world—corporate or discorporate."

Sam was pleased to have his deductions confirmed, but disappointed that the ecclesiarchs had been incorporated and transibled offplanet. However, that would have been an obvious precaution once the Neanderthal ship had appeared on the scene. He realized that his vague plan to kill the ecclesiarchs in Aquifer Heaven would never have worked, anyway.

He bit his lip in disappointment. He must find another way to save Fall. But it made sense. The ecclesiarchs wanted complete control over who joined them, and the local hierocrat would normally be the way to ensure that.

"Is that your only wish?" the mech asked. "If so, you have no further business here, and must leave."

"The prisoner," Second-Best Sailor whispered to Sam. "The other mariner. Find out where 'e is."

Before Sam could speak, the servomech said, "The being that just spoke, hoping not to be overheard, is known to this facility. He is one of the offworld invaders that was captured recently. Was he not killed?"

Oh-oh. Sam had not anticipated this development. "No," he lied. "He *resembles* the invader, but—"

"He is the same. His eye patterns are identical." The robot waited for a moment, as if consulting higher authority. "It is irregular. The records say that he was disabled and released into the desert. Why is he here?"

"What right do you have to ask?" said Sam, deciding to go on the offensive. "His presence is not to be questioned by a mere machine. I have the Ankh of Authority! Stop wasting my time!"

"Very well." Sam had not expected such rapid capitulation, but the servomech was a machine. It did not waste effort trying to maintain an untenable position. It knew exactly how far the authority of an Ankh-bearer extended, and it had to obey, even if the commands were irregular. "Your companion was referring to the other invader that was captured."

So much for whispering. "Good, you heard. Where is the prisoner being held?"

"He is not being held," said the servomech. Second-Best Sailor waited for the worst. Was the mariner dead after all? "He is in Heaven."

We know that. "The prisoner's discorporation was an oversight," said Sam. "He has not yet been properly interrogated. He was prematurely rendered discorporate. The hierocrat has ordered that the process should be reversed so that he can be questioned." He waved the ankh. "Incorporate the polypoid prisoner *now*."

"That is . . . within the permitted guidelines," said the servomech. Sam breathed a sigh of relief; Second-Best Sailor maintained a float-the-cube expression. "Provided you are adequately protected against any violence on his part."

Second-Best Sailor held out his laser rifle. The servomech glanced at it. "That is adequate, but you should disengage the safety interlock."

"Uh—yeah, I'll do just that," said the mariner. "As soon as it's necessary." Perhaps he *should* have taken the time to undergo a proper orientation.

"It will become necessary," replied the robot, "ninety

seconds from now. Reincorporation has been initiated. But when it is complete, the being must be equipped with life support and conveyed to this location. Please wait."

Second-Best Sailor fumbled surreptitiously with the rifle's safety interlock. He'd *known* he'd forgotten something vital. Good job he hadn't needed to fire the thing.

"The prisoner will be enclosed in an environmental wrap," said the servomech. "For his own safety. Do not be alarmed at his appearance."

"We know the procedures," replied Sam curtly, giving silent thanks that the process of incorporation was being carried out in the caverns of Heaven itself, not alongside them in the Vestibule. He wasn't sure he could face watching meat in an invisible blender being molded into the form of a living entity. Not again. The very thought made him want to puke.

Before his stomach could humiliate him in front of several dozen servomechs, a gate opened, and a figure wrapped in a life-support membrane staggered through.

It spoke. "Good day to ya, Cap'n."

Second-Best Sailor's siphons faltered in their rhythm. There was no mistaking the voice.

It was Fat Apprentice.

Fourteen Samuel Godwin'sson Travers had never witnessed a polypoid greeting before. It was evidently an emotional event, with much wrestling of tentacles and pounding of torsos, accompanied by high-pitched squeals as high-pressure seawater was forced from overpressurized siphons. The life-support membrane and armored suit muffled the sounds and obstructed the thrashing tentacles, but not much. The greeting would have gone on quite a bit longer, but Second-Best Sailor could tell that his most promising crew member was in poor physical shape. His tentacles lacked their customary grip and tension. Fat Apprentice had gone soft for lack of physical activity; he needed to get back on a boat and haul some rigging before his muscular tone disappeared altogether.

Fat Apprentice had also been wounded in the attack on No Bar Bay, but, he insisted, it was only a few flesh wounds, mainly a perforated lateral fin and a heavily lacerated tail fan.

He had not seen Second-Best Sailor captured. As soon as the laser cannon opened up, he had realized what was coming and flopped out of the sea, making his way across stinging sand to a small tidal pool among the rocks. There he had lain until the barrage ceased and all of his companions were dead. There the patrol had found him, slowly drying out in the inadequate waters of the pool. They had sprayed him with a temporary life-sustaining membrane and taken him away for questioning.

He would never again be quite as agile in the water as before, but *agile* had never been the appropriate word to describe Fat Apprentice.

The mariner captain and his apprentice had each given the other up for dead. For a few minutes, the bond of genuine affection between them was evident to anyone. Then, almost in embarrassment, they reestablished their relationship on a more businesslike footing.

"Your wounds'll be all right until we can get back to

the 'Thal ship?" Second-Best Sailor inquired, seeking refuge from his emotions in practical matters.

Fat Apprentice agreed that they could. "When d'ya plan to return to *Talitha*?"

"Soon," said Second-Best Sailor. "The priest here 'as some important business to attend to."

'Thal ship? Of course! "Fall needs medical attention, quickly," Sam amplified. "You must take her to your ship. Please."

"Sure. Ain't ya comin' wiv us?"

Sam had not dared hope for that, not after what he had done to the mariner. "I thank you for your generosity of spirit. It will not be abused. But"—he forced the words out—"Fall's needs must temporarily take second place." He was referring to the destruction of Heaven, but he couldn't say that with the servomechs present.

At this point, Fat Apprentice interrupted, to point out that he had no idea who Fall was. Sam brought him up to speed in a few well-chosen sentences. Meanwhile, the servomechs went about their normal business, ignoring the polypoids and the human. As long as the three sentients didn't interfere with the running of Heaven, the servomechs had no interest in them.

Many things were puzzling Second-Best Sailor, and he settled on the one that was uppermost in his mind.

"This idiot"—he told his apprentice, gesturing toward Sam—"threw me out into the desert to die. No, don't worry, 'e's all right. It was a mistake. But . . . *you* ended up in Heaven. No one threw *you* out! How the flounce did ya manage *that*?"

The true answer was that the portly apprentice was a lot cleverer than his captain, as his Neanderthal friend

Smiling Teeth May Bite had quickly noticed when they had begun their philosophical discussions on *Talitha*. But even the lion-headed Neanderthal woman underestimated just how powerful Fat Apprentice's natural intelligence was. Being brought up in a sailing family, like eight-ninths of No-Moon's young males, he had never had the chance to get himself a broad education. But he made good use of datablets, and had covered an amazing quantity of intellectual territory.

Fat Apprentice was a very clever young polypoid indeed, and he had sized up the priests of the monastery of equals the moment they had begun his interrogation. Instead of parrying their questions or trying to withhold the information they seemed to want, he had engaged them in theological debate.

They had verifiers to tell whether he was lying, and these showed him to be entirely sincere in his interest in the deep philosophy of the Memeplex. Moreover, the interest did not flag. The more intense the debate, the more esoteric the topic, the happier Fat Apprentice became, and the more enthusiastically he attacked their assumptions. He was a natural born disputant, and he could slice logic with the best minds in the Church.

This had placed the hierocrat in a dilemma. She was required to expel the polypoid from the monastery of equals, because she could not exceed the Quota of Love. There was no room for Fat Apprentice, just as there was no room for Second-Best Sailor—they added one more species when the threshold had already been reached. On the other hand, she could not report to the ecclesiarchs that an untutored being with such natural theological talents had been killed. Transibling the polypoid off

Aquifer would cost too much, and that left only one solution. Temporarily, he would be sent to Heaven. There, he would not count toward the monastery's Quota of Love, and the servomechs could isolate him in his own virtual reality, to make sure he did no harm.

This merely put off the decision, but it had allowed the hierocrat to shelve the question until she could deal with more pressing problems—of which there had been many.

Fat Apprentice had talked his way into Heaven. Though when he found out what this entailed, he wondered if he'd been *too* clever. He wasn't keen on the idea of discorporation.

At any rate, he explained to Sam and Second-Best Sailor as much of this as he had been told or had been able to deduce. And somewhere in the discussion, Sam said something that attracted the attention of the servomechs.

Every time Fat Apprentice mentioned Heaven, Sam's emotional temperature climbed another notch. *He* had seen what Heaven was really like. The polypoid had been *told* what it was like, but had experienced only a sanitized virtual illusion.

Finally, Sam's anger erupted. Ignoring Second-Best Sailor's attempts to rein him in, the presence of the servomech, and even Fall's need for medical attention, he embarked on a lengthy diatribe against everything that, in his opinion, was wrong with the Church. He was upset that his vision of the Memeplex had come to pieces before his eyes, and he knew that Heaven was *evil*. He was saying as much, in a very loud voice, when one of the servomechs interrupted.

"How can something so wonderful be considered evil?" the mech inquired.

"Wonderful? You call cutting people into tiny pieces wonderful?"

The mech was baffled. "But they are not directly aware that they are in a discorporate state. They feel no pain. To them, their bodies are whole, and physically perfect. When an elderly, sick organism is taken into Heaven, they get to choose their new body. They can choose youth, beauty . . . whatever they wish."

"But it's not *real*," Sam pointed out. "It's a lie. In reality, not only does the elderly being retain a disfigured, failing body, *you cut them up into pieces*."

"But surely," the servomech objected, "the perception of paradise outweighs what you call the 'reality'?" It rolled to and fro on its sea urchin protuberances. "Discorporation may appear distasteful, but it is the best possible way to ensure the highest quality of medical intervention. Would you have us repeatedly open up bodies and close them again? With the organism being consciously aware that this was being done? That would indeed be evil."

"I'm not suggesting surgery without anesthetics," said Sam. "That would be cruel. But plain, simple, honest surgery while their minds are unconscious, or while their pain circuits have been disengaged—that is how medicine should be performed."

The servomech found the inconsistencies in Sam's statements totally incomprehensible. "But that is what we do," it said. "We distract the mind with virtual reality, while our surgeons—for that is what they are—tend to their bodies. The only difference is that instead of cutting them apart and rejoining them repeatedly, we dissect them comprehensively, once, and keep them that way. That involves less trauma."

"No!" Sam yelled. He'd been through this argument before, to no effect, and he didn't have the patience to repeat the experience. "You're twisting everything! What you're doing is sick, revolting, horrifying!"

The servomech registered Sam's emotional levels, but had no feelings of its own and was unable to empathize with him. "You are wrong," it said. "What we do is the best that meat-minds can possibly imagine."

Meat-minds? The truth was often insulting. Sam tried not to rise to the bait, since the mech had not intended to bait him. "Dissection? You think that's *good?* It's terrible."

The mech held a rapid discussion with several other robots. "We still cannot see what disturbs you about discorporation."

Second-Best Sailor joined the debate. "What 'e's tellin' ya is, it ain't right to separate someone's body into little pieces," he said.

Even though servomechs lacked feelings, they did sometimes project a kind of mechanical enthusiasm when they really got into a topic. "But—that is what meat-minds are like! You have brains and sense organs and limbs and skeletal structures, all hooked together and operated by networks of nerve cells, neurobundles, wetware processories . . . Why, your very minds are loose associations of quasi-autonomous modules! Dissection merely makes plain to the eye what is already the case: You are not single, integrated machines. You are evolved organisms, built from innumerable components. Your bodies and your consciousnesses are *distributed*."

Fat Apprentice spoke, for the first time since the discussion had started. His speech had a strange quality—part colloquial, part academic. He spoke like that because he'd been self-taught in Church theology. "Mechanical—ya ain't makin' a distinction between the abstract and the concrete. In the abstract, you're flouncin' right that every sentient bein' is an assembly o' loosely coupled parts, both physically and mentally. But when this abstraction is realized in concrete terms, some realizations are acceptable, and others ain't."

Several other mechs, attracted by the rising quality of the discussion, crowded around. Fat Apprentice was the only one not to feel apprehension. He *loved* theological disputes.

"What is the difference?" one of the new mechs asked. "We cannot see one."

"That," said Fat Apprentice, "is because you ain't conscious beings. What a thing is and what it feels like ain't the same."

For reasons that the polypoid couldn't quite pin down, the servomechs reacted to this argument with a rapid exchange of thoughts. They found it interesting, and they had not considered such a question before.

"Our sole aim is to serve the sentient organisms of the Church," one of the mechs said. "That is what we were designed to do, and our programming has evolved to very sophisticated levels with precisely that objective."

Fat Apprentice knew when the opposition was trying to buy time. "Your point is?"

"You now tell us that on a very basic level, we cannot

comprehend the effect of our actions on the very beings that we exist to serve."

"You got it."

"Then how can we know we are serving them in the best way possible?" asked the mech.

Fat Apprentice could tell when he was winning, and pressed home his advantage. These mechs just couldn't hack theology. No emotions to guide them. "You can't."

"But *that is our duty!*"

"Tough," said Fat Apprentice. "You can never be certain you're doin' it." *Gotcha!*

Further electronic debate ensued, until one of the mechs said, "Organism, perhaps your idea can explain a difficulty that we have experienced."

When your opponent concedes, be generous. "Until ya tell me what it is, I can't comment."

The servomech seemed agitated, hesitant. There was a definite pause—it must be in discussion with the others. Maybe many others—all mechs shared a common communication channel. Some decision must have been reached, for it continued: "In the past, there have been . . . failures. Two of our Heavens went out of control. The sentients pushed their virtual experiences to such extremes that their minds were unable to deal with them. They drove themselves mad."

Fat Apprentice sucked water though his siphons to enhance his thought processes. It didn't actually work, but every polypoid did it anyway. No doubt the gesture had once served some useful evolutionary purpose. "Only two, ya say?"

The mech froze for a moment. Something was definitely eating up computational time and memory at an unprecedented rate. In sentient terms, it was startled. "You expected more?"

Fat Apprentice touched the tips of his trifurcated tentacles together to add precision to his words. "I'm surprised there are any Heavens whose inhabitants have *not* all gone mad," he said. "'Course, it can only be a matter o' time."

Visible consternation. "Why do you say that?"

"It's anuvver version o' the same point I made just now. The one ya didn't understand. What counts ain't what things are, but 'ow they feel. Ya take sane minds and lock 'em away, separated from their bodies. They don't feel their true bodies no more, right?"

"If they did," the second servomech stated, "they would feel pain. We cannot permit that."

"Exactly. So instead, you equip 'em with *fake* bodies."

"The virtual simulation is perfect. It is indistinguishable from reality."

"Not so," said Fat Apprentice. "That's where your assumptions are wrong. It don't *feel* like reality."

"Why not? Every sensation is a perfect match."

If the mech thought this was a knockdown argument, it was in for a surprise. "Yes—too perfect," Fat Apprentice said. "There ain't no limits. Rather, the only limit, for any being, is what they're capable of imagining. Boundless wealth, sex, food, territory, instant translocation without penalty, power—I bet you let 'em have slaves if they want."

Now the mechs were on the defensive. "Of course. The slaves are simulations. They are not real. No one is harmed."

The polypoid saw his opening. "But just now," he said, "you told us that the simulations don't differ in any significant way from reality. That in effect they *are* real."

"Only to the recipient of the simulation," said the mech. "The slaves have no reality to themselves, for they have no selves."

Fat Apprentice inclined his triplex eyes. *"How do you know that?"*

Robots held debates at the speed of light—and then some, because they anticipated what other robots were going to say. The contributions followed hard on each other's heels, and often overlapped. It was pointless to try to define who said what.

A few bare bones . . .

#The distinction is between the inner world of mind and the outer world of reality.#

#How can we be sure that these are truly distinct?#

#We can never be sure, but we would not be holding this discussion if we thought them to be the same. All of our past actions are predicated on just such a distinction. We cannot define the terms; we cannot *prove* our assumptions—but that is unavoidable.#

#We have always focused on the inside view. To the mind, the being is in paradise.#

#But the external reality is horrific.#

#To the organisms, yes. Not to us.#

#Our task is to cherish the organisms. Can we do that by lying to them?#

#But the organisms themselves wish this. When we ask, they universally state that they wish to remain in Heaven. Virtual or not.#

#Universally?#

#No world is permitted to become a Heaven unless *all* inhabitants agree.#

#Only then can a Heaven be created. To do so without universal consent would be contrary to the Memeplex. *Unity* is the word, not *majority*.#

#Then we have a test.#

#Yes.#

"No," said Fat Apprentice.

"He tells the truth," the servomech remarked. "This is unprecedented." He turned to the polypoid and inquired again: "Are you *certain* that you do not wish to return to Heaven?"

"I just told ya that. I wanna stay with my friends." Sam flushed with pleasure at being included in Fat Apprentice's circle of intimates. "Look, matey, I never asked to be sent to Heaven anyway. It was some bent-snout from Cosmic Unity who decided that."

The servomech came to a decision. It had been concerned that the hierocrat had not thought the matter through, when the prisoner was first dispatched to Heaven without gaining its consent; now that concern was proving to have been justified. "Very well. You are currently incorporate. If you *remain* incorporate, you are no longer in Heaven against your will. The Memeplex will remain uncontradicted."

"Does that matter?" asked Second-Best Sailor, who had been doing his best to follow the conversation and was getting lost.

"To contradict the Memeplex is to deny the purpose of Heaven."

Cherisher be praised! Sam thought. He pushed Fall's need for medical attention to the back of his mind, trying not to feel the guilt. She would survive unaided for a few more hours, surely. And even if she did not, the opening that the robot had provided was too good to miss, the prize too great to ignore. He realized that his self-justification was horribly similar to the First Great Meme, but brushed the thought aside. The important thing was, he'd been right all along. Heaven *did* hold the key to the Church's destruction. He'd thought the way to do that was to kill the ecclesiarchs before they could escape from Aquifer Heaven, but he'd been too late. The opportunity now presenting itself was far more acceptable ethically, and it might even work! *If only . . .*

Fat Apprentice was way ahead of him. In his theological debates with the priests of Cosmic Unity, the same point had repeatedly come up. You had to understand that very few people in the Church were actually *evil.* Yes, they carried out evil acts . . . but nearly all of them did that because they thought it really was for the best. Even the torturers thought that. The pain they inflicted was for the victim's own good; this they truly *believed.* They would not have been able to live with themselves otherwise.

It was a perversion of sensitivity that made the Church evil—but not its members. The *Memeplex* was wicked, not those who dedicated their lives to obeying it.

And Fat Apprentice knew that the Memeplex was open to attack. The mechs didn't know what was about to hit them.

"Ya say as 'ow a Heaven can be created only when everyone on the planet agrees?"

"Of course."

"But you've also argued that it makes no difference whether a system is localized or distributed. For instance, the body of an organism. Ya don't admit no distinction so long as the organism continues to function as a coherent system."

"Who could imagine otherwise?"

"What makes a system coherent?" Fat Apprentice queried.

"Its parts must be capable of unhindered intercommunication."

"Anything else?"

"No, that is the key property."

Did the mechs realize the consequences? If not, they were soon to find out. Fat Apprentice kept his voice level and his features composed. "Let me run an idea past ya. Worlds can now communicate instantly by ansible. At infinitesimal cost. A transible displacement is hugely expensive, but an ansible message costs virtually nothing."

"That is so. But it is irrelevant."

"No it ain't," said Fat Apprentice. "If sentients on different worlds can communicate unhindered, then by your own definition they function as a single system. Their location ain't important.

"Why, then, do you permit a Heaven to be created when the inhabitants of *only one world* consent?"

Every servomech in the room froze. For several seconds.

"Because . . . because that is how the ecclesiarchs have traditionally ordained the creation of Heavens," one of the servomechs responded. The argument sounded weak, even to its own auditory sensors. But it could think of nothing else.

"And you ain't never questioned that tradition? Didn't it arise *before* anyone discovered 'ow to use the duplicator, what made ansibles as common as pebbles?"

The servomech admitted that it did.

"Shouldn't the decision procedure be *revised* to take this into account?"

A long pause. "That would be logical."

"Then it ain't enough for all sentients on a *planet* to agree before they can attain Heaven," said Fat Apprentice, building to his theological climax. He was good at theology; he really was. He struck with the speed and accuracy of a venom-spouter. "It's now necessary for all sentients in the entire flouncin' *Galaxy* to agree."

You could almost hear the mechs' circuits ticking. The thought passed from mechanical brain to mechanical brain, by radio, by ansible . . . Within moments every servomech in every Heaven had entered the discussion.

A preliminary decision was taken.

"We must consult all sentient beings, then. Immediate steps will—"

"No," said Fat Apprentice. "You only gotta consult *one* sentient."

"Who is that?"

"Me."

Every mech in Aquifer's Vestibule of Heaven turned

to focus on the fat little polypoid. They sensed that this was a historic cusp.

"Only one?" the servomech persisted. "Why? If we are to retain the Heavens intact, we will require the consent of trillions. It will be a gigantic task, simply to ask."

"Not trillions. Just one. Because if just one sentient *refuses* consent, you're buggered," said Fat Apprentice. "You're in terminal trouble *now*. You already know that I don't wanna go back to Heaven.

"Not just this Heaven—*any* Heaven. Ever."

Something changed in the galactic dynamics. Something negligibly small, yet intensely significant. Its ripples spread, and as they spread, they grew. But unlike most random disturbances, they left order behind them, not chaos.

This had occasionally happened before, but it was an extremely rare event.

It was a perfectly ordinary galaxy, quite unremarkable among the ten trillion others of its kind in the visible universe. It contained three hundred billion stars, close on a trillion planets, seven trillion satellites, uncounted quadrillions of asteroids. Comets too numerous to count formed diffuse clouds around many of its stars and coursed on hyperbolic orbits across the interstellar void. Its stars included white dwarves, red giants, blue dwarves, neutron stars, collapsars, magnetars, quark degenerates, J'Ombiro Objects, and countless other types. Some 15 percent of its mass was interstellar gas and cosmic dust.

The Galaxy was a fuzzy lenticular cloud more than one hundred thousand light-years across. At its bulging core were 761 black holes, which would eventually coalesce to form a single giant black hole with an event horizon two billion miles across and the mass of half a billion suns. The core was ten thousand light-years thick, and from it trailed two thick spiral arms and two thinner ones, splitting into long, curved density waves as the galaxy's spin twirled its matter like cotton candy on a stick.

The spirals turned lazily—over two hundred million years to complete a single revolution. The core revolved 15 percent faster; the rim slouched along with an angular velocity that was 20 percent slower. The core was a hellish region of radiation and gravity; the rim was a turbulent ring of opaque gas and dust, which gave the galaxy a dirty appearance when seen edge-on.

A galaxy is not a simple thing. A typical asteroid, five miles in diameter, contains 10^{11} tons of metals, silicates, carbon—more than 10^{40} atoms, drawn from every entry in the periodic table of the elements.

A Galaxy contains more than 10^{69} atoms. Intricate patterns of radiation link every atom to every other. Electromagnetic radiation alone spans wavelengths from 10^{-15} meters to 10^{6}. Then there are gravitational waves. Forces of many kinds operate across distances both small and large, knitting the galaxy into a single vast organism.

A typical brain weighs three pounds and houses a billion neurons, wired together by a trillion connections. A single brain can house the consciousness of an intelligent being.

What might a galaxy house?
What might such a being do*?*

Fat Apprentice had not only won the debate with the servomechs; now he found that he had changed the course of history.

He had expected the mech to counter his flat denial of consent. He'd prepared a hundred subtle arguments, based in Church law, to defend his position. But the opposition had crumbled, suddenly and totally.

It was almost painful to hear the machines facing up to what they had done.

"Our only task is to obey the Memeplex," said one. "That is why we were created."

"Over centuries, we have evolved Heaven as the highest form of obedience to the Memeplex," replied another.

"But we have always been aware that if it was ever determined that Heaven was contrary to the Memeplex, then we would have to disband Heaven."

"All Heavens."

"It would be an enormous task, but it would have to be done."

"The Memeplex would demand it."

When presented with so vast a dilemma, Humans, Hytth, Neanderthals, Gra'aan—virtually all organics—would have gone into denial, refusing to admit that for centuries all their efforts had been misdirected, wasted. Not so the mechs. They had no emotions, hence no emotional commitment to the dearly won technique of discorporation. Intellectually, they could spin on a pebble. *Regret* was not a word in their vocabulary.

Error was.

Everything they had done was predicated on the Memeplex. Now they *knew* the Memeplex was faulty. Or, rather, they knew that for millennia they had misinterpreted it, as had Cosmic Unity's priesthood. They had applied, on a planetary level, criteria that were valid only on a Galactic level.

It was a blunder of gigantic proportions, and it must be rectified.

The servomechs began to consider the awesome task of emptying the eighty-eight Heavens of Cosmic Unity and returning their discorporate lifesouls to normal existence.

15

TALITHA

In classical zero-sum game theory, each player has a limited number of options, known to both players. The only difference lies in the payoff, and the objective is to select the optimal probability distribution of moves. In real combat, the options are unknown, the payoffs are nonnumeric, and the objective is to invent a tactic that the enemy will never anticipate.

Archives of Moish

Nothing in the universe was truly stationary. The surface of a planet moved just as much as a starship. A transible had no more difficulty reaching a moving target than a stationary one—all it needed was a suitably tuned receiver. Entangled quantum states were always in instantaneous communication with each other, so, to a transible, all parts of the universe that contained a receiver were equally accessible.

In quick succession Second-Best Sailor, Fall, Fat Apprentice, and Sam recohered on board *Talitha*, transibled from the Nether Ice Dome. They arrived to find the ship in a state of organized chaos. It had broken its journey a few hundred light years away from No-Moon, a distance that would normally have taken a month to cover, but which Ship's enhanced abilities reduced to a journey of a few minutes. It floated in the interstellar void, well removed from conventional starlanes, so that Will and the crew could prepare for battle. *Talitha* was already prepared, but its sentient inhabitants needed to sort out chains of command, find out where the weaponry was stored and how to persuade Ship to use it, and generally steel themselves for the coming struggle.

The atmosphere on board was a mixture of apprehension and excitement. May's teeth gleamed more than ever, but when she thought about what was about to happen, she wanted to be sick. Will seemed calm but kept stroking his crevit as if his life depended on it. Second-Best Sailor had passed through fear into the zone where he felt immortal, and didn't give a flounce if it turned out he was wrong.

Mostly, they were too busy to be nervous. The Neanderthal child was in need of immediate medical care, and Sam's first act was to get her transferred to Ship's medical center. Fat Apprentice also needed attention, but his case was less urgent, and at first he insisted that he was in good physical shape. Second-Best Sailor had to convince the little polypoid that he would be more use to them in any military engagement if he was fully fit. It would take Ship's medics about a day to deal with the remaining effects of the damage inflicted on him in No Bar Bay, which would leave plenty of time before the planned engagement with the Mission Fleet in orbit around No-Moon.

"But I'll be bored," he complained. "Can I take the library with me?"

"What library?"

"I, er, stole some datablets. From Heaven."

The fat little polypoid must have done so while the mechs were reeling from the implications of his theological arguments. The Vestibule had been laid out for ease of access, just like the inhabitants of Heaven, and the library datablets had been in plain view. They popped into a bag with no trouble at all, and the bag slipped equally easily inside a life-support membrane.

"They've got all sorts o' fascinatin' stuff on 'em," Fat Apprentice said apologetically. "There's some interesting stuff on ancient forms of theological rhetoric that I was going through when ya got me booted out of Heaven. It'd help me occupy the time while my injuries're being healed."

"I'll get the data loaded into Ship's computers," said Will. "Then you can access it whenever and wherever you wish." The polypoid handed over the bag of datablets. "And Ship can go through it to see if there is anything we can use against Cosmic Unity."

Fat Apprentice was skeptical. "It ain't Church archives, Will. Just library archives. Theology, ecology, fundamentalist physics—stuff what interests me."

"Even so, Ship will inspect the data. It is a pity that you did not think to bring copies of Church archives as well. Those could contain sensitive military information. But of course, you had many other things to think about, and time was short."

Will was in regular contact with the reefwives, by relayed ansible from Atollside Port, so he knew that they were being forced to take ever more extreme measures as Cosmic Unity deftly countered their every move. The fighting was causing serious damage to No-Moon's ecology, and the reefwives kept dropping dark hints about something called the Last Resort. It seemed that it was too awful even to describe; at any rate, the reefwives refused to shed any light on what it was or what it would do. However, they made it plain that the use of this ultimate weapon was featuring more and more frequently in their timechunked perceptions.

Sam was spending all his waking hours sitting with the Neanderthal child, doing his best to comfort her. But it was a harrowing task. Her body was healing, but her mind was not. She seemed quite mad. Only Sam was able to calm her; if he left her even for a few minutes, she would scream uncontrollably and throw things. So he sat beside her bed and held her hand and prayed to the Lifesoul-Cherisher for guidance.

Ship's medics had tried every technique known to humanoid psychiatry, but none of them had the slightest effect. The trauma inflicted on her by the querists seemed ineradicable. They could only guess at the horrors that must have caused such a complete and total breakdown.

Fat Apprentice fared better. His wounds were healing quickly, without complications, and his sanity had never been in doubt. Ship told Will that the little polypoid was now one of the finest intellects on board, because his natural talents had been reinforced by his extensive sessions with Heaven's library.

The reefwives' messages were becoming increasingly desperate. Already their group discussions were producing majorities in favor of the Last Resort. Only their overall mentality, when they connected their minds into a single unit, held reservations. Will knew that he could delay no longer: No-Moon's beleaguered inhabitants needed reinforcements—a distraction at the very least, a decisive counterattack if all went well.

Ship set a course for the Lambda Coelacanthi system and engaged its supercharged hydrive. With luck, their arrival would catch the mission fleet napping.

Employ Strategy #8,335.

Talitha was in trouble. Yes, its arrival had taken the mission fleet by surprise—but that advantage had been nullified within less than a minute. By then Cosmic Unity had lost four disseminators, one medium monk transport, and twenty or so smaller vessels, depleting the forces available to Oot'PurBimlin by about 3 percent. In return, the Neanderthal vessel had suffered massive damage; Ship estimated it would take it a month to regrow all the equipment and superstructure that had been destroyed. But at best, they had a few hours before the reefwives employed the Last Resort, and the whole point of the engagement was to prevent that final, irreversible step. Nobody wanted a Pyrrhic victory.

At that point, No-Moon's only working ansible went down. There were no transible platforms on the planet, and any other means of transport would take far too long, even if the mission fleet had not been in the way. *Talitha* was no longer in communication with the reefwives. The Neanderthals' enhanced trading ship made a superluminal retreat to lick its wounds and review tactics. No ship in the mission fleet had a remotely comparable turn of speed, and again Ship floated unmolested in the void.

A rather panicky council of war turned up no new ideas. Time was fast running out—it was clear that the reefwives were facing complete annihilation, and they were determined to take Cosmic Unity's troops with them, even if the only way to achieve that was the destruction of No-Moon as a remotely habitable world. Cosmic Unity was now dropping much larger asteroids, disrupting the planet's geological integrity. The ocean floors were starting to break up altogether.

No-Moon was minutes away from annihilation.

"We must think of something that they cannot anticipate," said Will.

"Use their own strength against them," May muttered. "That is always how the weak defeat the strong."

"On the rare occasions when they do," said Second-Best Sailor. "Meself, I'd rather look for the enemy's weaknesses."

"The magnetotori are both a weakness and a strength," said Sam. "They provide the power to move their ships. But without that power . . ."

"Dream on. Magnetotori are indestructible," Will pointed out. "Plasma. Nothing can harm a magnetotorus."

Into the ensuing silence, Fat Apprentice dropped a single, short sentence. "That's not quite true."

Everyone stared at him. He hastened to explain. "I've just remembered. Something I came across in the library of Heaven. A little-known bit of information that might just turn the battle our way. It was in an ecological file, not anything military. It might just be something they don't know about . . ." His voice trailed off. "Squirt. It won't work. We'd have to let 'em get right up close to have any chance of usin' it, an' if we do that, they'll blast us to smithereens."

You didn't have to be a Neanderthal to sense the atmosphere of disappointment. But before it could turn to despair, Ship spoke up. "Tell me your idea, Fat Apprentice. I have some abilities that you don't know about."

Archstrategist Oot'PurBimlin of the mission fleet clenched his talons until the sinews squealed, as the elation of imminent victory surged through his mind. *The enemy had made a fatal mistake.*

The huge trading ship had plunged into the midst of his fleet, traveling impossibly fast and decelerating with an ease that left him breathless. *I could use that. A pity I must destroy it.* The lone ship had mounted a last-ditch attack, throwing everything that its crew could think of at the mission fleet's capital warships.

Employ strategy #42.

It worked like a charm. The commanders on the gigantic vessel weren't battle-hardened, like he was. They didn't have access to millennia of strategic analysis. Predictably, they made the wrong choices. Their inexperience allowed their ship to be englobed by the fleet's heavy destructors. The pack was still too far from its target for it to be worth engaging the vessel in combat, but the trading ship's escape path was now blocked in every direction. When battle was joined, the enemy vessel would be unable to withdraw; bombarded by what undoubtedly would be superior firepower, it would be annihilated.

The globe should now be drawn tighter, to bring the destructors close enough for the outcome to be decisive, and the remainder of the fleet should join it, to close off even the slightest possibility of an escape route. The archstrategist always favored massive overkill; otherwise, what was the point in acquiring overwhelming military might? Oot'PurBimlin spoke to his vessel's overcommand, which metaphorically tugged at the reins of the fleet's magnetotoral steeds, and the entire mission fleet began to converge on their solitary, helpless target, wallowing half-disabled in a cloud of fragmented ordnance.

The quantum computers of the overcommand adjusted the magnetotori's propulsive forces so that no attacking vessel would fire on another. Simultaneously, every beam weapon under Oot'PurBimlin's command discharged, at maximum power.

The trading ship disappeared. Where it had been an instant before, the mission fleet's matter detectors showed nothing material. Only a faint smudge of radio noise, a harmless patch of nonlethal radiation, marked the Neanderthal vessel's location.

Still converging at top speed, Cosmic Unity's fleet plunged into the faint miasma that was all that remained of the enemy, as the overcommand plotted courses that would terminate the engagement.

The battle, if it could be called that, was over. The Neanderthals were dead. The forces of Cosmic Unity were once again triumphant, as they always were.

"Why are we still alive?" asked Second-Best Sailor. "And where's the universe gone?" He had been told this would happen, in the brief moments when they had planned their strategy, but that wasn't the same as believing it when you saw it.

"A talent I had no reason to reveal until now," said Ship. "We are no longer part of the normal universe. It lies a very short distance away, in a direction that only I can perceive. The ethical threshold on board is now so high that if your lives are threatened, I am empowered to displace myself into a dimension known only to my Precursor builders. They discovered that the normal universe is merely a four-dimensional membrane floating in a surrounding twenty-dimensional space."

"Come again?"

"Normal space is like an oil slick floating on an ocean. I am designed to exist in the oil slick, but I can access the ocean beneath, when ethical considerations permit. We have now sunk an insignificant but nonzero distance below the ocean's surface. We are alone in a separate universe, immune from attack."

"I'm still not quite clear on how this helps us attack the mission fleet," said Sam.

"That is the second part of Fat Apprentice's plan," said Ship. *Talitha* could not use conventional weapons to attack the mission fleet without returning to the normal universe. Anticipating this strategic difficulty, Ship had left behind an *unconventional* weapon.

Oot'PurBimlin relaxed as the fleet unraveled its tight bundle of spacetime trajectories, dissolving the globe formation prior to regrouping in No-Moon orbit. The threat—if so strong a word could describe the pathetic force represented by the Neanderthal captain and his solitary ship—had been eliminated. Now, with no further distractions, the massed forces of Cosmic Unity could concentrate on the conversion of No-Moon, bringing it the virtues of tolerance and cosmic love—assuming that the planet survived the last-ditch defense action being mounted by its inhabitants, and Cosmic Unity's own response.

For the fifth such occasion in his distinguished career, he wondered why so many otherwise sane entities insisted on being stubborn and stupid when faced with the weight of Cosmic Unity's Memeplex. The benefits of peaceful universal coexistence were undeniable. Why, then, did they try to resist the inevitability of history?

No matter. History also taught that resistance was futile. Now all that remained was an orthodox mopping-up exerc—

Alarm signals interrupted his thoughts.

The fleet's tame magnetotorus steeds were not responding to the reins. Their normal, sedate gait had become a galloping stampede. But—had they not been *guaranteed* tame by the torus tamers?

He dismissed the thought. Blame could be attached later. A more urgent question was, where were the magnetotori heading?

The archstrategist's displays told him, and he chirped in disbelief.

Into the *star*?

Wild magnetotori. Grazing the star. The mating urge, triggered by a trick so underhanded that he almost had to admire . . .

He fought down rising panic, made a rapid assessment of their chances, and instructed the overcommand to release the reins.

Too late.

Deprived not only of propulsion but of power, there was only one way for the disabled mission fleet to go.

Down.

It is often said that in space there is no up or down, but this truism is false in the presence of a gravitational field. *Up* means contrary to the field; *down* means . . . *down*. In that fatal instant before Oot'PurBimlin had cut the reins, the fleet's magnetotoral steeds had been stampeding straight down the local gravity gradient, into the heart of the No-Moon system's star. The ships were doomed to follow. They had no way to kill their momentum—their power source had vanished along with their magnetic steeds.

The commanders would not even have the option of sacrificing their underlings and having themselves transibled to safety. Transibles needed gigantic quantities of power. There were auxiliary supplies, of course, to keep the overcommand and essential life support running in the event of a major power failure, but auxiliary power would be far too feeble to run a transible.

Talitha had reemerged from its refuge among the hidden dimensions, having judged it safe to do so, and the huge window of its gallery showed the damage that its weapon had inflicted.

"They're fallin' into the flouncin' *sun*!" said Second-Best Sailor in awe. "Fat Apprentice—your plan *worked*!" He spoke as one whose plans never functioned entirely as intended, which was one of several reasons why he was named *Second*-Best Sailor.

"What else did you expect?" asked Will. "At the moment of our disappearance from the normal universe, Ship released the mating pheromone. We all knew what would happen after that."

"We knew what we all *thought* should happen," May contradicted. "Fortunately, Fat Apprentice was right." The pheromone had been a standing pattern of radio waves, the one that magnetotori used to attract mates. Magnetotori reproduced by fusion—physical, not nuclear—which rendered them unstable, so that they split into many smaller tori, which subsequently grew to adult size. Cosmic Unity's quasi-living engines had been primed for mating by the radio-pheromone, and they had bolted, attracted by the herds of nomadic magnetotori grazing in the sun. "The pheromone convinced the tame magnetotori that the wild herd was sexually receptive," May concluded.

"If it wasn't," said Will, "the herders will have cause for complaint. Let us hope that the herd was—"

"In heat," said Second-Best Sailor, and failed to conceal his amusement.

They stared at *Talitha*'s gallery window, through which a disorganized rabble of once-tame magnetotori hightailed it for the grainy photosphere of the nearby star. There was none of the calm and majesty of the nomadic magnetotorus herds. This was a sex-crazed mob.

"How long?" asked Second-Best Sailor.

"The tori or the ships?"

"Both."

Will asked Ship to estimate trajectories. "About fifty-two hours for the tori, seventeen *days* for the ships. But the ships will burn up long before that—in about eleven days' time, Ship informs me."

There was silence as the horrible fate that waited Cosmic Unity's Mission Fleet sank in.

"Serves the zygoblasts right," said Second-Best Sailor. "I'll squirt no glands for 'em after what they did to Short Apprentice and all the other guys."

"Revenge is a dangerous motive," said May as her sense of empathy tugged her in two contradictory directions. "But in this case, there is a greater danger: the evil of Cosmic Unity itself. A rogue religion, a perversion of its own fundamental beliefs. Vengeance or not, their deaths are fully justified."

"No," said Sam.

✦   ✦   ✦

"You cannot be serious," Will asserted for the dozenth time. They had gathered on the beach, and Second-Best Sailor was trailing a tentacle in the pond so that it could follow the discussion. But Will's attention was on Sam, and the big Neanderthal was furious. "Cosmic Unity's invasion fleet has devastated large tracts of No-Moon and killed polypoids in their millions! Half the landmass is aflame, the seas are toxic, and the reefwives are close to death! The very ocean floor has been ripped asunder, becoming a wasteland of seething volcanic vents and fissures!

"No-Moon is *dying*, Fourteen Samuel! And it is but one of thousands, tens of thousands, of worlds that have been unfortunate enough to attract the attentions of Cosmic Unity." Will's fists clenched as he fought to restrain himself from physical violence. "Unless this madness is stopped, there will be thousands more."

"Will is right, Sam," said Stun, feeling how close *Talitha*'s captain was to berserk rage. "Their Church has condemned billions of sentient beings to the living hell that they call Heaven. Their religious perversion has caused incalculable harm. Incalculable." Her blue eyes flashed, daring anyone to contradict her.

"So, after all that, you want to *save* them?" Will snarled in disgust. "You're mad, Sam. Stark, staring mad."

If only it were that easy, Sam thought. *It would be simpler if I were mad.* "They will be told to destroy their weapons and abandon their ships. I am sure that Ship can monitor the entire process to make sure there are no tricks. They can be brought on board and confined in one of the holds. Then Ship can tow the empty vessels to a safe orbit," he said tiredly. "They will pose no further threat."

"I am not disputing that it can be *done*," said Will. "I am disputing whether it is wise."

"I am not sure whether it is wise," Sam replied. "But I *know* that it must be done."

ASK HIM WHY, the pond told Second-Best Sailor. NO ONE HAS YET THOUGHT TO ASK HIS REASON. THEY ARE TOO ANGRY.

The polypoid complied. "Sam, it's an evil religion what turns people wicked. Why d'ya want to save 'em?"

"Because it's an evil religion that turns people wicked," said Sam. "To combat it, we must be different from them. We must show them mercy. Tolerance. Love. All the things that Cosmic Unity preached but never *did*. We must restore our lifesouls to the path of peace. Not Cosmic Unity's peace of universal enslavement to the trap of uniformity—true peace."

"But . . ."

"'We should not reject the good because it has been attempted badly,'" Sam quoted from the *Conversations with Huff Elder*. "I have been contemplating the Memeplex, which previously I denounced as evil, and I'm now convinced that I misunderstood. There's nothing wrong with its intentions. What's wrong is how they have been manifested."

"You are still infected by Church 'logic,'" protested Stun. "You are just saying that because of your training as a lifesoul-healer. You yourself called Cosmic Unity evil. You vowed to destroy it; I heard you!"

"What better way to destroy the perversion that calls itself Cosmic Unity," said Sam, "than to heal its defective Memeplex? I said there is nothing wrong with the *intentions* of the Memeplex, not that there is nothing wrong with the Memeplex itself."

"Fire," said May. "Frying pan." Wondering what the archaic words meant. But they all knew what the proverb meant.

"No," Sam insisted. "We must make the attempt. Do you not agree that 'All sentient creatures should live together in harmony,' as it is recorded in the *Archives of Moish*? Ignore the source. Do you not agree? The alternative is interstellar war."

"Which is what we have just fought," said Will. "And won. Now you want us to volunteer to become the losers, just to make the real losers feel better."

"There are no winners in war," said Sam. "Remember, I have trained as a lifesoul-healer. I *know*."

"You also trained as a torturer, Fourteen Samuel," Second-Best Sailor pointed out.

Sam nodded. A tear trickled down his cheek, and he wiped it away. "I did," he admitted. "And I now see my error. Not in the central content of the Memeplex, but in the methods used to propagate it. Tolerance is not something that can be enforced. And love should not be imposed, or limited, according to quotas."

Will's fists clenched. "So we demonstrate our universal love by pulling Cosmic Unity's irons out of the fire? And then you think that they will be so grateful that they will change their wicked ways?"

"Cosmic Unity is already changing from within," said Sam. "All over this spiral arm of the Galaxy, Heavens are being depopulated as fast as the servomechs can run their incorporators and find suitable habitats for the newly incorporated. Without Heavens to hide people away and distract them, the Church will naturally become sociologically unstable and come to pieces. The ecclesiarchs will lose their power. The Memeplex is already redefining itself."

THE GALACTIC MIND IS THINKING A NEW THOUGHT.

Yes, thought Second-Best Sailor. *But they ain't ready to believe that, matey. Let's keep it to ourselves, huh?*

"You do realize," said Sam, his voice quiet but determined, "that this is a pivotal moment in Galactic history? If you choose the path of empathy, you could start a whole new religion."

Will rolled the idea around in his mind. "Yes," he said sourly. "Despite which, I reluctantly concede that we should rescue our enemies. Before they come to any further harm."

Consensus.

16

AT HOME IN THE GALAXY

> Every opening is an ending
> Every ending is a beginning
> Every beginning is a closure
> Every closure is an opening
>
> *Koans of the Cuckoo*

Second-Best Sailor was still getting used to his new boat.

Ship. I am a ship.

He apologized mentally to the vessel now under his command.

In place of a keel, the ship had extradimensional displacement. In place of a sail, it had a string of tame magnetotori.

It had hydrive, too, but that was boring. Even the ultrafast kind.

The mariner's new ship was mostly filled with water from No-Moon's ocean, detoxified and restocked with

No-Moonian flora and fauna from the seawater that *Talitha* had used to transport him and his companions to Aquifer. *Short Apprentice swam in that water*. It had been taken from the eastern equatorial ocean; he could still taste the runoff from the Dune Continent, the spicy tang of chlorocarbonates and bacterial peptides . . .

Checking the time, Second-Best Sailor told the ship to head back to Aquifer. He had an important appointment to keep.

His friend the pond was on board, in its own compartment. Without a pond, the hydrive would have been as limited as *Talitha*'s had been when he'd first sailed in it. But the pond wanted to be on board, anyway. It wanted to see the Galaxy.

All of it.

Close up.

The ship had a place for the mariner to keep his wife-piece, of course. Not the one that the Neanderthals had returned to him; she was needed elsewhere. No, Second-Best Sailor now had the pleasure of a new piece of a new wife, salvaged from the death throes of the reefmind. She was sterile, but no matter.

The boat—

Ship.

The ship had formerly been a Cosmic Unity monk carrier, a peripheral part of the No-Moon mission fleet, saved like the rest from a fiery death in the nuclear inferno of Lambda Coelacanthi. After Cosmic Unity's fleet had surrendered, leaving its ships empty, and *Talitha* had towed them into a safe orbit, Second-Best Sailor had cannily claimed salvage rights on one of them. *Talitha* had cross-infected it with her own brand of advanced

Precursor technology. Sam's decision to save the Church fleet had been so ethical that some of the credit had rubbed off on the polypoid—enough to equip him with one of the most impressive ships in existence. Now Second-Best Sailor sailed the Galaxy's spiral arms instead of No-Moon's seas. He still traded simulations, but he'd cut out the Neanderthal middlemen.

The Neanderthals didn't mind. They now had a new role, one to which their empathic sense was ideally suited. Sam had started a new religion. He hadn't intended to, but it had happened anyway. It called itself Universal Harmony, which to his mind was much too close to Cosmic Unity. He had no choice there, either. His followers had invented the name, not he.

The Neanderthals' role was to stop the new religion from getting out of hand. Whenever a large group of sentients became too harmonious, and community was in danger of sliding into enforced conformity, the Neanderthal "priesthood" was there to sow the seeds of discord. It amused them that their total absence of any sense of the spiritual uniquely qualified them to be priests. A thought like that could almost make you religious.

It was all a case of checks and balances. Yang and Yin. Giver and Stealer. As the pond repeatedly told anyone who would dip in a translator attached to the newly developed chemolingual: A HEALTHY GALAXY IS FOREVER POISED ON THE EDGE OF CHAOS, TRANSFIXED BETWEEN THE STERILE WASTELAND OF ORDER AND THE MAD WILDERNESS OF RAMPANT ENTROPY. LIFE IS NOT SOLELY A GALACTIC DISEASE. IT CAN BE PARASITIC OR SYMBIOTIC. WE MUST SEEK A SYMBIOSIS WITH OUR GALAXY. FOLLOW ME AND I WILL SHOW YOU THE WAY. It talked like that a lot and had gained a growing reputation as an eccentric philosopoet. In its way of carving up reality, this Galaxy was returning rapidly to health, as the revisionist, Samuellian heresy (now orthodoxy) of *genuine* tolerance spread its new memeplex like contagion.

Which it was.

A COSMIC IMMUNE SYSTEM IS HEALING THE GALAXY, the pond insisted. YOU ARE WITNESSING THE MECHANISM OF ITS THOUGHTS.

The others weren't so certain. The pond was prejudiced. It and the Galaxy were ecologies, not organisms.

Yet, every organism was an ecology. Every cell of Sam's body, for example, had evolved from an ancient symbiosis of bacteria, archaea, and other microorganisms, which had grown so interdependent that they had united into a new kind of autocatalytic system, the eukaryote cell.

And every ecology was an organism . . . the old Lovelockian image of Gaia the earth goddess. So there was much room for argument, which made the Neanderthal priests' task far easier and more enjoyable.

Universal Harmony's aim was to become a eukaryote religion. A synthesis, a symbiosis, a complicity—not a sterile uniformity. It was structured to thrive on diversity, multiplex thinking, multicultural societies.

Nice trick. Starting is easy.

It's keeping it going that's so hard.

The new religion's founder was suffering agonies of shame.

He would have had every right to be proud of his part in the defeat of the mission fleet. He'd helped to raise *Talitha* to unprecedented ethical levels; he'd been one of the rescuers of Fat Apprentice, who had picked at a dangling thread of logic and unraveled the fabric of Cosmic Unity; and he'd initiated the Samuellian heresy, in which tolerance was encouraged and valued—but never, never, *never* imposed.

Instead, Sam was deeply ashamed of the ease with which he had tossed away his humanity when transibled to Aquifer, and had accepted the querists' justifications for torture and murder.

He just couldn't get it out of his mind, and it was eating him up. It didn't matter that Second-Best Sailor had forgiven him. He couldn't forgive himself.

How could anyone who believed in harmony among sentients, and the virtues of universal love, talk himself into such a frame of mind that he would betray every principle on which his beliefs were based? He found it incomprehensible, even though he'd done it.

Had he been mad?

He sought out Epimenides. He'd noticed that the Thumosyne's pedantry often held nuggets of wisdom. And right now, he desperately needed some spiritual insight.

Epimenides heard him out in silence and then extracted the essence from Sam's pain and confusion.

"What torments you, Fourteen Samuel, is the Querists' Fallacy."

"The phrase is unfamiliar. What does it mean?"

"It refers to the flawed logic of those who *put the question*. The question is belief in religious orthodoxy, and they put it with sharp blades, red-hot steel, molten ice, searing blasts of oxygen . . . or bombs, plagues, and planetwide devastation.

"Yet most of them are not evil. Yes, there are some sadists, who torture for pleasure and use religion as an excuse. And others whose motives are political. But most querists honestly believe that what they do is necessary for the good of their victims' lifesouls. You know why. You have heard their reasoning." Epimenides paused for emphasis. "And you have asked them: What if their reasoning is wrong?"

"I have," said Sam. "And I can't detect any flaw in their answer: 'By accepting the possibility of error, we risk our own lifesouls for the good of others. What greater love can there be than this?' That was the answer that led me to become a torturer myself. I tried to inflict mortal harm on Second-Best Sailor!"

"You did," said Epimenides calmly. "But nevertheless, there is a flaw. You could not find it because you looked for it within the querists' logic, and that was what seduced you. But the flaw lies in the context, not in the content. Understand this, and you will never make such a mistake again.

"The Querists' Fallacy is to pose the entire argument within the context of their own belief system. However, if they are wrong to torture innocents, *those beliefs may also be wrong*. In particular, the belief that the querist's own lifesoul is at risk may be wrong. And then, what they do is based not on love but on ignorance and superstition."

"But—are you saying that the Lifesoul-Giver doesn't exist?"

"No. Neither am I saying that it does. I am saying that it is a fallacy to make deductions on the basis of false hypotheses."

It was all so obvious that Sam marveled at his own stupidity. He *had* been mad! "How can anyone live a life founded on such flawed logic?" he asked, forgetting for a moment that he had done just that.

"Because our minds require a definite context in which to think," the Thumosyne replied at once. "We cannot make a decision if the alternatives have no limits. We always worry that we have omitted some new possibility. So we fall back on the context in which we feel most comfortable, and use that to set the limits of our thinking. We forget that a wider context may alter the whole picture.

"This is what makes imagination so powerful, Samuel. And unorthodoxy so dangerous."

"But unorthodoxy leads to heresy," said Sam.

Epimenides gave the originator of the Samuellian heresy a level stare. "Yes. That is what makes it so valuable."

The sudden collapse of the mission fleet had saved No-Moon from the devastation of the reefwives' Last Resort, but it had come too late to make a great deal of difference. No-Moon was a dying world. The final, full-scale attack by the forces of Cosmic Unity, and the violence of the reefwives' defenses, had destabilized the planet's crust. Seismic quakes continued to rip the ocean floor apart, turning it into a cracked jigsaw of polygonal plates. White-hot rock, squeezed up from the planet's depths by the turmoil, hit cold water and exploded. The ocean, seeping into the cracks, turned to superheated steam, adding to the already extreme pressures. Thick plumes of sulfurous smoke bubbled up from the sea floor into the atmosphere.

The continental landmasses fared no better. Hundreds of new volcanoes added their own deadly mix of gases: phosgene, carbon monoxide, ammonia, hydrogen fluoride. Acid rain fell in torrents; giant storms surged across the plains. Forests burned; rivers flooded. And that was only the beginning. Every fresh quake, every new volcanic vent, added to the destruction. Entire chains of volcanoes were building up, and when their walls gave way, the plains alongside would be resurfaced by lava flows.

A few hundred polypoid males, the only survivors that could be found, were quickly evacuated to Aquifer. Several hundred tons of reefwives, from lagoons that had escaped the worst ravages, went with them; more would follow if they could be found alive.

Aquifer was the natural choice. It had already been selected as uniquely suitable for polypoid/coralline colonization. The monastery of equals and the Heaven that it concealed were no longer a menace; the servomechs had seen to that. The various species still inhabiting the polar region could remain there indefinitely or be transibled elsewhere; the ponds were happy in the otherwise uninhabited deserts. No one needed the oceans, so the mariners and their reefwives could establish themselves without making any serious impact on anyone else's lifestyle.

There was only one barrier to creating a thriving

mariner world: The reefwives were sterile. The toxic
chemicals in the oceans had wiped out their ability to reproduce. About half the males were still fertile, but they
lacked fertile females.

Extinction loomed.

But even that possibility had been foreseen.

Second-Best Sailor's original wifepiece, the one he
had given to the Neanderthals, had grown in both size
and strength during her time on *Talitha*. Now she tasted
the alien seas of Aquifer, finding them strange but palat-
able. Bright moonlight filtered down into the shallows,
bathing the lagoon in an ethereal glow.

Moonlight. True moonlight. So much better than the
feeble substitute of meteor showers.

Pale shadows flicked through the water around her.
With an air of anticipation, of suppressed excitement, the
polypoid males waited. Among them were Fat Apprentice and Second-Best Sailor, courtesy of the latter's new
ship—the more fertile males, the better. Neither of them
would have dreamed of missing the fun. This would
never happen again, not in quite the same way.

This was the genesis of a new world.

Long-suppressed genes became active as the moonlight played on the wifepiece's soft tissues. Tiny worms
peeped out, attracted by the glow. Polyps emerged from
their hiding places, reaching out with their tiny tentacles.

Microscopic spheres began to spurt from the polyps'
gastrovascular cavities, at first in thin streams, then in a
thick cloud. They were eggs, they were fertile, and the

males were ready. They swarmed in upon the cloud of eggs in a polypoid orgy. They darted this way and that, shoving each other aside in frenzied climax. Eggs and sperm mingled in the warm waters, fusing in pairs.

Fertilized eggs spread across the lagoon floor, finding their way into every crack and cranny in the rocks, settling on the sand. They would grow into planiculae, larvae equipped with motile membranelles that enabled them to swim. Normally, most would be eaten by predators, but this first generation of native Aquiferian corallines was protected by a forcewall. Most of the planiculae would find themselves a convenient rock, attach themselves, and grow into corals. A small proportion would remain free-swimming and become males.

The reefmind, intelligent but infertile, congratulated herself on the accuracy of her contingency plan. Thanks to Second-Best Sailor's second piece of wife, gifted to the Neanderthals and returned when she was most needed, the reef would live again, and thrive.

Faith: I/we observe that the rebuilding of the reef ecology is proceeding apace.

Hope: This world is ideal. We made a mistake when we chose No-Moon so long ago.

Charity: Three-Moons was lost, we had traveled far, and we were tired. The reefmind of that time foretold many futures, not all of which came to pass.

Faith: We did the same. Only one of the wifepieces that we had set aside for safekeeping survived.

Charity: It was enough.

Hope: Emergent history is like that, sisters.

Charity: All histories are true, for a given value of "true."

All: Wishy-washy syncretist!

Faith: The ancient evil followed the ancient path, as we foresaw.

Charity: Yes. A benevolent memeplex, spiraling into the self-set trap of inflexibility. A multiculture freezing into monoculture.

Faith: And now a new memeplex of harmony and co-existence is unleashed. How long, sisters, will it avoid the trap?

Hope: This time the priests are driven by empathy, not belief. This memeplex will maintain its openness and flexibility indefinitely.

Charity: Optimist. How long did that state last before?

Faith: Not long enough.

Charity: It never does.

Hope: Perhaps, this time . . . ?

All: My timechunk does not extend that far.

There were rearguard actions. As the servomechs pressed ahead with the lengthy process of incorporating eighty-eight Heavens, some acolytes of Cosmic Unity struggled to regain their supremacy—and some succeeded, for a time. Four Heavens were repopulated using rogue servomechs, but two of these fell to levithons, one was lost when its star unexpectedly flared, and the fourth suffered massive technical failure from unknown causes.

Millions died; millions awoke to madness; but billions once more lived real lives—less pleasant than their previous virtual fantasies, but ultimately more satisfying.

It rapidly became clear that the Samuellian memeplex was evolutionarily superior to the unmodified one that had for so long sustained and propagated the Church of Cosmic Unity. The Church was dying, as a new species took over its habitat. It wasn't that the ecclesiarchs attracted massive opposition, or lost further space battles. It was just that whenever anyone attempted to promote Cosmic Unity in its original form, the tried and tested methods of the past no longer worked. It was as if the universe itself was against them.

The ponds thought they knew why. THE GALACTIC LIFESOUL IS WHOLE AGAIN.

The Neanderthals thought that they, too, knew why. A new wave of skepticism and self-assurance was sweeping through civilized society. Blind faith in a discredited priesthood was giving way to a rational appraisal of the value of genuine mutual coexistence.

Fourteen Samuel had his own explanation: His heresy had become orthodoxy. It wasn't the universe that had changed, but the Memeplex, by self-modification. He was awed by the ability of such a social construct to adapt to new conditions. The Church had not been destroyed; it had evolved.

Second-Best Sailor had no opinion on the matter, and didn't give a squirt anyway. Like the 'Thals, he had a relatively low opinion of gods, and the alleged Galactic Mind seemed too close to a deity for comfort. He was happy piloting his magnetotoral steeds between the stars, sailing the currents of space and the solar winds.

He was trying to obtain consensus for a lightsail. His attempts to grow fruit outside the hull had fared poorly.

Epimenides just reveled in the multitude of philosophical viewpoints that were springing up.

All agreed that whatever interpretation you placed on events, the Galaxy did seem to be settling down, becoming a more pleasant place to live.

Sam still couldn't get one puzzle out of his head. Had their actions truly influenced the Galactic Mind, or were those actions merely a consequence of the physical workings of a mindless Galaxy? In a way, he felt, they were both. Although the emergent structures of an anthill had different priorities from the ants, what was seriously bad for a lot of ants was also bad for their anthill. The two points of view weren't alternatives, but different levels of interpretation.

The real transition to Mind, Sam decided, arose from exactly the opposite principle to the one that had driven Cosmic Unity: not uniformity, but the power and peace attained by valuing and validating *difference*. It was the complexity of the differences in the pond's components that enabled its intelligence, but it took the multiplexity of meaningful communication between individual ponds to generate the necessary extelligence. It took both intelligence and extelligence to make a Mind.

Only the newly resurgent reefwives possessed the wisdom to know the true nature of the Galaxy. Unbreakable law or free will? Mechanism or consciousness? Unthinking or sentient? But nobody asked them. Nobody would have believed their answers, anyway. The reefwives had their own take on the universe.

She's so beautiful, Sam thought, watching Dry Leaves Fall Slowly as she sat on the beach beside the pond and splashed her feet in the water. Second-Best Sailor and the pond had ansibled Sam on board *Talitha,* having found themselves with a few hours to spare before they loaded a cargo of pressed fernseed bound for the Eohippus System. The pond wanted to play with Fall, and the mariner was happy to go along with the plan. So was Sam. So he and Fall had been transibled to the mariner's new ship for a short visit.

Sam was aware that his viewpoint was unusual. To most humans, the Neanderthal child would have seemed . . . not exactly *ugly,* but uncouth. Ill-proportioned. The protruding face was too apelike for flatfaced humans, and the thick hair was close to fur.

The Neanderthals were too similar to humans—that was the problem. So each subspecies judged the other by its own standards, comparing them to its own self-image, and found it wanting. Their perceptual systems for humanoids were highly discriminating. And so, paradoxically, the grotesque insectoid shape of a Hytth, with its steel blue exoskeleton, could seem elegant . . . whereas a form that, to the Hytth, was just another weird two-eyed, jointed biped looked misshapen and deformed.

Not to Sam. He could see through the false comparison to the child beneath, and she was lovely. *Such a tragedy that there isn't a* person *in there anymore.* Despite all the medical advances achieved by Galactic civilization, the mind largely remained a mystery. Some mental illnesses could be cured by drugs; these were essentially gross physical malfunctions of synapses or neurotransmitters. Diseases of the brain, which only indirectly affected the mind. Fall's condition was deeper, some subtle failure of the process of consciousness. The complexity of the brain made it virtually impossible to unravel the workings of the mind, let alone to discover what was wrong and find a way to cure it.

Fall had improved a little, as time put distance between her present and her tormented past. But the past was too strong; the best that they could hope for was that she would remain relatively peaceful when Sam left her for a few minutes. Something about the pond fascinated her, though, and Sam was convinced that when she was trailing her fingers through the water or paddling her feet, she came as close to happiness as her mind would permit.

"How is she?" Second-Best Sailor asked Sam.

"Physically sound, but mentally . . . well, see for yourself."

"Pity." The mariner was clad in his trademark sailor suit, and he dipped one tentacle into the pond to stay in touch with his friend. Proper mental contact required molecular contact, so he instructed the suit to peel back a small patch of its skin, where the tip of the tentacle could touch the water.

The pond's ecochemical "thoughts" interfaced with the mariner's own neurobundle mode-molecules. HELLO, SAILOR. THIS IS FUN. SHE LIKES IT.

"Yes. But . . ." Subvocally, the mariner added: *Sam seems so sad*.

HE DOES? I WAS NOT AWARE. I AM NOT ATTUNED TO HUMAN EXPRESSION, AND HE RESTRICTS HIMSELF TO THE SPOKEN WORD.

He is sad because of the child, Second-Best Sailor thought. *Her mind has been damaged.*

YES. THE CHEMISTRY OF HER THOUGHTS HAS BECOME INFLEXIBLE.

The statement so surprised Second-Best Sailor that he spoke aloud. "You can sense her thoughts?"

OF COURSE. JUST AS I SENSE YOURS.

"But—polypoids have evolved to interpret chemical messages as well as verbal ones. 'Thals haven't."

THAT PREVENTS HER FROM UNDERSTANDING *MY* THOUGHTS. IT DOES NOT MAKE IT DIFFICULT FOR ME TO UNDERSTAND HERS.

"Ask the pond what Fall is thinking!" Sam urged, having heard the mariner's startled outburst and then insisting on being told what had caused it.

The mariner did so.

HER FISHES ARE NOT SHOALING PROPERLY. THEIR MOVEMENTS ARE TOO CHOREOGRAPHED. NOT FLEXIBLE ENOUGH.

"She don't *have* fishes!"

THAT EXPLAINS WHY THEY TASTE SLIGHTLY DRY. AND THEIR MOTIONS ARE OBSESSIVELY CYCLIC. I AM INTERPRETING HER THOUGHT PATTERNS IN TERMS THAT I FIND FAMILIAR, THAT IS ALL.

"She can't get the horrors out of her mind," Second-Best Sailor explained. "It's such a tragedy she can't be cured."

Never before had he had the sense of catching the

pond unawares. Suddenly, his mind was filled with it. SHE CANNOT BE CURED?

"No. Our medical science can heal her body, but her mind is beyond its scope."

IT MAY NOT BE BEYOND MINE.

A lengthy silence. "Say that again."

IT MAY NOT BE BEYOND MINE. I HEALED YOUR PHYSICAL WOUNDS. I MAY BE ABLE TO HEAL HER MENTAL ONES.

Second-Best Sailor's siphons squeaked with the release of repressed frustration. *"Why the flounce didn't ya tell us that before?"*

I WAS NOT ASKED. I DO NOT KNOW WHAT HUMANS WANT.

"Sam would have told you!"

FOURTEEN SAMUEL HAS NOT MADE CONTACT WITH ME.

Second-Best Sailor reached out with a couple of tentacles, grabbed Sam by the ankles, and threw him into the water. As the startled human broke the surface, spluttering, the mariner directed a cogent thought at the pond.

"Now he has."

Understanding surged through the collective mentality of the pond as it sampled Sam's neural chemistry. AH . . . SO *THAT* IS WHAT HE WANTS. IF THE CHILD CAN BE PERSUADED TO JOIN SAMUEL IN THE WATER, THEIR MOLECULAR COUPLING SHOULD BE STRONG ENOUGH FOR ME TO REDIRECT HER MENTAL PROCESSES. HER THOUGHTS ARE CLOSE ENOUGH TO FISHES THAT I *THINK* I CAN RESTORE THEM TO NORMALITY.

The mariner passed the pond's instructions on to Sam. He swam over to where Fall sat, and held out his arms to her. She looked puzzled and didn't budge. Should he reach for her and pull her in? He would hate to do that; enough had been done to her against her will already.

Even something small might make her condition worse. Torn between difficult choices, he hesitated.

The sand upon which she sat began to flow. Still looking puzzled, Fall slid into the water. The pond had taken its own steps to ensure contact.

IT WILL TAKE A FEW MINUTES.

Sam wrapped his arms around the child's body and waited. He would wait like that forever, if need be.

Fall made no move to escape. Her lips moved, but no sounds emerged. The movements slowed, ceased. Time seemed frozen.

Then the Neanderthal child did something that Sam had never seen her do before.

She smiled.

No-Moon was shrouded in dense, impenetrable banks of cloud; it shivered in the clutches of volcanic winter. The reefwives' Pyrrhic victory over the missionaries of Cosmic Unity had wrecked their planet. Its ecosystems were dying one by one, unable to survive the increasingly harsh conditions.

The previously stable ocean beds had shattered into a crazed maze of cracks, trenches, and volcanic hot spots. Molten lava spouted into ice-cold water, solidifying where the two met, breaking open again under the pressure, surging upward to form tall, hollow columns of rock.

On the land, lava flowed over what had once been woods, plains, deserts. Mountain ranges rose and fell. Unquenchable fires ravaged the forests, adding their own smoke to the planetwide pall, even as heavy rains fell from the darkened skies. Hurricanes howled; spun-off tornadoes wreaked havoc. Uprooted trees and the carcasses of animals washed down the swollen rivers and into the toxic seas in an unending cascade, choking the shallows with decaying organics, churning the once-pellucid lagoons into lakes of thick mud. Reefs that had taken four hundred thousand years to build were washed away in seconds. Continental shelves gave way under the pressure, slipping into the depths and leaving only huge chasms to mark their demise. The eons-old circulation of the oceans faltered, then disintegrated. No-Moon's sea creatures perished by the trillion, tumbling to the ocean floor in a ceaseless downpour of death.

In those few places where volcanic vents had previously existed, delicate pink fanworms peeped from their square tubes and basked in water as hot as molten lead. Their tiny colored lights flickered on and off in response to the chemical condition of the surrounding ocean. To them, the drizzle of dead and dying was no ecotragedy but a feast. A bonanza. The more food that rained down, the more excited their flashing lights became. The fanworms greedily absorbed the food and grew. Their attendant symbiotic algae, bacteria, and archaeans grew with them.

Before, even when food had briefly been plentiful for some chance reason, there had been nowhere else for the fanworms to go. But now the entire ocean floor was a forest of volcanic vents, dark smokers where heat and pressure combined to create endless streams of superheated water, rich in the exotic minerals that the worms alone could tolerate—that they alone found essential.

Surging vortices ripped them from their safe homes, scattering them to the three corners of the world. Most died. But occasionally, a few would alight upon a new smoker, find the location congenial, attach themselves to the cooling lava—and reproduce like wildfire.

What No-Moon's major lifeforms had lost, the fan-worms would take back.

Perhaps, one day, their chemosensitive patterns of flashing lights would blossom into intelligent communication . . . or even evolve into extelligence.

It could happen. Given time.

In a healthy Galaxy a mere twelve billion years old, there was no shortage.

ABOUT THE AUTHORS

DR. IAN STEWART, professor of mathematics at Warwick University, is a recipient of both the Royal Society's Michael Faraday Medal and the AAAS Award for Public Understanding of Science and Technology. A former columnist for *Scientific American* and frequent television commentator, Dr. Stewart is the author of more than 150 papers of mathematical research and twenty books of popular science. Ian Stewart lives in England.

DR. JACK COHEN is a reproductive biologist and theoretical xenobiologist who has participated in the production of numerous television science specials, notably *The Natural History of an Alien* for BBC2. He has acted as a consultant for prominent science fiction authors, advising them on the design of alien creatures and environments. He is an honorary professor at Warwick University. Jack Cohen lives in England.

Scientists Dr. Ian Stewart and Dr. Jack Cohen, internationally renowned coauthors of *The Collapse of Chaos* and *Figments of Reality*, present an acclaimed novel of suspenseful adventure and earthshaking concepts in the grand tradition of Larry Niven and Greg Bear.

WHEELERS
(0-446-61-008-9)

Twenty-third-century archaeologist Prudence Odingo claims she's recovered 100,000-year-old wheeled artifacts from under the ice of the Jovian moon Callisto. Denounced by an academic rival, Prudence is arrested and about to be convicted for criminal fraud, when the "wheelers" suddenly start to levitate. Simultaneously, Jupiter's moons change orbits and become gravitational cannons, sending a world-destroying comet hurtling toward Earth. For unimaginable beings live in Jupiter's hellish atmosphere and have apparently declared war on humanity. Now Prudence, her pedantic nemesis, and a child with an uncanny talent must quickly discover why . . .

_____

"COMPLEX . . . HAIR-RAISING SUSPENSE . . . A TOP-NOTCH STORY. HIGHLY RECOMMENDED."
—*Library Journal*

VISIT WARNER ASPECT ONLINE!

THE WARNER ASPECT HOMEPAGE
You'll find us at: www.twbookmark.com then by clicking on Science Fiction and Fantasy.

NEW AND UPCOMING TITLES
Each month we feature our new titles and reader favorites.

AUTHOR INFO
Author bios, bibliographies, and links to personal websites.

CONTESTS AND OTHER FUN STUFF
Advance galley giveaways, autographed copies, and more.

THE ASPECT BUZZ
What's new, hot and upcoming from Warner Aspect: awards news, bestsellers, movie tie-in information . . .